TRICKSTERS AND ANGELS

A NOVEL

RONALD C. MEYER

MARK REEDER

HANGAR 1 PUBLISHING

Copyright © 2021 by Ronald C. Meyer and Mark Reeder

All rights reserved. This book is protected by copyright.

No part of it may be reproduced, stored in a retrieval system, or transmitted in any form or by any means, electronic, mechanical, photocopying, recording, or otherwise without written permission from the author.

ISBN Paperback: 978-1-955471-22-0

ACKNOWLEDGMENTS

We would like to thank the people who gave us input on the writing of this book: Our brilliant editor Byron Belitsos who made this book a reality; Dr. Alexander P. Murphy, the University of Oregon's extraordinary human geographer who taught us the 'importance of place' in making sense of the world; Alan Combs who showed us the connection between divine intervention and the Greek God Hermes, the Norse God Loki and the Native American trickster, Coyote; and our first reader, David Bartsch. A special thanks to Diane Evans, Ron Meyer's wife and beloved life partner, and to Diane Anderson.

1

———

March 24, 2019
Rio Chama, New Mexico

Jonathan Ramsey drove into the parking lot of the Rio Chama de Milagro Shrine and stopped in front of the whitewashed, adobe-bricked arch that formed the entrance to the so-called healing place. Rows of white stones marked parking spots in the dirt. He pulled into a space beside a silver pickup truck with New Mexico plates.

It was dawn—a chilly Friday in March.

As Ramsey stepped out of his car, he could see his breath. He looked westward. The Milagro Shrine occupied a high ridge overlooking the Rio Chama River, a fast-flowing tributary of the Rio Grande. It was surrounded by stubbled meadows of rabbit grass and sage that swept in broad curves toward the darkly forested Sangre de Cristo Mountains. In the near distance the faint tinkle of bells spilled into the morning's silence as Hispanic sheepherders rose to tend their flocks. The area was sleepy and dry, and bordered on being withered and empty—except for the Rio Chama de Milagro Shrine itself, which stood majestically under the breaking light. Only a short time ago it had been the greatest healing center of its kind in North America.

Ramsey closed the car door, and pulled his soft-leather jacket tighter around his shoulders against the morning chill. High above, a cold wind blew clouds from the mountains to the high plains and beyond. As the sun rose, a red band limned the hills in the east. Although he would be late for his meeting in town, he did not hurry. He stared through the high arching entryway at the hill where the shrine's sacred cottonwood tree stood.

Focusing his camera, he began filming the shrine's Visitor Center at the base of the hill. It was a single story, white stucco building, built by local contractors, using post and beam construction and hay bales. A glass dome soared above the entry. Though he had not yet set foot inside the shrine, Ramsey knew all about it. Over the past week he had read every article about it on the web and watched on YouTube every eyewitness account of its miraculous healing powers. He pushed the record button, taking advantage of the morning light. When he finished with the Visitor Center, he suddenly found himself thinking again about the late-night phone call he had received from Myriam St. Eves a week earlier.

"How soon can you make it?" she had demanded, her voice both earnest and worried.

"I have a weeklong conference in D.C.," he had answered.

"Not sooner?"

"I can be there Friday morning."

"That will have to do." The phone went dead.

Myriam St. Eves had been his principal advisor for his postdoctoral research fellowship. *And now?* He let the thought run no further, other than to wonder why she would call him of all people.

Ramsey was a thin man, brown-haired with a dark beard. His eyes were slate gray. His leather jacket was patched and his trousers faded, the cuffs flopping carelessly over worn Nike running shoes. It was an image he cultivated when he taught his classes at Grinnell College in Iowa. Quite different from his corporate image of Canali wool suits,

Salvatore Ferragamo shoes, and Paul Smith London shirts. He was forty-one and unmarried.

Startled by a coughing engine, Ramsey whirled to watch a 1970s Volkswagen Microbus drive up the narrow one-lane road. It pulled into the space next to Ramsey's rental Prius. The engine sputtered then died with a soft backfire.

A young man and woman got out. They were dressed in gaily-colored flannel shirts and blue jeans and wore clogs. The woman had a bright red bandana covering her head. The man wore a battered Stetson and carried a sleeping toddler in his arms, a two-year-old boy with a mop of dark hair.

"After you," the young man said, indicating that Ramsey should go first since he was already here.

He shook his head. "I'm in no hurry. Go on ahead."

"Have a good day," the woman said.

As the couple passed through the arch, she unwound the bandana. Her head was bald and it displayed a livid horseshoe-shaped scar above the occipital bone.

"It was a long trip, but thank God we made it," the young man said as he drew her towards him. "I know you're going to get better."

The woman turned to him, her mouth set. "I have faith."

The sun topped the surrounding mountains and shone golden on the crest of the hill, where the cottonwood tree rose bright and shining into the sky like a beacon. It was massive and looked as if must be a thousand years old. Impossible for any species in the genus of *Populus* to survive for so long, and yet there it stood, ancient and venerable.

The woman stopped and stared. Her breath caught in her throat. The cottonwood beckoned her forward. "It's as beautiful as I imagined."

The young man gripped her hands. "I know it's going work."

Ramsey watched the couple hurry up the path toward stone stairs leading upward to the shrine's famous tree. Straightening his shoulders, he started forward. The moment he crossed under the Milagro Shrine's high arching entryway, a rush of freezing cold swept through him as though a glacial wind buffeted his soul. His vision narrowed to a single dot and he lurched against the adobe brick, crying out.

"You all right?" the young man called out.

"It's nothing." Ramsey smiled. He pushed himself up straight. Internally he was on the ledge of a deep dark canyon fighting the demand to fall. It almost felt like a memory. Since he was a senior in college, entering sacred spaces had affected him in unusual ways. This time the transition from the outside world to a sacred one was particularly strong and he knew in that instant that his life would never be the same again. He walked on toward the Visitor Center.

Myriam St. Eves read the text on her iPhone a second time. "i'm at the shrine. see u in 30. jonathan."

Asking Jonathan Ramsey for help put Myriam on edge. She hated feeling beholden to him. But she couldn't refuse the request of the man she hoped to marry. Her partner Hiram had specifically asked for Ramsey. So she stood on the steps of the Café Rio waiting for the encounter she thought would never happen.

The mellow scent of sage hung in the air, the morning was now clear and crisp with no hint of being overcast, and all around her were the old western Hispanic buildings of the town of Rio Chama. The place was one of those Wild West mining towns that had survived as the center of commerce for outlying ranchers until recently, when the Milagro Shrine brought in people by the thousands from across the country and the world. The influx had made the town's local businesses prosperous. Two new motels had sprung up at the edge of town as well as a modern Safeway, a 24-Hour Fitness Center, and a movie theater. Bank of America had built a small office complex on Main Street, its glass, steel, and concrete clashing with the wood buildings of the courthouse on one side and the James Brothers Mercantile Store on the other.

Just three months ago the Milagro Shrine was a must stop in

north-central New Mexico along with Taos, Santa Fe, Georgia O'Keefe's Ghost Ranch, and the nearby mission ruins. But the shrine's pull was mysteriously fading. A large "Office Space for Lease" sign hung in the bank's front window, and the mercantile store had gone back to its original hours of 10 to 4, three days a week.

Feeling the cold especially in her right leg, Myriam climbed up the wide steps and inside the Café Rio to its atrium. Painted in the dark reds, sharp blues, and fire orange of a New Mexico sunset, it stretched half the length of the building. Pueblo pottery and ornate masks were everywhere, and in the center a round fireplace took away the chill with a mesquite-log fire. Once crowded at all hours with pilgrims and curiosity seekers, this morning the place was nearly empty. Rosa Cisneros, the Café's owner, was talking with Raphael Núnez, Rio Chama's only real estate agent and chairman of the Board for the Friends of the Shrine. From the way she stood with her fists planted on her hips, and the way Raphael spread his hands supplicating, palms up as if asking for forgiveness, the conversation didn't look to be a happy one.

Myriam crossed the tiled floor, seating herself at a table near the windows with a view of the street. She glanced at the time of Ramsey's text to her. It came in thirty-five minutes ago. She tapped her turquoise-colored nails on the Mexican-tile tabletop, and idly arranged the blue and orange salt-and-pepper shakers on different squares. She rubbed her right calf where it ached. The recent doctor's diagnosis troubled her and added to the anxiety surrounding her meeting with Jonathan. She couldn't shake the feeling that her former student was going to turn her request down. *Yet he made the trip here, which is more than I could've hoped for.*

"Myriam."

Startled, she looked up. Rosa set a carafe and a small pitcher on the table. "Decaf, skim milk, no cream." She pulled out a small notebook and pen and began writing. "The usual?"

"Somebody is joining me. I'll order then." The darkness in Rosa's eyes made Myriam shiver. "Anything wrong?"

Rosa shrugged. "I'm fine ... it's just business."

"I'm sorry, so many good times here."

"I keep asking myself, did I do something wrong? God blessed me and then he took it away. I don't understand. What can I do to bring the shrine's power back? I pray every night."

A shaft of ice shot through Myriam's stomach. "Has the cancer returned?"

Rosa kissed the cross hanging around her neck. "No, I'm fine. I've been so fortunate." A smile came over her face.

"Is something else going on?"

"I don't want to jinx it. I'll tell you later."

Myriam studied the Hispanic woman as she walked toward the kitchen. *What does she mean by "I don't want to jinx it"?*

Her gaze drifted across the empty street to the weathered Rio Chama Hotel, its white-painted clapboard siding faded from the sun. Its second-story balcony made it look like a building out of an old Western movie. She remembered how she had said those exact same words ten years ago to her lifelong friend Nancy Bloomberg in that hotel when they visited the shrine for the first time. It had been on their thirtieth "girls' trip."

Every year after graduating college the two of them had taken a week away from husbands and children to explore some new place. The trip ten years ago was supposed to be their last, as Nancy's MS was growing progressively worse, but she insisted on one more trip before she became wheelchair-bound. The night before they went to the shrine, Nancy had begun to shake, the tremors starting in her delicately boned hands and spreading until she fell onto the hotel room's double bed unable to stand any longer. Her frantic weeping and pleas for help made no difference. Myriam had held her until after midnight when the shaking stopped. By then Nancy's bubbly personality was replaced by a dull, confused look. They had slept in each other's arms until almost checkout time.

Dressing slowly the next morning, each movement registering in a spasm of pain on her face, Nancy had said quietly, "Myriam, do you believe in miracles ... a higher intelligent healing power that we can access?"

At the time she had smiled. Nancy was a born-again Christian and Myriam did not want to deflate her friend's hope. So she responded, "I don't want to jinx it."

Myriam fell out of her reverie just for a moment as a car drove along Rio Chama's deserted main street in front of the Café Rio. Dust spun in tiny whirlwinds from its tires. *I didn't believe in any of that miraculous healing stuff back then. How wrong I was.*

In the morning the two women had driven to the shrine. The day was overcast and a light rain fell. The grass and piñon pine glittered bright green. The air smelled of burned copper, though no lightning crisscrossed the dull gray clouds.

The only other car in the lot was a gray Toyota pickup with New Mexico plates. Myriam had parked across from it and got out first, helping Nancy to stand. In town at the Mercantile they had bought a cane. Nancy grasped the handle but also leaned on Myriam for support.

Passing through the adobe archway, they had stopped at the base of the hill. "Are you sure you want to climb all the way up there?" Myriam had asked her friend, more afraid of the walk down than the hike up.

Her face set in a determined grimace, Nancy answered. "I need to."

She had just put her foot on the first step when a man came out of the Visitor Center. He was tall and muscular with graying red hair. A broad smile spread across his weathered face. He introduced himself, his voice a strong baritone. "I'm Adam Gwillt. I'm sort of a caretaker here. Do you need some help?"

"Do you know what I'm supposed to do?" Nancy had asked.

It seemed as if the caretaker understood what they needed.

Making warm inviting eye contact, he answered, "You made the journey. That is often enough."

Nancy instinctively took his arm and he led them around the back of the Center to a small bench sheltered from the weather by a large mesquite tree. The rain flicked off the grass all around them and splattered the rock path but none hit the bench where they sat.

"You can see the cottonwood from here." He pointed to the top of the hill where the giant tree swayed gently in the breeze. "And beside it is the Christ Chapel. Local artisan's are volunteering their time and labor to build it. It'll be magnificent when it's finished."

Myriam and her friend had sat for hours, chatting sometimes or sitting in silence, always watching the tree. Adam checked on them twice, each time gently touching Nancy on her shoulder. By noon the shrine was bustling with tourists and the first of many busloads of pilgrims. The clouds had parted and the sun had come out. A shaft of soft golden light lit up the cottonwood.

Later that afternoon Adam had stopped by again. He studied the two of them. "I suspect that you are finding what you came for," he said knowingly and walked away.

Myriam looked at Nancy. "Is he right?"

Nancy nodded. "I'm tired, but something has changed." She paused; a smile came over her face. "I'm no longer afraid. It's as though Jesus has reached inside my heart and given me new life and hope."

Being at the shrine had done nothing for Myriam, and she thought Nancy looked worse after they returned to the hotel. However, each day for the rest of the week Nancy insisted on visiting the shrine and sitting on the bench, gazing at the cottonwood.

A month after returning home, Myriam had received a phone call. The caller I.D. said it was from Nancy's husband, Sid. Myriam steeled her nerves against the worst, but when she answered, Sid's shout of joy echoed from the phone through the room. "Nancy's symptoms are going away, the doctors say it's a miracle."

~

From the parking lot the Rio Chama de Milagro Shrine complex spread out beneath the hill like a vast English garden.

The Visitor Center, built as the shrine's healing power drew ever more pilgrims and tourists, was typical of such buildings at national parks. Upon entering, tourists walked up to a long counter where receptionists helped answer questions and gave them small maps of the shrine complex. Beside the counter was a small gift shop, where a sign said 100 percent of all proceeds go to the Rio Chama de Milagro Shrine. Behind the counter was an auditorium where pilgrims could watch a short movie about the miraculous founding of the healing spot more than a decade ago. At the back of the building and on the east and west sides, doors opened onto a labyrinth of pathways that wound through the xeriscaped grounds of cactus, rabbit grass, mesquite, and piñon pine. Visitors could walk the path to the base of the hill and the stone steps leading to the cottonwood tree or find one of the many small nooks from which they could sit and look at the sacred tree at the top of the hill.

Ramsey wandered along the paths, occasionally taking pictures of alcoves with benches for people to sit and pray or meditate. Almost all of them held small treasures— baby shoes, ribbons, war medals— the kinds of tokens believers leave when prayers have been answered. Fifteen years ago he and Myriam had been doing research on the rapid diffusion of Hispanic traditions of sacred places as this phenomenon moved north from Mexico. Such traditions were even common in Iowa today. There was even a sacred Hispanic place outside of Grinnell College's main entrance. *Someday I'll have to figure out how governments have let these little sacred places spring up without objection.*

Coming to the last alcove, he stared at a cross made from dried pink roses. A dusting of sunlight through the wicker of overhead beams and flower blossoms gave them an ethereal hue. Ramsey took a deep breath. The same vertigo that had occurred when he passed through the entrance settled into him again. It was a feeling of standing on a ledge, stronger this time and even more like a real memory this time. He wanted to snap a picture but all he could do was stare.

"Beautiful, aren't they?"

Ramsey turned to face a short, thin man in blue jeans and work shirt. He had an ascetic, acne-scarred face, hidden mostly by a dark beard slowly turning gray. Graying hair was pulled back in a long queue down his back. He wore a brightly colored vest. A bola tie, the cord held together with a large piece of tourmaline, partially obscured a priest's collar.

"Sorry if I startled you. I'm Father Michael, though I suppose it isn't 'Father' anymore. I was pleasantly defrocked more than ten years ago." With a twinkle he chuckled and held out a hand.

Ramsey shook it. The grip was strong. "You still wear the collar."

Father Michael shrugged. "I suppose they can kick the priest out of the church but not the priest out of the man." His thin face lit up with an infectious smile. "I just wanted to say that many of our visitors were drawn to this particular alcove. They say it's where many healings took place."

Ramsey nodded. "I felt something as well."

"Just now?"

"Yes."

"Wonderful. So what brings you here?"

"Actually I might investigate what happened here."

"Journalist?"

"Human geographer ... What are your thoughts about the power of the shrine to heal?"

"I've always put my faith in the words of Jesus." He pointed at the top of the hill. "I suggest you visit the tree or perhaps the Christ Chapel. You may find the answers you seek there."

He turned and walked away.

Ramsey watched him disappear along the winding paths leading back to the Visitor Center. Raising his camera, he pirouetted to snap the picture of the flowered cross but the sun had moved slightly and he no longer couldn't capture its true beauty—at least not digitally. He lowered his camera and backed away. He discovered a trail on the edge of the garden and followed it. At last he found himself at the foot of the gray stone stairs leading to the Milagro Shrine's giant cottonwood. He walked the ninety-nine steps to the top and stared at the great tree. Deep purple catkins hung from every branch. A large number of petal-less flowers ready to bloom were hidden within each fingerlike spike. According to native legend, the flowering of the cottonwood signaled the beginning of new life.

Sweat trickled down Ramsey's ribs as the past loomed up suddenly and he was transported to the last time he sat underneath a sacred tree.

Twelve years ago, during his visit to a sacred spot far north of Cuzco, Peru, a shaman had taken him to the holiest of holy Palo Santo trees in the Amazonian rainforest on the eastern slopes of the Andes Mountains. The old man had told him that, by sitting under this tree and imbibing sacred medicine, he would open up like a flower and get the answers to his deepest questions. Instead, after drinking mixture of plant medicines that the natives called *Ayahuasca*, he was instantaneously gripped by the most primal feeling of fear he had ever experienced. His mind was swept into a dark vision of shadow and light filled with nightmarish creatures. Mercifully, he had passed out. After spending nearly a month in a Lima hospital recovering from what doctors had called an extreme psychotic episode, and still unwell, he had returned to his home in Eugene, Oregon.

It had taken Ramsey a year to convalesce enough to begin his life again. But the damage was done. He dropped his postdoc research on sacred places and took a job with the State Department as a human geographer. Two years later he had acquired enough contacts to go into business on his own with a partner, Ron Grange. Very quickly, they had built a multimillion-dollar business spanning the globe, allowing Ramsey to operate out of the small Midwestern college town of Grinnell, Iowa where he had done his undergraduate work. Remarkably, once he had returned to the town, his recovery accelerated at an astounding pace.

From his base of operation in Grinnell he had been able to deal remotely with most of their clients and travel the world when necessary. At the same time, Ramsey was able to keep in touch with academia by co-teaching an economic and political geography honors seminar at the private college that was the focal point of this small town.

Pulling a catkin from a branch, he recalled one of the cardinal rules of his profession. *Human geography stops at the doorstep.* Yet, here he was doing it again, breaking that rule without knowing why. Was it that the Milagro Shrine was such an anomaly in the history of sacred places? Unlike many other Christian related shrines, it had not started with a vision of Jesus or Mary. Instead, its focal point was an icon of Native American spiritual quests—the cottonwood tree. It was recent. Or maybe he hoped to get a personal apology from Myriam. *She owes me*, he thought bitterly. All these thoughts ran through his head as he examined the flowers tucked in the cottonwood catkin.

"You are like that catkin ready to sow the seeds of a new life."

Ramsey wasn't sure if the words came from inside his head or from the air around him. He instinctively asked, "What?"

A shadow appeared beside him. Backlit against the bright morning sun, it was hard to make out. Ramsey shielded his eyes and the rugged outline of a man came into focus. He appeared to be in his fifties with questing blue eyes and graying red hair. In spite of the rough, home-spun quality of his clothes draping his body, Ramsey could see the man was naturally big-boned and muscular. His eyes were set above high cheekbones, and Ramsey observed that he had a thin Roman nose and full lips. When the man smiled, all of his teeth were white. The mysterious visitor had an air of confidence; he clenched and unclenched his fists like a man straining to keep the confidence bottled up so as not to overwhelm everyone around him. With a jerk of surprise, Ramsey had the sudden thought that the stranger was the kind of man he always wanted to be.

The stranger smiled. "Not many visitors do that ... pull a catkin from the sacred tree."

Ramsey felt pressure building in his head, like something working desperately to get out. He wondered if he were hallucinating. He licked his lips and stared into the stranger's face. Everything seemed magnified. The man pointed to a spike of purple petals, his hand translucent and wavering like a mirage. The muscles rippled in his jaw and lips elongated as he formed the words, "Why did you take it?"

Ramsey stretched his neck, trying to fight off the strange illusion, but his head tightened, ready to explode. He answered, the sound loud in his own ears, "I don't know."

The stranger smiled and nodded. "That's what everyone says who does that. I know because I've been here from the beginning."

The syllables punctuated the clear air and all at once the pressure within Ramsey eased. "So you were healed?" he rasped.

"Some would say that." A car alarm blared in the still morning. Ramsey winced and turned away, looking down the long flight of steps toward the parking lot. Half dozen visitors climbed steadily upwards. "What did you say?" he asked turning back. No one was there to answer his question. He craned his neck around to see. The stranger had vanished.

Ramsey shuddered. He threw the catkin away, watched it pushed by the wind across the grass until it lay still on the steps of the Christ Chapel. Caught in the strangeness of the experience, he mindlessly continued documenting the shrine's famous tree and the small chapel with his camera. Then he was back to normal awareness. His mind flipped into research mode, mentally taking notes.

It's obvious the shrine developed organically. Its origins will prove most important. It was a chance to study first-hand the question he had long grappled with in his research: Do sacred places somehow capture powerful forces or are they just cultural or religious artifacts?

He suppressed a gasp and stepped back as if distancing himself from these thoughts. He was quite surprised at how easily he had been influenced to accepting the challenge of his former academic advisor.

~

Myriam sat at the table watching Ramsey get out of his rental car. *He hasn't changed much in all this time*, she thought. *How long's it been ... ten ... no, twelve years.*

Rosa came by and switched the coffee carafe for a fresh one. She followed Myriam's gaze. "Is that your guest?"

"Yes. His name's Jonathan."

"A friend?"

Myriam nodded. She kneaded her leg, trying to dampen the pain that flared suddenly. It had begun to occur without warning from time to time over the past few months. She concentrated on Jonathan. *This has to work. I have to make it happen.*

"Will you show him here, please?" she asked keeping her voice even.

Rosa nodded and headed for the entrance. She eyed the rugged-looking, middle-aged man as Ramsey searched in his pocket for change for the parking meter. Every couple of seconds he glanced at the café with a look both bemused and apprehensive. She looked back at Myriam who was studying the tabletop with great care. *What's between those two?* she wondered.

"Good morning, Jonathan," Rosa said.

Ramsey looked up startled. He stuffed two more quarters in the meter and walked up the steps, grasping the Hispanic woman's hand when she extended it. It was soft and smelled slightly of peanut oil.

"Welcome to Café Rio," she added, her English lightly accented. There was a purr beneath it like she was inviting him to more than just the restaurant. "Senora Eves is waiting for you. Right this way."

"Do you meet all your customers like this?" Ramsey asked, warming to her.

"Just interesting men like yourself."

Myriam rearranged the salt and pepper on different squares, trying to figure out how to deal with what happened between her and Jonathan twelve years ago. His troubles in Peru had eventually brought about a loss of funding for her research project. Looking up, she saw him at the entrance talking to Rosa. *Let the past go*, she commanded herself.

Rosa motioned to the table where Myriam sat. There were a few townsfolk eating breakfast and they watched him suspiciously as he crossed the atrium. The room smelled of pico de gallo, cilantro, and mole sauce. He counted twelve four-tops and sixteen doubles, automatically totaling the number in his head. He had worked as a bus boy while he was an undergraduate at Grinnell College. He had received his masters and PhD at UCLA while studying under the famous American geographer Jared Diamond before working on his postdoc at the University of Oregon with Myriam. He noted there was no wait staff on duty and surmised that Rosa was the owner. *An owner in distress.*

Driving into Rio Chama he had seen all the telltale signs of a boom and bust cycle. Only a few cars on the street and all the businesses closed, except for the restaurant, in spite of it being Tuesday. His mind quickly put two and two together. *It has to be the shrine. It lost its mojo, impacting the town's population, causing an economic decline. Is that what Myriam's interested in—what's happening to the town geographically?*

And then he was in front of the table. Myriam waved at the chair opposite without smiling.

Ramsey took it and studied her, trying to gauge her mood. They hadn't talked in twelve years, and yet now she had demanded he fly down here and speak with her.

"Your trip here was fine?" she asked.

He nodded. "I flew into Albuquerque, drove up. Signs of a bad drought everywhere."

She nodded. "I have a place down here now. I've watched the area go from a Piñon pine forest to a short grass and scrub ecosystem. I'm on the county water board."

Myriam is one of those people who don't seem to age, Ramsey thought. She had the same dark hair, her skin smooth except for a few wrinkles around her eyes. He remembered she had inexhaustible energy. She knew everybody who could make things happen. Myriam was the ultimate facilitator, the kind of person every academic department needed. During their two-year association Ramsey was never sure if she was manipulating him for her own gain or if she really cared about him. But she got him his postdoc appointment in the country's most prestigious human geography department. The contacts he made there served him very well after his recovery. In spite of what had happened in Peru, he owed her and they both knew it.

Myriam began speaking in her rapid-fire style that was characteristic when she wanted something. "I know we've never properly resolved what happened in Peru and your departure from Oregon. We can set that aside, as far as I'm concerned." She studied him for a second then went on before he could respond. "I've followed your career. I'm impressed. What you accomplished in the Middle East was not only innovative but provided big kudos for human geography ... Tell me what you think of the shrine?"

For a moment Ramsey felt like the prodigal son returning home. He still relished her acceptance and praise. *All right, so it's still there*, he thought. "What do you want, my professional analysis?"

With a sort of quizzical smile, she answered, "Of course, you were always brilliant when it came to –"

"Sacred places?"

"That's right."

Ramsey took in a deep breath and gave her the thumbnail sketch he'd been working on since he left the shrine. "It's is similar in its characteristics to every other Southwestern Catholic shrine and grotto. Larger than most. The landscape features are not special. The 'Bodhi Tree effect' is cool, but in general it's quite ordinary."

She nodded knowingly.

"But it was once a big deal." He gestured to the restaurant, indicating his understanding of its economic impact on the area.

"Right again."

"And last, in all the stories I read about the shrine your name doesn't show up. I'll bet you work behind the scenes, as you always have."

"Three for three," Myriam said.

Ramsey eyed her over the rim of his coffee cup. Something didn't seem right. She was a classically trained administrator, better suited to large institutional operations than a once thriving healing shrine. He said, "Why would Myriam St. Eves spend her efforts here?"

Myriam shrugged. "It's seemed a good idea at the time."

Ramsey smiled. As a human geographer he knew people loved to tell stories. He just had to ask Myriam the right question to get her to speak. "Why would you put all of your well-known talents in to making this place work?"

Myriam could feel the story being tugged out of her by Ramsey's easy-going manner. She almost couldn't help herself by answering. "It began with a trip with my friend Nancy Bloomberg to the shrine. You remember her?"

Ramsey nodded.

Myriam told him everything that happened during the visit and the miraculous healing a month later. "I saw that this place had great potential and I wanted to help it thrive. The shrine had a need for a good administrator and I knew I could fill that role. Besides I wanted to get away from Eugene. Things had gone sour at the University of Oregon. As you know, after your misappropriation of funds, I lost the post-doc research money at the university. Officials weren't too keen to keep me around after that."

Ramsey bristled at the taunt. "Well at least you didn't have to worry about money, what with your husband's wealth," he mocked. "It would have been nice if you'd used some of that money to visit me in Peru while I was convalescing."

Myriam felt her cheeks heat up. "We went through a divorce at the time. Money wasn't exactly available."

They paused, studied each other. As if arriving at the same conclusion, they both spoke at the same time. "Let's start over."

Myriam smiled. 'Agreed."

Ramsey answered her smile with one of his own. "Did you ever experience the shrine's healing powers?"

"Not like Nancy did, but it had a miraculous effect on me in it's own way. It gave me my life back after all that had happened."

Ramsey nodded. "So what's next?"

"I want to hire you. That's what you do now, isn't it? Work for hire."

Caught off guard, Ramsey leaned back in his chair, "Hire me to do what?"

"If you've done your research, as I suspect you have, then you already know."

"Find out what was behind the shrine's remarkable healing powers and its sudden loss of those powers."

He sat silently, trying to figure out what she really wanted. His sense was that she wasn't telling him everything. Memories of mistrust flooded back. The awful row with her over his unapproved trip to Peru overwhelmed his mind for a moment. She was still watching him, waiting for his answer. He hardened his voice to see how she would respond. "Why me? There are a dozen others who could set up an investigation without any of our personal baggage."

Myriam didn't flinch and said evenly if not convincingly, "You're the one for the job. You have that rare combination of geographical understanding and spiritual background."

In spite of a strong voice telling him to walk away now, he felt himself back at the cottonwood tree, slowly being reeled in by the mystery. *What did the strange man at the shrine say? "You're a flower ready to bloom." Is that why I'm here?* He decided to test her. "Will you pay whatever it takes?"

"We will," she answered without hesitation.

Ramsey thought for a moment. "Who's 'we'?"

Myriam didn't answer and instead motioned to Rosa. "We're ready to order." She was pleased that their breakfast passed pleasantly over small talk. What happened to this or that person ... the state of University of Oregon's geography department ... the emergence of human geography as a force in economics, political policy, and climate change.

The rhythm of the conversation felt good to Ramsey. It was like old times, but underlying it was that nagging uncertainty and anxiety that had characterized their relationship from the beginning. Although Ramsey was flattered by her claim that he was the only one who could figure out the great mystery of the shrine, in the end he said he would think about it but had already decided he wasn't coming back.

She paid the check and left a twenty-five percent tip. He got up to leave and was quite surprised when she didn't persist. *Does she know me better than I know myself?*

Rosa overheard the whole conversation and watched as Ramsey got up, shook Myriam's hand, and left. She noticed that the tension in the room when they first met had subtly shifted. It was as if he had found what he came for, a kind of closure. And yet, there was something unfinished in the way the two Anglos parted. Myriam was tapping her fingers on the table, eyes glancing at Ramsey and back to her smartphone as if undecided what to do next. Ramsey's shoulders were set, his back ramrod straight. He was done, through; yet, his steps hesitated at the door as if expecting Myriam to come after him. *He knows something about what happened to the shrine's healing power,* Rosa thought. *Something he didn't tell Myriam.* Rosa smiled to herself. *Maybe this gringo can help bring it back.* She rushed after him.

Outside the Café Rio Ramsey fished for his car keys. He heard the soft patter of shoes on the steps behind him, followed by the hand on his sleeve. He turned, ready with his excuse. *I'm sorry Myriam, but it's not for me. Peru was enough. I don't need or want that again.*

The words died on his lips. "Rosa," he said, taking a step back. He studied her and the eyes that looked back appraised him equally. They were dark brown with russet lights. Short dark hair framed an oval face. Her olive skin was perfect, and the corners of her generous mouth had no wrinkles. He judged her to be somewhat younger than himself.

"Is something wrong?" he asked.

Her eyes narrowed. "You tell *me*."

Ramsey took another step back and found himself pressed against the rental car. She hadn't moved forward and yet he had the unmistakable feeling of being held not against his will but by her design. "I'm not sure what you mean."

She handed him a card. "Call this number. She was there that very first night nearly fifteen years ago."

"Call her?"

Rosa nodded. "Go with the Lord." She hurried back into the restaurant.

That was strange. Ramsey held the card between his middle and forefinger. A city garbage can rested against the side of the building ten feet away. With a simple flick he could make it without touching the rim. It was an old magician's trick he had learned as a kid. He stopped mid-throw. Taking a deep breath he turned the card to read it. The name written on the back was Carlotta Moore and beneath it was her number.

He looked across the street to the old hotel where he had already booked a room for the night. The sun was almost at the meridian. It had already been a long day and the need for sleep gripped him. Still, Rosa's entreaty hung in the air like a gentle breeze pushing him to take the next step. It seemed to him as if all day there had been pushes and nudges bringing him to a decision point. He shivered thinking of Peru and his mistaken belief at the time that he was supposed to be there. Still ... he shot a look at the Rio Café. Rosa was bussing the table, speaking with Myriam. It wouldn't hurt to call. Fishing his phone from his pocket, he dialed the number.

～

Carlotta Moore stood on the porch of her adobe home. She was a tall, large-hipped, big-busted woman, sculpted like the ancient depictions of Gaia, the Earth goddess. Hair rolled down her back in a waterfall of white and yellow curls. She wore a circlet of olive wood around her head and a gauzy white dress that flittered upward in the afternoon breeze, revealing legs shaped like muscled pillars. Her eyes were dark and piercing, and yet she held out her arms and hugged Ramsey to her like an old friend.

"Let's sit outside," she said and led him to a side porch where a carafe of coffee and two cups sat on a glass table. "I was glad you called. I'm happy to talk about that first night."

Ramsey raised his eyebrows at the mention of *first night*.

She sat facing the Sangre de Christo Mountains and the Milagro Shrine, which Ramsey, looking over his shoulder, could just see in the distance. The large cottonwood tree seemed brighter from here, and yet ethereal. He suddenly felt as if its essence had crossed the miles of rabbit grass and mesquite and now hovered about him in whispers of wind. Ramsey paused for a moment, trying to translate what the breeze was telling him.

"So you're a human geographer. Remind me again what they do."

"We study the importance of place in every kind of human activity. Some of the most important places in the history of humanity are sacred places."

"Like you said on the phone, you might study the history of the shrine?"

"I'm interested in how it got started. It'll help me decide if I want to proceed."

"So, what would you like to know?"

If Ramsey had a special skill it was his ability to listen. To listen to a place. To listen to people while setting his personal preferences aside. "It is perhaps the most important skill a human geographer can have," Jared Diamond had told him when he arrived at UCLA. From that moment on Ramsey consciously practiced developing that capacity.

Ramsey said, "Rosa Cisneros said you were at the Milagro Shrine from the beginning."

"There was no shrine then. I'm the only one left from the original group."

"What happened to the others?"

"They've all passed on."

"They're dead?"

She laughed lightly. "I meant they've gone out into the world. That night changed us all." Carlotta took a sip of coffee. Ramsey did the same and pursed his lips against the strong taste. "I brew it until a wooden spoon can stand up in the mix by itself. Then I add a little water. It's better for you that way." She set hers down and leaned back.

Ramsey relaxed, his smile inviting her to tell him all about the original group and that first night.

"Back at the turn of the millennium a group of us teachers from our county started coming up here in August during the Perseid meteor shower. We thought of it as a way to inaugurate the new school year. If you've ever taught you know there's something special about the beginning of a new year. Gathering together to watch the meteor shower became sort of a ritual or pilgrimage. The place was special because it had a single cottonwood growing on a dry ridge. Plus, the owner of the land didn't mind us being there. Then in 2003 we trooped up to the top of the hill and something different happened this time. It was August 12th at the height of the meteor shower. They were zipping across the night sky like Fourth of July fireworks. They seemed brighter than usual as though the gods had breathed fire into the night sky. The cottonwood tree shivered with every meteor that passed behind its massive branches.

"We are all gathered, sitting at the base of the tree, and that's when it happened."

"What happened?" Ramsey asked.

"It was like a benediction ... a feeling of deep peace and love fell over everyone. We all felt joy and goodness. Not just the good you feel waking up every morning glad you're still above ground, but good like you can go out and tackle the world. You believe in that kind of possibility?"

Ramsey gave a slight nod. "Go on."

Carlotta smiled at him and said, "Guess how old I am."

Ramsey sat back. In some of the Indian tribes he studied in the Amazon, a woman's age was a mark of respect and wisdom. Women in the U.S. weren't so blasé about getting older. "I'm thinking forty-five," he ventured, ready to take it back in an instant.

She laughed loudly and said, "Fifty-five, but I feel half that age and have every day since that night. I have the energy of people thirty years younger than I am. The feeling has never gone away."

"That's remarkable. Can you tell me what happened to the others?"

"The most amazing transformation was a teacher from West Fork, named William Benedict. He had rheumatoid arthritis. By the time we walked down to the cars he was flipping coins in the air and catching them. It was a true miracle."

"Any other 'miracles'?"

"Within a month Agnes left a bad relationship. My best friend, Francis resigned and went home to take care of her ailing parents. It was like we all experienced our own special miracle. I would say *transformational* miracle."

Ramsey's mind was racing. *It was the old paradox—did these people make the place miraculous or did the place make the miracles?*

"Then what happened?"

William was a science teacher and wanted to test to see if it would happen again. The next night he brought some other people with different illnesses and some of them got better. The shrine grew from that time to what you see out there now. People coming here getting healed finding new direction in their life, until ... I'm sure you know what's happened."

She stopped, reached for her coffee. Her hand shook slightly as if a great sob entered her chest. Ramsey could see there was something more about the first days of the Milagro shrine she wanted to share, something that brought a touch of sadness and uncertainty to her life. He let his eyes smile, sending out gratitude and support to her. It was an interview technique he'd honed to get people to relax so they would speak more honestly about issues.

She tapped her fingers against the cup. "There's something I believe you should see." Carlotta got up and went into the house, bringing back a picture. "Here's the original group a couple years later."

Ramsey studied the photograph. Ten people were clustered about the cottonwood tree. It was late summer, judging by the dark brown grass. The sky was dark blue without a cloud. Everyone was dressed in shorts and t-shirts. They smiled brightly and a couple on the far left held up fingers in a 'V' for peace. He was drawn to a man standing next to the couple. He was standing a bit apart, as though he wasn't really a member of the group. *That looks like the person I saw under the cottonwood this morning.*

He pointed to the man and asked, "Who's that?"

"My half-brother. He wasn't part of our teacher's group, but I brought him along because I thought the exercise would do him good. He'd been in a terrible motorcycle accident a few months earlier while living in Des Moines, Iowa. I brought him here to convalesce. At the time he could barely walk and couldn't talk at all. It was like his brain and body had been pulverized. My two sons and me are his only living family. As he got better, he became sort of the unofficial caretaker of the shrine. That is, up until around two months ago."

Ramsey raised his eyebrows. "Where is he now?"

Carlotta's jovial manner deadened and she shook her head. "Don't know. He just disappeared. A tear fell from her eye. "No explanation, no good bye. At the shrine on a Tuesday and gone on Wednesday."

Ramsey briefly wondered if he should say anything to her about the man he saw, but he couldn't be sure it was the same person, and he didn't want the conversation to get stuck here. Instead he asked, "His name is–?"

"Gwillt," she answered. "Adam Gwillt. His father was a Scot. He died two years after Adam was born. Mom returned to the states and married Clement Moore, my father. I wish Adam were here, he could tell you a lot more about the everyday working of the Milagro Shrine than I can. Of course, you can always talk to Father Michael."

"I might," Ramsey said, remembering the former priest he'd met at the shrine.

"Good." Carlotta frowned, the sudden disappearance of her brother still quite painful. "Call him ... Father Michael can answer the questions I can't."

Ramsey nodded, wondering what those questions might be. In the next instant, he stifled a yawn, realizing he would never call Father Michael to find out. The visit with Carlotta was interesting, but it didn't change his mind any about taking the job.

He got up to leave. "Thanks for the coffee and I'm so sorry about your brother. I hope Adam turns up."

She followed him out to the driveway where he'd parked his rental car. As he started to get in, she put her hand on his and said, "You really should call Father Michael. I have his number."

"Thanks. If I come back, I'll get it." Ramsey was anxious to leave. The correlation between the person who spoke to him under the Cottonwood tree and Adam Gwillt had shaken him. He searched his memory for what he knew about apparitional experiences. Apparitions were at the heart of many sacred sites. Appearances of Mary or even Christ at holy Christian sites were common phenomena. In some cases, mass apparitions were at the center of a sacred site's beginnings. He also remembered that many people experience ghostly apparitions of recently departed lovers, friends, and family members. A few months ago he had read an article about how quantum scientists postulated that our linear time is flexible in higher dimensions and that we can on some occasions slip in and out of our four-dimensional world and experience apparitions of celestial beings. One researcher even speculated these dimensional shifts could account for phenomena such as the sudden appearance of guardian angels. Ramsey reasoned that if he just experienced an apparition of Adam Gwillt it meant that he must be dead. Or did it?

2

———————

July, 2012
Abilene, Texas

"I just got another demand from Reverend Billy Paul," Hiram Beecher said, shaking a huge fist at the notebook computer and its collage of photos from the Rio Chama de Milagro Shrine in New Mexico. "He wants us to investigate this supposed new Christian healing shrine in New Mexico. He thinks it might be an opportunity for us."

He was standing in the boardroom of the Brothers of the Lord, a worldwide Christian ministry, whose regional headquarters for the Southwest United States was in Abilene, Texas. The top floor offices looked down on historic Cypress Street, once busy with cars and pedestrians visiting its small shops. But the district was still as empty and dusty as it was during the first year of the Great Recession. Clustered around him were the eleven other members of the board, all of them waiting for Brother Beecher to tell them what he wanted.

Beecher enjoyed his position of power in the Brotherhood. He was a giant, florid man, in his mid-60s, as hard as the oilrigs he had worked on as a teenager in Gregg County in Eastern Texas, and as tough as the Airborne Rangers he'd joined at the height of America's war effort in Vietnam. His clothes were plain; his dark beard was flecked with gray like his hair. The last two fingers were missing from his left hand. They had been mangled by twisted parachute lines during a jump into Laos. He'd cut them off, bandaged the hand and completed his clandestine mission.

"What does he want, Brother Beecher?" Sam Conklin asked. He was the youngest board member. He was shorter than Beecher and not as thick. "I hear the shrine heals the sick and gives peace to all who visit. It's located near the ruins of a sacred mission, where God's priests were slaughtered by heathens."

Beecher was surprised that Conklin knew a lot about something he had never heard of. Conklin was headstrong at times, blurting out whatever he thought instead of watching and waiting, but Beecher needed his connections to the oil and cattle wealth in central Texas.

"He wants as much information as we can find on this shrine," said Beecher. "The New Mexico region is part of our responsibility for the Brothers of the Lord. I'll take the lead on investigating the shrine's healing powers. I want the rest of you to find out who owns the land. Is it for sale? When did the shrine start?"

3

———————

August, 2015
New York City

"I am the archetype of transformation. I am Hermes, I am Loki, I am Coyote."

His human name was Edward Caine and he loved hearing himself say, "I am Coyote, the creator of the world." But today he would be Coyote the Trickster.

Edward Caine waited patiently for the battle to begin. The sky was clear and the morning already warm. By noon it would be hot and humid but by then it would no longer matter. He smiled to himself. This was a milestone in his life—4000 years of prodding humanity forward, of shaking humans from their complacency. The event he planned for today was magnificent, and worthy of Hermes, messenger of the Greek gods; of Loki, the Norse god of fire; and of Coyote, the Lakota creator of the world. *And why not*, he thought. *Are they not come alive again in me?* He breathed in deeply, felt the first rays of the morning sun prickle his skin. *Thank you Helios for your gift of light so all can see when I let loose the dogs of havoc. For is not Hermes also the Thief? ... is not Loki the God of Chaos, and is not my favorite, Coyote, also the Trickster?*

Caine often appeared as a man of thirty-one, five feet, ten inches tall, a trim 150 pounds, dark haired, with green eyes. But today he looked like a modern-day Falstaff—long hair the color of wet sand pulled back in a ponytail with a length of tarred hemp; plump cheeks crosshatched with the blue streaks of broken veins from drinking too much. A huge belly pushed through the patched sackcloth tunic and overflowed the motley pants he wore. He limped across the field, leaning on a staff for support.

Edward Caine took great delight in what he was about to do. He marveled at the brilliance of his plan. Today he was playing a common soldier in the army of Henry Tudor, leader of the House of Lancaster and rival to Richard III, head of the House of York and King of England. Both sides were made up of re-enactors from the Society for Creative Anachronism, staging the Battle of Bosworth Field at Sheep Meadow in New York City's Central Park on the 530th anniversary of the real contest.

Caine had not yet spied his quarry, Frank Ketterman. He was playing the role of John Howard, First Duke of Norfolk. A supporter of King Richard, Howard died at the Battle of Bosworth from an arrow in his face while defending his liege lord. Ketterman, the top asset manager at Citibank, had been the Bank's principal overseer of the subprime mortgage market throughout the first decade of the millennium. The government bailed out Citibank and the others but did almost nothing for the homeowners. Seven years later Ketterman was Wall Street's principal representative in secret negotiations with the U.S. government to settle all liability issues that might be brought against the banks.

Caine took his eyes off the Yorkists and checked the onlookers behind the police barricades who had come to watch a medieval battle reenactment. A few policemen on horseback rode quietly through the crowd. Other cops were scattered throughout, most paying no attention to the people but gazing at the field, grinning and pointing.

Easing forward through the Lancaster lines, Caine positioned himself at the front.

The battle's start was fifteen minutes late. The combatants were waiting for the re-enactors, King Richard and the Duke of Norfolk, who had not yet emerged from the Yorkist's ornate pavilion. It rose golden behind the lines of troops. A standard with the Royal Coat of Arms for England fluttered at the entrance. The top half beneath a jeweled crown bore three French crosses and three *lions passant* while the bottom half-reversed the same images. Beneath the shield in lettering large enough for all to read was the monarchy's motto in French: *Dieu et mon droit* ("God and my right").

The Trickster nodded. *Very apt. The bankers think of themselves as barons and untouchable. But I can bring every one of them bad fortune whenever I please.*

The tent flap swung open and Caine watched Ketterman stride through the men at arms. He wore a metal cuirass over chainmail armor, mailed gloves, greaves, and a helmet with a face guard. On his shoulder was a white rose surrounded by the colors of his house— black and red. He yelled at everyone and kicked the young page who held his sword.

Caine took his eyes off his target and checked the field. The armies were lining up on opposite sides, readying for the horn blast that would send them hurtling across the field at each other. The early morning sun glinted off chainmail and helmets. Pennants showing the red rose of Lancaster and the white rose of York fluttered in the breeze. These were anachronisms, of course. In the real dynastic wars for control of England, neither the House of Lancaster nor the House of York had chosen a rose as their emblem. To which gods each side prayed, Caine was not sure, but he was sure the Trickster had been there, bringing good and bad fortune to each side.

Any moment now, Caine thought. A horn sounded once. The re-enactors readied themselves. Another blast and they raised their weapons—harmless foam maces and broadswords—high into the air. He checked his own weapon. The staff concealed a tiny needle coated with *ethyldichloroarsine*, a nerve agent that caused burning pain, sneezing, coughing, vomiting, and pulmonary edema—followed by death.

A third wail from the horn and a great yell rose from nearly five hundred throats. The lines charged each other.

The Trickster zigzagged through the melee, never taking his eyes from his quarry. Reveling in the chaos, he avoided battle with Yorkists when he could. When forced, he quickly dispatched opponents with sharp blows from his staff to the soft tissue behind the knee, knocking them down and leaving them unharmed. But at last Ketterman stood in front of him. The man's faceplate had swung open. He was four inches taller than Caine and sneered at him.

"Henry Tudor dispatches a fat old man to fight me. Let the usurper send a champion who is worthy." He raised his foam broadsword to strike.

"It isn't Henry Tudor I fight for," Caine said.

Ketterman's blow halted in the air above the Trickster's head. "" What is this?"

Taking advantage of the bigger man's hesitation, Caine jammed the staff into the armpit at the weakest part of the armor and released the dart. The thin needle slipped easily through the chainmail's linked metal rings. Ketterman jerked once. "What!" he gasped. He tried to take a step and fell to his knees. His face contorted in a grimace. Hands clawed at his cuirass and he cried out against the sharp itching pain. He slid over onto his side. Violent coughing wracked him and his arms fell shaking to the ground. "Who are you?" he rasped.

The Trickster watched the banker struggle, his movements growing weaker. Panic filled the man's eyes. He could no longer speak. Bloody foam rimmed his mouth. Caine leaned in close and whispered, "Today I am your bad fortune." He closed the faceplate. Turning slowly, he saw that the battle had by-passed him. He stared down at Ketterman who now lay still as a corpse, though he wasn't yet dead. That would come much later after much pain. He walked away casually toward the northern edge of Sheep Meadow and the Neil Singer Lilac Walk. Tomorrow there would be a slight downtick in the financial markets and the public would not know why. But those in power would.

Ketterman was the third principal bank negotiator he had dispatched in a year. Bringing bad fortune to these people was Caine's way of destroying and re-creating the world. *I have done well and had fun doing it.*

During the preceding few weeks Caine had shocked a number of people who in one form or another were in conflict with Ketterman with the tweet "Ketterman will soon join his ancestors." His death would work to their advantage if they prepared to act quickly. One of those people was Sam Conklin. That's how the Trickster and Conklin met over a simple tweet. Conklin thought it was a miracle, but Caine knew better.

4

———

April, 1950
Edinburgh, Scotland

Caine was walking on Calton Hill. To the west lay the Salisbury Crags and beyond them the Firth of Forth. The sounds of traffic were muted this early in the morning. He loved the slow walk. The infrequently traveled path was lush with gorse and everywhere around him were lochs and glens. He thought it was as if God had brought to the Scottish lowlands a wild piece of the highlands to remind all Scots of their true heritage. Each step brought him upwards, out of the mist that had settled over Edinburgh and hid the 400-year-old cemeteries of the capitol city's Old Town. Holyrood Palace was barely visible. It'd been sometime since he had ascended Calton Hill to walk among Edinburgh's prized collection of monuments—Nelson's telescope, the city observatory, and Caine's favorite national monument, the unfinished copy of the Parthenon.

He sat atop the tall hill and breathed in deeply, wrapping the clean air around him like a blanket, and settling within its crisp folds like a babe nestling to its mother. *The gods are near,* he told himself, and sighed contentedly.

In times past, he had sat here for hours, under the night sky waiting to be called. He always knew the best times to be alone. But today was not one of those times. The King was in residence and the cultural center of Scotland was buzzing with excitement. His Majesty's presence had brought thousands of tourists from the kingdom and around the world. *It can't be helped. Transitions happen when they happen.*

He stood up and rested a slim fingered hand along the gray bricks of Nelson's Telescope. The monument pointed north toward the Firth of Forth as if spying on the sea and what dangers it held. As he waited, the sun rose above the fog settling in the low parts of Old Town, brightening the cobalt blue sky. Somewhere out of the mist a bell tolled. He counted the peals—seven o'clock. *It's nearly time.*

The sound of lorries chugging up the main road, engines straining with the loads of tourists coming to visit Calton, made a plaintive counterpart to the rustle of the wind in the shrubs. Then into the dark blue heaven splashed a sound like God playing bagpipes. Caine looked skyward straining to hear. The sound, like breezes to anyone else, brought him a new task. He listened. *There on the steps of the old observatory a woman is in labor. A baby is coming.*

The message ended. Caine had walked over to where the crowd had gathered. The terrified husband was yelling for somebody to help. A handful of onlookers gathered around helpless.

Caine threaded his way through the tourists. He gazed at the mother. Her hair hung in stringy wet curls; her face was a blotchy patchwork of bright red and pasty white. Her breathing came in labored gasps, dampening, slower, slower with each contraction, each push weaker than the last. A young man began running down the hill, shouting he was going for help. The nearest phone booth was miles away and the ambulance miles beyond that. They would never arrive in time.

Caine knelt down and gently placed his hand on the woman's rippling belly. At once the muscles in her neck tightened. Her hands gripped the ground, tearing out handfuls of sod. She screamed and with a giant push, the new baby emerged from the portal of the womb into his hands. A small woman rushed up with a white picnic cloth and took the baby.

"It's a boy," she cooed to the mother.

"His name is Adam," Caine said.

He walked away, the crowd parting for him like the Red Sea. Arthur's Seat, Holyrood Park's highest peak, loomed ahead of him, its barren rocky outcrop thrusting upward to form a rugged throne. He headed toward it, the crowd forgotten, but the baby's presence loomed in his consciousness. He breathed in deeply, recognizing the beginning, like all great beginnings marked by wailing and crying. The wind veered and rushed toward him, the breeze whispering words only he could hear: *Change is coming ... Change is coming.*

5

———

December, 2015
Edinburgh, Scotland

Caine stood at the top of Arthur's Seat looking past the dark green and yellow of the blooming gorse of Holyrood Park into Edinburgh below. The sharp tang of salt air mingled with the oily trace of car exhaust. He frowned at the smog layering the city with a thick haze.

It took only sixty years to change from that idyllic summer morning to this dreary winter day. More change was coming now and he loved it. He looked skyward as if he could somehow see limned against the dark blue of the Scottish highland sky the old Celtic gods—Llyr, god of the sea, and Math, god of wisdom. *Do you remember me brothers? He thought also of Dwyn, god of mischief, lord of change.*

The dark buzz of his phone shook Caine. The sudden appearance of smart phones reminded him of the marvelous changes happening in the world and even greater ones on the way. Caine was suddenly exhilarated. *How wonderful! So much change in so few years. New ways coming, nearer and nearer.*

He pulled himself from his musing and glanced at the number, recognizing it. He let his face ripple into the familiar features the caller would remember. Then pressing connect, he let the caller's face appear on the screen. He said, "So did you grab the opportunity I handed you?"

Startled by the question, it took Conklin a moment to answer. "Yes, you were right."

"I take it you were able to regain control of your family ranch?"

"Yes."

"And the oil shale rights below."

"Yes."

"You're a rich man now."

Caine heard the hesitation in Conklin's sudden breath. Then the man was saying, "They're saying Ketterman was murdered."

"I would call it bad fortune. But bad fortune for someone is good fortune for another. Wouldn't you agree?"

Caine's all but admitting he killed the man, Conklin thought. "Can we meet?"

"How about next Thursday 2 o'clock in Austin? I believe the gay bar three blocks off the capital would be a fine place. . . .You know the one?"

"Yes."

"Bring that fellow Hiram Beecher with you. Until then."

Caine slipped the phone back into his pocket. *Another piece of the change.*

Looking out upon the gorse, its flowers turning from yellow to golden as the sun rose higher in the sky, he smiled, reveling in the knowledge of change whipping across the world.

6

———

March 26, 2019
Grinnell, Iowa

It was just past midnight when Ramsey pulled into the driveway of his restored Victorian house in Grinnell, Iowa. The small Iowa college town was a place where he felt grounded and at peace. Ramsey always maintained that the best days of his life had been his four years at Grinnell College. The quiet beauty of the small town suited him perfectly. After recovering from his psychotic episode in Peru, Ramsey had used a portion of the substantial inheritance from his father to set up his consulting firm with a remarkable young man from Myriam's postdoc research team. Not only was Dr. Ron Grange brilliant, but his father was a highly successful and connected lobbyist in D.C. As the firm grew, Ron wanted to move their offices to the East Coast, where most of the world's geopolitical powerbrokers were located. But the idea of living in a large metropolitan city had not appealed to Ramsey. The two men compromised. Ron chose to live in Bethesda and Ramsey returned to Grinnell. He had found the Victorian house on the edge of the campus and had rented office space on the upper floor of a local bank.

Parking his car in front of the garage, he carried his bags to the back entrance. A motion light flicked on, bathing the house's large portico in a soft light. The back door was unlocked. Inside a note from the housekeeper was pinned to the refrigerator. "Dinner is ready; just heat for two minutes in the microwave. Gladys."

Food would have to wait until tomorrow. He went into his office, and after pouring himself a snifter of fine cognac, stood in front of the French doors that opened onto the backyard. The soft scents of spring filled the crisp night air. Somewhere in the trees beside the garage a barn owl hooted. He tipped his glass in salute, glad to be back amid familiar sights and sounds. But even as he took a sip of the fine brandy, his thoughts kicked him out of the comforts of home and back into events of the past two days. The memory of what happened beside the Cottonwood tree was losing its vibrancy, and he could have called Myriam and graciously decline her offer. But then there was what had happened at Chicago's O'Hare airport late this afternoon.

While waiting for a connecting flight to Des Moines, he had looked up Adam Gwillt on the Internet. But after twenty minutes of searching, it was as if man didn't exist. The only information he found was a short article in Rio Chama's local newspaper about his disappearance—along with a picture of Adam—that was probably placed at the request of the sister, Carlotta. Otherwise, nothing. He had recalled again how the apparition beside the cottonwood tree had looked remarkably like the picture of Adam that Carlotta had shown him. But was it really him? The question was becoming both perplexing and intriguing. Then the strangest thing had happened. While sitting in O'Brien's Restaurant & Bar enjoying a burger and fries, he had overheard the name "Adam Gwillt." Looking over his shoulder, he saw a man talking on his cell phone. By his fine clothes, Ramsey surmised he was a successful businessman. Just as he got up to ask about Adam, the man had looked at his watch, grabbed his computer and dashed off.

For a moment Ramsey had thought about chasing after him.

Then he noticed the man's credit card receipt on his table. Walking over casually, he had read his name: Malcolm Grossinger. A quick Internet search revealed he was the president of Midwest Cable based in Des Moines, Iowa.

Ramsey wasn't sure how he felt about coincidences. He knew that the famous Swiss psychologist Carl Jung had built a whole theory of psychological development around meaningful coincidences that he called synchronicity. Taking another sip of the fragrant brandy, Ramsey felt like he was being steered along some path much like what had occurred on his journey to Peru. *Back then I was led astray by some mysterious forces. Is the same thing happening again? Am I misreading what happened in the last two days? Or, as Jung might say, "are these signs that providence is at work in my life."*

But today the problem at hand was quite different. What should he do about Myriam's offer and what were all those coincidences around Adam Gwillt about? It came down to rationality versus intuition, he supposed. So he settled into the large wingback chair before the fireplace in his office. Around him on the walls hung beautifully framed historical maps collected by his father from around the world. Ramsey senior had been a physical geographer and his appreciation of cartography was not lost on his only son. *For that I am grateful*, Ramsey thought.

Cradling the brandy snifter in both hands, he studied the last picture of his father before he suffered a massive, fatal heart attack in Ramsey's junior year in high school. It hung in a frame over the mantle. His father's face was sallow, the eyes hollowed, the once-sharp neckline layered under fat. It was taken while he was standing in his study, one hand resting pretentiously on a globe of the world and the other inside his favorite blue-checked waistcoat. It was a pose he'd always wanted to make, standing like the nineteenth-century-British Empire's imperious Prime Minister, Benjamin Disraeli. After the picture, he had wheezed into the chair behind his desk and clucked at his son's disapproving frown as he pulled out a cigar from the humidor on the shelf behind. "I'm a dying man so give me my pleasures and listen to my advice," his father had said. After lighting up, he leaned back into the soft leather and blew a smoke ring into the air, and said thoughtfully, "Jonathan, geography is the one reliable way of making sense of what is happening in the world, and it will be the overarching field of the twenty-first century." He had died a week later.

"So what would you do, old man? Would you take this job?" Ramsey asked, nodding toward the picture.

He could hear his father's old chuckle, the same laugh when he'd asked him to sign the permission slip to play football in junior high school. The old man had lit one of his cigars and said, "Jonathan, you have both rationality and intuition. When they come together, you'll know how to decide."

Ramsey reviewed Myriam's offer for the hundredth time since leaving New Mexico. His rational side told him to accept the challenge. *I could take the job. Businesswise there is neither gain nor risk.* The two young staffers in his company, recent geography graduates from the University of Kansas, could handle the campaign in Ecuador to incentivize locals to preserve a large portion of the unique rain forest ecosystem. Both were familiar with his methodology and strategies. Also businesswise, Ron Grange could handle the upcoming D.C. and LA meetings on resource use in the Arctic. The only possible hiccup was the weekly undergraduate seminar on the geopolitics of newly emerging ethnic and religious identities he was teaching at Grinnell College. But his co-teacher could easily handle the class.

Ramsey took a sip of brandy, savoring the mellow sweetness. On the other hand, his gut feeling was unclear. *Better not to peek behind old doors.*

He set the brandy onto a low table. The wall clock said twelve thirty. It was still not too late to call the one person who could give him the perspective he needed. Picking up his phone, he punched in a number. It answered quickly, not going to voice mail. A dry chuckle and then, "Jonathan."

It was good to hear his old mentor's voice.

Ramsey rode down Main Street to the Frontier Café. The day was windless, but gray clouds covered the sky and there was a hint of an early spring snowstorm in the sharp sting of the air. Leaning his bike against the rack out front, he glanced inside. Professor Orensen was already waiting for him at their favorite table.

The professor had two PhD's—a doctorate in divinity and another in political science. Most importantly, he was the man who had steered Ramsey to follow in his father's footsteps. Now an emeritus professor of religious studies and international relations, he had changed little since Ramsey walked into his class over twenty years ago. That first day he had noticed the man's shock of white hair that rolled behind his ears and down his back in long braids. He was thin and ramrod straight and dark complected, like his mother. She had been one-sixteenth Lakota. A large curved nose dominated his narrow face, slightly pocked from childhood measles. He had stood in front of the class like a Plains Indian warrior challenging everyone to be smarter than he was. And when it happened, which was rare, it was like *counting coup*—the ancient Lakota way of besting someone without hurting him.

Throughout the years of graduate and postgraduate work, Ramsey had stayed in touch with his old mentor through emails and the occasional Christmas card. Everything seemed fine, but he was unprepared for what he found when he returned to start his business twelve years ago. Professor Orensen had lost much of the color in his face. The bounce was gone from his step and he merely walked to his classes, whereas before he had galloped. In talking to him, Ramsey discovered the once vibrant personality had become bitter and old. Though he was up for retirement, he kept on teaching. However, it was like a routine, a rut worn in the carpet of academia. Twice Ramsey had approached him about it, only to be shrugged off. Only much later did he learn that the man's wife of fifty-three years had died of brain cancer a year earlier.

Then four years ago the professor had seemed to get a second wind. His old vitality returned and Ramsey discovered their mentor student relationship was deeper than ever. It had since developed into the most rewarding friendship Ramsey had. They even co-taught his class in emerging ethnic and religious identities.

Ramsey waved as he threaded through the crowded restaurant, the savory smells of hot soups and warm bread filling him with a pleasant sense of being home, its stark contrast with the Café Rio underscoring the problem he'd come here to discuss. The two men shook hands and he grabbed the menu as he sat down. "Give me a moment."

"I already ordered the usual. Burger and fries," the professor said.

Ramsey closed the menu and let it fall onto the table. "Have I become that predictable?"

Orensen chuckled. "About your dining habits, maybe. Can't say much about the rest of your life." He took a sip of hot tea. "So why the meeting?"

Ramsey was grateful Orensen had never been one for small talk, especially when he sensed a person needed advice. "Some things have come up. Remember my postdoc fellowship at Oregon and the program administrator, Myriam St. Eves?"

"The one you said was both the best and the worst person that ever entered your life?"

"That's the one. A week ago she called and all but demanded I meet her in New Mexico where she has a second home. While I was there, she offered me a job. She wants me to investigate some unusual phenomena surrounding a healing spot called Rio Chama de Milagro Shrine."

Orensen's eyebrows raised and his eyes narrowed. For a moment Ramsey thought the professor might get up and leave.

"Did I touch a nerve or something?" he asked.

Orensen shook his head. "You just surprised me. I happen to know it very well."

"Really? How come you never told me?"

"I had an experience there I don't tell anyone about because . . ." He licked his lips and took a sip of tea. "It just sounds too crazy."

The waitress came and set two orders of burgers and fries in front of the men. She placed a dish with salsa beside Orensen's plate.

"Thanks, Pam," he said.

"No problem, professor." She looked at Ramsey. "No pickles and French's Mustard?"

"You got it."

She left and neither man touched his food. They looked across the table at each other and Ramsey wondered if he should ask what had happened there. He could sense the man's expression telling him it was very personal and had something to do with the difficulties after his wife died. He decided to wait.

Orensen took a deep breath. He felt the sweat bead up on his brow and wiped it away with the napkin. His thoughts raced. *We don't speak openly about the shrine, and now this. What should I do?* His ancestors on his mother's side would have called this unexpected meeting a sign, an omen to be heeded. *I didn't believe in that stuff*, he reminded himself. *At least not until four years ago. Now I'm on the lookout for such things.* He took a sip of tea; the warmth in his throat spread through him. *It's a good story. Somebody should hear it before I die.*

Just then the restaurant's door blew open and a gust of cold air rattled through the room. The waitress closed it, apologizing to the customers.

The professor smiled. *And it would seem the universe has selected Jonathan as the one.*

"I'll tell you what happened. I was at a conference of religious instructors in Santa Fe. I was receiving one of those honorary awards for distinguished service in my field. You know the plaque they give to washed-up old folk. It was the anniversary of Melinda's passing. I felt horrible, wishing she could be there. The award was as much hers as mine. She put me through school, moved from her family in San Diego to the Midwest and never complained ... not about the harsh winters ... the small town. We used to joke that one lifetime was not enough for the two of us."

He sipped his tea. "That afternoon the conference had a free day. There was a story about the Rio Chama de Milagro Shrine in the information packet. I had nothing planned so I decided to go. I even imagined it as a kind of a pilgrimage."

Ramsey's eyes widened and he didn't bother to keep the incredulity out of his voice. "You? You were never religious."

"Imagine that, a doctor of divinity with no religion," Orensen said ironically. He said. "When you get older things begin to change."

"I get it. What happened next?"

"The short version is a mind-blowing, transformative experience. But that's just to set it up. I'll tell you this: I would never have accepted it from anyone else as anything more than a hallucination. But I'll tell you there was nothing hallucinatory about the experience at all. It was as real as you and me sitting here."

Ramsey reached for a fry, then set it down. He had never heard his old mentor speak so openly before. He realized that though they were close, the old man had kept things from him and now was opening up. He settled back and listened.

"When I got there," Orensen continued, "I walked along the paths looking at all the little curios left behind. At one point a man made eye contact with me. He was tall, muscular and redheaded. He came over and laid a hand on my arm. The next thing I know I'm being pulled up in some sort of light lattice. I tried to resist. I was scared, and then the light went away and I'm no longer outside. I'm sitting in a chapel. Then another light, blinding this time, and when it goes away, Melinda is sitting next to me, her hand is in mine." He licked his lips, felt the tears come to his eyes again the way they did on that afternoon. He didn't bother to brush them away.

"She looked just like she did the year before she got sick."

Ramsey felt his own pulse quicken. He was afraid to speak, feeling an onrush of tears would follow if he did. Melinda had been a second mother to him after his own mother died when he was eighteen. He nodded.

"What happened next I can only describe as a miracle. You see, during her illness I was her caretaker, setting up doctor visits and chemo and radiation treatments. I gave her medicine, cleaned up after her. I was always the caretaker, never the husband. I had walled off that feeling part of me because I knew if I ever let it peek out I would lose it and be no help at all. And because I didn't ever want to admit she was dying. So I never took the chance to tell her how much I loved her, how much she meant to me.

"When she died, all that grief and love and all the feelings I had stuffed inside for six months poured out. I cried every day for a year straight. And every day in the years that followed I had to decide just to live. I'll tell you, there never was a day I was happy. Living without her was the most wretched time of my life.

"So here she was sitting next to me, smiling. She leaned over and kissed me on the cheek and said, 'I've been waiting a long time to speak with you.'"

"I said, 'I thought you would never want to speak to me again after the way I acted when you were sick.'"

"'I always knew you loved me,'" she said.

"'I did ... I still do. A day doesn't go by when I don't miss you ... when I want to hold you once more ... do a crossword puzzle together ... go out for a walk.'"

"'Those were wonderful times, Roger. But now you have to stop holding me in grief and instead hold me in love.'"

"'How can I do that?'"

"Melinda then put her hand on my heart and said, 'In here.'"

"Jonathan, at that moment it was like a warm wind went through me. It lasted maybe a minute and when it was gone, my grief was gone with it, and in its place were love and gratitude for the fifty-three years we had together.

"She smiled at me and I smiled for the first time ... I mean truly smiled from my soul, from the very core of my heart, for the first time in six years. At that moment we were both satisfied and she disappeared.

"I opened my eyes. Strangely I was once more outside on the ground and that man I told you about was helping me up. He said, 'I see you got what you came for.' I began to thank him, but he shook his head. 'It's you,' he said and walked away.

"I can honestly say everything changed for the better after that day."

Ramsey pursed his lips. He studied his mentor and friend. His face was shining like an angel from a Raphael painting. He didn't know what to say, afraid any comment would destroy the moment.

Then Orensen picked up a sweet potato fry. He dipped it in the salsa and ate it with gusto. He chose another, basting it the same way but stopped before bringing it to his mouth. "You should eat these before they get cold," he said.

Ramsey smiled. "You're not asking me whether I believe your story or not."

"Doesn't matter whether you believe or not. What matters is that I believe. It happened to me and it changed my life."

Ramsey reached out to the old man and touched his hand gently. "I had my own non-ordinary experience at the Milagro Shrine, but nothing as profound as yours."

Over the rest of the meal, he related what happened and all the coincidences around Adam Gwillt. They finished and Ramsey picked up the check.

They sat a few moments and Orensen said, "You didn't come here to listen to an old man talk about his dead wife ... or did you?" He waved away Ramsey's response. "You want to know if you should take the job. Well now you have another coincidence, another piece of synchronicity as Jung would say. You have your answer. I'll cover your class for you until you get back."

Ramsey's mind and gut were now in harmony. "I don't know how long I'll be."

"So much the better."

As they were about to get up, Orensen motioned for Ramsey to sit down. "There's something bigger than the shrine. Do you know about it?"

"No."

"In the beginning there was a big controversy over whether the shrine should become part of the Catholic establishment since the Roman Catholic Church is very strong in northern New Mexico. But eventually it became a nonsectarian site supported by donations and run by a group called the Friends of the Shrine. A local priest actually rescinded his vows. But gradually something new emerged—an internet-based group called the New Gnostics, people impacted by the power of the shrine. I'm one. It's a religious movement totally different than anything else. We communicate through a password-protected website. I'll let you use my password if you like."

Ramsey's eyes widened in surprise. "That would be fantastic. But wouldn't I be getting you in trouble?"

"The New Gnostics believe in the power of the shrine and now that it's gone, we'd like to know what happened."

"You're certain I'll take the job."

Orensen smiled. "I can see you're already on your way, and you're the only one who can do it."

"Myriam said the same thing."

"How far do you trust her?"

Ramsey weighed what he knew about her against his own anger toward her, and pangs of guilt over flaunting the rules of her program and causing it to lose its funding. He wanted to trust her but he couldn't be sure. She was a facilitator and manipulating people was part of her way of getting things done.

"I'll have to be careful," he admitted.

Orensen nodded. "I'll do what I can to help."

Orensen waved goodbye and Ramsey watched him cross the street to his car parked in front of the historic Louis Sullivan Jewel Box Bank. The bank's odd diamond-like façade was a city landmark. The

Masonic-looking emblem seemed to point its tip right at the professor. Ramsey shook his head. The synchronicity contained in his friend's story and its connection to the shrine gave him a new jolt of energy. He checked his watch. The call to Des Moines would have to wait. He ordered a cup of coffee. He needed some time to think about all the coincidences that had led up to this point, coincidences that went back twenty years to a meeting with Orensen in his office.

Sitting behind a huge desk, littered with papers, tapes, post-it-notes, and strange curios, Professor Orensen had said, "I suspect your father has encouraged you to go into physical geography."

Ramsey had nodded an agreement. It had been a wonderful academic and practical field of inquiry in America for over one hundred years. Geography's roots went back to the earliest mapmakers in Mesopotamia and Greece. Maps throughout history told the story of human development and that appealed to Ramsey. But what the professor said next changed his life forever.

"Human geography is where the future of the planet lies, Jonathan. Especially sacred places. Unwrapping the mystery behind their power will offer a guide to navigating through the troubled waters humanity will face as we approach the new millennium. Sacred geography is where the physical environment and spirit meet. If I were starting a career in geography today, that's what I would set my sights on."

Ramsey took a sip of coffee and recalled the question that had niggled at him ever since his father had him read, at the age of sixteen, the writings of Lucien Lévy-Bruhl. The famed anthropologist had written, "The land is a living book in which the myths are inscribed. A legend is captured in the very outlines of the landscape."

·   ·   ·

Like Ramsey, it turned out that Orensen's urgings tied into a question that arose after the professor's own reading of Lévy-Bruhl: Do sacred places have an embedded and detectable power to transform and heal people?

A couple of years later when Ramsey had begun his graduate studies in human geography, there was a great intellectual debate over the validity and resurgence of interest in the principle of environmental determinism. Led by Jared Diamond's breakout book, *Guns, Germs, and Steel*, the idea was that the physical environment was the primary factor in the development of human cultures, deeply affecting consciousness as well as economic development. Place, in the geographical sense, was driving history.

Following in the footsteps of Lévy-Bruhl, Ramsey's initial research had centered on how sacred places had organized primitive societies. In these cultures, the whole natural world was alive with magic. Mountains, rivers, trees, almost anything could become sacred to a tribal group. Urged forward by Diamond, Ramsey had achieved a great insight. He discovered that a major factor in moving from nomadic tribal groups to primitive agricultural settlements was the establishment of permanent sacred places. Early on they were often burial grounds. He had written a paper on the effigy-mound builders, who prospered over 1,000 years ago in the upper Mississippi Valley. He demonstrated how critical these sacred mounds were to their success as agriculturalists. What became known as the Ramsey Principle stated that at least three percent of any early agriculturalist territory needed to be devoted to sacred places for it to become prosperous agricultural society.

So when the postdoc opportunity at the University of Oregon had come up, Ramsey proposed to Myriam that he would try to prove or disprove the possibility that there were inherently powerful spots distributed across the planet, which humans have fashioned into sacred places. This had led him to investigate with the latest scientific energy detecting and remote sensing equipment some of the world's most famous sacred places.

Beginning in the United States, he had gone to the Medicine

Wheel National Historic Landmark in Wyoming. From there he had traveled around the world. First to Jokhang in Tibet, then to Lourdes in France, India's sacred Elephanta Caves on Gharapuri Island, and the Minoan Caves in Crete. At each place he had used his ability to feel. As he often had described it to other researchers, "I was able to listen to the geographical story the place is telling. When listening deeply, I saw and felt the power of the place with new eyes and ears."

It was like what Ramsey heard at a talk by one of the astronauts who had walked on the moon, Edgar Mitchell, who described the mystical experiences he and his fellow astronauts had when they saw the Earth from outer space. Mitchell had said, "On the return trip home, gazing through 240,000 miles of space toward the stars and the planet from which I had come, I suddenly experienced the universe as intelligent, loving, and harmonious." At times Ramsey found himself wanting to understand this sort of experience more than he wanted to find answers to his research questions.

Ramsey felt the air pressure change around him, the slight prickle of static electricity. A faint rumble of thunder echoed against the dark clouds closing in on Grinnell. It reminded him of Glastonbury and a coincidence during his research trip that had ultimately led to the shrine and the growing mystery around Adam Gwillt.

The last stop on his travels had brought him to England. By this time he had collected a great variety of anomalous readings associated with a number of sacred places. He was sure that a number of these readings had to do with nearby massive crystalline structures but no clear pattern or correlation between the sites was evident. He was tired and was ready to head back to Eugene where he would make sense out of all the data he had collected. It was at Glastonbury, the last stop on his British itinerary, that the coincidence happened.

A major pilgrimage site for spiritual seekers in the twenty-first century, Glastonbury at one time had been touted as home to the fabled Isle of Avalon. Arthurian legend stated it was here that Arthur Pendragon had received the legendary sword of Excalibur. Later he came back here with Morgan le Fey to recover from wounds he suffered after defeating his mortal enemy Mordred at the Battle of Camlaan. Glastonbury was also reputed to be the final resting place of the Jesus Christ's Holy Grail, brought to the sacred isle by Joseph of Arimathea, who later became the first Christian bishop of Britain. Archaeologists generally downplayed these claims as being a publicity stunt by the monks to raise money for a new abbey after the original Glastonbury Abbey burned down in 1184. The town, itself, located 20 miles south of Bristol, had been an Iron Age village and was over 3,000 years old. The fact that early agriculturalists had created a town on this spot was more than enough to pique his interest. The later tales of Arthur and the Holy Grail were little more than icing on the cake. Ramsey had gotten some unusual low-frequency electromagnetic readings near the ruins of the old abbey.

One day while walking through the town square carrying his equipment and gauging the sky that was roiling with thick with dark clouds, a breeze whipped up, screaming of a downpour in just a few minutes. He had just decided to go to a pub, where he could wait out the storm, when an old man reached out a claw of a hand and snagged his windbreaker. "You need a guide," he said flatly.

Ramsey turned and started in surprise. The man was bent and twisted like a goblin, with a sharp nose stuck out from a gaunt face. Hair sprouted from his ears in tufts and his bushy eyebrows shadowed deep sockets that gleamed with a dark inner light. A long beard flowed down his chest. When he looked closer, Ramsey saw one of the man's eyes had been plucked out, as if offered in a sacrifice like Odin at the well of Mimir. The other was slate gray and burned with the intensity of an exploding star.

Ramsey set his equipment down. "Why do I need a guide?" he asked, amused at the man's boldness. He thought he was just an old drunk who needed money and like the twelfth century monks of Glastonbury Abbey was concocting a need where there wasn't one.

"You'll never find what's important here unless someone points you in the right direction."

Ramsey scratched the beard he'd been growing since the field research started three months ago. The old man looked harmless, so why not wait out the storm inside with him. "What's your name?"

"Loki."

Ramsey hid his surprise. Loki was a shape shifter and the trickster of the *Aesyr*, the Norse gods.

The old man said, "My family has lived in these parts since Glastonbury was a muddy jumble of thatch-roofed huts. We came here during the Iron Age. Not many can recall that far back."

For a sharp breath Ramsey thought the old man might be crazy, but there was something interesting—not just about the town—but about the man himself. His senses honed in on the old man. He stood on the sidewalk by the short wooden bench, as though he owned this spot on the town square. Others seemed to walk around him, not out of fear but respect. Some even nodded. "Mr. Loki, let's go inside to the brew pub before we get drenched by the storm and you can tell me what's special about this place."

The ancient man leaned back against the bench. He looked up and his good eye narrowed as though it were some kind of laser piercing the thunderclouds forming overhead. After a minute they roiled away and sunshine came through. The ever-curious aspect of Ramsey's character sparked his interest in the old man. And what the old man said next rewarded his curiosity.

"What you're trying to detect, that equipment can't find," the old man said. He smiled and his teeth were all white and solid, not like the old yellowed and broken teeth of a man who was supposed to be ancient and wizened. Ramsey realized also his voice was not raspy and shattered like so many old people who drank or smoked too much. It held a touch of lyricism, like a wandering minstrel, and seemed to match the man's tattered clothes, a motley of leather jerkin, a ruffled shirt, and coarse wool pants. The name "Loki" nagged at something in his memory but he couldn't place it.

"Some say they can feel it in their bones," Loki added. "Right now, you're poking at the edges, trying to see if there are any hornets in the nest. You have to go inside the nest, boy."

"Where can I do that here?"

"Not here. The place for that is Peru. That's where you'll find the meaning of what you experienced many years ago in Iowa." Ramsey started in surprise. How could the old man know about his experience during his college days at Grinnell? Before he could ask him about it the old man stood up and Ramsey realized he was as tall as himself. Loki looked back at the sky. The clouds were gathering again. "Time to go ... and time for you to return to the States and journey south to Peru. There is a shamanistic practitioner in Santa Fe ... José Luis ... who can get you there. You should look him up and tell them the old trickster sent you. He'll understand."

Loki crossed the square. He felt the young man's eyes on his back watching him. He could sense the rising certainty in the man's desire to make the journey. He laughed gleefully to himself, danced a jig and spun around. The young man was gathering up his equipment, his eyes darting in Loki's direction. *It is time for you to cross over,* Loki giggled in his mind.

Ramsey had watched Loki cross the plaza. The old man seemed to get bigger and darker with each step, like the gathering thundercloud. Ramsey grabbed his equipment and set off after him. Rain suddenly rushed down like Noah's flood. Instead of following the old man, he hightailed it to the nearest pub. Inside by a roaring fire, he ordered a black and tan. He waited an hour for the rain to stop. When he went outside, he saw no trace of the old man. It was then that Loki's boldest deed as a member of the Norse pantheon clicked in his memory. He was the Norse god who brought the gift of fire to mankind.

Ramsey hadn't thought about that day in a long time. He heard another deep rumble of thunder and looked out the café window. Gray clouds now enveloped the sky above Grinnell. Yet another rumble seemed to go on forever and when it ended, the clouds opened up and a cold slushy rain fell. He looked at his bike leaning against the rack outside the café. On the sidewalks, people scurried to get under cover. He ordered another cup of coffee and waited. *The power of synchroncity,* he thought. *Events are bringing me back to my starting point twenty years ago. Only this time I'm more prepared.* He sipped coffee and came to a decision. It was time to call Malcolm Grossinger, the man he had overheard in the airport.

Surprisingly, when Ramsey explained his rather unusual story about needing to speak with Malcolm to the woman who answered the phone, he was immediately connected. It was almost as if Malcolm had been waiting for the call. After Ramsey mentioned that he had overheard him in the airport conversing on the phone about Adam Gwillt, to Ramsey's surprise once again, Grossinger said he remembered the conversation he was having in the airport with his wife about Adam's belongings. He was not only happy to meet with Ramsey but seemed eager to talk about his longtime best friend Adam Gwillt. They arranged to meet outside of one of his condo complexes the next day.

7

———————

March 27, 2019
Des Moines, Iowa

Des Moines, the capital of Iowa, was one of those Midwestern towns that had gone through radical ups and downs over its life. Many would say its primary business is the presidential primary, as it is the first stop of every presidential campaign. Founded in 1851 as "Fort Des Moines," it had undergone a revival the 21st century. Part of that revival was the transformation of the old Simpson Chair factory into the Malcolm Grossinger Lofts—sixty-one loft apartments located in the heart of the Court Avenue cultural district. The charm of the exterior of this historic building has been a model for the gentrification of downtown Des Moines.

Malcolm Grossinger, the owner of the lofts, was an upper-middle-class only son of a Sioux City physician. He had graduated from Drake with honors and went into business, eventually marrying the daughter of a small upstart cable company executive. The cable enterprise was just the beginning. As the company grew, Malcolm's personal wealth climbed into the upper one percent of the country as he acquired many landholdings across

Iowa. He was one of the rich and powerful in Des Moines and board president of Des Moines's mega-church, the Evangelical Covenant.

Now in the gray mist of a cold March morning, Grossinger, with Ramsey by his side, buzzed himself into the Malcolm Grossinger Lofts.

Ramsey immediately liked the man while at the same time recognizing there was some agenda in play that he wasn't being told. Almost immediately Grossinger began talking about his friendship with Adam.

Grossinger and Adam had developed one of those lifelong relationships that to most people would seem a mystery.

Adam and Malcolm were roommates as freshmen at Des Moines' Drake University. An immediate and deep bond formed between the two young men. Adam had a scholarship from a private fund that supported foster children. He was a self-driven, self-taught philosophy major. But as Grossinger would quickly find out, he was a person incapable of dealing with the social milieu of university life and dropped out after only one semester.

Grossinger gave Ramsey a snapshot of Adam's life. Adam could've done anything he set his mind to, even play football at the pro level. During his adult life he worked mostly in a bookstore, and as a stock boy in a grocery store. When Malcolm needed something fixed on his house or his apartments Adam could do it all. They hunted together. They were passionate University of Iowa football and basketball fans, attending hundreds of games together.

Grossinger turned to Ramsey. "As you might have guessed by the name on the building, my family trust owns these apartments. When the restoration was complete, I let Adam stay here for free. Why not? He was my best friend. It's hard to believe he just disappeared. I've kept his place just as it was the day of his accident. I always thought he would come back."

"Did he?" Ramsey asked.

"No, instead I visited him three times down in New Mexico. The first time he was just beginning his convalescence. Still bedridden.

His memory was really foggy and he asked me to tell him stories about his life. Which I did for three days."

"Second time?"

"He had changed dramatically. He was anxious that I come down because he wanted to take a trip with me to Albuquerque. Said he wanted to see the ancient rock art. But when we got there he asked me to drop him off on the edge of the poorest Hispanic neighborhood in the city. Told me he would be fine and to pick him up in six hours. Which I did."

"What do you think he was doing? Did you ask him?"

"He said something about needing to be among the poor and the sick."

"That was it?"

"That was it."

"You said there was a third time. What did you guys do?"

"Nothing special."

Ramsey's highly practiced intuition again told him Grossinger was hiding something, but he didn't press it since they had now reached room 356, Adam's apartment. Grossinger pulled out a key and unlocked the door. It was a small loft. Books were everywhere. Every philosophical book that was ever written seemed to be here in one grand collection. Taking in the room, Ramsey grasped the organizing principle. Logical positivism in one place, transcendentalists in another, existentialist and moral philosophers —all were brilliantly grouped and alphabetized. *Adam must have been a stickler for order.*

"As I said, I kept the room for him just as he left it. I always assumed he was coming back. But now?" He shrugged.

Grossinger walked over to a large metal filing cabinet. He opened the upper drawer and inside were reams of handwritten notes, yellow pads filled with mathematical symbols and file folders stuffed with papers.

"Adam wrote constantly all his life. Said he hoped someday to write the quintessential philosophical treatise. Somebody should go through these and see what's here."

"You?"

"Of course not. Maybe you know somebody who might like to be paid to organize this stuff?"

"I might." Ramsey thought of a bright young graduate from the nearby University of Wisconsin who he just interviewed for an internship.

Grossinger's mood shifted. He was no longer the jovial storyteller. "Tell me again what you're up to?"

Ramsey wondered how Grossinger would respond to the story of his paranormal experience but he decided to risk the truth. "Do you believe in apparitions or visits from spirits, angels, or even the dead?" Ramsey waited for a reaction but Grossinger's steely gaze never shifted. "When I was at the shrine three days ago I had what could be called a visitation from Adam. He gave me a riddle about how it was time for me to sow the seeds of a life. I'm trying to make sense of this experience and the riddle. Can you help?"

The smile returned. "I believe I already have. I have an appointment I must get to in ten minutes." He then disarmed Ramsey when he said, "Stay as long as you like, lock up when you leave. And when you get back to the Milagro Shrine, tell Carlotta I love her."

Ramsey knew Grossinger was playing with him and enjoying it. "A last question. When did you take Adam to Albuquerque?"

"I believe it was in June of 2001. By the way, no one could ever figure out why Adam was driving Sam's motorcycle that day. Adam always said he had no recollection of what happened."

Ramsey spent another hour carefully studying the room. Eventually he was drawn to the book on the table alongside Adam's bed. It was William James's *Varieties of Religious Experiences,* and it was open to the page with a quote underlined: "There are two lives, the natural and the spiritual, and we must lose the one before we can participate in the other." The idea of him trying to commit suicide immediately popped into Ramsey's mind. *Is that what he was doing on the motorcycle?*

Ramsey tried to make sense of some of Adam's writings. *He's either a genius or self-deluded.* The last thing he noticed on Adam's desk were books on Scotland and travel logs and maps of Edinburgh. What was it Carlotta had said? His father was Scots and he'd been born in Edinburgh practically on the steps of Holyrood Palace.

He sat in the wingback chair by the window. The leather was shiny from use and it was obvious Adam had spent many hours reading here. As often happened at a time when he was sifting through clues to puzzles, his thoughts drifted to his old girlfriend, Paige Ripperton, and he wondered what she would think.

8

———————

Summer 2004
Eugene, Oregon

Ramsey listened to the phone message a second time. "Jonathan, I'm flying into Portland this morning. Don't bother coming up to get me. I'll rent a car and drive down. I have something important to tell you." He'd tried calling her back but she didn't pick up.

This is probably not good, he thought. Both of them always looked forward to the reunion that occurred during the hundred-mile trip from Portland to Eugene. It was sort of their thing. Besides, he had something important to tell her too. He was disappointed he would have to wait.

Paige and Ramsey had met at UCLA, while he was working on his doctorate. She was getting a Masters in psychology. A mutual friend introduced them at a Christmas party. They were perfect for each other. Neither had had any real serious romantic relationships before so everything was experimental and exciting. Paige was bumptious and playful in strong contrast to Ramsey who often displayed a serious and often dour demeanor. Paige was Southern California through and through. She talked and he listened. She described her parents as late baby boomer hippies living in the hills above Los Angeles.

Like many such children, she went in a different direction than her parents. She was open and liberal on social issues while at the same time being ultra-conservative in many of her religious beliefs, in contrast to Ramsey's agnosticism. Yet the glue that held them together was that they shared a strong sense of justice and basic goodness. Their relationship grew stronger and closer when Ramsey supported Paige through a dark period. Her beloved sister had suffered a surfing accident that left her paralyzed. An infection had led to a slow death. Where the couple disagreed was over children. She wanted children, but he wasn't so sure. And they argued about religion. Ramsey had no respect for those who took religious dogma on blind faith. As he told her, "I plan on becoming the world's greatest human geographer of religion and I'll do it while never stepping inside a church."

Paige countered his argument with, "I can't become a complete psychologist knowing that people's problems are always in part problems of spiritual growth. I have looked everywhere for the best way of bringing spirituality into my practice and I found it in the words of the Desert Mothers and Fathers. They said, 'Jesus spoke about God, Jesus spoke to God, and Jesus spoke as God.' I have tried to practice that everyday since."

At that time Ramsey gave her a little smirk as if to say *if you say so.*

Now after six months of travel around the world he was eager to tell her he understood, or at least he was on his way to understanding what she meant.

There was a knock on his office door. She looked more beautiful to him than ever. Her splendor was not in her physical appearance but in a radiant spirit Ramsey felt as love for him. The smile she gave him when they saw each other melted his heart afresh each time. He stood to hug her but she held up an umbrella. "I bought this in the airport. Let's walk. Coming from sunny southern California I love Eugene's gray mist."

They walked across the campus until they came upon the arboretum. It was Paige's favorite spot in Eugene. Ramsey said, "I know you have something important to tell me, but I have something important also."

"I do, but you first."

Ramsey recounted his mystical experiences at a number of the sacred sites he studied and how this unusual man in England had directed him to a shaman practitioner in Santa Fe. "Here's the best part. I signed up to travel with a group to Peru to participate in a weeklong ceremony with his teacher Don Julio Davila. He is a master of visionary medicine."

"I'm surprised and a little worried," she said.

Ramsey shook his head in confusion. "Why? I thought you'd be excited. I'm starting down a spiritual path. Isn't that what you wanted me to do?

Turning away so their eyes didn't meet, she said, "It just doesn't feel right. You have the money to do this?"

Ramsey looked around as if he was fearful somebody might be listening. "I talked Myriam into having the grant pay for it. I told her I needed to go to Machu Picchu. Which is sort of true. Some of the people in the group are going there after the ceremonies."

"Why are you doing this?"

"Remember you told me that one day the divine would call me and if I answered our relationship would move on to a whole another place. It's happening."

"Shit."

"What do you mean, shit?"

"What I came to tell you is I've fallen in love with somebody else, an older Christian man who shares my values. He asked me to marry him and I said 'yes.' We set a date in August."

Ramsey had spent the next week before his departure for Peru in a state of endless anger at himself. For the first time in his life the fire and drive that had moved him forward was gone. Yet he had to go. The flights, the accommodations were all paid for and nonrefundable.

José Luis the Santa Fe shaman practitioner led the group of about 20 men and women of all ages. Ramsey kept to himself on the plane and during the bus ride to the camp where they met up with guides and llamas that would take them into the rain forests. It wasn't until they entered the jungle that Ramsey suddenly came alive. There was something about the light, the beautiful butterflies, and the monkeys in the canopy that transformed his experience into a world where everything held magical potential. This was so much unlike the mystical experience he associated with the sacred sites, and more like returning to the simple joys of childhood.

Eventually the party reached a small village. Everybody was excited and happy to see Don Julio the great Peruvian shaman. José Luis introduced Don Julio to the group. The two men couldn't have been more different in appearance. José Luis was a small bulldog like man. His Hispanic features were like those of an itinerant farm worker. Yet he spoke fluent English and held a PhD from San Diego State. Don Julio was tall. He had a perfectly symmetrical long face with an aquiline nose and flawless smooth skin. The facial grooves paralleling his mouth projected a perpetual welcoming smile. Ramsey sensed he was like a force of nature shifting the state of everyone in the group to a higher level of awareness.

For Ramsey the shaman seemed to glow with a bluish luminosity. He noticed that José Luis spoke to Don Julio while pointing at Ramsey. Almost instantaneously and without a word everyone began an elaborate purification ritual centering on Ramsey. They smoked *mapacho*, jungle tobacco, profusely while he prepared a brown liquid. There was great laughter and happiness. Ramsey took a giant puff from what appeared to him like a stubble of burning straw. He coughed so deeply that he thought he was going to lose consciousness. But the tobacco had done its job. The world became like a dream for Ramsey. He felt radiant love emanating from everyone and everything. When they were done, Don Julio took Ramsey by the hand and led him to a large Palo Santo tree outside of the village. There he handed Ramsey the sacred Ayahuasca liquid.

As he swallowed, Ramsey's perception of the world changed even more dramatically. He saw himself with a resplendent golden body. He felt invincible. Peering around him, Don Julio and the others had disappeared. The verdant rain forest was whisked away and before him appeared a swirling multi-faceted gateway. At first it seemed impossible to pass through the razor sharp edges of the doors whirling in the entryway. It seemed they were rotating so fast they would slice his skin to ribbons in seconds. But as he watched, an unknown force entered his body, coursed through him, and shot straight for the gateway. Each door it touched slowed and then stopped twirling until all of them hung like a beaded curtain in front of him. He easily strode past the jeweled-doors and walked out onto a precipice. A westering sun shone down upon a lush valley where palaces of pulsating light waited. Each one beckoned with whispers of untold knowledge awaiting within. Ramsey found a wide stair zig-zagging down the cliff face. He climbed down, his heart and mind overjoyed to enter the first golden palace at the bottom. Suddenly the furious beat of many wings filled the air. He looked up and saw circling above him the strangest people he'd ever seen. They were beautiful, voluptuous women, their hair streaming golden behind them. Wings sprouted from their well-muscled backs. They seemed to be escorting him down the steps. He took these angelic beings as a good sign that he was on the right track and that the Ayahuasca liquid was indeed opening a new dimension for him.

He continued downward happily. But as he descended, the sky blackened. The wind turned cold. The sound of his winged escort slashed through the air. He looked at the bird-like women again. Their cherub-like faces were gone. Their full lips were pulled back over fangs and their eyes gleamed with the rapacious look of hawk predators. Long-tipped claws sprouted from their hands. They swirled around him more and more tightly. Too late, he knew he had been fooled. These weren't angels but *harpies*, female monsters from ancient Greek myth.

Plummeting down the stairs, he tried to reach the palace before the bird-women attacked. The palace gate slammed shut moments before he reached it. The harpies tore at his golden body. The pain was unbearable. Terror gripped him. He couldn't move. He couldn't scream. In a terrifying moment just as he disappeared, the harpies flew away and a strange, gray, swirling cloud dove out of the trees and swallowed him whole. That was the last thing he remembered until waking up in a Lima hospital.

In the days following his recovery, Ramsey discovered that during the ceremony he had physically disappeared. Nobody from the group could say exactly how it happened, but within two days elaborate search parties had been sent out to scour the jungle for him. His disappearance became an international story. Finally on the seventh day a party of leopard poachers found him barely alive sitting by a small stream. Unable to speak he was rushed to the hospital. By the time he got there he had fallen into a coma that lasted for two weeks.

When he finally woke up, Ramsey had no memory of what had happened. However, the first thing he said was, "Tell Paige I entered the temple."

9

———

March 24, 2019
Rio Chama, New Mexico

Myriam waited until Ramsey's rental car disappeared down Rio Chama's dusty main street before making the call. The deep baritone voice on the other end said, "Did he take the job?"

Myriam hesitated. She didn't know if Ramsey would take it or not. The way he brushed off any of her subtle probes to see how he felt suggested he didn't want it. And then there was their history. His body language seemed to be screaming that he still hadn't forgiven her for never coming to his aid personally after Peru. Yet there was something about the way he had stood beside his car looking off in the distance toward the shrine that intimated he was interested in uncovering the facts behind the mystery. Then, after Rosa spoke with him, he turned his car around and headed out of town toward the shrine instead of across the street to his hotel.

I wonder what she said? Myriam would have to ask, but not now. Hiram wanted an answer and she could practically hear his impatience coming out of the phone.

"I don't know, Hiram. It's hard to tell."

"I should have been there," Beecher grated.

"No ... no that would have turned him away for sure. Give him some space."

"How long?"

"A couple of days. Come over to the café, we'll talk about it."

The phone went dead.

Myriam took a deep breath. She loved Hiram Beecher for his masculinity and strength. He was a natural-born leader and self-made millionaire. He could be as hard as nails, befitting for the CEO of a major West Texas company. But he could be as soft as a box of newborn puppies.

They had met in Dallas four years previous. He was the keynote speaker at a sustainability conference where his company's recycling and landfill practices were presented as a model for the future. She had just lost her funding at the University of Oregon and had been hired by the city of Portland to investigate whether Beecher's company, Great Western States Waste Management, should bring their innovative practices to increase Portland's already green image. Beecher had just lost his wife to breast cancer. Myriam had not been in in a serious relationship since her divorce, unwilling to take the risk again. But something about Beecher had made her fall for him deeply. They had been together ever since.

Now sixty-five years of age, Beecher was a man of contradictions. He loved to hunt and fish but was a vegetarian. He married his high school sweetheart while on furlough from Vietnam. She had been a rock for him but there was very little love reciprocated and no children. And there was a strong streak of moral righteousness that ran through him.

His father had been an itinerant, evangelizing preacher in east Texas, with a heavy reliance on the spare-the-rod-spoil-the-child rule of parenting. Beecher had left home at sixteen and never looked back. After his stint in the army, he returned, bumped around Texas and finally ended up in Abilene. The missing two fingers on his right hand were a constant reminder of the war and the bad things that had happened over there. His Christian faith was one the first casualties.

The only thing that had saved him was his uncle's garbage collection business in Abilene. It was a steady sunup-to-sundown job. Nights were a blur of bars and women. But two years into it, he had attended a Reverend Billy Paul revival prayer meeting with a group of guys who drove dozers at the local landfill and a few bar girls they'd picked up in town. At one point, half drunk and falling out his chair, he heard the preacher call for witnesses. The girl he was with said, "You're pa's a preacher why don't you go on up and show 'em how it's done."

Reeling, Beecher got to his feet and stumbled toward the small stage. Some bouncers tried to escort him out but it was as if nothing could stand in his way. They seemed to brush past him or trip over their own feet. He found himself unmolested at the foot of the short stair leading to the stage. He climbed the steps and when the preacher reached out, Beecher was all set to tell him to go to hell. But the man's hand was like a match and it was as if it set him on fire, burning all the alcohol out of his system in an instant like a piece of flash paper. Beecher stood blinking at the crowd. He saw his girlfriend and the other boys from the garbage hauling business, hooting at him to "give 'em hell."

But as he had staggered toward the stage, a voice spoke to him in resonant tones. "Be healed, Brother Hiram, and go make a garden of the Earth."

Struck dumb by the otherworldly command, which he heard inside his head, Beecher swayed on his feet. His friends jeered at him, but their voices were tinny and small compared to the one in his skull. "Be healed, Brother Hiram," it repeated.

Beecher fell to his knees and prayed for forgiveness. He became a born-again Christian that night. With Billy Paul's help he reformed. He stopped drinking and whoring. He dove in to his uncle's business learning everything there was to know about running a trash collection company. Then three months later he walked into the shop one morning and found his uncle dead from an overdose of heroin. Spurred by his uncle's untimely death, Beecher decided at that moment he would dare to be even better and succeed. Over the next fifteen years he had built the small garbage hauling business into the leading waste management company in Texas and the third largest firm of its kind in the country.

The door to the café swung open and Beecher strode in. He smiled at Rosa and said, "Coffee." His boots clicked against the tile floor, the metal taps sending sparks in front of him like fireworks at a parade. Myriam stood and he gathered her into his arms. "Babe!" he said and kissed her on the cheek.

She held on, liking to be close, enjoying the smell of him like old leather, warm and agreeable.

"So," he said, "Ramsey's unsure of what he wants to do."

Myriam nodded. She sat down and watched Beecher straddle a chair as if he was riding a horse. She kept the amusement from her face. Beecher hated horses even though he owned a ranch with ten-thousand head of cattle and cowboys to run them. When out on the range, he rode a Harley and could make it do anything a quarter horse could.

"Are you certain I can't do anything to sweeten the pot?" he said.

"I'm sure you could incentivize him, but it would be better to have him reach the conclusion of working for us on his own. Ramsey has always been like that. When he believes the project is his own, he'll work like the devil's after him to find the answers." She smiled at Beecher. "He's a little bit like you that way."

Beecher returned the smile. "You know everything about me, babe," he said.

The warmth of his smile drew her to him and she reached across the table and squeezed his hand.

He studied her face. Strong with a softness about the eyes that hid her true strength —the ability to get a project working and find the right people to make it move along smoothly. Once Myriam had joined his company, she streamlined the operation until they became the most profitable waste management company in the world. She never took a cent in salary. She was five foot seven inches tall, the perfect height for him: Tall enough to nestle in his arms but not tall enough to look him straight in the eyes. Her other quality, complete loyalty, was something he thought he'd never find again after his wife Samantha passed away from cancer.

Beecher squeezed Myriam's hand in return. *I'm blessed, oh Lord, by thy bounty.* He kept the smile on his face, the words coming automatically to him, yet he no longer felt them in his heart as he had at the beginning after his conversion in front of the Reverend Billy Paul.

Eight years previous an unexpected visitor had come into Beecher's office in downtown Abilene. It was the Reverend Billy Paul. The hair on the nape of his neck had stood up when he first saw the renowned evangelical televangelist. The man's face glowed, cherubic-like, and he had a long gray beard, riven with dark streaks like Moses.

"Christ! What are you doing here?"

"The Lord opens doors whenever necessary, Brother Beecher," the Reverend Paul had answered softly.

Beecher overcame his surprise and said, "You remember me?"

"Of course."

Beecher settled back in his chair almost as if a gentle hand had pushed him there. Accustomed to running a multi-million dollar company and issuing orders daily, Beecher suddenly found himself unable to speak. Finally he managed to ask, "What do you want?"

"I am here to invite you to a special meeting this evening."

"I ... I have plans."

"I'm sure you can cancel them."

"And if I don't?"

"Then you will miss the greatest opportunity of your life." The Reverend's eyes narrowed. "This is your big chance and if you don't grab it, you will end out your days behind this desk growing ever smaller until you are a used-up bit of flesh with no purpose but to keep on living your three score and ten."

Beads of sweat had trickled down Beecher's cheek. The Reverend's words sounded like the voice of God and yet there was no danger behind them. At least no danger as he had experienced in the jungle trails of Cambodia and Vietnam, or in the soft-carpeted boardrooms of Texas billionaire oilmen. The man spoke mellowly as though offering an invitation. Beecher believed he could have declined and the Reverend Paul would have thanked him for his time and walked away. And yet, Beecher found himself nodding and saying yes.

He had buzzed his secretary and told her to cancel his afternoon and evening meetings.

That night, Reverend Paul had taken Beecher to a clandestine meeting of the Brothers of the Lord. Hardened by the destruction of the Twin Towers on 9/11, the group was focused on attempts across the country to water down the strict interpretation of the Bible. When they found such wayward churches, they worked to bring new mega-churches into the neighborhood. They even created their own seminary to produce ministers to fill the open positions in each new neighborhood. Beecher had quickly risen to a leadership position. That leadership had brought him to Rio Chama and the Milagro Shrine.

"So we leave Ramsey alone for a few days," Beecher said to Myriam.

"Yes, that'll give him time to get back to me and say he'll take the job. And we can set up people to help him."

"Clever girl." Beecher smiled.

Myriam basked under the warmth of his smile. It made her feel as though she belonged.

·   ·   ·

All her young life she had strived to become the leader of every high school and college club she joined. But once out in the real world, she had never been quite good enough to join the upper elite of the paradigmatic and theoretical thinkers of human geography. She had chosen human geography because it was open to women and because as a facilitator she could make things happen for other people's projects. Ever pragmatic, she had married for wealth, not love, and now had two grown sons. She was well off as a result of an amiable divorce settlement.

With her children out of the house, she had gone back to work at the urging of a longtime friend and of the chairman of the Geography Department at the University of Oregon to manage a major research grant directed at understanding the geographical distribution and migration of religious minorities in the country. Like everybody else who managed grants, she had used the money for many projects beyond the stated purpose, including her private project in Borneo, studying the effects of modernization on indigenous tribes living in the island's rain forests. When Ramsey nearly died in Peru without fiscal accountability, the National Science Foundation had investigated her entire project and rescinded the money.

The University would have kept her on teaching a summer class for teachers of Advanced Placement human geography, but lecturing wasn't her strong point. Managing people and projects was. So when Portland offered her a position managing the city's sustainability efforts, she took the job.

Beecher squeezed her hand again. "Penny for your thoughts."

"I was thinking of when we met."

He laughed. "I bet you thought I was a fourteen-carat asshole."

"Not at all." His eyes narrowed. "Well, maybe a little bit. But then you bought me carnations."

"Your favorite."

"How did you know?"

"I guessed."

"It's been a good four years."

"The best," he agreed. Beecher sipped his coffee.

The first three years of their relationship had flown by in a whirlwind of trips around the world. He quickly learned that she shared his deep and abiding interest in protecting the world's special places, from endangered ecosystems to ancient ruins. Throughout their courtship Beecher had resisted visiting the shrine because of its purported commerciality. But then a remarkable twist of fate occurred right after Reverend Billy Paul had ordered he look into the Milagro Shrine.

Beecher was astonished by the power of the sanctuary. For him it emanated an aura of purity that no other place on the planet could match. He was overwhelmed and immediately put up $50,000 of his own money to help maintain the shrine. And of course he assured the Reverend Billy Paul that all was well. That was all in the beginning before he discovered the truth.

Myriam had become more involved with its caretaker Adam, taking a personal interest in his physical recovery from the motorcycle accident that had left him nearly dead and in a coma for six weeks.

"He's like nobody I've ever met. There's even a sort of luminescence to his presence," she had told Beecher. She began spending more and more time there and with Adam. Often Beecher would join them as they strolled around the grounds chatting with visitors and pilgrims who were eager to talk about their experiences.

Beecher had never once been jealous of her attention to the man. There was no need. For one thing, Adam didn't appear to have an agenda with anyone. He devoted himself entirely to the shrine and its visitors. And it was clear that Myriam was as much in love with Beecher as he was with her.

. . .

Beecher sipped his coffee. Myriam leaned forward and kissed him lightly on the cheek. "I need to powder my nose, honey." He rose as she did. She smiled and said, "That's what I love about you. You're old fashioned, like a wild west cowboy."

"I have a white hat, too," he said, loving her.

Watching her walk off, he murmured, "It has been the best."

All her adult life Myriam had had trouble sleeping. After a particularly bad night she wandered around the grounds of the shrine and had come across one of the many vendors who set up shop on a small strip of land beside the parking lot. These were mostly Native Americans and a few others who sold their wares to pilgrims and tourists. She approached a battered old Ford pickup with blue doors and red stripes across the hood, like a painted face. The owner had erected a makeshift ramada from a tattered, blue plastic tarp. It stretched over the bed and on either side and past the back. He sat on the tailgate, a faded, black ten-gallon hat covering his head. He was an old man with silver hair in long braids down his back. Behind him in medicine bags were his wares. If Carlotta Moore had not told her he was the one whose Indian medicine was the best, she would have passed him by for one of the newer looking gaily colored stalls further along the road.

"Excuse me, sir. Do you have any wild chamomile or sage tea?" Myriam had asked.

The man raised his head and gazed at her quietly. Gray eyes scanned her like a benediction. "You're having trouble sleeping?" he had asked.

She nodded. "I seem to fall asleep right away but then I wake up, maybe forty-five minutes later and I can't get back to sleep. It's happened three days in a row and I'm exhausted."

He had smiled, his teeth white and even. He reached behind him and pulled a beaded bag from among the others. It was the color of tanned deer hide. The adornment was porcupine quills in the manner of plains Indians before the arrival of Europeans to America.

She recognized the style from artifacts she had acquired for the University of Oregon's Museum of Natural and Cultural History.

"Here, a gift from Coyote to help you sleep," he had said, his voice soft, the words cadenced like he was saying a prayer.

Myriam's eyes widened. "Are you sure? Coyote is the trickster. Perhaps it will have the opposite effect."

"Among the Lakota it is *iktomi* the spider who is the trickster. Coyote is the bringer of change. Tonight, you will sleep and you will dream I am sure."

She quickly replied, "I'm one of those people that never dream."

With a gleeful twinkle the old Indian reached out and touched her forehead. "Make a tea just before bedtime with a spoonful of this. Steep it fifteen minutes then strain it and drink it right away."

"How can I pay you?" When she offered him money he shook his head.

"Got to go." The Indian suddenly danced off laughing and talking to himself. He walked into the sage and piñon pine surrounding the shrine, never looking back.

Myriam had thought him a very odd character and might not have heeded his words, but that night, being desperate for sleep, she followed his directions. The world of dreams descended upon her like a vision. She found herself in the middle of an ancient city of mud and straw and bricks. The reek of sewage and the stink of humans and animals were overpowering. She brought her hand to her nose and saw the skin was white and some of the fingers shortened and deformed. She touched her face and her nose was a stub, the cartilage eaten away. She gasped in fear as she recognized the disease— leprosy. She started to wail when a figure clothed in white approached her.

He stopped and stood before her. Reaching out with a long fingered hand, he touched her forehead and said in a deep voice filled with compassion, "Be clean."

Immediately the leprosy disappeared and she was made clean. Myriam recognized, from within her dream, that this scene was repeating the biblical miracle of the cleansing of the leper. She looked up, expecting to see the shining radiance of Jesus Christ. Instead it was a stranger whose face was covered by a dark haze. Only his eyes shown through with benevolence that warmed her. The eyes were strangely familiar and she thought they might belong to Adam.

The stranger said, "See that you tell others who I am. Go, show yourself to them, for a proof to them."

When she woke the next morning, Myriam remembered the dream and had called Beecher right away. She told him all about it.

Myriam returned to the table. "I have to go, dear," she said, opening her purse. Beecher put out his hand. "It's on me." She pouted and said, "One of these days you're going have to let me pay for something." She kissed him on the cheek and walked out of the restaurant.

Beecher watched her drive off. *She doesn't suspect*, he told himself. Ironically, her request to be allowed to pay had in its own way already been granted. After all, her dream had inadvertently set in motion a bizarre, spiraling set of events.

After she had told Beecher about her dream, he had decided to contact the popular cable television show *Psychic or Psycho?* This popular series based in Phoenix, Arizona featured investigators who debunked psychic phenomena. Paying them a sizable advance, he persuaded them to explore the Milagro Shrine. Working under the guise that the results would soon become an episode in their popular series, the three-man, two-woman team had agreed to his proposal, and spent four days with their equipment, examining every aspect of the place and shooting copious amounts of Polycentrism Interference Photography. PIP was a remarkable new video processing technology that captured bioenergetic fields invisible to the naked eye. A scientist named Harry Oldfield invented PIP in the late 1980s, using advanced microchip technology. Oldfield developed a scanner that could provide real-time moving images of the energy fields associated with living things. He believed that the future of medical diagnosis lay in finding an effective scanner that could see imbalances in the body's energy flows. Beecher had even provided the crew with the money to purchase the most advanced form of this technology available.

The film crew had initially focused their attention on the cottonwood tree, spending two full days and nights following groups of pilgrims who had traveled from the East Coast to spend a week at the Milagro Shrine. Though a number of men and women glowed with reports claiming they had been healed in the presence of the tree, none of the equipment registered even the tiniest anomaly in the biofield surrounding the cottonwood. The Christ Chapel was next, and then the xeriscape garden with its maze of trails. Again nothing out the ordinary had been detected emanating from any of the structures or plant life at the Milagro Shrine.

The only hiccup had occurred on the second day of filming. The film's producer, Gil James, had approached Beecher, his jaw set and an angry glare in his eyes. He wasted no time complaining. "Hiram is there any way you can keep that little shit Raphael Núñez from following us around?"

"What's he doing?"

"Asking a lot of stupid questions and getting in the way of the crew's interviews with the pilgrims. I'd like to wring his neck." The producer's beefy hands squeezed an imaginary foe.

"I'll see what I can do, Gil. But really Raphael's just a small time opportunist. He's the chairman of the Board of the Friends of the Shrine and the local real estate broker."

Gil raised his voice. "Keep him away from my crew and equipment, or," he laughed harshly, "he's going to find out firsthand if this healing stuff works or not."

Beecher had spoken to Núñez and the man had backed off, watching the production crew from a distance.

·   ·   ·

After they had finished taping, Beecher accompanied the crew when they returned to Phoenix, where the footage was carefully examined on the production company's HD screens in their studio. What he saw had amazed him as much as it did the psychic busters. The cameras had definitely caught a number of people whose bioenergetic signatures displayed well-recognized ailments such as cancer and other diseases in black and dark red auras. One elderly gentleman, whose prostate initially appeared like a giant red cantaloupe on the screen, had his condition return to normal by the second night of filming. Others showed significant brightening, with the blackness dissipating and their bioenergetic fields moving towards more symmetry. Sometimes people's bioenergetic fields were closed. For a few nothing had happened. As astonishing as those revelations were, the most remarkable aspect recorded by the technology was an unusual energetic background signal that permeated all the footage.

The next revelation had rocked Beecher even more. It was footage taken by a woman intern who had walked around the Rio Chama de Milagro Shrine with a small hand-held camera. She had caught the caretaker, Adam Gwillt, on camera in the presence of two young girls ages ten and twelve. They were sisters, both suffering with Hodgkin's disease.

As Adam talked with the two girls and their parents, the film captured the largest and most perfect bioenergetic field surrounding the caretaker that the show's team had ever recorded. In fact, it was larger and clearer than images recorded of long-time Buddhist meditators or even the Dalai Lama. But even more astonishing was the effect of his aura on the two girls. Their fields had merged with his for a short time, and by the time the crew finished filming, the dark mass indicating the lymphoma had disappeared.

After much discussion and tweaking of the PIP's processing technology, the conclusion was that the pervasive background had somehow come from Adam.

Myriam's dream had been prophetic and now Beecher had proof Adam was the source of the shrine's healing power. Shaken by the findings, he had immediately taken possession of all the footage and paid an additional large sum of money to the producer to keep everything quiet.

Returning to Abilene, he had contacted the Reverend Billy Paul, telling him what he had discovered and about Myriam's dream revealing Adam as the next Christ.

10

———

December 2015
Amarillo, Texas

Hiram Beecher sat in his Amarillo office shaking his head at the Reverend Billy Paul's latest email—'Has that matter been taken care of yet?'

He clenched his fists until the knuckles cracked. His brain felt clogged at what the televangelist was asking of him. He reread the email. *How am I going to do this?*

The leader of the Brothers of the Lord had changed dramatically from the once-charismatic leader who awaited the second coming of Christ. Now the Reverend seemed old and bitter. *It has to be the pilgrimage. Something happened to him that day*, Beecher told himself. It was a wonder the man had survived.

At first, Reverend Billy Paul had been skeptical when he read Brother Hiram's report regarding Adam Gwillt's powers. After all, Beecher had given nothing but positive reviews about the Rio Chama de Milagro Shrine, touting it as a Christian center for miracles, the North American equivalent of France's Lourdes and Portugal's Our Lady of Fatima. It was what the Reverend had been waiting for since founding the Brothers—a place in America for followers to worship and experience the power of Christ. He had even confided in Beecher plans to switch the worldwide headquarters to the small community of Rio Chama in northern New Mexico.

But later, as he had reflected more deeply upon Beecher's information in the privacy of his megachurch's inner sanctum, something unexpected occurred. Reverend Billy Paul suddenly felt a strong summoning, a voice inside him telling him to visit the shrine for himself. Excitedly, the Reverend gripped the armrests of his ornate desk chair. Carved from obsidian and oak, the chair glowed under soft lights positioned to cast it in an unearthly halo of light. His followers in the Brothers of the Lord joining him here often fell to their knees and began praying when they saw the Reverend sitting in this chair behind his desk on the small dais raised in such a manner it appeared as if he were floating in the air supported only by divine will.

Reverend Paul felt his heart beat quickly; its thumping pulled at the scars of his recent bypass surgery, causing an ache his chest. *Could this be what we've all been waiting for? The second coming?* he asked himself breathlessly.

Reverend Paul had opened the laptop on his desk and pulled up the events calendar for the Milagro Shrine. The announcement of a holiday procession to honor the birth of Jesus Christ glowed eerily on his screen. It was a celebration with a pilgrimage starting in the valley below the shrine. Worshippers, pilgrims, and members of the shrine would carry a wooden cross to the Christ Chapel. Everyone would take a turn bearing Christianity's most humble symbol of salvation the five miles from Rio Chama to the shrine. An inner voice declared to Billy Paul that it would be perfect if he participated. *If Adam is who he says he is, he will be waiting for you at the Christ Chapel*, the voice declared.

Immediately Reverend Billy Paul had called Beecher and

enthusiastically told him of his plans. To his surprise his most loyal lieutenant did not agree.

"It's unwise, Reverend," Beecher had explained. "The high altitude where the shrine is, coupled with your bypass surgery less than six months ago, makes it unwise for you to carry the cross. It's very heavy and the way is slippery in many places. I'm afraid for your health and safety. It would be better for me to arrange a meeting with Adam through Myriam."

"The Lord will sustain me, brother Beecher," Reverend Paul had said, dismissing his concerns. "Adam will only reveal his true nature if I come to him in a state of pure faith." Beecher implored the leader of the Brothers of the Lord to reconsider, but in the end, Reverend Billy Paul insisted he drop the matter. "I am coming to New Mexico to participate. Make the arrangements, brother Beecher." In the end Hiram Beecher had agreed and the Reverend felt a glow of anticipation that he would make the pilgrimage.

On The Sunday after Thanksgiving, the afternoon was sunny and the temperature had hovered just above freezing. There was no wind and it was going to be a glorious pilgrimage to the shrine. Hundreds of worshippers and followers gathered at the starting point. Brother Beecher and other Brothers of the Lord were also in attendance. Reverend Billy Paul had stood with them. He had dressed in a simple white, woolen cassock, similar to what Jesus had worn on the day of his crucifixion. The cross had been constructed from nearby trees the weekend before by local artisans. As the time approached, Rio Chama's local choir sang *Adeste Fideles* in the original Latin. The sonorous and joyful words filled Reverend Billy Paul with exultation as he joined the group of men and women preparing to carry the cross on the long march to the shrine. As the final notes of the song drifted through the thin mountain air, the first of the worshippers lifted the cross to their shoulders and proceeded to drag it forward along the road to the shrine. At intervals of about a hundred yards, the heavy cross was passed to the next person who would carry it the next length.

Billy Paul had walked along with the others with his head held low like a penitent, waiting his turn at the back of the procession. He would be the last one to carry the cross. His placement was not by accident. He had wrangled his turn at the end, where he would triumphantly carry the cross to the front of the Christ Chapel, hoping to see Adam there waiting for him.

Spontaneously the group had begun singing Christmas hymns as the burden of the cross passed from one person to the next. As they entered the long gravel drive to the shrine's parking lot, the short, middle-aged woman in front of Billy Paul stumbled under the burden of the cross and fell to her knees. Amid gasps from the crowd of onlookers, the aging Reverend reached out to steady her. "Let me take this burden from you," he said, feeling the spirit of Simon of Cyrene filling his limbs with strength.

Hoisting the heavy wooden cross to his bony shoulders, he trudged forward. By the time Billy Paul was navigating the last steps to the front of the chapel, the sharp edges of the cross had bitten deeply into the flesh of his shoulders. His breath came in aching gasps and his heart labored against his ribs like a jackhammer. He dragged the now-painful burden toward the chapel entrance, his mind and body reeling under the weight and from the thin mountain air. The woman he had helped joined him and whispered, "This is going to be a special Christmas like the first." One by one, others in the procession came forward, each touching a part of the cross, some lifting it with their hands while praying.

The group swept forward, singing hallelujahs and chanting prayers. By now Billy Paul and his burden were being half-carried along by the crowd caught up in the exultation of Christ's final journey on Earth and oblivious to his gasping wheezes and staggering steps. At the small rock path leading to the now open chapel doors, one end of the cross lurched sideways and slid heavily on Reverend Paul's shoulder, breaking the skin. Blood trickled down his back, staining his white cassock red. A sharp pain lanced down his leg. He lost his balance and stumbled away from the group grabbing a hold of a small wooden sign identifying the Christ Chapel. The men and women carrying the cross left him behind as if he didn't exist. Even the bulk of the crowd—engulfed in a state of spiritual excitation—passed him by unnoticed.

Deeply saddened by this callous dismissal of his fellow cross bearers, Billy Paul sank to his knees. Moments later a gentle hand touched his shoulder.

"Are you okay?" asked a deep voice.

Turning, the TV evangelist immediately recognized the speaker from the video clips Beecher had provided. "Adam," he whispered. A sudden blissful joy filled his body and then, just as suddenly, excruciating pain gripped his chest and he crumpled into the shrine caretaker's strong arms.

The pain vanished in an instant. A sense of ease filled Billy Paul with a simplicity and strength he had not experienced since the time, as a teenager, when he had swiped oranges from the groves surrounding his Southern California home with his pals. Accompanying the peace and calm was a sense of floating in a bright white cloud. He looked down on a brown, dusty earth, now slowly receding. He recognized the cottonwood tree and the nearby Christ Chapel. They glowed with a soft inviting light. Beside the white gravel walkway leading to the chapel's entrance he saw his limp frail body cradled in the lap of Adam, his limbs curled up in a fetal position. Faceless human forms were gathered around the two of them. *They seem to be attending to me!* thought Billy Paul with great surprise. *Who are they?* But a sudden dread filled him, and the tranquility he had experienced only moments before vanished. The faceless beings darkened. They bent down toward him, talons extended, ready to grasp and rend his flesh. *NO! DON'T LET THEM TAKE ME!* he shouted at Adam.

The figure of Adam did not move. Billy Paul shouted until his voice was hoarse, but Adam ignored his pleas and continued to rock Billy Paul's lifeless body to and fro without a care in the world.

Frantically, Billy Paul drew up his legs and kicked forward, his hands making desperate swimming motions as he tried to swim back through the air toward his body. He had to stop the dark angels from taking his soul to hell! He seemed to move imperceptibly through air that was thick as jelly. His breathing hoarsened. He could no longer move at all. The last thing he remembered as his hands beat futilely against the thick air were the demons descending on him, fangs and claws bared as they prepared to take his soul to hell.

Reverend Billy Paul had awakened in a dimly lit hospital room in Taos, New Mexico. Fortunately the shrine had paramedics on the scene for just such emergencies. He had been resuscitated and helicoptered to the hospital.

As full awareness returned, the Reverend had an overpowering realization. Adam Gwillt was *not* Christ. No, he was the worst thing possible. The world's people had to know that Satan walked in their midst, disguised as the Milagro Shrine's healer!

Beecher's email program chimed. He leaned forward and a second email from Reverend Billy Paul appeared. It was the same message— 'Has that matter been taken care of yet?' He noticed his hands trembled at the idea of what the leader of the Brothers of the Lord was ordering him to do. *That cursed pilgrimage is responsible for his changed attitude.*

A few weeks after the heart attack, Beecher had received an ill-tempered call from a highly agitated Billy Paul. The televangelist had started right in without saying hello or asking about Myriam. "That Adam caretaker is the secret leader of a heretic group and is able to transfer his divine power from his body to those who follow him. They're going to claim that this will be the equivalent of Christ rising from the dead. This two-bit hustler, Adam, can't be allowed to take on the robe of our savior ... He needs to be stopped for the salvation of our souls."

Beecher had reeled from the angry diatribe. "That's impossible!" he blurted.

"Do you doubt my revelations, Brother Beecher?" Billy Paul had asked, his displeasure clear at Beecher's lack of faith.

"Of course not. It's just—"

"Then heed my words. Adam has dark and dangerous powers."

"But ... but how do you know this?" Beecher had asked, the certainty behind the Reverend's words rattling him.

"I had a vision when I visited the shrine for the pilgrimage. It showed me that Adam is not the second coming of Christ. He is Satan." He paused. "It's time Adam Gwillt left the shrine. You're close to it and him. Take care of it."

"What do you mean? Take care of it how?" Beecher asked taken aback by the Reverend's hardline tone.

"Do I need to say more?" the Reverend mocked Beecher in an angry voice. "You're a resourceful former military man. Do what needs to be done. Am I clear?" He had disconnected without another word.

Beecher leaned back in his chair. Outside his Amarillo office, rain began to fall, hard enough to clean the dust off windshields. He wished it could clear up this matter for him. He hadn't liked the implications of Billy Paul's order. It was clear the televangelist wanted Adam Gwillt to disappear permanently. The idea was distasteful, but Beecher had always been a good soldier. *But how to carry out the order?*

He had wrestled with that question for a number of sleepless nights. He had not traveled to the Milagro Shrine nor spoken with Myriam except on the phone. If only he could talk with her, maybe he could find the answers he needed. But he knew that way was blocked. He was in way too deep with Billy Paul and the reverend's plans for Adam. If he told her the truth now about what he knew, he'd lose her forever.

He had wracked his brain finding a way to entice Adam to move to a more comfortable place. He talked to Carlotta to see if she could induce her brother to move to Hawaii to avoid New Mexico's bitter winters. She laughed at him, saying Adam had a permanent home at the shrine and wouldn't leave it if another ice age descended. Next, Beecher contacted Adam's longtime friend, Malcolm Grossinger in

Des Moines, to see if he would be willing to take care of him back in Iowa. However, Grossinger had danced around the question and his attitude just seemed troubling to Beecher. In the end no inducement could get Adam to leave the Rio Chama Shrine.

The email chimed again. Beecher read the third email from the Reverend Paul. 'Has that matter been taken care of yet?'

It was an old Comanche tradition that if someone made a request of you three times, you had to follow through. The odd superstition stated that bad luck would befall the man who failed to carry out such an earnest request. He didn't want to think about the reverend's order and yet he had to. As the leader of the Brothers of the Lord in the Southwest, troubles in New Mexico were his responsibility.

Then Beecher remembered Sam Conklin had mentioned a contact of his. "He's a miracle worker. He's known as the 'magic man'. Believe me he can make trouble disappear."

Could use some magic right about now. He made the call to Conklin. Beecher was both relieved and horrified by what he heard.

11

March 27, 2019
Des Moines

Ramsey walked toward his car parked in the luxury lofts' visitors lot. It was already late afternoon and it would be dark by the time he returned to Grinnell. But the trip to meet Grossinger and see Adam's loft had been exactly what he needed. He had already decided how to handle Myriam's request.

Pulling his phone from his pocket, Ramsey paused. He thought to himself, *How do I want to play this? I need to test these guys to find out how much they really need my expertise.* He decided to make an outrageous demand, one that no savvy business person would accept.

He texted Myriam. 'I'll take the job. Results totally my property. 50 K. I'll have my legal draw up a contract. If you agree here's a link to my lawyer. I'll let her know you'll will be contacting her.'

Ramsey paused again. *If they agree to my writing the contract and that the results will become my intellectual property, what does that mean?* There was the obvious. But there was something behind it they weren't telling him. Unexpectedly, a new concern filled him. The shrine project felt like crossing a boundary. Peru welled up in his thoughts but he quashed it. At the same time his interest was piqued, and in spite of the absurdity of the contract he knew they would accept his terms.

He then sent a separate text. 'Email what you know about Adam Gwillt.' Ramsey also sent an email to his lawyer explaining what was going on. He scanned through all the incoming emails of the day. Somebody had hacked his email and was using it to push cheap Internet firearms. But there was one from an old buddy, from his Eugene days, Pete Miami.

I wonder if Pete's still doing his crazy GIS stuff in New Mexico.

12

March 28, 2019
Grinnell, Iowa

Ramsey made himself breakfast. Things were moving fast. By the time he had arrived back home from Des Moines the promised signed contract was in his inbox waiting for his signature. He had confidence his lawyer had gotten the terms he asked for, so he gave it a superficial read, mostly interested in who the other party was. It turned out to be a group called the Abilene Friends of Rio Chama de Milagro Shrine. Research showed they were a nonprofit group incorporated in Abilene, Texas. The chairman of the board was a waste disposal businessman named Hiram Beecher. Other members were an assortment of Texas businessmen and of course Myriam. It was Beecher who signed the contract.

After a good night's sleep, Ramsey was ready to go to work. He started by reading over Myriam's response to his request for information on Adam Gwillt. He learned that the Friends of the Shrine had paid him a token amount to clean up trash every day at the site; at the same time, many visitors seeking miracles had reported that his presence greatly enhanced their experience.

Myriam also included the story of her friend Nancy and how she got involved with the shrine after her healing. Lastly, she made the observation that Adam's disappearance had brought "a big black cloud over the shrine."

Ramsey wondered what Myriam knew about Adam's disappearance. She hadn't mentioned it to him.

Myriam closed by assuring Ramsey he was making the right choice, and by summarizing his assignment in her own words. "I have poured ten years of my life into the goodness this place has brought to so many people. I need to know if there's some way this power can be restored. Is it somehow being blocked? I'm sure if anyone can figure this out, it's you."

Ramsey wondered if she was hiding something.

It was a complex assignment, and Ramsey knew he had to formulate a detailed plan. The world of geographical data collection and analysis had grown exponentially since his sacred-site investigation more than a decade ago. Having made his mark in political and economic geography, he only superficially kept up with advances in GIS. Geographical Information Systems was where all the action was for the bright boys and girls in geography. Employing supersensitive remote sensing equipment to capture in real time a multiplicity of geophysical variables, GIS programmers, using high-speed computers, were able to analyze and integrate the data collected in ways unimaginable just ten years ago. The result was the revelation of hundreds of geophysical patterns never before detected.

Ramsey knew that was the kind of capability he needed to research the Milagro Shrine, but was ill-equipped in every way to make it happen. Then he remembered the annoying phish email from his old postdoc drinking buddy Pete Miami. He was simply the smartest guy Ramsey had ever met. After getting his PhD in physics from Stanford at age twenty-one, Pete had moved to Oregon, where the two first met. The first night they had hit the bars together he told

Ramsey, "GIS is the cutting edge of scientific investigation. That's where I can make my mark, not physics."

Pete liked to call Ramsey "the old man," since he was already twenty-eight. The last time they were together was at a world geographic conference in China. China, more than any other nation, was embracing the analytical power of geographical thinking to guide decision-making at the highest level.

Ramsey recalled one odd thing about Pete's client work. Pete had said he was running a major watershed analysis of northern New Mexico. At the time Ramsey wondered why this ambitious and brilliant scientist had taken on such a low-level scientific investigation. Then the last night of the conference, after many drinks, Pete had let it slip out that a company named the DeVere Diamond Group had funded the project.

Laughing, Ramsey had chided him, "What are you doing? Looking for diamonds in the New Mexico high desert?" Ramsey recalled that Miami's reaction was, "Whoops, did I say that to you. If I did I shouldn't have." They laughed it off.

It dawned on Ramsey that this could be an important coincidence. A quick Internet search revealed a number of articles about *kimberlites*, the material in which diamonds are embedded, having been found around Raton and near the Colorado-New Mexico border. He dialed his old friend.

"Jonathan you old bugger, how the hell are you?"

"Fine, Pete! Hey, old bud, remember the time I talked that Eugene cop out of taking you to jail?"

"Only every time we talk."

"Well, this time *I* need the favor."

"Nothing about how are the kids and family, or about people you have kept up with from the old days?"

"What? Did you do kill them all again? ... But I really need a favor. It'll be fun. By the way, I figured out what you're doing, you're looking for kimberlite pipes without a whisper to locals and government. It took me a while to understand why you would relegate yourself to a mundane watershed project."

"Bright boy. Are you blackmailing me?" asked Pete.

"Me? I'm way too ethical. What have you got going there?"

"With the kind of money I have you wouldn't believe the kind of remote sensing instruments I'm developing."

"And I have a project made for it," Ramsey said. "I take it you have a lot of long-term data stored someplace. There is this area I need checked out. All you need to do is tell me if anything unusual has gone on in and around this area over the last 10 years. You know, any unusual readings."

"Like what?"

"Remember when I was investigating sacred places, looking for any kind of energetic or physical factors that might be responsible for so-called religious experiences?"

"You're not going there again, are you?"

"I'm going to let you do it. How's that?"

Pete hesitated. "As I recall, it didn't turn out so well for you last time."

"I guarantee you won't have to move a step from your armchair to do this for me."

"So, where is this place?"

"I'll send you a link. . . . You'll do it?

Pete hummed a little tune that Ramsey recognized from their drinking days. It was the old Jeopardy final round theme. When the last note ended, he said, "I'll do it. Maybe I'll find God for you. Then you'll really owe me."

"You'd like that. How long you think?"

"Maybe tomorrow I can get you some preliminaries."

"That's crazy."

"That's what they say about me. Stay free and silly, old man."

Ramsey texted Pete the Rio Chama de Milagro Shrine link.

The next thing he had to do was look up Orensen's New Gnostics website.

13

____

September 2015
Pretoria, South Africa

Greta Van Horn scrolled through the computer files the GIS expert showed her on his tablet. Eyes narrowing, she asked bluntly, "Are these numbers accurate?"

Doctor Philippe Lindstrom nodded. "The results of the computational analyses are quite remarkable," he said, his Danish accent a pleasant lilt.

She stared at the displays again. "Anyone else know about this?"

"I'm the only one who has seen these, Ms. Horn. You were the first person I called."

"Keep it that way. I don't see any reason to bother Pieter Haas with this until there's something more substantial."

"Yes Ms. Horn."

Greta quickly downloaded the files into her data stick. Pieter had to see this right away. She hurried down the hall to the elevator. Pressing the button, the door opened instantly. It was the only entrance to this part of building. No one knew of the secret research lab one-hundred meters beneath the soaring office complex of the

DeVere Mining Group except for members of the board of directors. Ignoring the elevator buttons on the panel, she pulled out a round shaped key and inserted it into the lock at the bottom of the panel. She turned it clockwise. The elevator hummed upward to the chairman's private office.

DeVere had been the largest diamond company in the world for more than a century. There were younger companies nipping at their heels, especially in North America where new diamond possibilities had reportedly been found in Saskatchewan, Michigan, Wyoming and New Mexico, where DeVere held substantial interests. *And now this*, she thought, glancing though the papers a second time.

The elevator pinged and stopped. She straightened her conservative dark blue silk suit before hurrying across the hall and entering the closed door without announcing herself.

Pieter Haas was starring out the window at Pretoria. He didn't turn around. "It must be important, Greta," he said. "You didn't knock." The chairman of the DeVere Mining Group was a thin, well-groomed South African of Boer descent. His family traced their lineage back to the Voortrekkers who had escaped English rule in Cape Town and moved north and east into the Transvaal nearly 200 years ago.

"You'll want to see this," Greta answered. She had been in the chairman's private penthouse many times, but the room never ceased to awe her. The suite was spacious with large picture windows on three sides giving an aerial view of the Magaliesberg Mountains forming a ring-like wall north of South Africa's third capital. Thick carpet covered the floor. Rare oil paintings of the Great Trek of the Dutch colonists, interspersed with Zulu and Ashanti art and artifacts, adorned the walls.

Haas turned slowly. His pale blue eyes narrowed as she walked across the room and handed him the thick file. "What's this?"

"Lindstrom, the Danish geologist who you have working with Pete Miami in America, gave it to me." She handed him the data stick and he downloaded the information into his computer. She waited patiently as he scanned through the files. When his eyes widened, she added quickly, "Lindstrom's the only one who's seen this and I made certain you and I are the only ones he'll speak with about it."

Haas nodded and strode to his desk. He gestured to Greta to sit down. "Does Doctor Miami suspect anything?"

"Not as far as I know. His drones have been sending us raw data looking for kimberlite signatures in the area of northern New Mexico. Lindstrom's the one who's been crunching the numbers."

"We need to follow up," Haas said. "Who's the man we've been using to buy land there for the company?"

Greta Van Horn didn't have to consult her notes. She instantly replied, "Raphael Núnez. He owns the Rio Chama Real Estate Company."

"Have him ask around. See if he knows anything."

She nodded, not taking any notes.

Haas smiled his pleasure at Greta Van Horn's abacus mind. She wasn't a smasher—too wide in the shoulders and hips, eyes slightly askew on her broad face—but she was precise and never forgot an order, a business contact, or the fine print in any contract. She never left an embarrassing paper trail of emails or memos, and on this project that was essential.

"Anything else, sir?" she asked.

Haas shook his head and watched her leave. Then he returned to the window. A low haze covered the mountain range. It was hot and humid outside. Inside his office the air and temperature were perfectly controlled, yet he could feel stickiness in his armpits. Unbidden into his thoughts came an image of the Samburu shaman he had met nearly forty years ago and the prophecy the strange old man had told him.

Maybe the old man was right.

14

———

January, 2019
Austin, Texas

The Southwest Airlines 737 jet touched down at Austin-Bergstrom International Airport with a screech of metal and a loud explosion. Passengers screamed and lunged against their seatbelts.

Caine, knowing his presence guaranteed the safety of the plane and passengers, leaned back and smiled hugely, relishing the excitement and fear rippling through the cabin. *I love being in control of death. I am the most helpful of all the gods to humans.*

He took the hand of the woman sitting next to him. She was trembling, her breath coming in short gasps. "You'll be reading bedtime stories to your little girl tonight."

Caine was counting her heartbeats, felt the fast staccato rhythm slow. Fear ebbed from her eyes. Taking a deep breath, she looked at him and said, "Wow! It's not about me, is it?"

"Not today."

The Captain's calm voice came over the intercom. "Nothing to be alarmed about, ladies and gentlemen. One of the tires exploded, but we're fine. We're heading to the gate now under our own power. We'll be there in a few minutes."

Ten minutes later Caine was striding through the terminal, thick with passengers and aircrew, a few heading onward to other cities, others walking to the exit. Many were young, high schoolers or a bit older, and they carried musical instrument cases—guitars mostly, though some horns and woodwinds. Nashville, Tennessee proclaims itself the music capital of the country, but Austinites call their town the *live* music capital of the world, with more live music venues per capita than any other U.S. city.

Outside at the taxi stand he motioned to the first one in line. The bumper sticker proudly declared, "Keep Austin Weird."

"Afternoon," he said, handing his bag to the black driver. "Driskill Hotel."

"Good choice, sir. It's a bit of historic Austin right next to the capitol and the Governor's mansion." The man smiled, revealing gold-capped front teeth with tiny guitars etched into them. "George Bush used to live there."

"One should never 'misunderestimate' Texas voters," Caine drawled.

"That be true, sir."

The rest of the ride was quiet. The driver accepted a fifty percent tip and handed Caine his card. "If you need anything give me a call. I can be here in ten minutes."

"I have a meeting at Oilcan Harry's in the Warehouse District this evening at 8pm. Pick me up at 7:30."

"Yes sir," the cabby said toothily and drove off with a jaunty wave.

Inside the desk clerk found his reservation and checked him in quickly. He was in room 714, a floor above Beecher and Conklin's rooms. Caine smiled to himself. *Somebody's going to leap across the threshold they've resisted all their life.*

The room was elegantly furnished. He laid his carry-on luggage on the double bed and unzipped the travel bag. The costume was there, unharmed by the long trip from Scotland. Checking his watch, he saw the time was 6:15pm. *Plenty of time to get ready.*

Caine loved disguise. There is nothing better at enticing people to cross thresholds than the correct costume, and he had a good one planned for this evening. Pulling his phone from his suit coat pocket, he placed it next to the TV and pressed play. Seconds later Dionne Warwick's voice came through the tiny speakers clearly and the first words to the song *I Say a Little Prayer for You* echoed through the motel room. Humming the tune, he carefully stripped in front of the mirror, studying himself. His skin was flawless and smooth. His muscles were well defined and yet not bulging like a bodybuilder's. He chose a dark wig with red highlights, the same color as the women Beecher was attracted to. He began to apply makeup, painting on eyebrows in a thin line, using a dark mascara for his eyelashes and a hint of smoky eyes to give him a sense of mystery.

He checked the time. It had taken almost an hour to prepare. But when he looked in the mirror, he could see the subtle undertones of Myriam St. Eves, Beecher's current mistress. *Perfect.*

The dress was a little black number that showed off his figure without revealing any cleavage or leg.

When he finished, the room's phone rang. Picking it up, Caine heard the manager say, "Your taxi has arrived, sir."

"I'll be right down," he answered.

With a final look in the mirror, he altered his voice to a husky contralto. "The name is Beatrice," he said, pleased the words came out sounding provocative and yet somehow demure. He also chuckled at the name. "Beatrice" was the name of the guide in Dante Alighieri's *Divine Comedy* who had led the Italian poet out of Purgatory.

The black cabby met him at the curb, the door to the yellow cab already open. The man straightened, his eyes wide in surprise.

Caine felt the man's awe grow as the distance between them closed. Then the driver smiled, the harsh lights of the hotel glancing off his gold teeth. He held out his hand and said, "Watch your step."

Caine settled into the backseat of the cab.

The cabby got in. He eased the car out of the driveway into the traffic on Brazos Street. He looked into the rearview mirror and caught sight of Caine. "A siren of splendor," he said and whistled appreciatively.

"You believe in voodoo?" Caine asked.

"Of course. You be casting a spell tonight. I get it."

Traffic was light and the driver reached Oilcan Harry's in just a few minutes. He got out and held the door open for Caine, giving his hand to help him out. Caine gave him two hundred dollars. "Be back here in an hour."

The cabby gave a low bow like a gentleman. "At your service, ma'am."

At first sight, Oilcan Harry's was typical of any upscale bar on the geographical fringe of the Austin Sixth Street music district. The booze behind the bar was lit by a plethora of multicolored lights. Opposite the entrance was a stage where a band began playing once the clock struck midnight. The center was open for dancing. The tables and booths were arranged in helter-skelter fashion reflecting the craziness that erupted every night at Austin's premier gay bar and restaurant.

Caine settled into the shadows at the far end of the bar and waited.

Beecher's lingering uneasiness about what the Reverend had asked him to do intensified the moment he stepped into Oilcan Harry's bar. The evening was early and the bar was mostly empty. The bartender, a slender young man with brilliantly dyed yellow hair, said, "You boys looking to have a good time tonight?"

Beecher's neck turned red and he replied heatedly, "We're meeting someone. It's business."

"Of course it is, honey. It's always business in here." The young man winked at him. "So, what are you boys drinking?"

Conklin looked at the distress on Beecher's face and said, "Scotch and soda for me and my friend will have double shot of Jim Beam straight up."

Beecher scanned the crowd. A drag queen at the end of the bar gave him a little friendly wave. He gasped and almost called out his wife's name. *It couldn't be. There was no one there a moment ago.* He shook his head and looked again. The transvestite was still there, still smiling. He almost bolted out the door, but on the ride from the airport, Conklin had told him this was where the meeting was taking place.

"Why a gay bar, for Chrissakes?" Beecher had bellowed in the back of the limo.

Conklin had said, "A Texas state senator invited me and some businessmen with fracking interests to meet here. You have to do what you have to do to get what you want in Texas. And it's where my contact demanded to meet us. I should've told you it was a gay bar."

On the ride to the bar, Conklin had told Beecher how he had used the information about the impending death of Ketterman to clear up all the legal issues around his family ranch. He repeated for the third time how, when he had asked Caine on the phone if he had killed Ketterman, he didn't deny it.

Beecher stared out the window at the dark Austin night flowing past the cab in shadows and neon. *Christ, this could be a motherfucker. . . . I don't care how necessary the Reverend Billy Paul thinks it is,* he thought.

Beecher had been in a state of internal agitation ever since the email from the Reverend Billy Paul asking if the task had been completed yet. The idea was distasteful, and yet here he was in Austin to set up a hit. There was no denying that that was the purpose of this meeting.

Over the years, Beecher had never experienced any great remissions or healings while at the shrine, only that pleasant sense of peace. *Sure, the video crew filmed the strange aura about Adam ... the merging of his aura with the two little girls. There's no denying he has some special power. But the power of Christ? Impossible!*

Conklin paid for the drinks and led them to a table near the back. The chairs were padded. The light was soft, seductive. He eyed the bar and smiled at the female impersonator, waving her over.

"What the hell are you doing?" Beecher asked.

"Wait for it."

The woman smiled and with hips swinging, walked over to their table. "Sam, where are your manners? Aren't you going to introduce me to your handsome friend."

Beecher gaped at the female impersonator. "This is Caine?"

"I told you he was eccentric." Then, "This is Hiram Beecher."

Caine walked behind the older man, the tips of his fingers caressing his broad shoulders, and sat down. He smiled as Beecher choked on his whiskey. "The pleasure's all mine," he drawled like a Southern belle. Then deliberately setting his full lips in a little *moue*, added, "I thought for a moment you didn't recognize me, Sam."

"It took me a second. Who are you tonight?"

"Beatrice." Caine turned to Beecher. "I love disguise. Don't you think I fit in perfectly? In my line of activity a *woman* needs to be careful."

The logic of Caine's reasoning didn't escape Beecher. At the same time he found himself unable to take his eyes off the woman. *Man*, he corrected himself. But the word didn't seem to mean anything. He watched mesmerized as the man calling himself "Beatrice" reached out a long fingered hand and caressed his palm, running turquoise fingernails along his little finger the way his first wife Delores used to. Heat soared to his face. Feelings of shame coursed through him. He wanted to jump up and slap the transvestite, but instead his manhood hardened. He wanted to run screaming but his legs were liquid. He tried to look at Conklin, but Beatrice's eyes melted into his. It was like a vacuum sucking his soul.

"I thought your name was Caine?" Beecher croaked, trying to dislodge the lust coursing through him and get down to business.

"Tonight I'm Beatrice."

"You leading me to hell?" he said jokingly.

"Out of it ... into paradise."

As if on cue, the young man with the bright blonde hair arrived at the table. "Oh my, I see you want to take this upstairs."

It was like Caine had put a spell on Beecher. The drag queen took his hand and led him to the back of the bar. They walked up a flight of stairs. Beecher was filled with intense anticipation and fear at the same time. Conklin was forgotten. The meeting was a distant memory echoing impotently in his thoughts.

They entered a small room dimly lit by a single green light. In the middle was a large round bed. The only other furniture was a small table covered with sex toys, lubricants, and condoms.

"This is what you been waiting for," Beatrice said.

Beecher no longer remembered her real name. He undressed her slowly. Felt her hands unbutton his shirt, unzip his pants. His underwear slid down his legs to his ankles. Beatrice smiled and stroked Beecher's genitals.

He was filled with excruciating erotic energy. Entangled, the two fell into the bed. Beatrice's lips were questing everywhere and Beecher followed in kind.

Then, a sudden state shift. Beecher froze, his hand stroking Caine's engorged member.

The man/woman smiled at him. "You remember."

Out of the hidden depths of his mind Beecher saw himself as an eleven year-old, tossing his beloved New York Yankee baseball into the air and catching it with his Mickey Mantle glove. His next-door neighbor and dad's fishing buddy, Big Jim Thompson, had invited him over to his rambling, ranch-style house. Big Jim was a tall man with a buzz cut. His wife was called the "shrew" of the neighborhood. She hated the kids and screamed at them. Beecher saw himself looking at nude pictures of women in a Playboy magazine. Big Jim had given him a beer—a "man's drink" he called it. "A man shouldn't be drinking any of that cow-piss milk." He heard big Jim saying, "You like those breasts don't you." When he looked over big Jim had dropped his pants and underwear. He took Beecher's hand and started rubbing his genitals with it. "It's all right."

"You remember," Caine repeated.

Beecher found himself drenched in sweat.

Caine had taken off his wig and was oddly playful in an almost childlike way. He stroked Beecher's brow and said, "It wasn't your fault. We all have a little of that in us. Nothing to be ashamed of. Some more, some less. And now ... you're free."

Caine rose from the bed and walked over to an armoire near the door. He pulled out men's clothes and began to put them on. He sat at the table and removed the makeup, eyeing Beecher in the mirror. "You know that Adam Gwillt thing you wanted done. He's gone. I can assure you."

"What?" Beecher's mind swirled under a load of feelings ... shame, lust, embarrassment, anger, desire. He couldn't process words unless he listened very carefully. "What?" he repeated. "What did you say?"

"Adam Gwillt is gone."

Caine stood up. All traces of Beatrice were gone from his face. He now wore Levis, a blue pastel shirt with a bolo tie, cowboy boots, and a dark gray Stetson.

Beecher thought, oddly, that Caine must have had a change of clothes in the room for afterwards. *But why? ... Unless he planned it. ... But how could he know about Big Jim? ... It's impossible. Jim died years ago and I never told anyone.* He shook his head, clearing the thought.

He tumbled out of bed, staggered to the chair, grabbing it for support. "What's going on?" he shouted. The room was empty. He found his clothes in a heap by the table and put them on. He shook his head again, chasing the last vestige of Beatrice/Caine from his mind. He didn't want to think about what happened, but at the same time he remembered what Caine had said, "You're free."

Beecher came down the stairs. "Let's go," he said curtly.

"What happened?" Conklin asked.

"Nothing."

The younger man's eyes narrowed. He craned his neck around. "Where's Beatrice ... umm, Caine?"

"Gone."

"What about Adam?"

Beecher breathed in deeply. Caine said he was free, but did he mean Adam or something more? "It's taken care of," he told Conklin.

15

———————

March 30, 2019
Taos, New Mexico

Ramsey normally accepted flying as a necessary evil, an integral part of being a modern human geographer. However, as the small regional turbojet screamed and bumped its way along the Rockies on his flight from Denver to Taos, New Mexico he couldn't help but reflect on his own death. It'd been a while since he had been absorbed by thoughts of his own demise. The last time was Peru.

Soon after he swallowed the ritual potion the shamans had prepared for him, he felt himself being devoured piece-by-piece into the belly of a monster. A part of him wanted to let go, but another part, driven by fear, fought back.

Fought for what? Ramsey asked himself. He remembered: *I fought to be.* It was like two forces pulling on a rubber band. It snapped. Then there was nothing. *I shouldn't have fought.* He knew that now.

A violent shudder racked the thirty-passenger cabin. An overhead bin popped open and a backpack crashed into the aisle. Several passengers cried out. The lone flight attendant stayed buckled into her seat, but spoke over the intercom. "Stay in your seats. As soon as this choppiness smooths out, I'll get the cabin ship-shape again."

The passenger sitting next to Ramsey chuckled. She was a young woman in a navy flight uniform. "That was a good one," she said softly and went back to reading her iPad.

Ramsey found himself smiling too. After the initial jolt of fear when the first of the choppy air slammed into the plane, he had settled into the sense of providence he had accepted over the past few years. While living in Grinnell he had come to understand that there were forces in play ready to guide him. Perhaps the same forces that were intensified at sacred places. Life had a plan for him if he would only listen. He understood now that the initial jolt of energy he got when he entered the Rio Chama de Milagro Shrine was another calling to cross whatever that boundary was that he had resisted so mightily before. *This time would be different.* His musing on his past life was replaced by excitement as he replayed in his head the fascinating text Pete Miami had sent him. "I found God. Come to Taos ASAP."

On the flight from Des Moines to Denver Ramsey used his time to handle his daily grind of business emails. Internet connection on flights was a godsend to people like him —movers and shakers who used the information technology of the twenty-first century to virtually travel the world. He also had time to reflect on the New Gnostic website Orensen had given him to explore.

Ramsey knew well the controversies surrounding the ancient Gnostics. For many scholars it meant something more, something radically different than the ancient Christian sect Dan Brown depicted in his best-selling novel *The Da Vinci Code*, in which he fictionalized the legend of a purported lineage arising from the romantic union of Jesus Christ and Mary Magdalene.

To some scholars the Gnostics were one of the first true Christian sects. They saw Jesus as a divine prophet and teacher. Because they refused to bow to the emerging Roman Catholic Church, they were hunted down and wiped out. *The key to understanding their perspective on Christianity was in their name*, Ramsey thought. It came from the Greek word *gnōstikos*, meaning "to know" —not in the sense of knowing the capitol of the Ukraine, but in the sense of experiencing the divine directly. Ramsey recollected reading that at ancient gnostic prayer meetings, any gnostic—man, woman, or child—could stand up and lead the group. The closest modern-day equivalent in Christianity was the Quakers.

However, Orensen's website was not particularly religious but rather typical of special-interest social media sites. It provided stories of healings along with before-and-after pictures, plus other news about the shrine and more recently, updates about its apparent loss of healing power.

At first the site seemed random, as though some child had slapped painted handprints on his parent's kitchen wall. But when Ramsey had settled back and studied the layout, he observed how the members and the place itself seemed to be connected in some systematic way. As a human geographer, he knew something important was going on that he didn't yet understand. *There's a geographical pattern. I'm not getting it yet, but it will come*, he reassured himself.

One tab on the site was of particular interest to Ramsey. When he clicked on it, it opened to a familiar quotation. "Except a man be born of water and the Spirit, he cannot enter into the kingdom of God." This Bible quote startled him when he read it because it had been a favorite saying of Paige. He wondered if she were a New Gnostic and was surprised to find himself disappointed her name didn't turn up on the website. He pressed the tab and the webpage turned like a book. Written in elegant medieval calligraphy were the words: "Join us people of the shrine and make the journey that will take you from darkness into the light." There was nothing else on the page, and when he clicked on the sentence or any of the words, nothing happened.

Ramsey skyped Orensen to let him know what he was doing and to asked him about the mysterious tab.

The professor emeritus shrugged and said, "I don't know what it means. The digital world baffles me. Let me know what your friend Miami found. Be careful."

Orensen's offhand denial of any knowledge of the mysterious tab troubled Ramsey because he was sure it was a portal to a deeper level within the site. He felt it was connected to the pattern he wasn't seeing.

Ramsey looked out the window and saw that the plane was following the Rio Grande as they descended toward the small single runway of the Taos Regional Airport. The bumpiness had disappeared and the backpack had been returned to its overhead compartment. Passengers were once more calm while the flight attendant reminded everyone to put away their electronic devices and make sure their tray tables and seatbacks were in their original upright positions.

Once more his mind drifted back to the New Gnostic site. What was overwhelming were the many kinds of miraculous healings. The number and the passion with which they were told were staggering. Then Ramsey was reminded of an obvious point: All sacred places, all religions for that matter, were based on stories of miracles, real or purported. *Could it be that a new religion is forming around the Milagro Shrine?* he asked himself.

He settled into his seat. Pete would be picking him up at the airport. *This is going to be fun*, he thought. *Pete is one of my all-time favorite people and if he said he found God, he found God!*

16

March 30, 2019
Taos, New Mexico

Beecher shaded his eyes as he looked out the window. The small regional jet was traveling over the windward side of the Sangre de Christo Mountains. Below him the lush forest was dark green with patches of late snow nestled beneath overhangs of valleys. The dense foliage reminded Beecher of Vietnam and of the dangers and slaughter he had experienced when half his platoon was wiped out in a firefight with the Viet Cong. *I haven't thought about those men in many years. Is that okay?* He didn't know. They had all been young and raw, draftees mostly, and had only been together for a week, everyone wishing they were home—except Beecher, who strangely found war more peaceful than his childhood. He did three tours before coming back to Texas and was not wounded once.

He looked out the window once more and saw Taos in the distance. It was late afternoon but still plenty of time to make it to the meeting after they landed.

"The plane won't touchdown for another ten minutes," Beecher said to Conklin seated next to him on the plane.

The younger man nodded. Conklin was a pragmatist, a businessman, and a bit of an adventurer. He was fascinated by the exercise of power. He had never really bought into the mission of the Brothers of the Lord, but the members' connections had proven useful to him on a number of occasions. After all, Conklin was a person who did what he had to do to grow and protect his financial interests. He was particularly fascinated with Beecher's wheeling for power and pleased that he had taken him under his wing.

Conklin was unsure why Beecher pleaded with him to accompany him on this trip. But he was sure it had to do with the Reverend Billy Paul, the Milagro Shrine and the disappearance of Adam Gwillt. It was easy to see something was wrong. Beecher was normally a take-charge leader, demanding immediate response to his orders. But ever since Reverend Paul had instructed him to remove Adam, he was sounding unsure of himself. In the last two weeks the lines around the man's eyes and mouth had deepened. His gaze darted around as Conklin imagined he did while on patrol in Vietnam. Conklin relaxed and waited, knowing Beecher would eventually tell him what was going on. *Isn't that what Caine hinted at?*

As the plane cruised towards the runway, Beecher ran through all the events that had led up to this point. He needed to be clear about what he was going to tell Conklin.

Two days after meeting Caine at Oilcan Harry's, Beecher had heard for the first time, from someone other than Caine, that Adam had actually disappeared. Myriam had been to the shrine for one of the frequent workshops given by the Friends of the Shrine. She had called him that night, her voice near tears.

"Hiram, you have to come up," she said. "He's gone."

"Who?"

"Adam."

"When?"

"Five days ago."

Beecher remembered how surprised he was that Adam had

disappeared before meeting Caine at Oilcan Harry's. "He's left the shrine before, hasn't he?" Beecher had asked.

"Never."

He flew into Albuquerque the next morning and picked up the truck he kept at a vehicle storage facility. An hour and a half later he was at the shrine. Myriam came out of the Christ Chapel to greet him.

She held him fiercely saying over and over, "He's gone . . . gone . . . gone."

"Are you sure?"

She pulled back and nodded. He saw the red face, eyes puffy from crying. "Can't you feel it?" she asked. "Everyone else can. It's why we're so worried. The energy is gone, like someone turned the stove off."

Beecher had never felt anything at the shrine except that sense of peace. As his gaze swept over the grounds, it had all looked and felt the same as always. Except today it was covered in snow. "What about his sister, Carlotta? Has she said anything?"

"She was inconsolable. She was hysterical, worried that maybe her brother had wandered off and was in danger. She told me, 'Since the accident Adam's never gone anywhere. He didn't want to and he couldn't even if he did. His best friend from Iowa, Malcolm Grossinger, took him once on a trip someplace, but they were back early the next morning.'"

"What about the authorities?"

"The County Sheriff deputies are leading search parties all over the area. Nothing has turned up."

The plane leveled off. Off the right wing, Beecher could see the Taos Pueblo below. As the jet began its decent, he recalled how the search had been called off after a couple of weeks. Since then the only mention of Adam's disappearance had been short updates in the local newspaper about how the beloved caretaker of the Rio Chama

Milagro Shrine had disappeared. It asked anyone with any information to contact the shrine.

The hardest part for Beecher at the time had been deciding what to tell the Reverend Billy Paul about the disappearance of Adam. He had thought about lying and taking responsibility for Adam's disappearance. But, what if Adam suddenly showed up again? He hadn't even wanted to think about that scenario. Instead he had told the Reverend he had had nothing to do with Adam's disappearance, saying he had set something in motion but Adam disappeared before the assassination could take place. Unexpectedly, the Reverend was nonplussed with the news. Beecher recalled thinking it was like he already knew. The Reverend had said he would get back to him. At the time Beecher was greatly relieved. Although puzzled by Adam's disappearance, he had assumed someone else had killed him. In addition, Beecher's suppositions about Adam's miraculous powers had been confirmed as he watched the Milagro Shrine immediately lose its healing capacity now that Adam was no longer there. In any case, Adam was no longer his problem.

Then to Beecher's chagrin, the Adam enigma had started all over again three months later. That's when the phone call from the Reverend Billy Paul had come.

"Adam's not dead," the televangelist had announced angrily. "His existence is a greater problem than ever. Here's what you're going to do. You're going to hire this famous human geographer Jonathan Ramsey. He's our best hope of finding Adam." Surprisingly the Reverend Billy Paul knew about Ramsey's relationship with Myriam. "Tell her she should bring him in to investigate what happened to the shrine," the evangelist had said. "Ramsey will lead us to Adam.

"I cannot stress, Brother Beecher, as I said before, just how important it is to the work of the Brothers of the Lord that we find Adam Gwillt immediately."

Beecher had agreed reluctantly, and brought the idea up with Myriam that night—to her great surprise. Beecher told her that some of his folks researched who could figure out what happened at the

Milagro Shrine and Jonathan Ramsey was at the top of the list. "My people believe Adam's not dead," he said.

Myriam had had reservations because she and Ramsey had not parted on good terms, but upon hearing the hopeful tone in Beecher's voice, she agreed that he should do all that Reverend Paul had asked of him.

The last call from Brother Paul had come two days ago. The Reverend had been upbeat. "Brother Beecher, hiring Jonathan Ramsey has already paid big dividends in the search for Adam Gwillt."

"I'm glad to have helped out," Beecher had answered. At the time he had thought he was free. And could go back to Myriam with no secrets.

Then Paul added, "I have another job for you. Go to Taos, where you will be met by people who need your help in ending the Milagro Shrine and Adam Gwillt's sacrilege."

Beecher was becoming angry with himself about how he had let himself get into this troubling situation. After the Reverend had hung up, Beecher realized he needed help. There was no one he could really turn to. Then it occurred to him that Sam Conklin was the only one he felt confident of. After the evening with Caine they had shared a bond that went beyond the Brothers of the Lord. And Sam was resourceful. So Beecher had made a decision. Assessing his reaction step-by-step, Beecher would let Sam Conklin in on what was happening. *I need somebody to cover my back.*

These were the exact words Beecher told Conklin as the plane taxied to a stop at the Taos airport.

Conklin scratched at the mustache above his long upper lip. *Now it all makes sense,* he told himself. *Beecher's out on a limb and he needs backup.*

He wondered how far he should go in helping Beecher once again. The man had been fanatical when Beecher asked his help in his pursuit of the aims of the Brothers of the Lord concerning the shrine and Adam Gwillt. But now Beecher's concern had shifted from Adam Gwillt to himself.

Conklin thought back to Oilcan Harry's. Caine had come down the stairs alone. He sauntered over to where Conklin was sitting, slid next to him and waited, his mouth in a patient smile.

Conklin recalled glancing at the stairs and not seeing Beecher anywhere. His heart had thudded in his chest, and his mind went inexorably to the murder of Ketterman. Conklin had wondered if Beecher would ever come down.

Then Caine had leaned close, his lips right at Conklin's ear. "Hiram Beecher has gone over and come back. He'll need your help just as I helped you with Ketterman."

Caught by the sincere authority in Caine words Conklin had only been able to say, "How should I help him?"

"You'll know when he asks you."

Caine had then winked and left.

The jet's passengers began to debark. Conklin studied the hard-lined face beside him, saw the plea for help in the drawn mouth. He felt closer to Beecher than he could ever let on.

Without hesitation Conklin said, "Whatever you need, Hiram."

After renting an SUV at the airport, the two men drove immediately to the chalet. On the way there, Beecher reminded Conklin how Caine had insinuated at Oilcan Harry's that the Adam issue that already been taken care of.

Conklin took a deep breath. "You mean somebody killed him?"

"That's what I thought at the time," Beecher said, letting his distaste come through. "But it turns out he just disappeared one day. I can't tell you how much relieved I was."

"But that wasn't the end of it?"

"No, the Reverend Paul has become obsessed with finding him. He demanded that I hire a former associate of Myriam's, Jonathan Ramsey, to investigate what happened to the shrine's healing power. Brother Paul was convinced that somehow Dr. Ramsey's going to lead us to Adam."

"And did he?"

"That's why I'm here, why you're here."

"They found him in Taos?"

"I think so. Dr. Ramsey supposedly led them here. In any case I'll soon find out. Brother Paul set up a meeting for me with some people from South Africa."

"South Africa, it doesn't make sense, I don't understand."

"Me neither; something's not right."

"What do you need me to do?"

Beecher thought, *So far so good. The real test will come when we get to the chalet.*

"I'll explain when we get settled." Conklin's confusion must have shown clearly on his face because Beecher instantly added, "I know this must sound puzzling to you, but all I can ask is that you trust me." He smile. "In some ways I'm becoming more like you."

Conklin nodded, weighing the unknowns around this trip with Beecher's uncharacteristic openness. He decided he was still in. "How's that?"

"I know you've never bought into the brotherhood's mission. I'm having my own doubts now."

Conklin registered no surprise. "Something to do with what happened at the bar?"

Beecher was not ready to tell anyone what happened upstairs at Oilcan Harry's. So he dodged the question. "Among other things."

Conklin sensed that Beecher needed something from him.

"You know, for a while after I met Caine, I gained a kind of calmness. You probably noticed that too. I'm here partly because of that." Beecher pointed to an inn on a hillside above the road. "That's where we're staying."

Located 15 miles from Taos airport, the Edelweiss chalet was closed for the season. However, the owner was an old military buddy of Beecher's, so accommodations for him and Conklin were easily arranged.

A middle-aged man with a heavy German accent greeted them. He managed the chalet for Beecher's buddy. He pointed to where they should park their vehicle.

The German manager provided each of them with a comfortable room and opened the kitchen, putting out coffee and pastries.

When they were alone, Hiram pulled out a smartphone from his coat pocket and handed it to Conklin. Next he took what appeared to be a large ink pen out of his coat pocket. "Here's how we'll stay in touch. It's the latest in personal communication devices," he explained. He pushed a button on the top of the pen and the smart phone's screen lit up with a map of Northern New Mexico. A neon green light appeared just outside of Taos. Longitude and latitude appeared beside it. "We'll be able to communicate by voice and most importantly you'll be able to track my movements. I'll contact you when I know more. I'm turning it off now. If it comes on and I don't communicate with you, start tracking me. You have your gun?"

"It's in my luggage." He picked up the handheld device. It weighed less than a pound. He chuckled. "And I thought James Bond had all the great toys. He sobered. "You expecting trouble?"

Beecher shrugged. "I don't know what to expect, so I thought I should be prepared."

Beecher started the SUV and drove away. He turned onto the road leading to Taos. Here, Highway 64 ran straight as an arrow and in the late afternoon was clear of any cars. He put the cruise control at 85 and drove easily with one hand on the steering wheel. He liked the feeling of a fast car, the way it knifed through the air. It helped him relax, and relaxing was something he needed to do right now.

The Taos city limits soon loomed ahead. Beecher tapped his brakes and slowed way down. The car rental agent had warned him the sheriff had a speed trap here. By the time he passed the deputy's car, he was five miles an hour under the speed limit. He waved cheerfully. The young man waved back. He passed the famous Indian Pueblo where Native Americans lived as they had for the past thousand years. Unlike the shrine, it was closed off, hard to get into unless you knew someone who lived there. He pulled into the Wired Cyber Café on Felicidad Lane, just off Paseo Del Pueblo Norte, the main road running through town. The Reverend Billy Paul had told him to wait in Taos for a tall man with pale blue eyes who would give him instructions.

Beecher went inside and took a table near the back where he had a clear view of the parking lot and the front door. He ordered a Grande Americano. Pulling his phone from his shirt pocket, he laid it on the table and waited. In his coat pocket he felt the outline of a Glock Seventeen 9mm.

A few months ago he had been a devout follower of the Bothers of the Lord. "A true believer," Reverend Billy Paul had called him. At that time he would have gladly followed the order to end Adam Gwillt. But now, he didn't know any more. What was it Caine said to him after their encounter at Oilcan Harry's? *You're free.*

You're free all right, old buddy, Beecher told himself. *But you no longer know which way the wind is blowing.* He squeezed into the corner a little more so no one from the road could see him. It was like being back in Vietnam and setting up an ambush on the trail. His senses were honed, listening for even the slightest sound or movement to tell him which way to jump. *But which way will I jump? That's the question.*

17

____

March 30, 2019
Taos, New Mexico

Pete Miami was the only redheaded friend Ramsey had ever had. He was a tall, lanky bundle of brains. Einstein on steroids, Paige had called him. He played the bongo drums and the bass, wrote music, and could do cube roots in his head. In his personal interactions, he was like a great Dane puppy, running around the house, skidding on hardwood floors, knocking over tables and chairs, barreling straight at you, and at the last moment sliding to a jackknifing, claw scratching stop. They'd met as postdocs studying under Myriam at the University of Oregon and it was deep fellowship at first sight. They became inseparable except when either of them was on what they euphemistically called a "mission." It was a kind of code they used when either of them was busy with something special. For Ramsey it was whenever Paige came for a visit. For Pete it was usually an all-nighter at the lab with a gallon of ninety-proof coffee and an idea that just wouldn't go away until he'd hammered it to death or the coffee ran out. More often than not the idea gave up its secrets long before the coffee was finished.

As Ramsey walked out of the terminal, Pete rushed up, still puppy-like though older, beard now tinged with gray, long hair still in a pony tail—but now much longer than during his Oregon days. His green eyes twinkled with merriment. He didn't offer to take the bag or ask about the flight. He started right in. "Don't know the fuck whether to thank you or shoot you, Jon."

"Good to see you too, Pete," Ramsey said and held out his hand.

Pete grasped it belatedly as though it were something he was supposed to shake and not quite knowing what to do with it when the pleasantries were over.

"It was three gallons of coffee before your shrine gave up the ghost, so to speak." He laughed. "More on that later. You've got to see this first."

He led Ramsey out of the building to the parking lot and stopped, his arms raised like a magician. "Ta da!"

Parked across three spaces was 1958 Nash Rambler, robin's-egg-blue with purple seats. "Ain't she beautiful? I call her Nellie Bell. I lost my cherry in one when I was eleven. It was with Pandora Krakauer." He winked and unlocked the passenger door. It opened silently and closed with a soft click. He turned the key and the engine purred like a Bentley.

"Got her for a steal from an old lady who worked for Georgia O'Keefe, true story. Only used it to buy groceries on Sunday."

"No church?" Ramsey asked.

Pete looked at him sideways. "In this part of New Mexico, church is wherever you look."

"So, what did you find?"

"That can wait. What I've got to show you is more important." Pete swung onto Highway 64 and from there onto a dirt road that wound through the hills above Taos. The afternoon was waning and as they climbed, the sun seemed to perch perpetually on the western mountains. At the top of one of the hills, Pete pulled into a ramshackle cabin that was as dilapidated as the car was immaculate. He hustled Ramsey out of the car, through the house, and onto the back deck. The San de Cristo Mountains had to begun to eat into the reddening disk of the sun, a snow-glistened peak limned with dark shadows showing its notches and ridges exquisitely like a Japanese painting. This time Pete didn't say anything. He just soaked in the view.

Ramsey stood beside him. The muscles of his jaw worked but nothing came out.

Pete glanced at him. A big smile creased his face. "I used to think this was as close to God a person could get." He winked.

Ramsey waited, knowing that Pete would tell him what he meant in his own sweet time. "What's for dinner?"

"Margaritas, some kickass chili this *mamacita* in Rio Chama makes, and fresh-baked tortillas."

The food was everything Pete said it was. By the time they finished, the sun had set and twilight was a dim purple line across the mountains. They'd caught up, each suitably oohing and aahing in all the right places as they told stories since the last get-together in China. Ramsey was impatient to get on with Pete's "discovery of God," but knew better than to rush him. Once during a conversation with Ramsey in Oregon, Pete had talked through two traffic light cycles while cars honked and steered around him. Then he waited yet again and went through on the yellow. "Everyone's in such a damn hurry," he'd muttered.

At last dinner was complete. Pete pulled out a pair of Cubans, passing one over. Ramsey held his breath. Pete had always celebrated a breakthrough with a good meal and a terrific breakthrough with a cigar. A meal and a cigar together meant something spectacular. He smiled and blew a smoke ring.

"Now," Pete said simply. He got up and led Ramsey to the other side of the house. It looked out over a canyon. The lights of Taos were far in the distance. Pete opened the door to the garage and flicked on the light switch.

Ramsey couldn't stop the gasp. The room was wall-to-wall ultra-high definition plasma screens. He learned from Pete that each one was linked by satellite to the most powerful high-speed computer in the world, a Chinese Milky Way-2. It was housed in South Africa.

"Why South Africa?"

Pete grinned. "The DeVere Mining Group hired yours truly. They store the data on on their banks of servers and I get to use the speed of their supercomputer to test my hypotheses I'm working with this Danish guy, Lindstrom. Smart fellow. Nowadays I often have him confirm some of my calculations. Of course, I never show him everything."

The screens showed northern New Mexico in various geographical modes. One laid out the primary topography. Others displayed multidimensional Geographic Information Systems modeling representations. What it all meant was way beyond Ramsey's ability to understand. Pete sat in a chair that looked more like a pilot's seat on an F-15 fighter. There was another one next to it. Pointing to it, Pete said, "Buckle up."

When Ramsey was situated, Pete pressed a couple of panels. The screens in front of them went dark, then flickered to life. "You remember how to play Aviator?" As a post-doc Pete had worked on the graphics for a flight simulator for the U.S Navy and had pirated the finished product. He didn't wait for an answer.

All of a sudden Ramsey heard a low whoosh and then the screen in front of him took on a greenish tinge. Coming quickly in to view was a large expanse of New Mexico landscape, now flowing toward and then beneath him.

"You're active, old man."

Ramsey grabbed the joystick in front of him. The remote-controlled drone screamed into a steep dive. "Is this real?" he exclaimed.

"You bet. Steady there," Pete cautioned, though he made no move for the controls. "You're flying the latest, industrial-grade drone available with high-definition night cameras. I have two at my disposal. Remember how we used to use helicopters and planes to do our GIS data gathering. Now we use these babies. They can go everywhere, hover over one place for hours, and carry loads of instruments. They are the best tools we geographers have ever had."

Ramsey eased back and the drone leveled off. He hadn't played video games since Oregon, but the reflexes came back quickly. Soon he was piloting his bird across the night sky.

"Not bad, old man. We'll make a flyboy out of you yet." Pete clapped him on the back. "I'm plugging in some coordinates. Enjoy the ride."

"What's the range on these babies?" asked Ramsey.

"At night, a hundred miles out and back ... about four hours. During the day, photovoltaics in the wings can keep them aloft for twelve hours."

"So this is the big surprise?" Ramsey asked, feeling let down.

"Not even close." Ramsey flew in silence for a few more minutes.

"There!" Pete exclaimed. He stabbed a slim index finger at the right-hand bottom of the screen. His other hand pushed a red button on the left hand side of Ramsey's console. The camera image steadied and zoomed in on the ground. The outline of the small Christ Chapel at the Rio Chama Milagro Shrine came into view. Pete fine-tuned the image so the entire shrine was visible. "Hover mode," he explained.

Ramsey was blown away. Pete reached over and pushed two buttons. "They'll come home on their own now."

Pete pulled out a blue tooth keyboard and typed "execute." A new image appeared. Ramsey knew it was interlocking wave patterns that resolved into patterns looking similar to field distortions he had seen during explanations of Einstein's relativity, but he couldn't say what they really were. He squinted at the screen. "What am I seeing? None of this looks familiar."

"Old man, since you first looked for physical explanations of the planet's sacred sites, GIS has changed completely how we look at our beautiful home. I can find any number of geophysical fields around a gnat's ass from 2,000 feet away if I thought it might prove useful. More importantly, I have figured out how to detect fingerprint-like electromagnetic radiation from the micro-fractures of the earth's materials."

"The Earth's crust is under constant pressure, as I recall. Shifting, moving ... continuous micro-earthquakes."

"Bingo. Therefore, the rock types in various regions generate their own magnetic and electromagnetic fields." He pointed at the screen. "Among other things, our Chinese computer in South Africa has been keeping a record of all my collected data. This means that I can put together a portrait over time of any area I've been gathering data on and see it in a way we could never see before. It tells me a story of what has happened there, geologically and environmentally. I can use that to find mineral deposits, coal, changing water flow patterns, vegetation shifts, human produced developments ... whatever you want."

"Diamond pipes containing kimberlites?" Ramsey asked. He remembered that diamond pipes were an extremely rare geological phenomenon—volcanic extrusions from the deepest part of the Earth's core. Small in size, these tiny volcanoes brought to the surface of the earth already formed diamonds. The only known diamond pipes in the United States were a commercial venture in Arkansas and the now defunct Kelsey Lake Diamond Mine near Fort Collins, Colorado. Their rarity and small size made them almost impossible to find.

Pete grinned. "Particularly kimberlites."

Ramsey shot him a questioning look.

"And yes, I have, at least I believe I have. The next step is to field-verify. The big shots from South Africa's DeVere diamond cartel are here and we're going to take a look tomorrow."

"All this begs the question: What about my 'God'?"

"Here's what I'd found when I put together a time-based representation of your coordinates over the last five years I've been collecting data." Pete's fingers few over the keyboard and graphic representations began to unfold on both screens.

Ramsey's jaw dropped when the image appeared. The screen depicted an amazing warping of overlapping field-lines. It reminded Ramsey of artist renderings of objects warping space around a planet. As he watched, it configured itself into an amoeba-like structure that pulsed and changed color and shape, growing in intensity over time, then disappearing to a small afterglow of its original form.

"What we have here is the interaction of normally unconnected random electromagnetic and magnetic fields that over time produce a single remarkable coherence pattern. At first I could see there was something strange going on around the shrine, but it wasn't until yesterday that I was able to—through some brilliant mathematical manipulations that I put together, I might add—explain what you just saw."

Ramsey remembered the classic example his physics professor had used during his grad studies at UCLA to explain field coherence. The professor had started a digital recorder, then instructed the audience to plug their ears and sing *Amazing Grace* whenever the mood struck them. After a few minutes he had the students unplug their ears and continue singing before being told to stop. The instructor then played back what happened. The group result of everybody singing on their own was totally discordant, in fact, painful to listen to. Yet when the audience unplugged their ears, almost instantly people began to pick up on each other's singing. Very quickly they naturally self-organized themselves into a beautifully harmonic choir. The audience had cohered into a temporary 'field' of a higher order, existing only as long as the singing occurred.

Ramsey could see what Pete was driving at but he was almost afraid to ask. Swallowing he said, "What does that mean for the shrine?"

"Welcome to God's abode, old man . . . or at least the most advanced GIS depiction of your shrine possible."

Ramsey was at a loss for words. Everything he had searched for twelve years was now right in front of him, lighting up the screen like a neon sign advertising "God" or some sort of transcendent force. "H–how?" he managed to ask, his excitement soaring.

"Somehow all the electromagnetic radiation, magnetic fields, and even the bio-energetic fields at the shrine have coalesced into a coherent structure. What did it, I can't say, but this is its manifestation. I suspect that if you had been there before it collapsed you might have felt something like the pleasure of listening to the Mormon Tabernacle Choir . . . or the New York Philharmonic . . . or songs of humpback whales, only magnified a thousand times. This massive coherence of nature certainly would affect each and every person's bioenergetic fields in its presence. It would be like being in the presence of God. Just joking of course, since I don't know really knows what that would be like. If the people inside the cohered field were aware of it, I can't say." He rubbed his chin. "Damn, I wish I had been there."

Ramsey couldn't take his eyes from the screen. His heart thudded wildly in his chest. His mouth was suddenly dry and he couldn't speak. One thought kept running through his head: *Is this what gives the shrine its healing power? An anomalous coherence of the earth's many energetic physical fields?* Ramsey let out a toneless whistle. *What in the hell could produce such a thing?*

Pete leaned back in his chair and laughed. "I told you I found God."

Ramsey's mind was racing. Could it be what he had tried so hard to find fifteen years ago was now being handed to him? He needed some time to think and digest what he had just seen and learned.

Picking up on Ramsey's mindset, Pete said, "I know that look, old man. I'll drive us into town. There's a bar just off the main drag that's very conducive to processing."

He took a winding back road through the mountains of Carson National Forest. During the ride, he connected his iPhone and played Iron Butterfly's *In-A-Gadda-Da-Vida*.

Ramsey only half listened, his mind working on integrating what he'd just seen. *Is it as simple as the number-one axiom of modern human geography? People shape place and place shapes people in an ever-expanding spiral.* Was it that somehow the open-minded nature of the people on pilgrimage created subtle-field coherences and these coherent fields in turn changed people's mental states, the biofields of their bodies, and maybe even their life directions? The idea was intoxicating. But he knew there was an even bigger question that had to be added to the mix. *How does Adam Gwillt fit in?*

Ramsey glanced at his dear friend. *How much should I involve Pete? Should I engage him anymore?* He knew he couldn't do what he wanted to do without Pete's skillset and equipment. He turned down the music and brought Pete up to speed on his investigation, starting with his conversation with the ghost-like Adam Gwillt. It was slow-going at first. Pete scoffed and wisecracked his way through Ramsey's story, particularly at every coincidence he brought up, like the chance encounter with Malcolm Grossinger in the airport.

But the coincidence that blew Pete's mind was that it was their old teacher and advisor, Myriam, who had hired Ramsey. He laughed and said: "Myriam was never the substitute mother for me that she was for you."

Ramsey grit his teeth, annoyed with the observation.

Pete must have noticed because in the next second he pounded the steering wheel. "Sorry about the mom reference. It was out of line."

True but it was also genuine, thought Ramsey. Certainly the memory of Myriam's refusal to see him in Peru had stirred up the old fear of abandonment he'd experienced when his mother died. Ramsey smiled ruefully. "No problem."

'Thanks." Pete paused. "Funny coincidence that she was only a hundred miles away from me for such a long time huh?"

By the time they exited the forest, Taos was right in front of them. Pete roared down the main drag and stopped in front of Murphy's Pub. "The porter here's like nectar. They make it themselves."

Savoring the first sip, Ramsey turned to Pete. "One thing puzzles me. How come you had so much geophysical information from around the shrine ?"

"Funny you should ask. One evening around five years ago, shortly after I began my research, I was sitting right here at the bar and this young man asked me if it would be okay if he sat with me. He was one of those city guys that come up here to push their limits biking and hiking. He said he was from Phoenix where he was a programmer. Guess I was getting a little drunk and I must've told him that I was looking for diamonds."

Ramsey remembered that Pete could never keep a secret. "How many slips of the tongue do your employers give you?" Ramsey joked.

"You're right, touché."

"Back to my weird little tale. He gave me this funny little wink and said, 'I'll be right back.' When he returned he was carrying a white sample bag. He pulled out some of the best-looking kimberlites I've ever seen. One chunk contained a perfect little blue diamond."

"Talk about coincidences," Ramsey joked.

"Indeed. So, naturally I asked where he got the kimberlite. He replied he found it someplace southwest of here. When I pushed him for more details he couldn't say exactly where he found it. He assured me he'd gone back dozens of times, but no luck. But he knew the general area. He joked that maybe I could find it. At one point the bugger jumps off his stool and shouts to whole bar, 'We'll be rich!'"

"Bet that went over well."

Pete shrugged. "A streaker ran through here once; a girl I think."

"You think?"

"No one even bothered to look up and stare." He laughed. "That's how interested folks around these parts are in strange goings on. At any rate, when this city dude settled down, he said he could give me the general whereabouts." Pete waited for a few seconds. "Then there's a funny part, funny in being strange-like. You've read Carlos Castaneda?"

"Every book."

"It was like when he described talking to the coyote. There were no words. It was as if my body was receiving a map of the area where he found the kimberlite. Weird. Then he handed me the largest piece of kimberlite and said, 'Keep this. I'll know if you find the kimberlite pipe and then we'll both be rich. I know I can trust you.' He got up without another word, handed me his business card and took off."

Ramsey's eyes narrowed. "And the search area just happened to contain the coordinates of the shrine."

"Bingo. So when you asked me to run the scans, the work had already been done. I just never noticed the big anomaly at the shrine site. "

That's crazy, thought Ramsey. *Another encounter with a mysterious bringer of information. What are the odds on that?* "So, what did you do with the kimberlite sample he gave you?"

"The sample was rich in micro diamonds, the telltale sign of a highly productive pipe. Using the kimberlite he gave me, I was able to build a rock microfracture signature by subjecting it to minor pressures delivered by my compression machine. Once I had that I could scan for the kimberlite signature with my drone as it flew across the landscape. Lo and behold– "

"You found something?"

"Indeed, in one of the most impassable areas of New Mexico, thirty miles due west of your shrine. How's that for a coincidence?"

"Anybody know about this?"

"Well, I hired this local Hispanic woman from Rio Chama to help me navigate through the property rights in the area. It's a hodgepodge of private, Indian, and national forest lands. By the way it's same woman who made the kickass chili. She owns the Rio Chama Café. Name's Rosa Cisneros"

"Get out of town," Ramsey said laughing. "I met her a few days ago when I went down to Rio Chama. Hey, one question. Did you ever contact your lucky guy?"

"The card was bogus. None of the numbers connected to anyone."

"And you didn't think it was odd he hands you a bag of diamonds, says he can trust you and you'll both be rich, but gives you a bogus card?"

"Hey for one thing it's northern New Mexico we're talking about. You can't throw a rock without hitting something strange. And in my defense, I was hammered."

Pete's binges were legendary and Ramsey could almost accept his excuse, but something nagged at the back of his mind. "What was his name?"

Pete pulled the card from his wallet and handed it to Ramsey. The name read "Reginald Hermes—special programmer." He looked on the other side. It was blank. On a hunch he held it up to the light and he could see a watermark in the lower left hand corner. It was an image of a coyote. He smiled to himself. "What did he look like?"

"I don't know. He was tall and thin, I guess, about your height. ... short blond hair. He looked like a Viking. I mean all he needed was the helmet with the horns and a war axe. He had these crazy kind of eyes. They were blue like a Norwegian fjord, and he never really looked at me when he was speaking. He seemed to stare at me from the side, as though he was seeing something other than just me, like my aura or something. At one point he even shouted at me, 'Quit the drinking or you won't live to see thirty!' It was then that Ramsey recalled Pete hadn't had any of the margaritas, nor had he touched his beer all night. Occasionally he looked at it or moved it around the bar.

Pete laughed. "I believed him."

18

———————

February 2019
Pretoria, South Africa

Rain slashed the windows of the DeVere chairman's private penthouse suite. Low clouds obscured the Magaliesberg Mountains. Pieter Haas half listened to the long discussion about the search for a productive diamond pipe located in northern New Mexico. The man delivering the report had briefed DeVere's CEO days earlier. Haas already knew the decision the Mining Group would make—continue buying as much property in the area as they could. But he was interested in much more than the diamonds.

Haas's narrow and ascetic face belied his many passions and multifaceted worldview. In business he believed capitalism was the only vehicle for unleashing the creative power of the individual. Yet he practiced gaining every competitive advantage, legal or illegal he could find, tilting the playing field to his company's advantage. Diamonds were a ruthless business and Hass was well prepared mentally and physically to deal with any adversity. He was accustomed to getting what he wanted and as long as he made enough money for DeVere he could do what he pleased.

The long report was finally ending. From the looks on the Board member's faces, the group was ready to call it quits. The boring geologic details of diamond hunting weren't the reasons these Board members sat through these meetings. At the end of the day, all they needed to know the research money was well spent and their annual bonuses would continue to grow.

George Rhodes, the man in charge of the company's North American interests, leaned back in his chair. He was a roughneck who'd started as a digger in South Africa's Premier Mine and worked his way up to become a manager and then a director. Rumor had it he could smell diamonds like a pig hunts truffles. Five years ago Haas put him in charge of North America and never regretted it. "The initial kimberlite chunks found by amateur rock hounds were richer in diamonds than any found South Africa," Rhodes told the others. "The source of the kimberlite could be bigger than all of Saskatchewan and Michigan put together."

The rest of the Board nodded approval.

"When will you know?" asked Haas.

"By July at the latest. Our researcher over there, Pete Miami, believes he's getting close. Hell, he keeps expanding the search area and I'd wouldn't be surprised if Miami has the entire Northeast region of New Mexico geo-magnetically mapped by then."

"What's happening on the land front?"

"We're at the point in the process where we have enough private land that we should be able to make a trade with the forest service if the diamond pipes turn up on federal land." Rhodes laughed. "We've become the largest private landowners New Mexico."

Haas smiled, pleased with the initiative Rhodes had taken. But he was also pleased that under the cover of diamond hunting, they had found an even bigger treasure no one on the Board knew of. *And they won't know it until we have it secured.*

Haas said, "Excellent. Is there anything else?"

Rhodes shook his head.

"Gentlemen, to success," Haas said. He bowed his head in prayer and the others followed suit. It was a custom DeVere's founder had initiated a century ago.

"Until next month, everyone," Haas said after half a minute.

The men filed out.

Greta Van Horn waited outside. When the others had cleared the room, she came in. She carefully closed the door.

For the thousandth time, Haas rued the company rule that didn't allow women on the Board of Directors. Greta could run circles around the others. "What do you have to report?"

"I have Lindstrom waiting outside, and he has something you'll want to see. It has to do with this parcel of land at the center of that region of strange readings I showed you last fall. I looked into it like you asked." She handed him a map of northern New Mexico with the town of Rio Chama circled in red and smaller circle just north of the town also circled. "In the process of acquiring land we were urged by our local real estate man Raphael Núñez to buy the property called the Rio Chama Milagro Shrine. For the last decade it's been touted as the greatest healing shrine in the world, better than Lourdes in France. We did as Núñez asked and at his request gave it a cash infusion and put him on the board to oversee our investment."

Haas nodded his approval "Smart man, drive up the local real estate values."

Greta continued, "Here's the interesting part. A man named Hiram Beecher associated with the shrine hired a crew from the popular cable television show *Psychic or Psycho* to investigate the shrine's paranormal healing powers, supposedly located in a 200-year-old cottonwood tree. The TV crew and the producer spent four days, interviewed dozens of pilgrims and shot about a hundred hours of specially processed video. The show was supposed to be broadcast but never saw the light of day."

Haas frowned. "Not unusual for a production company to pull the plug on a project if they didn't find anything interesting for its viewers."

"That's just it. They did find something. I urged our man Núñez to do a little digging. It cost him some money but he was able to pry loose from the producer what was really going on. It seems the healing power of the shrine was not in the cottonwood tree but in the shrine's groundskeeper, a man named Adam Gwillt."

Greta touched her iPad. She handed it to him. On it was a screen grab from a video captured during the shoot

Haas's heart seemed to stop. With his fingers he enlarged the center of the picture. It was electronically processed in a way he didn't recognize and the man's features were strangely blurred, but the otherworldly emanations surrounding the figure were unmistakable. His mind reeled. "I want to meet this groundskeeper immediately."

"That would be difficult, sir."

"Why?"

"Apparently, he's disappeared."

"I need to find him as quickly as possible."

"I anticipated as much. That's why Lindstrom is waiting. He has something that might be of interest to you.

Dr. Paul Lindstrom fidgeted with his hands. Pieter Haas spoke in low tones with Greta Van Horn, ignoring the Danish geologist. Above a long side table was an oil portrait of the Voortrekker leader Andries Pretorius, for whom Pretoria was named. He held a musket in one hand and a Zulu knobkierie in the other. A team of oxen pulling a covered wagon followed him. The artist had captured Pretorius's self confident smile as he looked out upon the Transvaal, the area the Boers would conquer and hold for a half century until the second Boer War ended in 1902. Rumor said the current DeVere Group's chairman was a descendant and just as much a visionary as the Transvaal's conqueror.

Haas looked up from the file Lindstrom had given him. His pale blue eyes cut through the geologist with the same icy stare of Pretorius. "These readings show us what exactly?"

Lindstrom hesitated before answering. "For want of a better term, they show a baffling energy anomaly associated with the Milagro Shrine."

"So?"

"It's been there at least since Doctor Miami's drones started collecting geo-physical data. And now it's gone."

"Where is it?"

"I don't know. Perhaps we can get Dr. Miami to initiate a search. Sir, if you want to track the anomaly or even possibly pinpoint its location, you need to have feet on the ground."

Haas smiled. "You mean boots on the ground."

"Yes, sir. You need someone who could work real time with Doctor Miami. What he's doing is way above my pay grade."

"Thank you Doctor Lindstrom, that will be all."

Haas waited until the geologist left. He turned to Greta Van Horn. "Find out everything about this Beecher fellow. I'm sure he didn't undertake the documentary on the Milagro Shrine by himself. There has to be an organization behind what he did. It could be they even have the caretaker. Find them and him. It's your number one priority. And you'd better call Goren. Have him get the team together."

Greta shivered. The ex-paratrooper was no one to cross. "Anything else, sir?"

"Tell him to meet us in Cape Town. Have him prepare for New Mexico, the terrain and the climate. Let's see if we can't find the elusive caretaker."

When he was alone once more, Haas went to the window. A sudden squall battered the glass, but he didn't flinch, loving the wild, hooting wind that descended on Pretoria out of the Magaliesberg Mountains. At that moment the clouds parted revealing a headland that looked remarkably like a cross. He shuddered inwardly. The electronically processed image of Adam Gwillt brought up something out of his past so long buried he thought it dead.

It was like an image from another time, before he had begun his meteoric rise in the diamond business to become head of DeVere. "They have to find him," Haas said aloud. "They will find him."

19

March 15, 2019
Indianapolis, Indiana

Haas strolled alone on Indianapolis's New Jersey Street toward the Old National Centre. Goren and his paratroopers remained in the van with Greta. They wouldn't be needed for this part of the job. It had been relatively easy for Greta Van Horn to find the information he'd wanted about Hiram Beecher. The trail led here.

The hundred-year old building was easy to find. A tall minaret at the front guided him perfectly. It was now an entertainment center and its 2,500-seat performing arts theater was where the Reverend Billy Paul televised his daily show for the faithful. He stopped and checked his watch. The taping of the show should be ending now.

The building was also oddly apropos for his meeting. Greta's research indicated it was originally known as the Murat Temple and had been built by the Ancient Arabic Order of the Nobles of the Mystic Shrine—Freemasons.

Once more the old memories surfaced.

As a kid Haas had been raised in the bush from the lush veldt of

South Africa to the wild plains of Ethiopia by his wildlife photographer parents. Much of the time his only companion had been his younger sister Madeline.

Another shiver rippled through him. *It's been a long time since I thought of Madeline almost dying . . . and now twice in less than six months.*

It had happened along the Kenya-Somali border in the Danakil Desert. His little sister had contracted malaria. Trapped by tribal conflicts, his parents could only look on in horror as she began to slip away. Then out of nowhere there appeared the Samburu shaman. He was as tall as a Zulu warrior, dressed in a leopard skin his face and neck and chest painted with red ochre earth. He had picked up Madeline's limp body, and while Haas's parents stood frozen in place, walked off towards an elephant watering hole. When he came back in what seemed to young Haas to be just minutes, the shaman was walking hand-in-hand with his sister. While she ran to her parents, the shaman had turned to Haas and said, "There will come a time when you will see me again and when you do you must act."

The man's voice was like a drum in Haas's head, beating in rhythm with his heart. Haas had mustered all his courage and asked, "Act how?"

"Act to save your world." The shaman had then walked out into the dry dust wash and disappeared.

As Pieter Haas strode briskly across the street toward the Old National Centre and his meeting with the Reverend Billy Paul, he was sure that Adam had to be the shaman who saved Madeleine 35 years ago. And he needed to act. Greta had learned all about the Brothers of the Lord, their mission and their leader Billy Paul. It had also been relatively easy to uncover that the Brothers of the Lord didn't have Adam Gwillt but that Billy Paul was obsessed with finding and killing the shrine's former caretaker. What was hard for Haas was to find a way to locate Adam. It finally came to him. The complex plan needed everything to fall into place at the right time and he had to convince Reverend Billy Paul to play along. The thought of aligning himself with a charlatan like Paul made him sick. But Haas was a master of using the lie to his advantage. In the end he felt certain that Billy Paul would do everything Haas would tell him to do.

20

———————

March 30, 2019
Rio Chama, New Mexico

Myriam sat at her usual table in the Rio Chama Café atrium. The night air was crisp. Snow lingered in the high plains under overhangs and along dry streambeds even though it was late March. She wrapped her coat around her to ward off the chill, but she couldn't stop the deeper cold that ached her heart.

She and Beecher had just had a grinding row over the phone.

"I'll be in Taos for two, maybe three days," he told her.

"That's four nights you've been away this week."

"It's business."

"It's always business," she said sharply, unable to keep the disappointment out of her voice. "What is it this time?"

Beecher paused and Myriam knew that whatever excuse he came up with was just another lie. "I'm trying to close the deal on a big project. It's important," he said finally.

So am I, she thought bitterly but kept it inside. "The shrine's important too. You said you wanted to see it succeed."

"I do, but tonight ... this week, work has to come first."

"Then just stay there, and don't think of coming home for a little nooky and then leaving again for your important deal!" Myriam had hung up and refused to answer Beecher's repeated attempts to call her back. But now she felt rotten.

She stared out at Rio Chama. A half moon filled the street with light. A lone car sped through town in the direction of the shrine. She knew she wasn't really angry with Beecher. This whole thing with Adam's disappearance had left her empty again. It was like pouring salt on old wounds from her university days, wounds she had thought healed forever. She longed to walk at the Milagro Shrine and feel that lost peace and joy again.

Rosa set a pot of coffee on a trivet and sat down. "So, tell me," the café's owner said. "What has you here alone on a Friday night? Must be man trouble."

Myriam smiled wanly. "That obvious, huh."

Rosa laughed, her dark hair came lose from its bun and fell about her face. She didn't bother to tie it back, just pushed it aside. "Wild guess, actually. So, you're having trouble with Hiram."

Myriam nodded. "He no longer takes any time to talk with me or go out for walks. He's short-tempered and snaps at me whenever I ask a question. Every time the phone rings, he jumps a little. He's a changed man." *Everything around here has changed*, she thought bleakly.

"You ask him about it?"

"He just laughs and apologizes. Says, right now his business needs all his attention."

"When did it start?"

"A couple of weeks. I remember we'd gone to see Carlotta about Adam's disappearance. She was a mess. I think Hiram was hoping she could help figure out what happened to her brother." Myriam stared down at the table. "I've never felt good about not helping Carlotta more through her loss."

Rosa nodded knowingly. "She certainly has been a wreck. She didn't leave her house for weeks. She's better now. I mean I saw her at the mercantile a couple of days ago and she seemed all right. Maybe we should pay her a visit, see if she could use some help." Rosa smiled. "It'll take your mind off your man troubles. And may be Carlotta will have some news about her brother. Whaddya say?"

Myriam nodded. "I'd sure like to know what happened to him. Maybe something with his disappearance ties in with my trouble with Hiram." Rosa said, "Or maybe see if there's something she knows about Adam she hasn't told anyone about."

Myriam's head jerked up in surprise. She studied her friend, spotting a glimmer of knowing a secret, deep in her dark eyes. She recalled Rosa's statement from just a few days ago. "So, that's what you meant when you said you didn't want to 'jinx' it, right? You think Carlotta's hiding something?"

Not wanting to reveal the truth, Rosa went with Myriam's suggestion. "I don't know why I said that. You're right, maybe there's something she knows and just needs somebody she can trust to talk to."

Myriam still had a sense that Rosa wasn't telling her everything, but let it go. She was more concerned for Carlotta and now wanted to see Adam's sister as soon as possible.

The ride to Carlotta's was over a bumpy gravel road with high banks on both sides. Only the moon overhead gave any illumination. The lights were all on when they arrived and Carlotta was already waiting by the front door when they walked up the old wooden steps.

"Heard Rosa's truck rattling down the drive."

"We just thought we'd check in on you," Rosa replied. "See how you're doing."

"I must have seemed out of it to everyone for a while after my brother disappeared. I'm much better now. Or maybe 'resigned' is a better word. I fear Adam's not coming back. Fortunately, I have to teach my class every day and it's forced me to keep it together." She turned partly away as if to say goodnight but changed her mind. She held the door wide open. "Truth is, I'd appreciate the company. C'mon in, I've got water in the kettle."

The three women sat around Carlotta's wooden kitchen table. The room smelled strongly of roasted chilis and fresh ground coriander. Beside the window hung a Mexican *rista*, the red peppers adding their pungent smell to the kitchen.

Myriam inhaled deeply from the coffee cup in front of her. "This is heavenly. It's as good as yours, Rosa."

Rosa smiled. "I can't quite put my finger on the spices though."

"Nutmeg," Carlotta said. "Add a little lemon and it really pops." She eyed the two women. *They could almost be mother and daughter,* she thought. Both had high cheekbones and their noses were slightly curved. Though Myriam was older, her hair was still dark, so black in places that it had a hint of blue in it. Carlotta was sure that Myriam had Native American ancestors. She smiled, also aware that this wasn't just a social visit to check up on an old friend.

"So, what's the real reason, you come to visit me at nine o'clock on a Friday evening?"

Rosa laughed, showing even teeth. "Busted. I dragged Myriam out here because, well ... maybe there's something here that can help us find out what happened to Adam."

"I'll try to help."

Myriam let out a long breath, suddenly aware she felt better than she had in a long time. Even if they couldn't find Adam, just talking about him buoyed her spirits.

"C'mon, let's take this to the living room. We'll be more comfortable there."

A mesquite fire burned in the fireplace giving off a sweet aroma. They sat in three large chairs facing one another.

"Where to begin?" Carlotta asked.

"Why not start at the beginning before his accident," suggested

Myriam. "Maybe there's a clue in his past that'll tell us where he went."

"Sure ... well ... right before the accident, Adam was withdrawn, reclusive ... a virtual hermit in his apartment in Des Moines, Iowa. He ventured forth only for coffee and to hunt down books in this old bookstore on Ingersoll Avenue. I think it was called Ancient Ways or something like that. I visited him once. He had a loft on the top floor of an upscale condo complex. He's always had this unique relationship with one of the wealthiest men in Iowa. Bookshelves lined every wall, and some of the books were hundreds of years old, original editions. He was really proud of the first English translation of Kierkegaard's *Fear and Trembling*. Kept it on a small stand by itself. Every surface was littered with notebooks, all in his handwriting. I teased him about getting a computer so that he could keep his writing well organized and get rid of the clutter. He said he needed to write longhand ... to feel the idea come out of him organically without a machine getting in the way." Carlotta laughed.

"What?" asked Myriam.

"Nothing ... just that he wrote everything in pencil as if a pen were too newfangled or something. At any rate, everything changed after the accident."

Rosa's eyes widened. "I never heard the whole story about the accident. Only that it was a miracle he survived at all."

"That's pretty much it. He was on a motorcycle. God knows why he was driving a motorcycle. A delivery van ran a stop sign and hit him flat on. Crushed his spine, his pelvis. Every bone on the right side of his body was broken. The ER doctors didn't give him a chance. They were just keeping him sedated so he wouldn't have any pain until he died. Basically he was in a coma for several months.

"Then one day he woke up. He could barely talk and he couldn't move. He didn't know where he was or what had happened. The doctors said he could go home, but his loft was out of the question since he couldn't walk. So he came down here and I took care of him."

"You did a good job," Rosa said.

Carlotta shrugged. "Maybe. You know, when he arrived, not only was his body in bad shape but there was extensive brain damage. His neurologist in Des Moines doubted he would ever be able dress himself and feed himself again. So, I fed him and changed his clothes and bathed him. I figured I'd be taking care of him forever. I thought it was going to be this enormous burden, but it became just the opposite. One day he came out of his dreamlike trance and was better and the next day better again, until a week went by and he could walk on his own. His mind was still foggy. He had trouble interacting with what was going on around him. It was clear that he was intensely sensitive to the world surrounding him. When I asked him to tell me what was going on in his head, he said he saw and felt stuff nobody else sees and feels. At first I thought his brain was still scrambled by the accident, but eventually he was able to get it under control and operate in the world. You know what he was like, never having an agenda, yet somehow knowing just what to do and say." She laughed again.

"What's so funny?"

"My brother who had never really engaged with people before suddenly would talk to anyone at the shrine. When Father Michael gave him the job of caretaker, he was there every day. He was kind and listened, even people who were obviously troubled and just wanted to complain. And he always seemed to have the right thing to say to them. And that's not the only thing that changed."

She got up and led them to Adam's bedroom. It was completely bare of anything except a simple futon on the floor. The closet was empty and so was the chest of drawers.

Myriam pursed her lips. "I don't get it. So he took everything with him when he left."

Carlotta shook her head. "He left his room the way he lived in it— no books, no notebooks. He had only one change of clothes. On Sundays he washed everything. He would sit outside under the ramada without a stitch on no matter what the weather, watching the mountains while I washed and dried his clothes. He'd always been quirky. But now his quirks were endearing instead of strange."

The women went back into the living room.

Myriam watched the flames for a moment. Adam's behavior reminded her of her youngest son. He was a high functioning autistic who had learned to live in the world though always on the edge, never really a part of it. She'd seen this sort of thing happen with other autistic children.

She asked, "Did the doctors ever say what was going on?"

"They said it might be acquired savant syndrome. I looked it up. In the thirty or so known cases, ordinary people who suffer brain trauma suddenly develop almost superhuman new abilities—artistic brilliance, mathematical mastery, photographic memory. The neuroscientists said that as part of the brain goes dark, the brain reorganizes itself in unpredictable ways, often allowing capacities that were in the background to move to the forefront.

"Even so," Rosa said, "He had to be thankful for all you did for him."

"Oh yes. Adam was always immensely grateful for me taking care of him. But all the thanks really goes to him. When he arrived I was at my wits end. My two sons were going to hell, out of control and using drugs. You know all about the meth problem around here don't you, Myriam? Adam connected with the boys in a way I didn't think possible. They came to love him and he loved them back. Now twelve years later, the youngest one, Brett, is in Caltech's early entry program and Alex is one of those IT entrepreneurs in Seattle. Adam turned their lives around." The corners of her mouth turned down in a sad moue. "They miss him too so much. They would do anything for him. Alex came back and spent time with him whenever he could. And, praise the Lord, they both have been helpful since Adam's disappearance. They both miss him."

Rosa said, "We all do. If you don't mind, I think we should pray for him."

They held hands and closed their eyes. After a few moments, Carlotta made a little "aah" sound. "It's almost like he's here." The other two women murmured "yes" in agreement.

· · ·

When they stopped, Myriam asked, "Did anybody ever visit him and did he have any friends beside you and the boys."

"His wealthy friend from Des Moines, Malcolm Grossinger, came around a few times, and of course Father Michael often stopped by and they chatted. One time I overheard Adam telling the Father that he had surrendered to the realization he had become the essence of the healer." Carlotta blushed. "Mind you, I normally respected Adam's privacy when Father Michael visited him. But this one time I listened in. He told him he had become a conduit to the other world. I think he said that he when he first woke up from his coma, he spent most of his time in the other world. When Father Michael asked him what it looked like, Adam said there was an infinite world of forces that hold and guide us just like a loving mother holds and guides her child. I remember his words after that exactly. 'I have become just as Jesus said, a child, trusting these forces.' When Father Michael asked him what was happening now, Adam replied, 'I'm being absorbed by these forces.'"

"Did that mean anything to you?"

"Over the last year, at times, I swear Adam had become transparent, like I could look right through him. I told myself I should get my eyes checked."

As the women were departing Myriam asked, "Has Father Michael been around?"

"Yes, whenever he can. He travels a lot you know."

Myriam nodded her head thoughtfully. "Over the past three years he's traveled almost constantly."

21

March 30, 2019
Taos, New Mexico

Beecher tried calling Myriam back but she wouldn't pick up. After the fourth try he didn't bother to leave a message. He cursed and tossed the phone onto the table. It lay there staring at him like an accusing finger. His anger cooled and with it came remorse. *She's right to be angry. I haven't been much of a doting lover lately. Maybe I should have told her at least about the mysterious meeting tonight.* He shook his head and banged his fists together. *No! You're not thinking clearly. The less she knows the less danger she's in. You have to keep her safe from all of this.*

Beecher was sure that he had lost favor with the Reverend and that the charismatic preacher no longer trusted him. His instructions had mentioned no names, only to meet a contact here tonight. Billy Paul was becoming more and more erratic and he couldn't help but wonder if this was some kind of payback for failing to get rid of Adam the first time. Beecher pressed his hand against the Glock and shifted his gaze around the room and into the parking lot.

The phone buzzed and he gave a little start. A text message appeared. It was from the Reverend Billy Paul. *Your contact has arrived.*

Beecher looked up as the door to the coffeehouse opened. A man dressed in an impeccably tailored Savile Row suit entered. Graying hair around the temples put him in his forties. His back was ramrod straight, his hands long fingered. His pale blue eyes quartered the room, questing. Beecher pegged him instantly as ex-military. When the eyes fell on him, the man smiled. He came over, his stride easy, confident. He stopped and bowed slightly. "Mr. Beecher," he said quietly in a clipped accent Beecher couldn't place.

Beecher rose and they shook hands. The man's grip was firm. He was an inch taller than Beecher and not nearly so broad. Yet there was something in the man's stance, the way he stood cat-like, that told Beecher here was a man who would not hesitate to kill.

"Sit please, Mr.—"

"Haas ... Pieter Haas. As quaint as your American custom of informality is, I think we would be more comfortable talking at my hotel. The El Monte Segrado. I've taken the liberty of booking a premier suite for you."

"I have a hotel already."

"Yes, but the Reverend suggested we upgrade you." He smiled, his teeth very even and very white. "I'm sure you'll find the accommodations to your liking."

The invitation was direct, couched in a way that was not threatening so Beecher could not refuse. In Vietnam he'd heard of men like this, though he had never met any. They were called "fixers" —men who were genteel and ultra-polite, and who could always be counted on to get the *difficult* jobs done with a minimum of fireworks.

The man motioned Beecher to precede him. The hairs stuck up on the back of his neck. *I'm getting too old for this kind of shit.*

Outside a black Cadillac Escalade was parked by the entrance, the engine running.

"I have my rental," said Beecher.

"Where are you staying?"

"The Edelweiss Chalet."

Haas nodded at the Escalade. A young man got out instantly. He was stocky, built like a linebacker. His blond hair was crew cut. He wore a dark turtleneck over dark pants. His shoes made no sound on the asphalt. "Make sure Mr. Beecher's car gets to the Edelweiss chalet."

The young man held out his hand and Beecher knew this wasn't a request. He dropped the keys into his palm. At that moment another man slid out of the vehicle and held open a back door for the two men. He hesitated and Haas said quietly, "The Reverend was very clear these are blessed steps we are taking and he wants everything handled carefully. He'll explain once we reach the hotel."

Beecher looked behind. His car was already leaving the parking lot. There was no escape and even the gun wedged into his jeans at the small of his back felt so remote as to be useless. *I feel like an extra in a Godfather movie. Well I won't go whining.* He straightened his shoulders and his hand slid part way around his waist. "I'm afraid you have me at a disadvantage, Mr. Haas. I have no idea who you are or your relationship with the Reverend Billy Paul and the Brothers of the Lord."

Haas tilted his head to the side and his eyes narrowed.

Beecher felt sweat trickle between his shoulder blades in spite of the chilly night air, but he didn't flinch. He returned the stare evenly.

Haas smiled and bowed slightly. "My apologies, Mr. Beecher. I assumed the Reverend had briefed you sufficiently. This must seem very cloak and dagger to you. I am the CEO of the DeVere Mining Group. Reverend Billy Paul and I share a passion for resolving the issue of Adam Gwillt."

Beecher thought back to a documentary he had seen on the cold-bloodedness of diamond cartels in Africa. *Of course. Who better to hunt down Adam. The DeVere Mining Group would have killers on their payroll! They are notorious for ruthlessly controlling the diamond market.* "Thank you," he said and entered the SUV.

Inside the nine-passenger Escalade were three more men dressed like the young man driving Beecher's car. They were all ex-military or para-military. The driver wore a windbreaker over his dark clothes. It had the image of a springbok, the antelope-gazelle of South Africa, on the back.

Beecher settled back into the soft leather seats and waited. He kept his hand away from the Glock.

The Premier Suite was exquisitely furnished in Hopi and Navajo artifacts. Haas motioned to the bar. "Would you like a drink?"

Beecher shook his head. The South African frowned. "Pardon me. I forgot the Reverend told me you no longer drink. How about coffee or tea?"

"I'll have what you're drinking."

"Irish breakfast tea." Haas smiled. "Afraid I'm still on Johannesburg time."

"Works for me." Beecher settled onto a large sofa that dominated one end of the room.

Haas called room service. Then, "The bathroom is through there." He pointed to a hallway on the left at the far end of the room. There was a knock on the door, and it opened instantly. A middle-aged woman walked into the room. She nodded to Haas. "Everything is ready. The video feed will come on automatically in here."

"Hiram, this is Greta Van Horn, our invaluable communications expert. In constant contact with South Africa." She greeted Beecher with a stern look and then broke into slight smile. "Everything's under control." She exited the room.

"What are we waiting for?" Beecher was becoming more nervous by the moment as a cloud of entrapment encased his emotions.

Haas checked his watch. "The Reverend said he would call at precisely nine pm."

That's three minutes from now, Beecher told himself. "Good."

"I'm glad you agree." The South African snapped his fingers and the three ex-military men left the suite. "We won't be disturbed."

. . .

At precisely 9pm, the suite's big-screen TV came to life. The Reverend Billy Paul appeared. Beecher thought he looked gaunt and anxious. He spoke with a clipped urgency. "Everything is working as planned. Ramsey has led us to Adam. Within twenty-four hours with your help Brother Pieter and his associates are going to put an end to this Adam Gwillt abomination. I don't have to remind you that we're close, very close to saving Christianity in the modern era, Brother Hiram." The televangelist paused, his breathing heavy as if the speech itself were a great weight. Then, "Brother Pieter, have you told Brother Hiram what's happened in the past few days?"

"No, I didn't think I should."

"Tell him now if you would."

Haas placed his teacup on a mesquite end table and settled into a large chair. "Pete Miami is this genius geographer that's been working in northern New Mexico for the DeVere company for the past five years. He's been trying to pinpoint the location of a diamond deposit that is responsible for all the diamonds that have shown up in this area over the years. He's made some remarkable technological breakthroughs that allow him to detect all sorts of geophysical information no one knew even existed.

"When the Reverend Paul sent us the video files you so beautifully captured, we concluded that the phenomena connected with Adam represented a new power and we already knew there was something unusual in Pete Miami's raw GIS data covering the shrine. Only it was too risky to go directly to Dr. Miami and have him refine it. His skills and knowledge are way beyond anything we have in South Africa. Like many genius scientists he saw patterns no one else could. Unfortunately he's a loose cannon. Ultimately, we wanted Miami to come up with something that would help us find Adam without his knowing and the best way to do that was to arrange for the Friends of the Shrine to hire Jonathan Ramsey. Ramsey and Miami were best friends during their postdoc work together at the University of Oregon. We made it nearly impossible for Ramsey not to ask Pete to process all the GIS information he collected on the shrine's location. A few days ago our belief was vindicated. Pete found an anomalous field structure connected with the shrine. A kind of Adam Gwillt signature that disappeared almost entirely the day after Adam disappeared."

Beecher was amazed at the scale and cleverness of Reverend Billy Paul's organization. "How do you know all this?"

Haas looked at the Reverend and he nodded approval. "You don't have to know the details, but everything Pete Miami does using our computer is transparent to us. We may not have the ability to understand it, but we see all of what he sees. Yesterday Miami refined some of his computational magic on an energy anomaly. Immediately our techies back in South Africa started using satellite sensors to look for the same anomaly outside of the shrine."

The Reverend Paul jumped in. "We've found him. Here's the strange and beautiful part. It's real close to where Miami believes the diamond pipe is located."

"That's really bizarre—that the timing and the diamond discovery and the Adam signature should be so close together. Maybe it's all a set up. Doesn't that bother any of you?" Beecher asked.

The Reverend shook his head. "No, it's the Lord's signal we are doing the right thing. Tomorrow Miami will lead us to both. It'll be our triumph."

Haas added, "The Gwillt signature is centered on what we think is an old Anasazi cliff dwelling. We should be able to see it from the kimberlite site that Miami has located."

They're going to kill Adam, Beecher thought. "Why do you need me?"

"My dear brother Hiram, none of us have actually seen Adam Gwillt. There are few photographs of him and the ones we own have become mysteriously blurred. We need you to tell us if it's him. Something is going on right now. It is the work of the devil. It needs to be stopped!"

My God, this sounds like me just a few months ago. Beecher was no longer sure this was doing the Lord's work.

The screen went blank.

Haas turned to Beecher. "Are we good?"

Beecher hid his loathing for Paul's sanctimonious bullshit. There was no arguing and no escaping. "Of course."

"All right then, in the morning." Haas left the room.

Beecher was afraid to turn on his transmitter while in the room. Stepping out on the balcony he decided to take the risk. The pen hummed slightly in his hand. Moments later he heard Conklin's voice soft over the micro speaker. "Is everything okay?" Beecher began telling Conklin that they were going to look in the morning for Adam under the guise of finding a diamond deposit.

Conklin responded, "Somebody brought your vehicle here to the chalet. I was worried."

Beecher said, "I'll start transmitting a tracking signal when I'm comfortable. Use the chalet van to follow at a safe distance." He clicked the device to standby mode and stepped back in the room, waiting for somebody to rush in. But all was good. At least he had one small advantage in the face of what was going to happen in the morning. Conklin was a bit of an enigma, but Beecher was sure he had made the correct decision to tell the man everything. *Odd how these things work out.*

22

————

March 31, 2019
Taos, New Mexico

Pete and Ramsey got up early and went for an exhausting run along the mountain trails that connected to Pete's house. Ramsey was glad for the chance, since he needed the time to think. Especially since he had experienced a restless night.

He had been wakened by one of the most vivid dreams he ever remembered. In the dream Ramsey was moving from a new house, which was to be where he would raise his family, and then was suddenly uprooted to another one and then to another one and then to another one, never able to find a home. Then in a sudden surreal shift, his father appeared. He pointed to something near the horizon. Ramsey saw an old factory, with blown out windows and crumbling red brick. In the next breath his father and the building disappeared.

Ramsey knew this kind of big dream was trying to tell him something. This was more than an intuition; it was like a divine message. And he also knew it had something to do with Adam and the New Gnostics. It assured him that he was on the right track and that all the missing pieces would suddenly fall into place if he just remained steadfast, and allowed himself to be guided by the forces pulling him forward. Letting others take the lead in his own fate was something he was loathe to let happen, however. He hadn't become one of the country's leading human geographer in the business world because he handed off projects to others and let them run the show. Taking the back seat while forces drove his fate felt like handing over control of a car to a teenager on a winding icy mountain road.

He saw Pete's lithe form running ten yards ahead and wondered again if his old post doc buddy was one of those forces. Ramsey chuckled. At least Pete was a grown-up part of the time.

Pete stopped and waited for Ramsey to catch up. He checked his watch. "We still have an hour. Time for another couple of miles before breakfast. Then it's work, work, work."

"What's happening?" asked Ramsey, bent over and panting.

"Me and my favorite drone are leading a party of DeVere people to what I hope will be the most fantastic diamond pipe the world has ever seen." Pete furled his lower lip with his teeth. "This could be the life-changing event that I've been waiting for. I'm getting antsy and ready to move on. I don't suppose you have a job for me, old man?"

Finally catching his breath, Ramsey said, "You never know. Am I going with you to experience your grand discovery?"

"Nah. It's all a big secret you know. You'll drop me off where I'll meet the pros from DeVere and then drive Nellie Bell over to Rio Chama. I'll meet you there later." He frowned. "I don't need to tell you not to mention the diamonds to anyone, okay?"

Ramsey smiled. "Already tweeted it this morning ... told all my friends and family to invest in DeVere."

Pete jerked in surprise, then, "Good one."

With that they took off running again. Ramsey began formulating his plan. *It's not about the shrine. I need to find Adam Gwillt. And I need to get the truth from Myriam. There's so much going on here that I'm not being told.*

· · ·

After a quick shower and breakfast, the two men got into the Nash Rambler. "In case you were wondering, I named this baby 'Nellybelle' after Pat Brady's jeep on the *Roy Rogers Show*," Pete said.

"Trigger and Buttercup were taken?" asked Ramsey.

"The two drones."

Ramsey laughed.

They drove along back-mountain roads until they came out onto highway 64, north of the Taos Airport. Ramsey saw they were headed toward Rio Chama. Then he remembered the kimberlite deposits were in the same general area as the shrine.

As if reading his thoughts, Pete said, "There's a logging road that goes into the backcountry on the way to the shrine. I'm meeting my contacts there." He hesitated. "Look, these guys don't know you from Adam, so just play it cool. I don't want them spooked."

Interesting choice of names, Ramsey thought. He didn't think Pete was trying to hint at anything. On the other hand, the man was brilliant and just might be trying to warn Ramsey about something.

A gravel road swung off the highway to the north. Pete pulled onto it and waited. Thirty seconds later a black Escalade pulled in behind them.

"There's my ride," Pete said.

Six men piled out of the SUV. All of them were dressed in backcountry gear. Pete pursed his lips. Four of the men were burly and carried military issue packs and combat camo-fatigues. They were paramilitary by the way they held themselves alert, checking the road and woods surrounding them. From his picture Pete recognized the tall thin man with pale blue eyes who stood beside the Cadillac SUV. He was Pieter Haas, the DeVere Mining Group's CEO. Beside him was a man Pete didn't know at all.

The military guys approached his car with one man taking point and the others flanking him. *Uh-oh . . . this could be going to be dicey,* mused Pete. He glanced at Ramsey who was studying the situation with great intensity. Pete shifted his attention back to Haas. *He's the brains, the one I've got to convince that Jonathan's nothing more than a friend.*

Pete got out of the car and approached the CEO. He did his best to ignore the four bodyguards. "You must be Mr. Haas. Good to finally meet you," Pete said, walking over to the SUV. "The DeVere Group security said you'd be the one meeting me. You're much better looking than that picture on the website."

Ignoring Miami's irreverence, Haas countered, "Good morning, Doctor Miami. I trust you are as excited as I am on this wonderful day when your years of hard work and our money are about to come to fruition." The two men shook hands firmly. Haas scrutinized Ramsey. Continuing the charade planned earlier with the Reverend Billy Paul, he said, "I hope you weren't planning on bringing your friend along. We only have room in our vehicle for yourself."

Pete smiled. "Sorry, this is Jonathan Ramsey. We were postdocs together at Oregon. He's dropping my car off in Rio Chama and visiting the shrine there." Ramsey waved. Pete looked across the hood of the car at the sixth man. He extended his hand. "Didn't catch your name."

"It's Hiram Beecher. I came along to protect my financial investment in the DeVere group." The two men shook hands. Beecher looked over at Ramsey, standing beside the Nash Rambler. The two locked eyes. Each recognized the other by name. For the first time, Beecher was in the presence of the man he had hired at Reverend Paul's urging. For his part Ramsey realized this was the man who signed the contract hiring him to work on the shrine. Neither wished to acknowledge the other beyond the cordial greeting.

Ramsey ended the awkward charade by stepping back behind Pete's car. From there, his eyes flicked from one bodyguard to the next. They were exceptionally fit, the thin air of the high plains desert not bothering them at all, as though used to trekking in the mountains. One word fought its way into his consciousness: SEALs. Only they didn't look American. They all looked European except for Beecher. And then it hit him like a fireball—South Africa, DeVere diamonds. *Shit. These guys are paramilitary.* They are merciless in protecting their control of the diamond market. He kept a stupid look on his face wondering if he should tell Pete about this extraordinary coincidence. But Pete seemed to be handling himself with ease and Ramsey had to believe he had checked these guys out and knew who they were before arriving. *Why else would he ask me to play it cool?*

Instead, he said to Pete, "If you're all set, I'd like to take off. I want to spend the day at the shrine. You know, soak up the healing powers. You be safe."

"Sure," Pete said tossing Ramsey the keys. "I'll just get my things out of the back."

Haas smiled and said, "We'll return him to you at the end of the day. Were you two going to meet some place in particular?"

"At the Rio Chama Café."

"This evening then." He motioned the others back into the car. Pete stowed his gear in the back and joined them.

Ramsey watched the vehicle fishtail up the logging road and disappear out of sight over a small rise. He waited for a few minutes before starting the car and pulling out on to the highway. In the rearview mirror he saw a large pickup truck with Hispanic men sitting in the back turn onto the road. He saw they had guns. He swallowed hard, suddenly afraid for his friend Pete, and wondered if he should go after him. *And do what?* He asked himself. *Tell Pete some Hispanic guys are following him? They're probably hunters.*

Even more perplexing and confusing was the question of why a man involved with the shrine was now involved with a group of men from South Africa looking for a diamond pipe? *One more question for Myriam.*

He tapped the Google maps app on his phone, and said, "Rio Chama." It was forty-three miles away, about an hour along these roads.

23

———————

March 31, 2019
Taos, New Mexico

The Escalade soon reached a secondary road that was little more than a beaten track through the wilderness. Branches and bushes sideswiped the SUV at every chance. Pete watched the driver negotiate the turns and the washed-out, deeply rutted road with an ease that told him these guys were pros. *What does the DeVere Group need with professional military men to confirm a diamond discovery?* Then it occurred to him. *They must think somebody else knows about the diamonds.*

The road ended at a small clearing and the group got out. While the others loaded up their gear, Pete pulled an iPad from his daypack and brought up a three-dimensional topo map of the area. Then he pressed an icon that was the image of a drone. Underneath it was the name "Buttercup." Instantly the screen was overlaid with the camera feed from the drone. Pete looked up and there it was hovering right over them. It was the length of a bicycle with a wingspan of a North American condor. Made from carbon fiber, it weighed only twenty pounds fully loaded with camera gear. Solar panels in the wings powered the two lithium ion batteries that ran the motor, ailerons, tail rudder, and cameras. Controls on the screen allowed him to not only pilot the drone but direct the cameras as well.

Pointing to the drone, Pete said, "Ordinary GPS can't show us the safest route to where we're going. The drone is our eye in the sky allowing me to pick out the fastest and safest route." Then he pushed a question just to hear the response. "It'll also tell us if someone else is out here."

Hass smiled thinly. "Yes, it would be good to know if there's anyone out here who shouldn't be."

Using his fingers and thumbs sliding across the screen, the drone's nose camera responded and zeroed in on Haas and Beecher, standing beside the SUV. They were in an intense conversation that ended when one of the paramilitary guys strode up to them. The man's pack was partially open and Pete could see the barrel of an Israeli-made Uzi. The man handed Haas a pistol. In the next instant his hand smashed against the hood of the car as he squashed a wasp with a casual air of brutality.

Pete licked his lips. *Ex-military, weapons, South Africans ... diamonds. Pete old son, what have you gotten yourself into?*

Haas motioned Pete over. "Dr. Miami, if you will please do the honors by pointing out the way."

Pete nodded. He punched a button on the tablet and the drone proceeded forward. "It's open country for about a mile and then we'll enter the Sangre de Christo Mountains. From there our only hope of finding the kimberlite site is for the drone to pick the least nasty route through the wilderness."

One of the ex-military men came up to him. He was tall with short blond hair and thick lips. He had the unmistakable air of authority. "My men and I can go anywhere you tell us to."

"This is Goren," Haas introduced the man.

"To hell and back?" Pete joked.

"If necessary." The man didn't smile.

Let's hope it isn't necessary, Pete thought.

Goren flashed a hand signal at the other men. Two of them dropped back. The team's only black man stayed at point. Goren motioned Pete to go first. "Flint will be right beside you."

To everyone else he shouted, "Saddle up. We'll break for five minutes in an hour." He turned to Haas and said, "Sir, when you're ready."

"Thank you, Goren. Let's move out."

The first hour was along a well-maintained National Forest Service trail. Rangers had even carved steps in some of the steeper places. At the first hour's break point, the trail veered sharply south, but the drone indicated they move straight ahead.

"The trail will take us way south of the kimberlite location into ancient Pueblo land," Pete explained to Haas. "We have to stay true as long as we can. According to the drone images, we shouldn't encounter any major obstacles for another five miles. Then there's a steep ravine. We may need climbing ropes to get in and out of it, but that will save us hours compared to going around it."

By midday they had scaled the cliff and stopped for half an hour to rest and eat. They settled on one side of a wide beautiful valley.

Haas turned to Pete. "We must be close."

"On the other side of the ridge there is a depression grown over with piñon pines. That's exactly the center of the strongest kimberlite signature. It's less than a quarter of a mile." What happened next surprised Pete.

Rather than pulling everybody together for the march to the kimberlite location, Haas gestured to his men. "You boys go with Pete and see what he has located. Beecher and I will wait here." The men gathered their gear.

Pete, recovering from his surprise, asked, "Sure you don't want to come?"

"It's bad luck for me to go. We'll just wait here for the good news. Godspeed."

Pete ran his hand through his hair. The reason sounded superstitious and Haas didn't strike him as that kind of person. Still surrounded by Uzis and thugs whose arms were bigger than his thighs, Pete wasn't going to argue. He just hoped he got out of this alive.

He ducked under some branches and headed towards the ridge. Hass's men followed. The drone hovered overhead then darted toward the other side of the valley.

Beecher watched them go, uncertain what was going to happen next. Suddenly he felt the strong grip of Hass' hand on his shoulder steering him to a vantage point where they could look out across the valley. He handed Beecher the binoculars and pointed. "What do you see?"

Beecher quartered the terrain. A long overhang caught his attention. It looked almost manmade. As he adjusted the field of view he saw the telltale architecture of an Anasazi cliff dwelling. Something moved among the ruins. Maybe it was a deer. Maybe a person. Handing the binoculars back to a Haas, he said, "I might've seen somebody. Do you think it could be Adam?"

"Hopefully," answered Haas. A slight smile crossed his face as he added, "After all, he's the real prize ... Adam Gwillt the super healer."

Beecher started at the reverent tone in the South African's voice. "You sound like a true believer."

Haas leaned against a gnarled piñon pine. He lifted the binoculars to his eyes. "Goren and the others are about half way to the objective." His eyes narrowed as he studied Beecher. "As I said earlier. You have to choose."

Beecher's stomach turned over at the sudden chill in the man's tone. "You know Billy Paul asked me to have Adam killed, and that I tried to carry out his orders."

"Your zeal was misplaced. Luckily fate interceded. Good for us, and I hope you'll come to understand, good for you."

"You *don't* want to kill Adam?"

"Not at all. I see him as an asset, just the same as I do our diamonds." Haas laughed, the sound over-confident in the thin mountain air. "You might say he's a very special diamond."

Beecher's mind was reeling at the news. "I don't get it. Why?"

"A power like his could help gain control of a piece of the global medical economy especially if he could teach others his gift."

Beecher reflected on what Haas said. The power to heal could certainly make believers out of millions of people. *Zealots more like it. Zealots who would do anything for their master.* He glanced at Haas. "What's your connection to the Reverend?"

"He's a self-righteous fool. We needed him to get to Jonathan Ramsey, to get to you and to your woman Myriam."

"For what?"

"From what I've learned, Adam knows you and he likes and trusts Myriam. When we find Adam, we'd like you and Myriam to befriend him, talk him into joining us."

Beecher was so confused he didn't know how to react. Everything was suddenly upside down. *All this time I thought this was about killing Adam. But it's much more than that.* He didn't want to argue with Haas, but he needed information to figure out what to do. Beecher said, "Gwillt's a threat to Christianity ... The second coming of the devil."

Haas let the binoculars hang from their leather strap around his neck. "You may have believed that rubbish once, but you've changed. I can see it. And there's a whole larger movement going on based on the power of Adam. The Reverend Billy Paul didn't tell you about that did he? They're called the New Gnostics. It's a new kind of Christianity. Very powerful." Haas looked Beecher straight in the eye. "Like I said. You have to choose."

Beecher felt anger and confusion well up in his gut, but he forced it away. He needed time to reconcile what he just heard, so he decided to ask a simple question. "How do you know all this?"

"We know everything that's going on in the area. It's standard operating procedure when we're investigating for a potential diamond mine. Plus we have an insider who knows all about Adam and who for now will remain nameless."

An alarm bell rang out in the still air. Both men whirled at the noise.

"Where's that alarm coming from?" Haas asked.

Beecher shrugged. "In these mountains, it's hard to say. He peered across the valley. Shadows moved among the ruins. They could have been Goren and the team. It was hard to tell with or without binoculars.

The alarm echoed a second time throughout the ancient Anasazi cliff dwelling. A young man in his late twenties walked into a ground-level apartment on the cliff. He wore blue jeans and cowboy boots and carried a 30.06 in his right hand. He went into an inner room and looked down into a chamber dug nearly ten feet into the floor. This was a *kiva*, a circular room built underground where religious ceremonies had been conducted by generations of Anasazi. He clambered down the crude wooden ladder and stood beside a figure sitting on the red dusty floor. He saw no breath or heartbeat. But the face was ruddy colored and looked in good health. He touched the shoulder. The muscle was firm.

"Adam ... we have to go" the young man said quietly.

A dry buzzing sound issued from Haas's pack. He walked over and pulled out a sat phone. He paused and listened. Beecher watched him carefully. Haas scratched his chin with a well-manicured finger.

"Anything?" Beecher mouthed.

Haas shook his head. There was a pause as Haas listened. Then, he smiled and said, "They found kimberlite ... lots of it and now they're looking for the pipe."

Beecher picked up the binoculars and focused on the ridge across the valley. A speck moved above it. He adjusted the lenses and saw the drone circling the Anasazi cliff dwelling. As he watched, its right wing exploded and the drone winged over, spinning toward the ground.

A gunshot from the ridge split the silence.

Haas dropped the sat phone into the pack and pulled out a pistol with his left hand. His other held the pistol Goren gave him. Beecher took it. Part of his brain registered the crash of the drone. The rest of him was settling into a place where he was protected. His eyes scanned the ridgeline opposite and the tree line nearby. He didn't see any movement.

"Are your men prepared for this?" he whispered.

Haas nodded. "They're the best mercenaries in the business. Saw action in Mali with the rebels fighting the French. Goren did three tours in Basra, Iraq as part of the British Expeditionary Force."

Two more shots came from the trail where Goren and his men had followed Pete to the kimberlite location. Beecher squinted against the westering sun, looking for some sign of intruders. The bolt action of hunting rifle sliding a cartridge home ripped through the small clearing. Beecher didn't move. The noise was deliberate. He glanced at Haas who'd heard it also. Instinctively both men slowly raised their hands in the air, pistols dangling from their index fingers. They turned and looked into the barrels of two rifles pointed directly at their hearts. The larger of the two Hispanic men gestured for them to put their guns on the ground. Beecher and Haas complied.

They were zip tied with their hands behind their backs and put in the center of the clearing. When Beecher opened his mouth to ask what was going on, one of the men said, "No talking Americano."

Ten minutes later Pete and the four South African mercenaries marched into camp covered by six more Hispanic men, all carrying rifles. One of Goren's men had his arm in a makeshift sling.

Haas's eyes narrowed and he asked Pete, "Did you find the pipe?"

The Hispanic leader shouted, "Shut up!" He unfolded a large sack and his men put cell phones, sat phones, food, and water inside. Watches and jewelry followed. The team's weapons were slung on their persons.

Pete stole a glance at Haas and shook his head negatively. He looked at the Hispanic men and froze. He vaguely remembered the smallest one. *He worked in the kitchen at Rosa Cisneros' café. What if he remembers me?*

The leader of the Hispanics looked to the small man and said in Spanish, "Julio what should we do now?"

"Go crazy like I said."

Pete tensed, his high school Spanish still good enough to translate. *Crazy could mean anything.*

Immediately the leader began strutting around the makeshift camp waving his rifle in the air and cursing at Haas's party. "Bastardos. . . . You think you can come up into our mountains and take what doesn't belong to you? You're gonna pay a price for trespassing."

The other Hispanic men were busy gathering the backpacks and the rest of the gear, while handcuffing each of the commandos with plastic zip ties. They were well-organized and prepared. In all the commotion they seemed to forget about Pete. He gradually slid towards the edge of the group. For a moment when all eyes were on the ranting leader, he dove down the side of the hill. Tumbling and spinning around the piñon pines and scrub brush, he finally landed in a heap at the bottom.

From all of the yelling at the top of the hill, Pete was able to make out that Julio had told the others he recognized him. He heard the man shout, "I'm going after him. Do what we planned."

Pete scrambled to his feet and took off running, dodging between trees and sliding around boulders, guided only by the fear that he had to put as much distance between his pursuer and himself as he could or he was going to end up dead. Branches whipped across his eyes, momentarily blinding him. Roots and rocks grabbed at his ankles. Miraculously he stayed upright. He rounded a large outcropping of rock and shot along a narrow ridge toward a pass maybe a mile in the distance. Once he reached the other side of the mountain he convinced himself he would be safe. The area was more heavily forested and easier to get lost in.

He doubled his speed, though he knew he couldn't hold on for much longer. He just needed as much distance as he could get. Maybe the man would become disheartened and give up.

Pete had gone nearly a mile at top speed. Sharp pains laced his lungs with every breath. He slowed momentarily and a rifle shot echoed through the late afternoon. A branch above is head splintered.

He redoubled his pace heedless of where he was going. Rounding a large boulder on the narrow trail, he came to a skidding halt. A sheer cliff face plunged hundreds of feet to a shallow stream. The other side was nearly thirty feet across. There was no way to jump and the only way out was back the way he came.

Cursing his luck, Pete knew he had to chance it. He eased around the boulder, hoping to catch sight of his pursuer, something that could tell him if he had a chance. A gun blast and the rock splintered by his head. A chip slammed into his temple and he fell backward, cracking his head on the ground. Stunned, he tried to move but his legs wouldn't respond. He had to get out of there. He tried to get up but all he could make were little scrabbling motions with his hands. His vision cleared and a shadow fell across him.

Julio pointed his rifle at his chest. "I'm sorry, man. But I can't let you live. You know too much."

Pete said the first thing that came to his mind. "You think Rosa would want you to do this?"

The man smiled, his teeth crooked and yellow stained. "She will not care, I can assure you." Pete winced as a stubby thick finger closed on the trigger. Then his dread turned to fascination as a feathered shaft blossomed in the man's chest. The Hispanic swiped at it and another arrow caught the hand, pinning it like a butterfly beside the first arrow. Julio stumbled forward, fell to his knees and keeled over. He lay still.

Pete tried to get his feet under him but his legs still didn't work. He put a hand to his head and felt a deep gash there. *I'm seriously hurt,* he thought with a dispassion he didn't know he possessed. It was like observing a dying rabbit—only he was the rabbit. He was amazed he could be so nonchalant.

Another shadow fell across him. The figure was backlit and it was hard to make out. The man wore a feathered headdress and a breechclout and carried a bow with a quiver of arrows on his back. His skin was red-bronzed by the sun. He knelt beside Pete and smiled. "Today is not your day to die."

The Indian went to Julio who lay on his back, breathing in shallow gasps.

Julio's vision was blurring. He knew he was dying and it filled him with such fear he cried out for his mother. Blood foamed at his mouth. Then a shadow swarmed in front of him, solidified, and appeared to him as a black-garbed priest. He recognized the face of Father Michael from the Rio Chama de Milagro Shrine. He reached out with a hand and grasped the crucifix Father Michael dangled before him. His courage welled up. Though his life was over, he knew his soul could be saved. "Father, forgive me, I have sinned," he rasped.

"Do you admit freely of your wrong doings, my son?"

The dying man nodded.

The priest intoned the Penance. "God the Father of mercies,

through the death and resurrection of his Son,

has reconciled the world to himself

and sent the Holy Spirit among us

for the forgiveness of sins;

through the ministry of the Church

may God give you pardon and peace,

and I absolve you from your sins

in the name of the Father, and of the Son,

and of the Holy Spirit."

Julio's hands squeezed the cross once then collapsed on the rocks.

Pete watched the Indian close the man's eyes and whisper, "All will be forgiven, my son." Then the newcomer slung his bow across his back and walked to him. "Who are you?" he managed to say, though the pain in his head was excruciating.

"I'm your ticket out of here."

He started to go and Pete grabbed his leg. The Indian gently unclenched the fingers. "I'll be back. I have an ATV at the top of the mountain. I have to make a stretcher. I don't fancy carrying you, it could end up killing us both."

Pete said, "What's your name?"

The Indian smiled. "That one called me father, I guided him across the threshold."

24

———

March 31, 2019
Rio Chama, New Mexico

The concern over the truckload of Hispanic toughs following Pete and the diamond hunters drifted away as Ramsey became mesmerized by the sun glinting in and out of the pines on his way to Rio Chama. It took him into a state of contemplation. He held the belief that sacred places arose out of some singular magical event, real or imagined, occurring at a particular place within a given culture. From that moment on people in that culture made the place sacred. They built shrines, pilgrimaged there, and connected with the presence of a higher power there. It became a gateway to fulfilling the hardwired drive in all humans for self-transcendence.

His thoughts drifted back to the University of Oregon and his talk with Myriam St. Eves when he first arrived.

He and half dozen other postdocs, including Pete Miami, had met at Eugene's Twisted Branch Tavern, a local brewery. Myriam held informal seminars here, where postdocs and graduate students talked about their theses and research plans. After a few rounds, the ideas flew thick and fast and no one could separate the chaff from the wheat.

Holding a St. Pauli Girl in one hand as a microphone, Ramsey harangued Myriam and the other postdocs with a certain religious fervor, aided by the alcohol, about an idea of his that he had formulated when he first started taking classes with Professor Orensen at Grinnell College. "The Protestant Reformation and its rejection of the trappings of the Catholic Church freed people to take their religion and God wherever they went. No longer attached to the old sacred shrines and pilgrimages, they could build churches anywhere and everywhere, creating sacred places out of whole cloth. I, Jonathan Ramsey, propose to revolutionize the understanding of America's dramatic success by what I am calling the 'Sacred Place Hypothesis.'"

Of course, all of that had happened before the Peru incident.

In the past week, with his investigation of the Milagro Shrine, those ideas took center stage once again in his thoughts. Now, while driving to the Rio Chama de Milagro Shrine, he had to rethink what they represented. How could the presence of a single living person, in this case Adam Gwillt, be responsible for so many miraculous healings and change the underlying physical structure of a place? It was mind-boggling. *What am I missing?* It was a refrain that had been with Ramsey since he first set foot on the shrine. Then it came to him. *I need to find Adam Gwillt. Christ, perhaps my whole life has been about finding Adam.*

A deep pothole in the road shook him out of his reverie. He glanced at the road sign. He was entering Rio Chama. *Has my life been headed down the wrong path since Peru?* He shook his head. *Maybe. Maybe it's always been about answering the question as to whether there is a supernatural power behind sacred places? Maybe after fifteen years Adam represents the opportunity to resolve it once and for all.*

Filled with a new sense of purpose, he began to formulate some questions for Myriam. *That'll be the place to start.*

Myriam could not meet until mid-afternoon. Sitting at an out-of-the-way table in the Café Rio, Ramsey caught up on business. He sent several texts to his business partner Ron Grange about an upcoming meeting at Blue Island, Illinois. The project was standard fare for their company—revitalizing a decaying urban neighborhood. They'd handled a dozen such ventures and pretty much had it down to a science.

It was late in the afternoon when Myriam arrived. He watched her get out of her car and walk into the café. She limped slightly, favoring her right leg. She joined him and waited for Ramsey to speak. Instead, he reached into his suit-coat pocket and pulled out a battered Ronson lighter and a half crumpled pack of cigarettes. He started to light up when Rosa came over. The restaurant owner was very apologetic but firm. "You can't smoke in here. You'll have to go outside."

Ramsey nodded and reluctantly put the cigarettes back in his coat pocket. He drummed the tabletop with the lighter.

Myriam smiled. "What's going on?"

"What do you mean?"

She pointed at the lighter. "As a post doc you always smoked when you became totally absorbed in what you were doing ... especially when something didn't sit well."

"Old habits," Ramsey muttered. He hadn't smoked in six years. "I need the truth from you. You remember Pete Miami? It turns out he's been doing some cutting edge research over the past five years looking for kimberlite pipes in this area. He operates out of Taos."

"I had no idea."

"I asked him to look at the shrine with his sophisticated GIS equipment. It revealed some pretty amazing energy coherences associated the shrine that I now believe are connected to Adam Gwillt."

Myriam looked around to see if anybody was listening. "I believe the same thing."

Ramsey was just about to ask Myriam about Hiram Beecher when his phone buzzed. "I should take this." He picked up and after a few words felt the color drained from his face. Hanging up, he said to Myriam, "That was an emergency doctor in Española. Somebody dropped Pete off at the hospital and told them to call my number. He's been shot."

"Is it serious?"

"The caller didn't say." He hesitated wondering if he should tell Myriam that the last time he saw Pete was with Hiram. He decided not to complicate matters. "I have to go."

Myriam pushed away from the table. "I'll drive."

Rosa came over. "Someone's been shot?"

Ramsey nodded. "I think you know him. Pete Miami from Taos."

Her eyes went wide. "Oh no!"

Ramsey looked at her. The worry on her face was more than simply for an injured acquaintance, but he didn't have time to ask her about that. Myriam was already rushing out of the restaurant and Pete needed him.

25

March 31, 2019
Taos, New Mexico

Beecher tried to lift his right arm but it wouldn't obey him. His left was just as useless. In fact his whole body was numb. His head was woozy and when he opened his eyes, the piñon pines danced until he felt sick and had to close them. After breathing deeply for several seconds, he opened his eyes again and the trees settled down once more on the earth. His head began to clear and he felt a coarse tingling in his arms and legs. The nape of neck burned as if he'd been snake bit. But a voice in the back of his head told him that if that had happened he'd be dead.

He managed to roll over and saw the bodies of Haas and the four mercenaries lying in a pile. Their zip ties had been removed but they weren't moving. Beecher wasn't even certain they were breathing.

He concentrated trying to remember what happened. It was right after Julio ran after the geologist guy. The leader of the Mexicans was waving his gun around, yelling all kinds of crazy shit. It had gone on for about half an hour until he finally stopped. Then the Mexicans had gathered around, chattering excitedly among themselves. He cursed himself for not paying more attention in high school Spanish class, but a few words came back to him. The men had been arguing what to do with them. A couple of them had wanted to kill Beecher and the others. The leader had vetoed that, but his solution wasn't any kinder. Beecher remembered them taking all their food and water, the phones, and rifles. The leader had laughed and said, "The Gringos won't last a day out here."

Then one of the Mexicans had stepped behind him. Beecher's mind cleared. He recalled shaking and writhing. His arm was working and he put his hand to back of his neck. He felt two burn marks.

"I was tasered!" he said aloud.

He got unsteadily to his feet and stumbled over to the others. They all had similar burns on their necks.

I have to get out of here. He reached inside his vest, felt for the communicator stuffed inside the hidden pocket. He breathed out a heavy sigh of relief. The Mexicans had missed it. He heard a groan behind him and he hastily shoved the communicator back into its hiding place.

Beecher turned. Haas was sitting up. Goren and one of the other mercenaries were already helping their fellows to their feet. The Mexicans may have gotten the drop on them, but they were tough men and soon they spread about the clearing, reconnoitering. Five minutes later, the men came back to report to Haas.

By that time Beecher and Haas were comparing notes. It had gone down the way Beecher thought. He was the first one tasered. The others were hit a few minutes later.

Goren came up to the two men. He saluted Haas. "It's as I thought, sir. They took everything. Didn't leave us any food, water, communications, or weapons."

"They intended us to die out here," Beecher said. He told them what he had understood.

"That raises some interesting questions. How did they know what we were doing? Whose side are they on?"

"They must've followed us," Goren replied.

Haas nodded in agreement. "That was a charade about trespassing on their land. In reality there are only two possibilities. They were after the diamonds or they were protecting Adam Gwillt. In any case they wanted us dead and for it to look like an accident."

"We're a lot harder to kill than those Mexicans think," Goren said, setting his mouth in a tight-lipped scowl.

"What do you suggest?" asked Haas.

"Stay with the mission, sir. We head out to those ruins and see what we can find. Before we were ambushed, I saw signs somebody was there at least this morning."

"The information we got in South Africa was that Adam's biofield signature was still there just before we lost contact with Greta two hours ago when all this happened. He may still be there. We'll complete our mission."

"Is that wise?" Beecher said, more as an accusation than a question. If Adam was there I'm sure with all the gunfire he's left by now."

"With all due respect, Mr. Beecher, we're thirty miles from the nearest road and there's not a hint of rescue coming our way. Our best bet is, if he's not there, to see if Adam's men left any supplies. Also, the drone went down in that area. We might be able to salvage some of its parts and build a transmitter. Unless you happen to be carrying a spare sat phone on you, that's our best bet."

Beecher kept his expression noncommittal. His communicator could reach Conklin, if not from this camp site, then certainly from the nearest high peak—perhaps half an hour away. But he didn't say anything to Haas or the mercs. He could see the suspicion in their faces. Haas especially didn't trust him. *Maybe he thinks I set up the ambush. Wish I had, you smug son of a bitch. Then I'd be on my way back to Taos and home to Myriam, a cold beer, and a shower.*

It happened that fast. One moment Beecher was wondering what he was going to do and the next he'd decided. He was no longer part of the South Africans or Billy Paul's insanity. It was as if the taser had been the crowning moment, clearing all the doubts and angst from his head. He now saw the Reverend Billy Paul and the Brothers of the

Lord for what they truly represented—a secretive, militant society that refused to grow spiritually into a beneficial brotherhood that helped mankind. And the DeVere group wasn't any better. They used the shield of capitalism to foster the exploitation of others to feed their need to maintain power.

But Beecher couldn't just walk away from them here. Haas and Goren would be too skeptical of his motives. Plus there was Myriam to think of. Just looking at the primal anger in Haas's face confirmed that the man was a killer. He'd have to go with them until he found an opportunity to separate himself from the group.

"Good enough reasons for me," Beecher said. "Let's head out."

Goren led them along the edge of the ridge. There was no trail, just rough rock that canted inexorably toward the valley floor. The team was zigzagging across a field of boulders when Beecher saw his opportunity. Goren halted at the top of a granite slab. "Stay off the rock face," he warned. "It's too steep."

The slab tilted at a sharp angle and was slick. He followed the others, staying at the edge, then faked a slip. Seconds later he was sliding feet first toward the bottom. He groped the rock face like he was desperate and even cried out. Actually he was in no real danger. He'd spotted a soft landing of pine needles and dirt at the base and hit it square. But he doubled over and grabbed his ankle screaming as if he was in pain.

Goren and another merc came to his aid.

"Idiot," Goren fumed, when Beecher cried out as Goren tried to ease his boot off. "I told everyone to stay at the top and not to cross the rock face. Now you've gone and sprained your ankle."

Goren squinted up at the rock face, then stared hard at Beecher. "We'd be hard pressed to get ourselves up there without the burden of carrying you."

"You can't leave me here," Beecher whimpered.

Goren barely hid his disgust at Beecher's whining. "We can't do anything for you now. Once we get to the ruins and find supplies, I'll send someone from the team back for you. You'll have to hold on until we get return."

Beecher forced himself to look frightened. "I can climb back up with just a little help." He made a show of getting up and trying to walk, collapsing like a rag doll after one step.

Goren shook his head. "Stay put. We'll come back for you as soon as we can."

The merc started to leave and Beecher grabbed his pant leg. "Don't leave me!"

Goren shook him off. "You'd better stay quiet. You don't want to attract any wolves or coyotes."

Beecher started to say something but went silent. His eyes darted around the area like a frightened rabbit.

The two South Africans scrambled back up the slope. At the top, Goren conferred with Haas. A few moments passed, and Haas then waved at Beecher. "Hang tight," he called out.

Beecher heard no warmth in the man's voice and he knew that if he really had been injured and had to stay put, they would never have come back for him anyway. He watched the five men march out of sight. He then waited another fifteen minutes to be sure they were well out of earshot and wouldn't be able to see him. Carefully he made his way up the slab without making a sound. At the top he retraced their trail to the clearing.

Retrieving the communicator from its hidden pocket, he activated it. He spoke one word. "Geronimo." He waited a few seconds.

Conklin's voice came through loud and clear. "Hear you five by five. I see your position. Follow the trail back to the logging road."

"Roger that," said Beecher. He settled back and looked across the valley. Without binoculars he couldn't make out the Anasazi cliff dwellings clearly or see if Haas and his men had reached the ruins. It didn't matter. By the time they scouted the area and decided they might as well try to hike out, he'd be long gone. The question was, what to do now?

26

———————

March 31, 2019
Española, New Mexico

Arriving at Española's small rural hospital, Ramsey and Myriam rushed to the front desk, asking about Pete.

The receptionist pointed down the hall to the emergency room. "First bed on your right," she said.

When they entered, to their surprise Pete was sitting comfortably on an ER bed. It was a quiet evening and he was the only one in the room. His head wound was bandaged. The instant he saw Myriam and Ramsey he leapt from the bed with the studied grace of a gymnast. He embraced his old-time buddy. "Nurse told me they called you."

He cocked an eyebrow as he recognized Ramsey's traveling companion. "Dr. Myriam St. Eves ... didn't expect to see you." She held out a hand and he swatted it aside. "Hugs all around," he said.

Ramsey shook his head in perplexity. "From what the Doc said, we expected you at death's door."

Pete disengaged from Myriam and waved the sentiment away. "Word to the wise, if you're going to be shot, come here. Best pharmaceuticals in the country. Make you feel like Superman and ten years younger."

"And a whole lot dumber," Ramsey said wryly.

Pete grinned. "There's that."

"Sure you should be up and around?"

"Doc just signed my discharge papers. I'm supposed to take it easy for the next couple of days." Pete pulled a piece of paper out of his pocket. "Concussion protocol right here. Though I got to tell you, I feel strong enough to wrestle a grizzly bear. Course, that's the drugs talking." He winked.

Looking down at Myriam, he said, "You look wonderful, haven't aged a bit. Jonathan told me all about you and your shrine." He frowned. "We have to talk about that, later." Then he was grinning again. "For now, let's get out of here before the Doc changes his mind." He grabbed his hat and coat. "Do I have a story to tell! My car?"

"We came in Myriam's car. It's–"

"Faster and more comfortable. Let's vamoose somewhere private so I can tell you what happened." He charged out of the room and down the hall.

Ramsey and Myriam exchanged glances as they quickly followed, caught like swimmers in his riptide wake.

Passing the receptionist, Pete suddenly stopped and starred at the TV in the waiting room. He shouted at the receptionist, "Turn this up." To Ramsey he said, "You have to catch this."

A Native American reporter from the Taos Bureau of a Santa Fe TV station was interviewing a woman with a thick South African accent. "My husband and his friends went into the mountains to hunt wild turkeys. There were supposed to be back hours ago. I lost all communication with them. I haven't been able to call them. Something is terribly wrong."

Pete chuckled. "That's an understatement."

The female reporter said, "I know this must be a hard time for you. Thanks for taking the time to tell us your story. We are all praying for their well-being." Turning to the camera, she continued her reporting. "The Taos County Sheriff's Department has informed me they are sending out search parties at the break of dawn. Live from Taos, I'm Julie Lone Wolf."

Ramsey was stunned. "They're talking about the guys you left with? Right?"

"The last time I saw them they were being bound up by a bunch of nasty Mexicans from across the border. I was running as fast as I could."

"Christ, what happened?"

Pete shook his head. "Somewhere away from prying eyes and ears."

He was so amped up, he shot out of the ER entrance, passed Myriam's car and was across the parking lot into a secluded grove of pine trees. Someone had placed a picnic table in the middle. He leaned against the edge and waited for them to catch up.

"Sit down," he ordered. When they did, he paced the tiny clearing, checking the trees. A fretful cold wind stirred the pine needles. Wreaths of white vapor plumed his narrow face as he squinted through the green boughs. "It's going to snow tonight," he said as if checking the weather was the only reason they had dashed outside. At last he stopped pacing, apparently satisfied they were alone. Settling onto one of the benches, Pete told the story of what happened during the supposed search for the diamonds.

Ramsey had never seen his usually laid back friend so pent up before. There was an urgency behind his words, as if he were working through the details until he came to the important stuff. So he stayed mum. Myriam, taking her cue from her one-time postdoc, said nothing.

"Me and the four South African mercenaries left the clearing a little after noon and headed toward the site of the kimberlite. That's when the shit hit the fan. Someone shot Buttercup out of the sky." He paused dramatically.

"Buttercup?" Myriam ventured.

"One of his drones," Ramsey explained.

Pete nodded. "In the next instant a half dozen Mexican

desperados materialize out of the pines and take us totally by surprise. They disarmed the South Africans and zip tied them. They must have figured I wasn't a threat because they left me loose. They marched us back to the camp."

Pete jumped up again and spun around. In contrast to his earlier cheerfulness, he was now more somber. With the drug effects wearing off, it was now clear how much he was shaken. "I could sure use a drink," he said, but instantly shook his head. "Can't touch the stuff anymore." He resumed his story.

"The ring leader recognized me."

Startled, Ramsey asked, "How?"

"His name is Julio and I'm pretty sure he works for the woman who owns the Rio Chama Café ... Rosa Cisneros. He was trying to kill me and he would've. Then out of the blue this Indian guy puts two arrows in him and saves my life. It was so weird. I mean, I thought it was one of those psychedelic trips I used to experience. This guy Julio is about to put a bullet in my brain one second and the next, this Indian guy is leaning over him and, I swear, it's like he's giving him last rites. I mean, how fucked up is that?

"Then I died. No seriously, the white light, sounds of angels singing. I was walking down this long tunnel. And here's the crazy part."

"You mean you're just getting to what's crazy?" asked Ramsey.

It was a testament to just how strange his experience was that Pete merely nodded and went on. "Instead of going back over my life or seeing my dead friends and relatives, I was moving into the future. The future was getting better and more beautiful and there was this voice telling me what the world could be. Telling me what I was destined to become. All the while I was trying to figure out whose voice it was. It was driving me crazy. I knew it from somewhere. I just couldn't figure it out. And then all of a sudden I knew. It was your voice Jonathan."

Ramsey felt himself stiffen at the revelation. "My voice?"

"Yeah, your voice. Crazy, huh man?"

Ramsey didn't know what to think. He didn't want dismiss his friend's experience, but being spoken of as a kind of oracle made him uneasy. Besides, he wondered why Pete didn't want to go to the police.

Pete shook his head as if reading Ramsey's mind. "No police, old man. Something big's going down here and I want to find out what it is."

"You were almost killed, Pete," said Myriam.

"I've a guardian angel," Pete said, grinning. He slapped the picnic table and danced a jig. "I get it now. My DeVere fellows weren't only looking for diamonds. They were also after your guys' Adam Gwillt. I think I know how too." He clenched his fists. "How fast can you drive?" he asked Ramsey.

"Why?" Ramsey said warily.

"I have to get back to the lab right away. It's beginning to make sense in an odd way."

"You've lost me."

"You know the guy Beecher, the one who looked out of place with Haas and the South African mercenaries?"

The color drained from Myriam's face. "Hiram was with you?"

"You know him?" Pete asked.

She nodded. "What happened to him? Is he dead?"

Pete shrugged. "I don't know, Myriam. Do you know the South Africans too?"

"Of course not." Her hands started to shake, her car keys rattling in the still night air.

"I'll drive," Ramsey said gently.

Gratefully, Myriam handed him her keys.

The two men rode in silence toward Taos, waiting for Myriam to offer up some answers about Beecher. She stared out the car window lost in the shadows pelting past them in the forest. Twenty miles outside of Espanola, the snow Pete predicted began. The Mercedes' temperature gauge showed the outside air temp had plummeted forty degrees to 28. With the icy wind it would be a lot colder.

"You called it," said Ramsey, setting the car's thermostat to 70.

Pete shrugged. "Gotta a pal who works for the National Center for Atmospheric Research. I share data from the drones with him."

Myriam fidgeted with her seatbelt, unbuckling and rebuckling the clasp every half minute.

Ramsey had never seen her so distraught. At the University of Oregon—even when her world began to fall apart around her after the Peru debacle—she'd been icy calm. Now she stared into the fat snowflakes, her body trembling. Several times she started to speak but withdrew into herself, sighing. Tears shined against her makeup in the green glow of the dash lights.

She said to Pete, "You're sure the man's name was Hiram Beecher?"

"Yes ... Why?"

Pulling a tissue from her purse, she dried her tears and sat up straight. She then slid the seatbelt clasp into buckle with a decisive click.

Ramsey read all the telltales pointing to her standing on the edge. With the right questions he could nudge her to tell everything, the same way he did in interviews as a human geographer. He hesitated for a moment, arguing with himself whether this moment was the time to push her about her relationship to Beecher.

He cleared his throat and said to Pete, "He's the same guy who signed the contract hiring me to investigate the Milagro Shrine." Then gently to Myriam, "Hiram will make it."

Pete added, "Those South Africans are the kind of men who are trained to handle these kinds of situations. They'll get your friend through it."

"Thank you, both of you. That's very reassuring." Myriam settled back into her seat. She knew what lay beneath the warmth in Ramsey's voice. He was a skilled interviewer, using compassion to draw her out. It didn't matter. She had to tell someone all she knew. *It's why we hired Jonathan in the first place.*

"Hiram is more than a friend. He and I have been together for over four years now. It was love at first sight. He even joined The

Friends of the Shrine and supported it financially when I asked him to, without any questions."

She swiveled in her seat. "Did he tell you why he was with the South Africans?"

Pete nodded. "Something about protecting his investment. Remember, we were looking for diamonds."

"As far as I know he never had any business interest in diamonds." Myriam pursed her lips. She flicked a glance at Ramsey and continued. "Hiram asked me to hire you to find out what happened to Adam. At this point we believed that Adam was the real power behind the healings."

Ramsey kept his voice calm though his fingers gripped the wheel at the news. "You didn't think it was important to tell me that?"

"Hiram said he wanted you to discover it on your own, and once you did it would lead you to Adam. That's what we were all hoping, that you would find him alive and well."

"Do any other members of the Friends of the Shrine believe Adam is the power behind the healings?"

"I can't say for sure. Whenever Father Michael, talked about the healings, he'd always refer to the shrine and not to Adam as possessing the power. At first I believed him completely. Though I suppose after a while most of us began to suspect Adam was the source." She frowned. "It was easier to accept that the shrine itself— rather than a human being—possessed an inexplicable convergence of healing forces. How could one person make so many different kinds of healings happen? Last night Rosa and I had a conversation with Carlotta and she all but confirmed that Father Michael knew a lot more about Adam as the source than he ever let on publicly or with me."

Ramsey nodded, trying to put together the pieces. There were still quite a few parts missing, but the picture was beginning to come together. *Father Michael ... Carlotta said that I should talk to him. He must hold the key.*

"Is Father Michael at the shrine now?"

"Not likely. In the past year he's spent more time away than there.

And since Adam disappeared, he's been mostly gone, skyping with the leadership of the Friends of the Shrine telling us to keep up hope and that all will be well."

"You have his contact information?" Ramsey asked.

"Yes. You should get ahold of him as soon as possible. Father Michael once said to me, 'There is nothing more powerful than a miraculous healing. It has always been the guiding force on the planet.' Then he went on to say, 'Jesus knew this. In one of the Gnostic Gospels he told his followers to organize their communities around this principle. Jesus was well ahead of his time. Now the Milagro Shrine is making it happen.'"

Ramsey glanced at Myriam. She slumped in the front seat, her dark eyes quiet. It was like a great burden had been lifted from her—and, exhausted from carrying it—she needed peace. He realized for the first time since Peru that he could see her simply as a human being, an ordinary person in pain. "Thanks, Myriam," he said quietly.

Snow started coming down hard. Large fat flakes stuck to windshield. The wipers could barely keep up, making it difficult for Ramsey to see the highway. The road was narrow and winding in spots. He had to slow way down. The darkness in the car was punctuated by the blue glow of Ramsey's phone as Pete searched the web. Occasionally he grunted an approval. Ramsey hoped he was finding what he was looking for.

The Mercedes fishtailed through a turn, the backend sliding toward the guardrail. The front tires caught dry pavement and everything shot forward. Then the snow stopped as if someone had drawn a curtain. They drove on in silence for several minutes. Overhead stars started to peek through the overcast.

"That was tough. Some of those curves were a bitch," Ramsey said, relieved they had gotten through it.

Pete said, "I've been here for five years and I'm still not used to New Mexico's springs. One day it's sunny and clear ... five hours later it's raining ... three hours after that it's snowing and then it's clear again. It should just rain like everywhere else. Hopefully those South African bastards will freeze to death." Realizing what he had just said, Pete touched Myriam's shoulder. "That was stupid of me. Look, they'll find them in the morning, this sort of thing happens all the time around here."

Myriam nodded.

Ramsey asked, "Do you have any idea how those Mexicans knew what your discovery party was up to? Did you tell anyone?"

Pete groaned and slumped back in the seat. "Julio."

"What?"

"Julio the ring leader. Remember, I said he works for Rosa Cisneros." Pete slammed his hands against the seat. "I called Rosa the night before. She's been so excited about the possibility of a diamond mine in the area I couldn't help telling her."

Myriam mumbled, "That explains it."

"What?" Ramsey asked.

"The other day she said there was something she didn't want to jinx."

"Damn, you know what's really crazy? The Mexicans that jumped us. They swooped down on us when I jokingly said to the merc leader Goren, 'Damn this'll make for a 10 carat diamond.' They must've thought they were robbing a jewelry store. There were diamonds in the kimberlite but most were teeny-weeny. Not worth the effort to dig them out. Those Mexican dudes were filling bags full of the stuff." He snorted derisively. "What fools."

Ramsey tapped the steering wheel. "You think Rosa set you up?"

"Maybe."

"Did you find the pipe?"

"No. I have an idea about that."

Ramsey replied. "Not now. When we get to your place. Driving through that snowstorm was exhausting."

A few minutes later they reached the turnoff to Pete's home. Myriam's phone buzzed. She fished it from her purse. She recognized the Texas area code but not the number. Her hands started to shake. She handed it to Pete. "I can't ... what if it's someone calling to tell me

Hiram's dead?" Tears welled up in the corner of her eyes and she clenched her hands so tightly her knuckles popped.

Pete swiped the screen. "Myriam St. Eves' phone." He listened for a pair of breaths. "She's right here," he said. He handed her the phone but Myriam shied away, shaking her head. He smiled broadly. "Good news." He pressed the loudspeaker icon.

"Myriam. It's Hiram."

27

April 1, 2019
Indianapolis, Indiana

Sitting in his office at his mega-church, the Reverend Billy Paul looked at the video Greta Van Horn had placed in his Dropbox. He watched the local Taos, New Mexico TV reporter sign off with the hopeful words that everyone was praying for the lost hunting party's well-being. He felt the knot in his stomach. He was facing total disaster.

The Reverend Billy Paul had brought a new, simple message to his parishioners. It was the message of the one truth, the truth of the Bible— Jesus is Lord and only through taking Him into your heart as your personal savior could one enter the Kingdom of Heaven.

Billy Paul's charismatic style of preaching and his simple practice of faith had found a large audience among those searching for a conservative religious message. His ministry extended beyond national boundaries. Billy Paul became a larger-than-life global preacher, loved and admired by millions worldwide.

But in addition to his general church, he had set up a secret society—the Brothers of the Lord. Rich people funded this clandestine group, mostly believers from the South but also from everywhere there was discontent with the lax morals and beliefs of ecumenical Christianity. The Brothers of the Lord had been modeled after the *Shuilkerken*, the clandestine churches of the sixteenth-century Reformation that exercised what was known as *exercitium religionis privatum*, private religious services. Working in small groups, the Brothers of the Lord had created a secret ministry to battle against those who taught false doctrine and watered down of the Scriptures. But now their super-secret mission to find and stop Adam from becoming the central figure of a new kind of false religion had gone grievously awry.

Billy Paul watched the video again. His heart began to pound at the thought of his evangelical empire collapsing when news of the attempt to kill Adam Gwillt got out. *It will all come back to me. My fingerprints are all over this effort to kill someone.* A sharp pain lanced through his chest. Billy Paul buried his head in his open hands and began to weep.

28

April 1, 2019
Taos, New Mexico

Beecher bit back a curse. Pain shot from his knee shoot through his entire body. *The fall down the granite slab must have actually wrenched something.* He tried to ease to a more comfortable position without giving away that he was injured but Conklin was watching him with concern all over his face. "We can rest."

Beecher shook his head, eager to get back to civilization. "I'll be all right. How much farther to the van?"

"Half mile maybe."

Once again Beecher thanked his foresight in bringing the younger man into the situation. *Otherwise you'd be freezing your ass off with the South Africans.* Earlier the sudden temperature drop had drained much of the desperate energy that propelled his escape from the South Africans. Conklin had met him on the trail with energy bars and water. It occurred to Beecher he knew little about the youngest member of the Brothers of the Lord, yet the man was helping him, and had, in fact, saved his life. "Thanks, Sam," Beecher said.

"No problem, Hiram. So what happened back there?"

He told Conklin about the attack by the Mexicans.

Conklin whistled tunelessly. "You're lucky to be alive."

"Don't I know it? But you know what was really weird; that the scientist I hired to investigate the Milagro Shrine, Jonathan Ramsey, showed up with the guy working for DeVere—Pete Miami. It was part of a bigger plan all along. How strange is that?"

Conklin nodded. "Very"

They hadn't gone more than a dozen steps when Beecher staggered against a tree. Conklin grabbed him by the arm. "You okay?"

Beecher nodded, but his heart was racing. "It just came to me. I knew I had seen the leader of the Mexicans before, the one who went after Dr. Miami. He works at the Rio Chama Café where Myriam and I always eat."

"And that means what?"

Beecher shivered and not from the cold mountain air. "What if the Mexicans are supposed to get rid of everyone connected to the shrine?"

"That's a lot of people and doesn't seem probable," Conklin cautioned. "It more likely has something to do with the South Africans."

Beecher nodded and resumed walking up the steep slope. "It's just that I don't want to take any chances with Myriam."

"Makes sense. When we get back to the chalet you can sort it all out."

"Sure."

Beecher wasn't convinced. He worried about Myriam and whether he needed to move her out of Rio Chama to somewhere safe from the Reverend Billy Paul and the South Africans. He moved faster and the rest of the trip to the van was uneventful.

Beecher tried to ease his leg so the knee wouldn't hurt. No position worked. The van's bucket seats were just too cramped. He finally settled himself as comfortably as he could. He stared at the dark shadows flashing by. Here and there flakes of snow started to fall, the van's headlights turning them into miniature shooting stars. They still had several miles to go before they reached the chalet, and with the snow it would take them longer.

Once more Beecher scrutinized Conklin. *Does he have a bigger role in all this?* Then his attention turned to what to do next. There was no clear course of action. He knew he no longer was working with the Reverend Billy Paul or the South Africans. But where did he go from here? Deep down he felt himself siding with Adam. It was all so confusing.

When they arrived at the chalet, Beecher discovered Conklin had called ahead. The caretaker had a warm meal waiting for them in the large dining room. As they were eating, Beecher was drawn to a breaking news bulletin interrupting the basketball game the caretaker was watching. Beecher watched for a few minutes and then leaned over to Conklin. "That's Greta Van horn. She works for DeVere and most certainly isn't anybody's wife."

Conklin thought for a moment. "Obviously they haven't made it out yet." He saw consternation spread across Beecher's face. "What are you thinking?"

"Should I tell somebody? They could all die. I can't be responsible for their deaths no matter what assholes they might be."

"If they are as tough as you say, they'll make it through the night." Conklin's words seem to placate Beecher. Once again he wondered why Conklin was doing this. *Why is he helping me? What does he want?* Then a nagging urge that had been with him since Conklin found him exploded. "Can I use your phone?" Conklin handed it to him as Beecher got up and walked to the far end of the large dining hall.

He called Myriam. To his surprise she knew about what happened. Even more surprising was that she was with Jonathan Ramsey and Pete Miami. Nothing made sense to him.

29

April 1, 2019
Taos, New Mexico

Pete was still full of energy and dashed off to his lab, leaving Ramsey in the living room of his cabin. He was alone. Earlier a handsome, middle-aged man had showed up at Pete's front door, saying his name was Sam Conklin and that he had come to take Myriam to Beecher. But the day's revelations had caught up with Ramsey and all he wanted to do was lay back and relax, going over what had happened. He settled on the couch with another glass of Courvoisier Cognac.

It had been a madhouse just a half an hour earlier before Pete had left. Myriam had spoken to Hiram, and though her anguish had vanished, it was now replaced by a somber confusion. Turning to Ramsey, she had said, "Hiram told me to tell you your job is done. You'll be paid in full. He said Adam has been found. I don't understand what he means by that, but if you're interested I'll tell you once I know more."

Pete's brow furrowed and he ran his fingers through his red hair. "Just like that … we're done, *finito*, over and out."

Myriam had said. "Hiram has a different message for you. He's greatly relieved you got out safely and says for you to be very careful how you proceed with the South Africans, even if Haas and his men don't make it out."

The lines in Pete's forehead deepened. Then his eyes flashed with understanding, "I have to go work on some stuff. Make yourselves comfortable." He dashed for the lab and Ramsey heard the click of the lock being thrown.

Myriam said, "Actually I won't be staying. Hiram said somebody's on the way to get me. Turns out he's nearby."

"Are you sure you want to see Hiram?" Ramsey asked.

Myriam nodded. "He has a lot of explaining to do but needs to do it face to face alone with just me. Do you suppose Pete has anything to drink here?"

Ramsey was going to say, "Of course … it's Pete." Then he recalled his old friend had stopped drinking. "I'll look." He found the Courvoisier Cognac kept for guests and poured them stiff shots in a pair of coffee mugs.

Myriam smiled and tipped her glass to Ramsey. "Pete always had class."

"I have a lot of questions," Ramsey said.

"I supposed you would."

"First, I don't think I'm done with this."

"I don't think you are either. It might just be the beginning."

"There's something I've been wanting to ask you. You never mentioned any healing experience of your own."

"I never had one, unless you count this odd dream I had a few months ago where a man I thought could have been Adam appeared as Christ."

"Why do you think that is? That you never had an experience of healing energy?"

"I really don't know, but I saw all the good it did for other people, and that was enough."

"You know this Adam shrine thing is really about a big change occurring in the world. He twirled the Cognac in the glass, smelled the fragrant bouquet. "Are you a Gnostic?"

Myriam's eyebrows knitted together. "What are you talking about? That Christian sect was wiped out by the Catholics 1800 years ago."

Ramsey smiled. "There's a twenty-first century group of people, calling themselves the New Gnostics. They've been influenced by the Milagro Shrine and are building something global in nature. I believe they are creating a new religion. I think it all revolves around Adam and his healing capabilities."

Ramsey pulled out his phone and punched the link to the New Gnostic website. He handed it to Myriam.

"I know nothing about this."

"That's hard to believe, you being so involved in the management of the shrine."

"Considering our history, I don't see any reason you should trust me, but it's true."

Before Ramsey could reply, Conklin had knocked. She was out the door moments later. The last thing she had said was, "I'll get back to you."

Ramsey settled back in his chair. Pete's living room was eerily quiet as though someone had gone to great lengths to give Ramsey all the privacy he needed. He couldn't help but notice the exaggerated limp in Myriam's step as she rushed out the door. It reminded him of the early stages of Parkinson's. He took a sip of the cognac. He hoped Myriam did not have the disease that had devastated his mother.

He took another sip of the cognac. The warmth filling his body demanded that he sleep. For the moment he was relieved to think he could be done with the shrine and Adam Gwillt. But he knew this was just his fatigue speaking. The whole question of Adam and his relationship to the New Gnostics gnawed at him. *There's more happening here than Beecher or Myriam or the South Africans suspect,*

Ramsey told himself. *It's like the proverbial tip of the iceberg.* But he was too tired to go any deeper at this point.

"I need a good night's sleep," he said aloud with a yawn.

Then the smart phone in his pocket buzzed. It was a text message. The header read, "Unavailable." He opened it. "Adam awaits you."

30

———

April 2, 2019
Taos, New Mexico

Ramsey woke up just where he had fallen asleep, on Pete's couch. He opened his eyes and Pete's wry smile beamed down at him. He held out a cup of steaming coffee. "Get up, old man. I have something to show you. It'll blow your mind."

Ramsey sat up. Taking the cup of Pete's special home-brewed coffee, he gulped down a large swallow. "I'm getting too old for this shit. Did you sleep at all?"

"Finish your coffee and we'll be off on our morning run."

Every muscle in Ramsey's body protested at the thought.

"Just kidding. Have any interesting dreams?"

Ramsey searched his memory for a few minutes. "There was something but it's gone." The coffee was working its magic as the cobwebs lifted. "I see you cleaned yourself up."

"Of course. You want to hear what I discovered about Adam."

"I'm off the case, remember? Myriam's old man fired me."

Pete grinned. "No you're not."

"Why is that?" Ramsey retorted sarcastically.

"I can see you're not going to let it go. Clean yourself up and I'll show you what this is all about. Remember the shower's down the hall."

As the hot water raced down Ramsey's body, steam swirled around him, bathing him in a warm fog. It tore away suddenly, like a veil had been lifted. He was transported back to Peru. He was walking in a rainforest yet at the same time he was looking down at it as though from another and higher world. What he saw dazzled his senses. His heart was beating rapidly and his limbs trembled. The ordinary jungle had turned luminescent; individual trees shone ethereally as if someone had injected phosphorescent particles in the sap; butterflies glowed and shot like meteors through the dense canopy; bird song filled the air with a glorious benediction. Somehow it was more real than anything he had ever experienced. An urge welled up in him to bring this indescribable numinosity into the world. It contained unlimited power. But in the next heartbeat the jungle vanished and a dreamlike vision of Adam and the strange old man from England named Loki appeared, nodding their approval. And just as quickly they melded into a heavy rain that washed away the luminescence until there was only warm water pouring over Ramsey's face. Then the rain ended and his consciousness focused on his hand as he turned off the faucet. The strange experience had been brief but powerful.

Refreshed, Ramsey dressed quickly and went into lab.

"I tell you you're not done at all," Pete said. "Come over here. Up until now the South Africans have been able to see everything I'm doing with my GIS work. By the way I have a third drone collecting data 24/7 from my research area. Its flight path takes it in a spiral spreading outward, covering northern New Mexico down to Albuquerque every twelve hours. The info has been collected and sent off to South Africa."

Ramsey looked puzzled. "Why let the South Africans see what you are doing?"

"Why not? They're paying for it all. What they don't know is I've been sharing all the data with a buddy of mine at NCAR in Boulder Colorado."

The reason hit Ramsey and he smiled. "Of course, for climate research."

"Naturally."

"What did you get out of the deal?"

"I get to date his sister whenever I'm in town."

"What's the real reason?"

"Time on their supercomputer."

"And the point of all this?"

"They didn't see what I did last night. I used the NCAR computer to do some investigating. Remember, two days ago I showed you how a large number of geophysical fields and forces cohered into one large harmonious field around and over the Milagro Shrine."

"You said you'd found God."

"Perhaps a bit overzealous. After what Myriam told us, I thought it was your Adam guy producing it. But it's more like he's a conduit for some sort of power that's organizing those fields. If I were writing science fiction, I would say Adam is a human wormhole to another universe."

"There is a peripheral theory in human geography that hypothesizes certain places are transparent to different kinds of forces," Ramsey responded.

"Not as trendy as wormholes, but I'll bite."

"In early Christianity, it was proposed that sacred sites were 'thin places' wherein the realm of normal appearances becomes transparent to the spiritual reality that lies outside of normal reality. This idea was recently expressed by Christian contemplative Thomas Merton who wrote, 'We are living in a world that is absolutely transparent, and God is shining through it all the time.'"

"That's some heavy shit."

"Not as heavy as wormholes."

Pete nodded. "I suppose. Look, when I refined my analysis of the data I was able to track the movement of what I call the 'Adam Effect.' Over the five years I have of data, the coherent field strength at the Milagro Shrine fluctuated a bit but stayed within some defined parameters. Except there were two days when the field greatly diminished. The coherence began to break down. Then on the third day everything was back to normal. I think Adam left the site for those two days."

Ramsey immediately remembered what Grossinger had told him about the time he took Adam to Albuquerque. "Can you tell me when?"

"I could but later. Today, the coherence at the shrine is pretty much gone. It started rapidly destabilizing after the first of the year." He pointed to a graphic representation of the Adam Effect on one of the screens. "Look there. Two weeks later in Taos, a coherence field is forming and it stays there gaining greater coherence for nearly a month and then it moves again to where new field coherence emerges right near the famous Catholic El Santuario de Chimayo. Then gone again until ten days ago when a new field starts cohering. Guess where?"

"Right next to the kimberlite site," said Ramsey excitedly.

"Not too shabby for an old man." Pete looked at his glass. He sighed. "Times like these, I wish I hadn't given up drinking."

"I haven't," Ramsey said grinning. "Got anything that goes with orange juice?"

Pete came back with tequila, gave Ramsey a shot, looked at his own glass and set the bottle aside.

"So Adam was there yesterday," Ramsey asked.

"I'd put money on that."

"And now?"

"It was a weak field to begin with and now it's nearly gone."

"He left?"

"Gone like the wind," retorted Pete.

"Where did he go? Can you follow him?"

"Unless he stops in an area long enough for a field to start to cohere, I can't say."

Ramsey added another finger of Tequilla to his glass. "So you think the South Africans know all this?"

"I'm sure they do. I'm remotely using their computer most of the time.

"So they were after Adam and not the diamonds?"

Pete pursed his lips. "My best guess is that they're after both. After all, diamonds are DeVere's biggest source of income."

Ramsey nodded his head. "Even so, this morning they'll be as much in the dark about Adam's location as we are."

Pete drummed his fingers on the desktop. He looked at Ramsey out of the corner of his eye and shook his head.

"What?" asked Ramsey?

"Don't know if I should say anything. It could be an error in the data."

"So tell me and let me decide."

Pete brought up a different screen showing a map of New Mexico. His house and the shrine were highlighted. Then Miami switched images. Ramsey could see embryonic coherent fields briefly building at both places. Ramsey studied the timecode on the display. His eyes widened as he recognized what it meant. "Is this for real?"

Pete shrugged. "It isn't the Easter bunny."

"So Adam was near your house a couple of days back and at the shrine a week ago?"

"Appears so, unless there's another explanation."

Ramsey shook his head. He'd had the experience of the Adam apparition at the shrine the day he first arrived there. Maybe it wasn't an apparition at all.

The search for another explanation would have to wait. Pete's phone buzzed and a text message tweeted: "Missing South Africans found alive. Unrelated Hispanic man found dead." He showed it to Ramsey. "New game, old man."

31

—————

April 2, 2019
Taos, New Mexico

Myriam walked out onto the chalet's porch that looked out on the ski slopes. Low-lying fog hovered near the piñon pines that lined the five runs. The dark gray envelope of mist suited her mood. She had stormed off the evening before into one of the chalet's guestrooms after Hiram revealed his involvement in the various plots to kill or capture Adam. The revelation had shocked her. At the same time she still longed to find herself in his powerful embrace. As he had told his story, she could see his pain and his hope that she would somehow forgive him. Myriam could also see that he was frightened. That was an emotion she had never seen in Hiram before.

As Myriam stretched, she realized she had hardly slept. Through the night she had played over and over in her mind the many "what-ifs," trying to make sense of the story she heard from the man that had become more than just a lover. A man who was her best friend. *Can grown men in today's modern world really act this way? How could Hiram be a part of such ignorance and evil?*

Unexpectedly, her attention was drawn inside the chalet where the German caretaker and Conklin gathered around the television. As she approached, Myriam could see a reporter interviewing two men. They were talking about their previous night's ordeal and the dramatic rescue efforts by the local Forest Service rangers. The man spoke with a smooth South African accent. She recognized him immediately. He had come to the Milagro Shrine a couple of months ago. Raphael Núñez introduced him on a shrine tour. She was amazed at how well he looked even after a sleepless night of fighting the rain and cold.

From behind her a voice boomed through the chalet, "That's Haas." Everybody turned and looked at Beecher.

Pieter Haas walked away from the newswoman relieved the interview was over. Skirting the news crew's truck, Greta Van Horn ran up to him and threw her arms around his broad shoulders in a mad embrace. She whispered in his ear, "I know this is embarrassing but play along. They think I'm your wife."

With the cameras now clearly focused on the couple, Haas smiled and gave a thumbs up. And then the two of them hurried off to the waiting SUV. Once inside the privacy of the vehicle, Greta resumed her normally distant attitude toward the CEO. "Two of the men are in the hospital undergoing tests and observation, and the others are back at the hotel," she informed him.

"Fill me in," Haas demanded.

"Everything's under control. We need to get you checked out."

He waved away her concern.

"How did the forest rangers find us so quickly?"

"I sent them the coordinates of where you were heading."

"Good thinking. Thank you. Did they find Beecher or Miami?"

"No word on either of them yet."

"What about Adam?"

"He's gone."

Haas's eyes narrowed. "Gone where?"

Greta shook her head. "He vanished into thin air."

Haas slumped in his seat. The news hit him almost as badly as the experience of spending the night outside in northern New Mexico's mountains. "Take me to the hotel," he said wearily. *I need a long hot shower and some rest*, he told himself. *Then I'll deal with all of this.*

Four hours later, looking as if nothing had happened, Haas entered Greta's hotel room. She had improvised a control center to stay in contact with South Africa. She had a cordless headset and was speaking softly to Dr. Lindstrom on the screen. She clicked off when he came over.

"Well?" he said, sitting in a chair opposite the dark-haired woman.

Neatly prepared as usual, Greta began, "First let me say Goren told me what happened out there. I'm glad you were able to make it out alive. Here's what's new. As you requested, we kept eyes on Miami's house and the chalet where Beecher is staying. He arrived early in the evening at the chalet with somebody we don't know. The report was he looked shaken, walked with a limp, but otherwise was okay. Five hours later Miami, who had a head wound, plus Jonathan Ramsey and Beecher's woman, Myriam St. Eves, showed up at Miami's house. Later the fellow who seems to be helping Beecher picked up Myriam and drove her to the chalet. All rather cozy don't you think?"

Haas shook his head in amazement. "So, Beecher made it out. I can't believe it considering the difficulty we had. It's almost as if there were divine intervention."

Greta watched her boss who sat looking up at the ceiling as if in prayer. After several seconds she cleared her throat.

Haas smiled. "What happened with Adam?"

"According to Lindstrom it appears Adam started moving about the time you were ambushed by the Mexicans."

Looking up from her notes, she snapped, "What in the hell was that about?"

Surprised by her uncharacteristic show of emotion, Haas

shrugged. "We were sloppy. They must have followed us from the moment we left Taos."

"Do you think they were there to stop you from finding Adam?"

"The slimy little bastards seemed to be thinking they were going to find a wealth of diamonds."

"So it was unrelated to the primary mission?"

Haas nodded. "So Adam just disappeared?"

"You remember it's impossible to track Adam when he's moving. So, either he's been on the go for twenty hours or he's left our coverage area."

"Where does that leave us?"

"Nowhere. But our analysts discovered something interesting. When they were reevaluating the data since Adam's disappearance, there was an interesting spike in the coherence at the shrine eight days ago."

"How is that possible?"

"The lingering or residual coherence field at the shrine had a spike upward in strength. It turns out that was the day Jonathan Ramsey visited the Milagro Shrine for the first time. Here's what's really interesting. We found what might be a similar weak coherence field two nights ago in the area of Miami's house. Our people think Jonathan Ramsey might have somehow produced it."

"Christ, where is Ramsey now?"

Greta touched her headset. "Tell me where Ramsey is right now." She listened, then, "It looks like he, Pete Miami, and Myriam St. Eves are heading back to the shrine. Remember, Miami's car is there."

"Call Goren. Get us one of those SUVs. I need to get down there."

32

———

April 2, 2019
Taos, Mexico

New Mexico's highest mountain, Wheeler Peak, rose majestic and snow-covered under bright blue skies and the Wheeler Peak Wilderness Area spread out before Ramsey like a dark green blanket as he found himself once again at the wheel of Myriam's car. Much had changed in less than twenty-four hours. In the backseat Pete, no longer energized by his discoveries, was curled up like a baby, snoring away. Periodically, as Ramsey remembered he was prone to do, he let out a strange growl.

Myriam looked at Ramsey questioningly. "Is he really sleeping?"

"Yep. He's always done that, at least since I've known him. He's like a dog chasing cats in his sleep."

Ramsey zeroed in on the road ahead. He was satisfied to wait until Myriam was ready to tell him what was going on with Beecher. It gave him time to think about the revelation of Adam's connection to the healing power of the Milagro Shrine. It raised more questions than it answered. He knew there was a vast literature about energetic healing powers, including techniques like shamanistic healing, chakra balancing, and Reiki. But these were direct hands-on procedures. Although he'd read about some healers who seemed to have an impact on electromagnetic fields, Adam was different. He somehow created a remarkably sustained geo-physical, bioelectrical, and electromagnetic field coherence that could affect many people over a broad area. Ramsey wondered too if the same phenomenon was present at other healing sites. Would the results be the same if Adam's sister Carlotta had lived along the Oregon coast, even though that region has a completely different geological substrate and processes? Would a healing shrine have emerged?

Pete had showed Ramsey how the field coherence over the Milagro Shrine gradually intensified and expanded. Was that the result of the interaction of the healed people? So that they too were sort of acting like a conduit to . . . Here Ramsey's thoughts faltered. *To what?* he wondered.

From the accounts reported on the New Gnostic website, people from all walks of life were affected by the shrine. Then it occurred to him that Adam wasn't actually mentioned in any of the reported healings.

More questions arose, flying through his mind thick as a hail storm and almost as painful, as he realized he had no answers to them: Have there been people throughout history who have had Adam's kind of superpower? How many? Christ? Buddha? St. Francis? Were their powers derived from where they physically lived, as he had once theorized? Or were these spiritual leaders doing something different? Something different than the way normal people lived their lives? Or did something unique happen to them that gave them their powers?

Ramsey locked down his thoughts. He had to stop the flood of questions before they overwhelmed him. More than anything he wished he could talk with Adam. For a moment he even imagined the kind of experiments he would like to perform on the healer—a thought he quickly dismissed as unethical. He recalled the strange text message from last night: "Adam awaits you." At first he thought maybe Pete was playing a joke on him, but his old friend insisted he wasn't. It was a nuisance and most likely some sick kind of joke, yet he found himself hoping it was somehow true.

He turned to Myriam.

She must have read the frustration and anger on his face because she said, "I didn't know anything about what Hiram and that bastard Haas were up to, and they were playing me and you. They used me." Anger turned her fine-boned features into a scary mask. "Hiram used me!" She looked at Ramsey. "They used both of us."

Understanding passed through Ramsey. "They tricked you into hiring me."

She nodded. "Hiram is a member of a group of secret Christian fanatics, known as the Brothers of the Lord, led by the televangelist Brother Paul. At first they were excited about the shrine, and then when it was discovered that Adam was the source of the shrine's healing power, they created a plan to kill him."

Ramsey was incredulous. "You're joking!"

"That's what I thought, but it's true. You were part of the plan to have Pete locate Adam through the advanced GIS technology of his."

"It worked; but did he say why they didn't just go to Pete directly?"

"Hiram didn't say and I didn't ask." She looked at the curled up geophysical genius on the backseat. "Maybe they couldn't trust him, or they figured they couldn't make him do it."

Ramsey started to swear and Myriam cut him off.

"They must've found out about your obsession with sacred places and your friendship with Pete." She looked back at him still curled up. "And the connection between the three of us."

Ramsey took a deep breath, thinking of the events that occurred since he stepped foot on the grounds of the shrine. "Christ, that means Malcolm Grossinger, Adam's college friend, and maybe even Professor Orensen were involved in the ruse." He pounded the car's steering wheel so hard, Pete snorted and half woke up, then curled into a tighter ball and fell back to sleep. "This is unbelievable," Ramsey swore. "I stupidly thought my call to investigate the power of the shrine might be some sort of divine providence."

Myriam reached over and touched Ramsey's arm. "I'm not so sure it might not be true. We know something very few people know—the miraculous healing power of Adam Gwillt. It's almost as if the fate of this incredible being has been put in our hands."

The gentle touch relaxed Ramsey and he throttled back his anger.

She took in a deep breath. "Regarding the shrine. I'm just an administrator and promoter." Her frown deepened. "And I haven't been a very good one lately, have I?"

Ramsey frowned too. "You're better than you think. I always blamed you for not supporting me totally after Peru, but honestly, it was my own shit there. I wasn't ready for it and ... I should've told you my whole plan."

In response Myriam smiled wanly. "You were always unstoppable. It's what made you a good investigator ... One of the best I had the opportunity to work with." Her tone shifted, "I'm so sorry I got you involved."

Ramsey thought for a moment. "Interestingly there's nothing to be sorry about. It's not as if anything bad happened to me or is going to." He shrugged. "So, what are you going to do now?"

"This may sound strange, but after I clean up, then I'm running over to the shrine to pray. And you?"

"I need a car."

Myriam looked at Pete who was now stretching. "What about Pete's?"

"There are some things I need to do alone."

"Hiram keeps a utility truck in my shed. Will that do?"

33

April 2, 2019
Taos, New Mexico

The morning was crisp and clear. Melting snow filled in the spaces around the trees and left the trail along the chalet's ski runs muddy. Hiram Beecher slipped on a wet slab of rock, banging his shoulder against a piñon pine. He righted himself and continued hiking upwards, barely noticing the tear in his jacket. Overhead the ski lift swayed in the morning breeze. It would have been easier to use the lift but the walk was therapeutic. *Testing my knee*, he told himself. To his surprise he felt remarkably pain-free, at least physically. His heart, on the other hand, felt ripped in two.

Myriam had left that morning, her face set in a grimace of pain, frustration, and anger. All of it directed at him. He accepted it as the price he had to pay for keeping secrets from her.

He reached the top of the hill. The valley spread out in front of him, peaceful and quiet. As far as the world knew, nothing unusual had happened in northern New Mexico's wilderness yesterday. That's how Beecher was coming to think about it. On the other hand, he was relieved by finally having told Myriam the truth about everything.

Now he had to live with the consequences. So it was with a heavy heart that he pulled out his phone and pushed the contact entry for Brother Paul. There was only a recording. He waited for the tone and left a message. "This is Hiram Beecher. I'm done. Don't contact me again." Beecher pushed the end call button. He could've said more—a lot more. About how Brother Paul used him and was as dishonest as the day was long, and that if the son of a bitch ever tried contacting him again, he'd tear his limbs off one by one. But confessing everything to Myriam had had a psychological cathartic effect, like a ritual cleansing of the soul and spirit. He had finally freed himself of the Brothers of the Lord.

As for the South Africans, his instincts told him that as long as he kept his mouth shut they would leave him alone. He was also sure their pursuit of Adam was over. Everyone was back to square one. And their relationship with Brother Paul—that was no longer any of his business.

The crunch of snow underfoot riveted Beecher's attention back down the trail. A shadow moved through the trees. Pulling his handgun from his belt, Beecher thought ruefully, *Perhaps I was wrong about the South Africans.* Then he heard the high-pitched voice of Conklin.

"Wait up," the man wheezed in the high cold mountain air.

Once again questions about Conklin's motivation for helping him shot through him. *Is he an ally or enemy?*

34

———————

April 2, 2019
Rio Chama, New Mexico

Holman Elementary School was located on Highway 518 about halfway between Moro and Rio Chama. Carlotta agreed to meet Ramsey at Eagle County Park during her afternoon break from teaching. The park was hardly more than a picnic area alongside the Moro reservoir. Its low-lying cottonwoods had already finished blooming. Ramsey sat at one of the picnic benches, pulled out his tablet, and began responding to some pressing business matters. It felt good to be engaged in some normal human geographical problems for a change. After a while he looked up with a wide smile at the large 2001 Dodge Ram pickup truck he had just parked in the lot. Ramsey had not driven a stick shift like this since his graduate field days at UCLA, when he drove across the Sonoran desert hunting down Native American sacred sites. It brought back memories of carefree days filled with love for Paige. It had been one of the best times of his life—a life, he realized with a dull pang of regret—that was now long gone.

. . .

After the drive to Rio Chama, it had been decided that rather than dropping Pete off at the Café Rio first. They would go to Myriam's home, grab the truck, and then Ramsey would deliver Pete to the Café. Ramsey had sensed that Pete had something to do that didn't involve Myriam.

Twice on the way into town Ramsey stalled the truck at stop signs.

"Sure you can drive this beast, old man?" Pete laughed.

"It's because I am an old man that I can. So what's happening in Rio Chama?"

"Rosa Cisneros."

Ramsey arched his eyebrows.

"When you all thought I was sleeping, I texted her. She says it's not her fault. The Mexicans and all that."

"And you believe her?" Ramsey asked, deliberately allowing skepticism in his tone.

Pete smiled. "I gave up the booze and the drugs. I'm not giving up on women."

Ramsey smiled too. "Sound wisdom."

When they drove up to the Café, Rosa was outside waiting.

"Wish me luck."

"Whenever did you need luck with the ladies, hotshot?"

Pete jumped out and came around to the driver's window. "Give me a buzz when you're ready to head back to Taos. I'll pick you up at Myriam's."

Ramsey watched Pete skip his way to Rosa. He could see their embrace represented much more than a business relationship.

"I'll be damned," Ramsey muttered.

He should've told me, Ramsey mused, wondering why Pete had kept his relationship with Rosa a secret. The sound of another vehicle pulling into the park's gravel parking lot told him that Carlotta had arrived.

Ramsey studied the schoolteacher as she walked from her car to the table. Backlit by the bright New Mexico sun, she reminded Ramsey of the Adam apparition.

She called out to him, "You have news of Adam. Good news you said."

"He's alive," said Ramsey.

Her only show of emotion was a hesitation in her step, then she walked more swiftly, sitting beside him in a single fluid motion. She cleared her throat. "I always knew it, somehow I could feel him. So where is he?"

"Some smart people with sophisticated equipment have been tracking him since the day he disappeared. Moving around from place to place, to Taos, the western side of the forest, finally into the wilderness near an Anasazi ruin."

"And now?"

"Yesterday the smart people came to believe that he's gone ... disappeared, not dead."

"I knew that too. And don't talk to me like I'm a fool."

"Of course, sorry. Could he be doing this on his own? Moving around I mean?"

"No chance."

"Then who do you think is helping him?"

Carlotta shook her head. "I wish I knew."

"I was hoping you could tell me."

Her brow furrowed and her eyebrows arched. "Why your sudden interest in Adam? Before it was the shrine."

"We ... I know now that he's the source of the shrine's healing power."

Carlotta nodded. "Father Michael told me a year ago. He also said not to mention it to anyone, but that soon many people would know. Might even want to kill him." Dark eyes bored into him and he noticed for the first time she had not removed her hand from the pocket of her blue windbreaker. Stenciled in gold lettering across the left breast was 'Moro High School Rifle Team'.

"Are you one of those?" she asked, her voice dead flat.

Flustered, Ramsey blurted out, "God no!" He recovered his poise and continued, "Did you ever talk with Adam about this threat?

"What do you think?"

"And?"

"I'm still uncertain about you. And you haven't talked to Father Michael like I told you to."

Ramsey felt embarrassed.

"I had dinner with Father Michael last night," she continued. "I believe if you go to the shrine and ask around you will find him."

Carlotta reached across the table with her free hand and took one of his hands in hers. "Trust your intuition more, rationality less. Thanks for the good news. The third-graders are waiting for a lesson on the orbits of the moon and planets."

As she walked off Ramsey called after her, "If I hear anything, I'll let you know."

Carlotta never stopped walking. Ramsey got up and followed her. "Was all that sorrow over Adam an act?"

Carlotta never looked back. She got into her car and drove away, leaving Ramsey pondering just whose side was anyone on.

35

April 2, 2019
Rio Chama, New Mexico

This time Ramsey strode through the high-arched entrance to
the shrine with purpose and energy. He was determined to
find Adam. Straightaway, he was aware there were more people than
the last time. A tour bus had unloaded around fifty seniors. Most had
climbed the long set of steps to the cottonwood tree. He thought to
himself *if they only knew.* Yet even he was drawn there, strangely.

As he mounted the steps, he scanned the site for Father Michael.
He'd only met him once and wasn't sure he would recognize him.
After seeing no one that might fit the bill, he continued up the long
flight of stairs.

Half way up the steep climb he ran into a chubby woman with
rouged cheeks. She was in her fifties. Silver hair hung in rings around
her head, forming a halo that gleamed in the bright daylight. A small
shrine nametag attached to her jacket said "Ichthys."

Greek for fish, Ramsey told himself. Then he noticed it was spelled
in ancient Koine Greek letters. They were laid out according to the
early Christian design that featured two intersecting arcs that made

the shape of a fish. It was like a clue pointing him where to go. He addressed her in a gentle tone. "I'm looking for Father Michael. Have you seen him?"

Piercing gray eyes stared hard at him. The woman pulled out her phone, scrolled down and touched a number and waited. She suddenly bellowed, "You'll find what you need at the Christ Chapel."

Ramsey winced. "Got it, thank you so much."

"It's across from the cottonwood!" she yelled.

Her scream seemed to catapult him up the remaining stairs. He quickly threaded through the tourists and crossed the hundred yards separating the building from the cottonwood.

The chapel was the one place Ramsey had not visited earlier. It was known as the Christ Chapel because of the impressive crucifix inside. The crucifix had come all the way from the Holy Land. It was a donation from a billionaire tech mogul whose wife had been healed at the shrine.

The door was slightly ajar and Ramsey slipped in. With only a single small stained glass window, it took a while for his eyes to adjust to the low light level. He jerked in surprise at the room's strange architecture. Visitors entered the apse first. Its domed ceiling soared above a small wooden altar. The nave spread out from there, with room to hold maybe thirty worshippers. Beyond the last pew was the crucifix mounted on the far wall so that everyone had to look up at it. Colored light from the stain glass window fell upon cross. The Christ figure was not typical of the golden-haired, light-skinned Jesus found in many Christian churches. Ebony curls fell upon shoulders so dark they were almost black. He was not nailed to the wood, but his arms were upraised and his hands cupped as if receiving a blessing. He wore no loincloth and was naked like Michelangelo's "David."

Ramsey swallowed his unease and called out softly, "Father Michael." Silence followed and then he felt the presence of someone behind. Turning, he was confused by the glowing man-shaped aura he saw. "Who are you"?

The voice was familiar. "Who do you think I am?"

"Are you Adam?"

"He who drinks from my mouth will become like me, and I will become like him, and the hidden things will be revealed to him."

The words seemed to appear in his mind as much as he heard them. Ramsey was so stunned he stupidly found himself asking, "Like what?"

"Jesus was always up to something new. He was a creative force like none other. Figure it out."

Then out of the corner of his eye Ramsey caught a slight movement in the shadows beneath the cross. A young woman was sitting on the floor, her knees up against her chest. For a moment he thought it was Paige. She looked up. Her eyes were luminous. She said, "I am praying and listening, please continue."

Ramsey turned back around, the Adam apparition was gone. He searched the room but there were no others except the woman.

Time ticked by in slow heartbeats. He realized he was staring straight at the eyes of Jesus on the cross. They were onyx and seemed to follow Ramsey as he was drawn forward. The Christ figure's full lips parted and he spoke directly to him: "I see you and love you." For the first time in his life Ramsey knew he was truly loved. It was a love Ramsey experienced as pure as the love a newborn receives from its mother, and at some deep level he understood how Jesus had taken all the evil in the world into his heart and returned it as love.

The experience freed Ramsey of all thought. He slid to the floor and tears of joy ran down his cheeks. He was only aware of air going in and out of his lungs as one with the breath of God.

Ramsey did not know how long he waited there, only that a rustle of movement entered his thoughts. He was sitting on the stone floor. He looked around and saw the strange woman had left. The sun must have passed midday because the stain glass window now sprayed light on the opposite side of the room. But the chamber's enchanting dreamlike appearance continued as though the sun's brilliance burnished everything in the room. He felt blessed.

He clambered to his feet, thanking God for the grace he had just received. Bowing to the figure on the cross, he turned and left the chapel. As he stepped outside, he felt a solid object pressed into his back.

A low voice with a South African accent whispered in his ear, "That's a 9mm Beretta aimed at your left kidney. Don't make a fuss. We're going to have a little chat."

The pistol propelled Ramsey toward the plain wooden benches circling the cottonwood tree. On the nearest one sat the man Ramsey saw with Pete two days ago—Pieter Haas.

He had taken only a few steps when to his surprise, his assailant let out a sharp gasp.. The gun fell away and made a soft plopping noise on the ground. Ramsey looked back. The gunman had fallen to his knees and a large black wasp perched on the man's neck. Before anything else could happen the young woman from the chapel grabbed Ramsey by the arm.

"Let's go. It's a spider wasp. Its sting is the most painful in the insect world. But its effect only lasts for four minutes. That's enough time."

"Enough time for what?" asked a shaken Ramsey.

"To have some fun before the shit hits the fan as they say. Come on, let's move!"

Now in the daylight Ramsey saw the woman for the first time clearly. She was astonishingly beautiful, nubile, and clad in skintight clothes that left nothing to the imagination. She was, Ramsey realized, the embodiment of Aphrodite the Greek goddess of love, beauty, pleasure, and procreation. She pushed him along like a gentle but insistent wave.

Ramsey asked, "Where are we going?"

The woman steered him in the direction of the older tourists leaving the cottonwood tree and heading down the stone steps. Soon they were surrounded by gray-haired seniors. Many of them walked briskly, belying their age.

"I feel great for the first time in years," claimed a man holding a cane. He twirled it like Fred Astaire and even danced a few quick steps. "My arthritis is gone."

As they picked up the pace Ramsey craned his neck to see Haas who had fallen in behind them at a distance. The man with the gun was back on his feet. Ramsey stumbled but the woman caught him before he fell.

"Who are you?" Ramsey asked.

With a twinkle in her eyes she answered, "My friends call me 'Puck,' for obvious reasons." She pulled blonde hair back to reveal slightly pointed ears. "You can call me Puck too—it'll be more fun that way."

"Why are you doing this?"

Ignoring the question she said, "I have a plan to help you. If we can stay close to the seniors, I can get you down to your truck and on your way."

Ramsey's mind was swimming with images and questions. He had no clue why Haas wanted him so badly that he would risk kidnapping him at gunpoint in a public place. Then there was this mysterious woman who was helping him escape. Another question popped into his head. "How did you know I came in a truck?"

"Isn't it obvious I've been watching you? Something happened when you looked at the crucifix. I like hearing about such things, making them happen, in fact."

Ramsey thought about running and escaping this strange woman, but her hand on his arm held him with a gentle but insistent pressure.

"I know what happened," she said. "I could see it. You felt the love of Jesus. He's been holding the door open for you to the other side your whole life. It's like your sacred places, the thin places to the transcendent that Thomas Merton talked about. That opening to the other side, that's what lingered after Jesus died. He's not alone you know. There have been many others through the centuries—Zoroaster, Moses, Buddha, Muhammad, Baha'ullah, Ueshiba, and many more, even Bill Clinton." She grinned. "Just kidding about him. Made you look, though. It's very real and not as rare as people think. Each of those individuals have changed the planet's geological structure by bringing the other side very close like what happened here and many other places like this one." She made a sweeping gesture that encompassed the whole shrine.

Ramsey was surprised at how confidently she provided an answer to his life-long question about sacred sites

"Who are you?" Ramsey insisted.

"I'm Puck ... a friend ... a guide. Right now I'm helping you get to the place you need to be. Come on, let's catch up with them," she said pointing to the seniors.

The older tourists were now walking back to their bus.

Ramsey seemed to have no choice but to follow Puck. Like being in a lucid dream, Ramsey was becoming aware that he was once more caught up in some sort of altered state. It was similar when he took LSD in high school. The drug ran the show until its potency wore off. Ramsey wondered if later he would be able to sort out reality from the illusion of what was happening to him. His back was still sore from where Haas' man had jabbed his gun into his kidney. That was surely real. And then there was Haas still watching every move. That was real too.

Puck said, "You're probably wondering if I saw Adam back in the chapel ... or at least what you call Adam."

Ramsey knew now that there was nothing to do but play along. "What do you think he meant by saying that Jesus is always up to something new?"

"That's what I call a statement of the 'Jesus Principle.' It's made my work so much easier." To Ramsey's surprise, the woman began dancing a little jig. "You tricked me. You could be good at this if you had only learned to pray. If you knew how to pray, Peru would have been a cakewalk. You won't be able to teach it if you can't do it yourself."

"Stop that!" Ramsey grated.

Puck smiled and settled down.

Ramsey continued. "I am not a Christian because I choose not be controlled by some archaic notions that no longer apply in the modern world."

The woman smiled indulgently like listening to a petulant child. "You'll change your tune about Jesus. There's a lot more to what He was up to than you can't possibly imagine now. But you'll figure it out."

Puck urged Ramsey past the seniors as they filed into the bus. She pushed him toward his truck. "Good luck," she called out. As she departed, she stopped and turned back to Ramsey. "Look up Matthew 18:20, it's a key that will open an important door for you." With that Puck glided gracefully toward Haas and the man with the gun.

With Puck's departure Ramsey shifted back into a normal state of mind. Clearheaded, he looked one more time for the beautiful woman. She transformed into a wisp of light that passed harmlessly between Haas and the man with the gun. All the negative emotions associated with being a hunted man swelled up in Ramsey's chest. *What the hell does Haas want with me?* It didn't make sense. But he didn't wait around to find out. He hurried toward Beecher's old truck, pulling out the keys as he ran. The door squealed open. A quick backward glance showed the two men were still fifty yards away. He slid the key into the ignition but nothing happened. Panic gripped him. He was about to lock the door when Haas swung it wide open. In his hand was a stun gun.

36

April 2, 2019
Rio Chama, New Mexico

Myriam had arrived at the shrine a half hour before Ramsey and with a troubled mind. She could not remember a tougher time in her life. There had been the divorce and the trouble at the University of Oregon, but nothing like this. She was feeling sorry for herself when she sat down on one of the benches near the cottonwood tree. The climb had been slow and painful. Her right leg throbbed and she was exhausted. She had wanted to tell Hiram about the diagnosis but was afraid he would abandon her. So much of their life together had been the joyful exploration of the world through long walks.

Three months ago she had been told by her doctor that she had early-stage Parkinson's. No tremors yet, but a weakness in her leg made walking difficult and her balance uncertain. She had come to the shrine to pray, for what exactly she was uncertain. *If only the shrine was as it used to be. If only Adam were still here!*

She sat for a long time with her eyes closed. When she finally opened them she began watching a large group of seniors as they crested the long set of stone steps and now milled about the cottonwood tree. Myriam studied them carefully. She had always feared becoming old and infirm. Now her greatest dread was coming true. She thought about telling them there was no hope for you here anymore. As two old men passed by, one of them exclaimed how his head pain had suddenly disappeared. *Power of positive thinking*, Myriam thought. She watched them descend the long flight of steps to the shrine's parking lot and the bus waiting for them.

Myriam returned to the reason she had come to the Milagro Shrine. She knew she didn't know how to pray. She was open and hoping for answers, for anything. Then, for some inexplicable reason she said to herself, "Fuck it." She let go; she let go of everything. Nothing mattered. She was amazed as she felt herself putting her fate in the hands of some great unknown.

Then she was brought back to reality by a loud female voice. "Myriam!"

Startled, she turned in the direction of the voice. A beautiful young woman stood in front of her. Her skimpy clothing ruffled in the light breeze. Myriam asked, "Who are you?"

"My name is Robin, but you can call me Puck. Father Michael gave me a message for you. Your friend Jonathan Ramsey is in trouble. He needs your help." Pointing toward the bus, the young woman continued, "See him down there?"

Myriam shaded her eyes and made out the familiar gait of her postdoc student, Jonathan Ramsey.

"Hurry, you need to reach him before he gets to the truck," the young woman said with a dramatic flair.

"My leg . . . I can't, why not you?"

"It's not my business anymore. You're wasting time." With that Puck winked at Myriam and bounded off in the direction of the Christ Chapel.

Myriam stood up and took a step, then another. No pain, her balance was good. *Adrenaline*, she thought. But even so, she couldn't stop the heart-felt joy coursing through her. She ran as fast as her 60-year-old legs would take her. Upon reaching the parking lot she stopped. There, unmistakably, was Haas and another large man putting what appeared to be an unconscious Jonathan into their SUV. She yelled, "What are you doing?"

Haas glared at her then turned away. Myriam watched helplessly as they drove off.

37

———————

April 2, 2019
Rio Chama, New Mexico

Ramsey awoke to the smell of new leather inches from his nose. His whole body ached. His brain was fuzzy. He shook his head to clear it and found that was the wrong thing to do. *What happened to me?* All he remembered was a shock tore through his chest and he felt as though he'd been picked up and slammed to the ground.

Bits and pieces of what happened came back to him then. *I was tasered. That's what happened.* His thinking began to clear as his brain's functions seemed to come back on line. The man holding the stun gun was familiar. He'd see the fierce pale-blue eyes when they met two days ago. *It was the South African . . . Haas!*

Slowly Ramsey opened one eye. He stared at the back of black leather seats. Sunlight glinted off a windshield. He heard the dull buzz of tires on concrete reverberating through the seat. Judging by the size of the back seat he figured he was in an SUV. A broad stocky man drove. It wasn't Haas. Then he heard a voice in a language he didn't quite recognize come from the passenger seat.

The big man nodded silently. The car sped up.

He stretched his muscles. Metal cut into his wrists and he realized he was handcuffed. He stifled a moan, not wanting to alert his kidnappers he was awake. He needed time to think. In a rush all the bewildering events at the shrine came back to him. For some unknown reason he settled on the wispy Puck dancing towards Haas and the large man with the gun. He thought she didn't do such a great job taking care of the "bad boys." Ramsey laughed at the absurdity of it all. Of course she wasn't real.

Then he came back to his current predicament. *What does Haas want with me?*

As if hearing his thoughts, the passenger turned toward him. The narrow ascetic face of Pieter Haas smiled at him apologetically. "Sorry about the stun gun. You proved more resourceful than I expected," he said gently.

"Apparently not resourceful enough," said Ramsey ruefully, staring at the taser in Haas's right hand.

The South African's smile widened. "Indeed." Then the man's face grew pensive. "We need to talk."

"You could have just asked."

"I didn't want to risk you saying no and not listening to what I'm about to tell you."

Myriam's first thought was to give chase in her car, but the SUV topped the rise on the narrow dirt road and sped out of sight before she could get her car keys from her purse.

Her next thought was to call 911. Pulling out her phone, her fingers hovered over its contact directory. *What am I going to say to the operator? That a scantily clad Aphrodite-looking woman warned me my friend is being kidnapped?* The absurdity of the situation fell upon her and she would have laughed except for the image of Jonathan's unconscious crumpled body being thrown into the back of the car.

But the situation *was* absurd. A strange woman warned her. Her leg had stopped hurting enabling her to run to the parking lot in time to see two men abduct her former post-graduate student. Confusion threatened to overwhelm her, as it had so often in the past few months as the Parkinson's steadily worsened. But in the next instant, her mind cleared. Her administrator's way of thinking kicked in. First, she needed clarity to deal with this kind of situation. She glanced around the now nearly empty parking lot. Parked beside Hiram's truck was the shrine's van, belonging to Father Michael. *He'll know.*

She strode purposefully towards the Visitor Center when the realization struck her. Her balance was perfect. She was walking pain free! Not in the way that Parkinson's sometimes disappears for a few moments at a time, but in the way of being totally healed. She knew without a doubt the disease would never return.

Her lips turned up in a smile. *After all this time, the miracle I have always been waiting for.* A chill rushed up her spine, bubbling into an ecstatic shout of joy. She heard herself shouting, "Thank you, shrine. . . . Thank you Adam!"

A couple emerging from the Center stared at her at first and then they too smiled, getting caught up in her enthusiasm, the older man proclaiming "Hallelujah!" as they passed. She was grinning widely now, not bothered at all by the idea that moments before she had uttered something that only a few hours ago she would never have imagined herself ever saying.

Just as she pulled on the door to the Visitor Center, a familiar voice seemed to come out of nowhere. "Did I just hear you say, 'thank you Adam?'"

Father Michael emerged from shadows near the entrance, his scarred cheeks rosy with mirth behind his gray beard.

"I did," Myriam said breathlessly. "But I need to speak with you. Something terrible has happened."

"You look like something wonderful just happened—not terrible."

"You're right. Something wonderful happened. I believe my Parkinson's was just cured by the shrine. But at the same time something terrible has happened. My friend, the person we hired to find Adam, Jonathan Ramsey, was just kidnapped right in front of my eyes by the men who want to kidnap Adam."

Father Michael gave Myriam a patronizing look. "Let's discuss the important things first. Tell me about your experience. Some of the seniors in the last group from Phoenix reported miraculous cures and insights. That hasn't happened in months."

Myriam peered at Father Michael as though seeing him for the first time. In that moment a terrifying thought shot through her mind.

Instinctively she clenched her fists and took a step forward. "You know."

"What are you talking about?"

"You know they took Jonathan. You already knew Haas was here, didn't you?"

"There's nothing to worry about. I'll take care of it."

"How?"

"You just experienced a miracle, so trust that. I do." Father Michael touched her arm and she shrugged him off.

He smiled at her. "Trust the miracle you've just had." He inclined his head and walked into the Visitor Center.

Myriam knew she would have to look elsewhere for help.

38

———————

April 2, 2019
Rio Chama, New Mexico

Pieter Haas drummed the fingernails of his left hand on the dash of the SUV. His right hand cradled his phone against his ear. The early afternoon sun blazed overhead and the car's air conditioning unit was at maximum. Still, he could feel the sweat from his armpits trickle down his ribs. He was anxious over his latest decision. He had gone to great lengths to try and salvage what he could of the debacle of finding Adam. Deciding to act boldly, he had kidnapped Jonathan Ramsey.

Now he listened carefully as Greta van Horn laid out the events that had happened with the shrine over the past forty-eight hours. "Lindstrom just reported to me that a weak version of the anomalous field-coherence associated with Adam had occurred in the area of the shrine just two hours ago." Greta paused in her report.

"Is it still there? "Haas asked excitedly.

"It's gone now."

Haas breathed in sharply. He glanced at Ramsey in the back seat. The man was eying him, a neutral expression on his face.

"Pieter, is everything okay?" he heard Greta say.

"Yes, I believe it will be. We'll see you shortly."

"There's one more thing. News reporters are at the hotel. They're asking lots of questions about DeVere and its reasons for being in New Mexico. Is there anything you want me to say?"

Haas thought a moment. The real reason wouldn't do, of course, but DeVere was a diamond company and that provided the perfect cover. "Say nothing overtly but hint at the possibility of a huge diamond discovery."

He ended the call and took a moment to settle his thoughts. He decided his boldness had been the correct move after all. He now figured his last chance to find Adam lay with Jonathan Ramsey and what he had learned of the shrine's groundskeeper in his investigation. Intuition told Haas that Ramsey had discovered some critical piece of the puzzle about Adam's healing power. But how to get the human geographer to reveal what he had learned was another matter. He needed Ramsey on his side, but how could he get him to willingly to join the South Africans and bring Pete Miami in as well?

Taking a thoughtful breath, he turned his attention to Ramsey. The handcuffs had been removed, and when their eyes met, Ramsey smiled. The earlier terrified man seemed transformed to Haas. He was calm, alert almost combative in his demeanor. *It is not going to be easy to win him over*, Haas told himself.

To his many friends Haas was often viewed as a chameleon, able to change his personality at the drop of a hat. It was a trait he'd noticed as a child. He had a special gift for truly understanding what others were saying, not only their words but also their gestures. It was like he could tell what a person wanted before even they knew. This capacity he had used to his advantage in all his business undertakings. Now he would have to put this unique talent to use in a last ditch effort to find the Milagro Shrine's missing caretaker.

Haas began, "I'm very sorry we had to do it this way. Given what you undoubtedly know about me, I felt certain that if I simply asked you to come with me—well, you know your most likely answer."

Acknowledging the truth of Haas' statement, Ramsey replied, "I'm here now. Start by telling me where we're going."

"Back to Taos. Miami's house, the airport, or wherever you want. I'm asking you to hear me out first."

Ramsey smiled. "It's not as if I have a choice."

Haas turned to Goren. "Stop the car." He waited until the mercenary pulled off on the narrow highway, hazard lights flashing. "I'll let you out right now. We're only a couple of miles from Taos. You can make it there easily." He paused. "But I hope you'll decide to listen to what I have to say." He waited. After several seconds, Ramsey nodded. Goren turned the warning flashers off and put the car in gear.

"Let me start by apologizing again," said Haas. "I'm largely responsible for bringing you to the shrine in the first place."

"I thought it was Beecher. Next you'll tell me you're doing all this for my benefit." Ramsey's voice was flat.

"Would that be so hard to believe?" Haas smiled at the surprise splashing across Ramsey's face. "I take it you've learned something about a group known as the New Gnostics?" he continued smoothly. He was pleased to see that Ramsey was interested.

"It's a social media group of people who've been impacted by the healing power of the shrine."

Haas nodded. "It's much greater than that. It's hundreds of communities around the globe, made up, as you mentioned, of people affected by the shrine, living in harmony with the world around them, but more importantly with themselves." He paused again. "I'm one of them."

He watched Ramsey take this in, his mind working, connecting pieces of what must have been a confusing puzzle surrounding the events of the past two weeks, and now fitting them into a larger picture of understanding.

Ramsey's brow furrowed. He asked, "You're not the only one involved in what I have been experiencing . . . all the coincidences . . . am I correct?"

"Malcolm Grossinger, Father Michael, Myriam. You already know about Dr. Orensen." Haas waited, watching Ramsey reflect on this strange turn of events.

Ramsey took a deep breath. "So, my involvement was all one big ruse. But why?"

Ignoring the question, Haas continued, "I want to give you some background so you can put this in context. Two years ago after I was healed at the shrine, I gave a large sum of money to the Friends of the Shrine. I met Myriam and she introduced me to Father Michael. He told me about the New Gnostics and we stayed in touch."

It took all of Ramsey's self-control not to register any surprise. His senses, honed through thousands of human geography interviews, told him Haas was mixing truth with lies. He could have gotten out of the car and walked away, but the man's attempt at candor made Ramsey stay. Somewhere in the tale he was certain lay the means to sort through the fiction if he only stayed patient enough and listened carefully and asked the right questions.

Falling back on his skills as a human geographer and interviewer, he asked, "So you were healed at the shrine two years ago?"

Haas nodded. "Then one day I got an urgent call from Father Michael. He told me that Adam was in danger. We were making plans to protect him when Adam disappeared."

Haas was surprised and pleased at Ramsey's calm acceptance of this story. Oddly, he couldn't tell if Ramsey believed what he was being told or was just going along so they would let him go.

Silence stretched the moment.

Finally Ramsey spoke. "So you weren't responsible for his disappearance?"

"No. At first we thought that a radical religious group, the Brothers of the Lord led by the Reverend Billy Paul, might have killed him. We weren't sure. Malcolm Grossinger suggested I befriend this Reverend Paul, and I did. With some big money and even bigger bold-faced lying I became one of his most trusted confidants."

"You learned they weren't responsible for his disappearance?"

"That's right. Eventually it came to me in a rather bizarre way that I should use Miami's highly developed GIS system for finding kimberlite to look for Adam. I remembered how a paranormal investigatory film crew had discovered some strange biogenic fields around Adam and the shrine." Haas noticed that Ramsey appeared to take particular interest in how the idea came to him. For a second it looked like Ramsey was going ask a question and then dismissed the idea.

Haas continued. "Unfortunately, Pete and I had a strange relationship—even combative at times—especially when I visited him to check on his progress in searching for the kimberlite. It was during one of those trips that, at my sister's urging, I went down to the shrine. I was dying. A month later when I saw my doctor I was nearly cancer-free."

"When was that?" Ramsey asked, now certain that the South African was painting a picture of himself that would seduce Ramsey. *He wants me to believe in him . . . to support him. But why? I need to see where he's going.*

Hass continued. "Two years ago. Anyhow, the next time I saw Pete he was in a good mood. Talkative. Perhaps he picked up on my improved condition. He talked about you, your search for the mystery behind healing places. He told me that you were his only true friend and how you'd grown apart since your experience in Peru. And how that separation had been painful for him." Haas caught a fleeting sense of regret cross Ramsey's features.

"The next time I visited I was hoping for more of the same. Instead, for some reason he was more hostile than ever."

"He can be like that," Ramsey said to keep Haas talking. "So you couldn't go to him directly?"

"I remember what he said about you. Like I said, the idea came to me in a strange way."

"Tell me about that," Ramsey asked.

Haas was surprised by Ramsey's tone and wondered if he should tell Ramsey about the Samburu shaman who had healed his sister in the Danakil Desert. Firmly, he said, "Another time."

Haas waited to see if Ramsey would push the matter further, but he didn't.

"The connection between you, Myriam, Beecher, and the Brothers of the Lord made it all so perfect. Reverend Billy Paul was so obsessed with finding Adam he easily went along with my plan. Through your help, along with Dr. Miami, we were able to locate Adam as I suspect you already know. We didn't know who had him so I had to be prepared for any contingency. Then the damn Mexicans showed up and ruined everything."

Haas stopped. He took sip of water from a plastic container, offered it to Ramsey.

Ramsey shook his head. "So, I was just a pawn," he said, his anger getting the best of him.

"In an odd way just the opposite."

Ramsey's head snapped up. "What do you mean?"

"There's something bigger going on here and I believe you're the only person who can help us find Adam."

Goren turned into the drive for the El Monte Segrado Hotel. He parked in front and turned off the engine. A crowd of people, media, and Sheriff's deputies had gathered outside the lobby entrance.

Haas looked into the rearview mirror, saw Ramsey alert, looking out the window at the crowd. "You ready to come in?" he asked.

39

April 2, 2019
Taos, New Mexico

Ramsey stood less than three feet away from an overweight county sheriff's deputy. The man's face was ruddy from the unusually warm day and sweat trickled from beneath his white hat down his pudgy cheeks. He leaned against his cruiser with a bored expression on his face. Ramsey's immediate impulse was to tell him what just happened.

When the SUV arrived at the lodge, press and television were waiting for the man whose identity had been revealed to be Pieter Haas, CEO of the DeVere Mining Group. Word had spread quickly that the lost hunting party was a ruse. The rumor that spread through the region was that the missing hunting party had been on an expedition to lay claim to a new diamond discovery. The excitement over the possibility had caused such a stir that television crews as far away as Phoenix, Arizona had arrived on the scene. The county sheriff had dispatched four units to control the scene.

Before the media had gathered around the SUV, Haas handed

Ramsey back his phone. "I put my private number in there, you're free to go. Do you need a ride?"

Taking the phone, Ramsey had replied, "No."

He exited the car and walked off as if nothing had happened, stopping briefly at the crowd's edge to look at the mob scene around Haas.

The sheriff deputy looked at Ramsey with curiosity. Smiling, Ramsey shook off the urge to tell the deputy what just happened and walked away. Free of the crowd, he clicked on his phone's cab app. Victory Royal Express was the first listing in Taos. *I'm far from victory,* thought Ramsey, gingerly rubbing his chest where Haas tasered him.

Five minutes later he was on his way to the airport to catch a commuter to Albuquerque and then a late-night flight to Chicago. It would be expensive but a limousine would be waiting to drive him back to Grinnell. Ramsey needed desperately to ground himself in the mundane world of human geography that up until two weeks ago had been his entire life.

Once in the privacy of the cab, he opened up his text message threads on this phone. Haas had used it send to send a message in Ramsey's name to Myriam. "I collapsed from the heat and exhaustion. Haas took me to the emergency clinic in Taos. All okay now. Truck key under the seat."

Myriam had replied, "Call me."

Right now he was too tired to call Myriam. He needed to be home and settled.

40

____

April 3, 2019
Grinnell, Iowa

Disoriented from having slept in his disheveled clothes from the previous day, Ramsey opened his eyes and saw slivers of bright light cutting across his bedroom wall. He reached for his phone. The time read 11:12am. Arriving around four in the morning, he had fallen into his bed. The trip home from Taos, New Mexico was exceptional by its uneventfulness: no visions, no coincidences, no mercurial women, and no one kidnapping him. It gave Ramsey time to think about what to do next. One train of thought told him to drop the whole Adam pursuit, forget about what happened the past week, return to life as it was before. He argued to himself that contrary to what Haas had said, there was nothing special about himself, nothing he could do to help find Adam—even if he wanted to. His job was done. The mystery of the shrine's healing power was resolved. Adam was a one-time anomaly whose power would vanish like the morning fog when he passed. On the other hand, the real mystery was the truth about his own role in the events of the past two weeks. This was totally unclear and he felt the strong need for answers.

As he walked to his bathroom he recalled that before he fell asleep he had decided to take one more step. Since he needed to retrieve his car at the Des Moines airport, he would try to get some answers from Malcolm Grossinger. But first he had some unfinished business. Cleaning out the pockets of his pants, he found the key to Myriam's truck.

Once Ramsey got some food and coffee he called her. She didn't pick up so he left a message saying Haas had sent the text about collapsing from heat and exhaustion and she should call him back as soon as possible. Within minutes a relieved Myriam responded.

"You're safe?"

"At home in Grinnell."

"That's a relief. When I saw Haas putting you into his car, I thought for sure he was kidnapping you."

"In a way he was. He wanted to talk to me about Adam. Wants me to help find him."

"Will you?" she asked.

Ramsey heard the hint of desperation in her tone. But he couldn't be sure if it was for finding Adam or keeping the shrine's caretaker out of the clutches of the South Africans. He decided he could ease her fears either way. "I'm through with that. Adam's alive and I wish him an obscure life away from South Africans and anyone else trying to exploit his powers."

Myriam said, "I understand. I'm just glad you're all right. I feel so responsible."

"No worries," Ramsey said in a comforting tone. "Like me, you appear to have been a pawn in some grand scheme by Haas and his Brothers of the Lord buddies to find Adam. In many ways my part in the whole business, my whole involvement in the way it went down, doesn't make much sense to me."

There was a pause and then Myriam said, "At the time it all seemed simple and clear what I had to do, but I see what you mean. I have to tell you something. I suspect you noticed the tremor in my leg."

"I could see you were trying to hide it. Parkinson's?"

"Yes. Yesterday something remarkable occurred at the shrine when a young woman told me you were in trouble. I suddenly found I had regained my balance and strength and was able to run down the hill to the parking lot. Unfortunately not in time to help you, but the Parkinson's is gone. In fact, yesterday afternoon at the shrine was like before Adam disappeared. Many healings and realizations were reported."

"Interesting. I'm very happy for you," Ramsey said.

"Those healings and my own healing raise interesting questions, don't they?

"Perhaps. Is it still happening today?"

"I don't know. I haven't been there yet."

"So what's your next step?"

"Hiram's on his way here. We'll see. By the way, I have another key. Keep the one you have just in case you come back."

"You need to work it out with Hiram," Ramsey said.

"I know."

"I have to run. Take care." Ramsey wondered for a moment what the return yesterday of the Milagro Shrine's healing power meant. He thought about calling Myriam back and asking her to check. Was it just another anomaly in a world full of anomalies? He shook his head. *Remember, you're letting all that go old buddy, after you speak with Grossinger.*

Next Ramsey called Pete, deciding not to tell about his abduction. They arranged for Pete to send Ramsey's stuff he left in the cabin back to Grinnell.

Then Ramsey made the most important call of all. He wasn't surprised when Grossinger agreed to meet him on such short notice. Once again they decided to meet at Adam's old apartment.

Ramsey arranged for one of his new employees to drive him to the Des Moines airport. The drive turned out to be highly productive. The young man was able to bring Ramsey up to speed on the company projects—particularly the upcoming visit to Blue Island, Illinois, on behalf of one of the company's urban clients. Ramsey also took care of a number of calls and emails.

Normality felt good.

41

April 3, 2019
Seattle, Washington

In many ways, Alex Moore was the spitting image of his uncle. Like Adam, he was tall, large-boned, and muscular—but instead of red hair he had long, jet-black, dreadlock extensions.

He gently closed the massive door of the isolation chamber. It was designed for PSI experiments by one of the world's leading paranormal investigators, Patrick Rhodes. Its two-foot-thick lead walls were impervious to all known electromagnetic radiation, sound, and bioenergetic fields.

To an outside observer Alex could be described as possessing the sort of presence that would draw the attention of every person in a crowd. He briefly scanned the empty room that acted as a gateway to the chamber, and then opened the second door.

Looking out the window with his feet up on the desk was a bespectacled young man dressed in a t-shirt, faded blue jeans, and sneakers. A mop of brown hair stuck out in all directions. He had a two-day growth of beard that covered his narrow face in dark brown patches.

Alex said, "Not long now."

Rhodes looked away from the window and the rain clouds enveloping Seattle's downtown landscape. He pushed horn-rimmed glasses up his long nose. "Can I go in the chamber?" He asked with reverence in his voice.

"Of course." Alex smiled. "I'm going for some coffee."

42

———————

April 3, 2019
Rio Chama, New Mexico

Myriam once again sat on her favorite bench that allowed visitors to gaze upon the shrine's venerable cottonwood tree. The catkins had dried up and the majestic old tree's spray of new green leaves glistened in the sun. She took a deep breath and let it out, but it did not release the anxiety that held her body tense against the chill spring wind. As she began to shiver, Myriam thought to herself, *Shivering but not trembling. What a relief.*

Then she saw him. He thrust his hand in the air signaling he saw her. He stopped, waiting. The anxiety disappeared and Myriam vigorously waved back. With that Beecher strode quickly up the rest of the slight rise toward her.

As he got closer, Myriam could see the openhearted smile of her lover. It was all she needed. She raced to the man she held so dear for so long and fell gently into his embracing arms.

At first nothing was said, each content to savor the touch of the other as they walked towards the small Christ Chapel. The breeze died and the morning sun felt like a blanket engulfing them in radiant, loving warmth.

Finally Beecher spoke. "Your Parkinson's, it's gone?"

Myriam was surprised. "I didn't think you knew."

"I could see what was happening and I researched the symptoms."

"I didn't want to tell you. I thought you would turn away."

Beecher looked her in the eyes. "I wouldn't have. And I won't now if you'll let me stay."

"Hiram," she said as tears filled her eyes. They walked on.

Finally Myriam said, "It went away! The only way I can explain it is that I was healed by the shrine two days ago. I'm fine. Miraculously, everything is normal now."

When they reached the Christ Chapel, Myriam told Hiram the whole story of Ramsey's abduction by Haas, Father Michael's complicity, and Ramsey's safe return to Grinnell. She ended the story by saying, "Jonathan's done with the whole matter. He's really pissed that everybody played him. He had no idea why Haas was so convinced he could find Adam. But none of that matters." She twined her fingers in Beecher's. "Are we together?"

"We are," Beecher replied lovingly.

Myriam's mood changed and she asked anxiously, "Are you worried about Haas and Brother Paul?"

Beecher shook his head and took her in his strong arms. "I was a pawn too. They don't need me anymore, so they'll leave us alone."

Myriam hugged him fiercely, glad they were safe. "So what should we do?"

Beecher looked down at his feet. Shame threatened to overwhelm him. But he knew he had to tell Myriam everything. He took a deep breath. "I need to tell you something. It may change how you feel about me."

Myriam hid her anxiety and desperately hoped what he was about to confess wouldn't change their lives or her commitment to the man she loved. It was strange feeling this way when only two days earlier, she had been so angry she contemplated leaving him.

"I had a strange experience when I met Conklin in Austin in December last year," Beecher began. For the next ten minutes he laid out his encounter at Oilcan Harry's with the transvestite. He finished and waited for Myriam to say something.

Myriam rocked back on her heels. The story was hard to believe yet there was something in his contrite expression that indicated he was telling the truth. It was as though he had been transformed or some heavy weight had been lifted from his shoulders.

"Hiram, why didn't you tell me earlier?" she said softly.

"He shook his head. "Fear, maybe. . . . No, it wasn't only that. I was also ashamed of my life in the Brothers of the Lord. I saw that I had acted in a non-Christian manner, I suppose, but more so, I had acted without love for a fellow human being."

He looked at her with tears in his eyes. "I guess I'm asking for forgiveness for many sins."

Myriam felt the knot in her stomach slowly release. She saw in front of her a changed man but a man who could still be her friend and lover. "Truly you can only forgive yourself, love," she heard herself say, but she also knew she had to forgive him herself or their relationship might not survive his confession. "I understand," she said with compassion.

He closed his eyes and she saw the worry drain out of him. "Thank you," he answered. But there was one more thing Beecher knew he had to tell Myriam. "There's something else, but it's more of a question than divulging a sin. When I confronted Conklin yesterday, asking him one more time which side he was on ... why he was doing what he did, he told me he was in love with me. Said he had felt it since the first day he set eyes on me."

All the while Beecher had been telling his story about Oilcan Harry's, Myriam had listened intently holding back any judgment. She took a deep breath and said as matter-of-factly as she could, "Hiram, what did you say to him?"

"I told him that nothing like he wanted was possible between us."

"And how did Conklin take it?"

Beecher shrugged. "Said he understood."

She saw he was still holding something back and gently prodded him to tell her everything. "And?"

"I wanted to say we could still be friends, but the words never came out of my mouth. I'm wondering if I did the right thing?"

Myriam stood on her tiptoes and kissed him on the cheek. "There's plenty of time to answer that question, love."

"How did I get to deserve such a beautiful wonderful woman as you?" Beecher asked cradling her lovingly in his arms. "Let's go home."

Myriam smiled. "Let's go home."

43

April 4, 2019
Rio Chama, New Mexico

After a glorious night, Hiram and Myriam found themselves relaxing around her breakfast table.

Myriam said, "I had a revelation last night. Something came to me in my sleep. It was like a dream, only more intense—as though it were really happening."

She took a deep breath, ready for Beecher to laugh at her, but the big man put down his coffee and leaned across the table taking her hand in his broad fingers. "Tell me about it."

"A coyote came to me and began speaking. He asked me, 'Why are you crying, little one?' I told him, 'Because I was leaving New Mexico in the morning.' He laughed gently and shook his head. 'The shrine needs a new caretaker.' He gave me a catkin like ones from the cottonwood tree." Myriam opened up her left hand. In it was a dried spike from the cottonwood. "I found this on the dresser this morning."

She paused, then said shyly, "I want to keep the shrine going." She waited for Beecher to say something.

The big man nodded his head slowly and said, "Agreed.

"You're so agreeable."

"It's my penance."

Myriam reached over and placed her other hand in his. "I love you so much."

44

April 4, 2019
Des Moines, Iowa

Ramsey parked on the capital grounds and studied the new urban architecture that seemed to float along the Des Moines River. He shook his head at the nearness of the development to the river. Heavy spring rains coupled with snowmelt had brought the river up and out of its banks. A surprising warm front had extended from the Rockies into Minnesota and was going to increase the flood danger. These buildings would be flooded unless city crews sandbagged the entire area. That was a stopgap measure at best. Next year if the city accepted his firm's watershed recommendations for the capital, they would build retaining walls to keep back the floodwaters. But the new design would spoil views and playgrounds. It was a win/lose situation unless he could find a way to make the new area special for everyone.

Every bridge needs to be crossed in its time, he thought. He started the car and pulled into the street heading for the Grossinger Lofts. For a moment he thought about calling Grossinger and saying he couldn't make the meeting. Ever since he decided to confront Adam's friend, he had been indecisive about what approach to take. That indecision had led to hesitation and waiting. He looked at his watch. He was almost late. Then it came to him.

As Ramsey walked down the hall he could see that the door to Adam's condo was slightly ajar. Carefully he pushed it open. "Hello," he called out.

"Come in," Grossinger said quietly.

Sitting in the large leather chair, Grossinger gestured for Ramsey to sit in the chair next to the computer table. To Ramsey, the older man seemed to have aged. His countenance was almost grandfatherly.

"What have you found out about Adam?" he asked.

Ramsey's plan was to go right to the heart of the matter. "You lied to me last week."

"What do you mean?" Grossinger seemed genuinely surprised.

"You knew all along Adam was alive. You and Pieter Haas cooked up this convoluted scheme to involve me in a search for his whereabouts."

Grossinger stood up. "I don't know any Pieter Haas. Are you crazy?" he said with a tinge of anger.

"You're denying you're a Gnostic?"

Grossinger turned away from Ramsey and walked over to the window. Tapping his finger on the sill, he turned abruptly back towards Ramsey. His anger had subsided "Okay, calm down and tell me what this is about."

Taking Grossinger's cue, Ramsey said calmly, "I was told you are a high level member of the New Gnostics, a global group of people who have been affected by the Rio Chama Shrine and Adam's healing powers."

"I can tell you truthfully I'm not a member of any such group." Moving ever closer to Ramsey, he added, "What did you say about Adam's healing power just now?"

Ramsey was confused. "Don't you know Adam was the source of the shrine's healing power?"

Grossinger appeared to Ramsey to be struggling with how to answer. Finally he nodded. "Adam figured it out eventually. Before I say more I need you to tell me what's going on."

Ramsey decided he had nothing to lose and told him about the strange sequence of events. Grossinger listened intently without asking any questions and when it was over said, "That's quite a story. But the part about my involvement is not true. The conversation in the airport was just a coincidence. I was talking with my wife about Adam."

As Ramsey was about to reply, Grossinger's phone buzzed. "I need to take this," he said, and walked into the bedroom, closing the door.

The call seemed to be taking forever. Eventually Ramsey noticed a photo album just to the right of the computer. He started thumbing through it. It was all pictures of Adam playing chess with different people. Above each opponent was a large black "W" or "L." Halfway through the album he was stopped cold. There was a picture of himself across from Adam. Above Ramsey's head was an "L." Later he would recall that the album wasn't there the last time he was in the condo and vaguely remembered during his college days playing an amateur chess competition at Des Moines' Drake University.

45

April 6, 2019
Grinnell, Iowa

Four days after returning from New Mexico, Ramsey's experiences and revelations about Adam Gwillt being the source of the healing power of the shrine were becoming more unreal and even improbable. Rather than clarifying his long search to understand the geographical power behind sacred places, the New Mexico adventure—as he was coming to think of it—had only muddied the water.

Rather than confronting his old mentor Roger Orensen, as he had planned to do right after returning from his confrontation with Grossinger, Ramsey decided to concentrate on his work. A project his company had been working on for over a year was coming to a critical point. It involved a trip to Blue Island, Illinois, a nearly all-black suburb of South Chicago. It was described in geographical literature as a social and food desert.

For months Ramsey's partner, Ron Grange, had worked to convince the Philip Thornton Foundation to partner with some Blue Island community members to create a pilot project for rehabilitating the beleaguered town. Grange had convinced Illinois' junior U.S. Senator that his company's geographical perspective would bring remedies to the problems where others had failed. Success would be a feather in the Senator's cap if he got behind it. The result was that state troopers would accompany Ramsey and Grange on a tour of the beleaguered city.

Over the last few days Ramsey had worked feverishly to bring himself up to speed on Blue Island. He only traveled from his house to his office, sometimes sleeping overnight there. New Mexico and Adam Gwillt receded from his mind.

The day before the planned visit, Ramsey met his partner at the Marriott Inn's four-star restaurant for dinner and to go over their plans for the visit.

At dinner Ramsey asked, "Who's meeting us?"

Grange replied, "Janet Furlong from the Philip Thornton Foundation. She worked with us on the low-income co-op deal in East Lansing three years ago. The Illinois Highway Patrol has assigned two state troopers to drive us around. We'll be met on site by Reverend Small from the city's largest Baptist church. He's the most highly respected man in town."

"Will we get to speak to the residents?"

Grange paused, a piece of apple pie teetering precariously on his fork. "I am told it might not be safe."

Ramsey pursed his lips. "We need to learn how the people of Blue Island see the world."

"You're right," Grange agreed. He washed down the pie with a swallow of coffee. "I'll have the reverend set up a meeting at his church. That should be safe."

Ramsey looked at his partner in a renewed sense of how brilliant Grange was at establishing a baseline of community-shared values that form the nexus for understanding family structure, neighborhoods, law enforcement, and social services—and their relation to the state and federal governments.

"Ron, I don't think I've told you enough how much I appreciate your genius for understanding and bringing sensitivity to how geographically isolated groups are trapped by their mental boundaries."

Grange gave a thumbs up in appreciation. "It only works because of your capacity to see how a place restricts opportunity or empowers people to escape those mental boundaries."

"We're a good team."

"Indeed." Grange set his fork down. His eyes narrowed slightly. "I see by our bank account that you completed the New Mexico project. Did you find what you were looking for?"

Ramsey thought to himself that Beecher had paid up just like he said he would. "It's a long weird story I'm still digesting. On the bright side I got to spend time with Pete Miami."

Grange chuckled. "Bet that was weirdly interesting."

"Lately that seems to be the way everything's going." Ramsey took the first bite of his dessert—New York cheesecake drizzled with an apricot brandy sauce. It was exceptionally good.

46

———————

April 7, 2019
Blue Island, Illinois

A gunshot rang out. Everyone in the lead state patrol car was startled. A second shot. The officer driving slammed on the brakes. The state highway patrol car skidded on the damp pavement and came to a halt in front of an old factory, its windows blown out and its faded red brick crumbling.

Through the patrol car's rain-spotted front windshield Ramsey and Grange watched a teenage black male stumble in front of an abandoned van and fall to his knees. The driver flipped on the cruiser's lights. "Welcome to Blue Island, murder capitol of Illinois, gentlemen," the driver said drily.

"Aren't you going to help him?" asked Ramsey.

"Not our jurisdiction. Besides it's a prime place for an ambush." The driver scanned the surrounding buildings warily. He keyed his vest mic and said, "Unknown black male, possibly armed, at the old brick factory on Kedzie Avenue. Advise caution."

As if overhearing his warning, the officers of the second patrol car, which had taken point, did not get out.

In less than two minutes two Blue Island police cars arrived at the scene, sirens blaring. Four officers, guns drawn, stepped out of their vehicles. They were aimed at the teen who had one hand wedged inside his coat.

"What're they doing? Can't they see the boy's hurt?" Ramsey asked the driver.

"They're protecting themselves. Stay in the car and let the police handle it," the State Patrol officer said.

Ramsey saw the policemen advance on the youth. Something didn't look right. His hand went to the door.

Grange put a hand on his arm. "What the hell are you doing?"

Ramsey shook him off. "They're reading this all wrong. The kid's not a danger ... he's in danger."

Ramsey leapt out of the patrol car and ran toward the slumping teen. One of the Blue Island officers yelled, "Get out of the way! He has a gun."

Ignoring the officer's command, Ramsey leaned down and steadied the teen. The boy looked up into his face. Tears streamed down his cheeks and his mouth was twisted in abject terror like Ramsey had never seen before. The teen's hand slowly began moving out from inside his jacket. The police sighted their guns. Ramsey shielded the boy.

When the hand came free the boy looked at bloody fingers and said, "I've been shot." He passed out and slumped against Ramsey's chest.

Reverend Small left the second state patrol car and knelt down beside Ramsey. "The ambulance has been called. I'll wait with him," he said with compassion and concern. Ramsey stood up. The rain had stopped and a light mist covered the ground. The shooting of the young black must have affected Ramsey's senses because everything around him seemed intense. He turned slowly, seeing the street scene more clearly than before—broken beer and whiskey bottles, dilapidated buildings, sidewalks strewn with filth, homeless sleeping in doorways. The van wasn't just abandoned, it had been jacked, it's tires gone, engine removed, windows smashed. He took a deep breath and the rancid odor of rotting garbage forced him to blink back tears.

It was eerily quiet now that the sirens had been turned off.. Ramsey broke the silence. "He must be somebody's son. Why isn't anybody coming?"

"There is no trust ... no trust in God ... no trust at all," the Reverend said.

A new siren was heard approaching in the distance. Ramsey waited until the ambulance arrived and then walked over to Grange. People from the neighborhood now ringed the crime scene. They watched. Several had their phones out, videoing the action. No one approached. As the ambulance sped off, Grange shook his head. "This isn't good."

Nodding, Ramsey said, "The boy couldn't have been older than thirteen or fourteen. He was terrified."

"Of what?"

"Me."

Grange pivoted on his heels. Yellow police crime-scene tape had just gone up. Beyond that a sea of black faces peered at them. He scratched his beard. "I don't know Jonathan. None of these folks look afraid to me. Angry maybe."

Ramsey wiped the blood on his hands across his jacket. " Obviously the police reaction to the shooting must be the norm here."

"So, what do you want to do?"

Ramsey pointed his chin at a group of black kids hanging apart from the crowd. "See those kids there by the canal? I'm going to go talk to them."

"Probably a gang. Might run. Might shoot you."

Curiously, Ramsey didn't have any fear. Not because he thought they couldn't be dangerous but because he sensed a wary curiosity coming from them as if they were waiting to see what was going down. He shrugged. "Let's see what happens." He started toward what he estimated to be a group of about ten black teens. The closer he got, the stronger the stench from the nearby canal. This waterway, known as the Calumet Sag Channel, had been constructed about one-hundred years ago to carry sewage and industrial waste away from Lake Michigan. Today the man-made canal was one of the country's most polluted bodies of water.

The boys did not run. As Ramsey came up to them, the tallest one stepped forward and demanded, "Who the fuck are you, dog?"

Ramsey looked at him. The way the rest of the gang held back in a kind of triangle formation, he surmised the teenager was the leader. "I'm Jonathan Ramsey. Do any of you know the MLK Baptist Church on State Street?" No answer. "Can you take me there?"

"Why?" asked the leader.

"I want to walk there and I need to be safe."

"Just go with your white killer cops," one of the younger members shouted.

Most of the others mumbled in agreement, but one them stood on tiptoe beside the leader and whispered something in his ear. Ramsey started in surprise as he realized the gang member was a girl. An older teen to be more accurate. She had close-cropped red dyed hair, strange blue eyes, a straight Roman nose and a generous mouth.

When she finished talking, the leader looked at her and said, "For real?"

She nodded.

"You stopped those po-pos from shooting Leonardo?" asked the leader, his voice less defiant than before.

Ramsey nodded.

The young black teen smiled. "Will you pay us?"

"I'll give you a hundred bucks now and another hundred when we get there."

"You're one fucked up white boy," chimed in a voice from the back.

Murmurs of assent rolled through the group.

Ramsey pulled out two $50 bills, handed them to the leader. "I'd like to talk along the way." He started walking, the black teens filled in around him. Pointing to the canal he said, "Does it always smell this bad?"

"This isn't bad. You should be here when it's hot." Gang members made choking and coughing sounds, amusing themselves.

Ramsey said "So, which way?"

They walked in silence for three blocks. Finally the leader stopped and pointed back at the crime scene. "Don't you want to know about Leonardo?

"Was he one of yours?"

"Is he gonna die? "

"I don't think so."

"It was a mistake."

"It could have been you."

"The dog's right," said a member of the gang. "We all gonna to die here."

"Maybe not. How many of you would like to get out of here?" Ramsey asked.

The smallest member snorted. "Nobody ever gets out."

Another added, "Except the dead."

Suddenly Ramsey shouted, "Man, what's wrong with you? You're the ones that are fucked up. Don't trust anybody."

The small teen pulled out a gun and waved it around. "Man, here you trust one thing ... Beretta."

Ramsey glanced at the state patrol cars that had been tracking him and the gang as they walked. One look at the pistol, and the lead car veered suddenly toward the group. Ramsey watched Grange vigorously telling the driver to back off. When the car pulled away, he started walking again.

"You believe you have a flaw, like something went wrong. Is that right?" said Ramsey.

The tall gang leader, satisfied there was no immediate danger, said in an angry voice, I've always known that I'm wrong, I shouldn't be here. But I am . . . wrong wrong wrong. I'm always wrong . . . just wrong."

Others nodded angrily in agreement. "Everyone says we're no good."

"There's something wrong with us when we were born and nobody can fix it."

Ramsey gestured at the police cars. "Do you think those men believe that?"

The leader answered immediately. "They know it. We're no good. Don't count."

"Like we're born no good," added the other one.

"That's what I mean."

"What do you believe, whitey?" asked the young woman. So far she had stayed out of the conversation and now was saying something important. The others quieted down when she spoke.

"You're speaking crap," said Ramsey. He jerked a thumb dismissively at the patrol cars. "Those cops, the other whiteys, they also believe they were born no good."

"Bullshit!" said the leader.

"It's true," Ramsey said, now softening his voice.

The young men eyed him. The whipsaw tones of his voice had captured their attention. Out of the corner of his eye, he saw the young woman's eyes size him up shrewdly before nodding and he knew she was the real brains behind this gang. Part of him wondered why a young black woman with her acumen would be caught up with a bunch of street thugs like these guys. She obviously wasn't a gangbanger. But he had to stay focused on the unfolding situation and the plan that had blossomed in his mind when the shot teen was taken away.

"We all think it down deep in places we don't let others see." His gaze swept the group and judged now was the moment to strike. "Whitey is just as much a slave as you."

"I ain't no slave!" yelled the leader.

"Quiet, Slim," said the young girl. "Tell us what you mean by that."

"Anyone's a slave as long they are too frightened to change themselves and the world around them."

"I'm not afraid of anyone!" cried the small teen and waved the gun around.

The girl swatted his hand down. "Put that gun away or I'll take it from you."

The kid glared at her but did as he was told. "Go on," she said to Ramsey.

"You think that by being *wrong* you're different. Those whitey are the same. The only difference is they, me, trust more people, trust a system to protect them, and maybe trust a higher power."

Ramsey saw something shift in the group's mindset. Pointing to the gun, he said, "If you're going to shoot me, let's go to the church first."

The young woman put her hand on the black teen's arm. Gently, she took the gun, tucked it in the back of her jeans, and walked up to Ramsey. She said in an almost mocking angelic voice, "My name's Magdiel King. People around here call me Maggie. What's yours?"

47

April 7, 2019
Blue Island, Illinois

"So what did we learn?" Grange asked Ramsey in the patrol car after the church meeting ended. It was early evening and the sun hung over the western edge of Blue Island like a searchlight laying bare the city's ruined landscape.

The meeting at the church had not gone well. The middle-aged and elderly people who came were filled with confusion and anger. They had watched their community dissolve into chaos over the past thirty years until the last shreds of hope and purpose had been wrung out of it.

While the rest of Ramsey's group piled into their escort patrol cars in front of the Baptist Church, he pulled the Thornton Foundation representative Janet Furlong aside. The concern on her face for the lackluster meeting was clear enough to see. He smiled at her and said, "A set of recommendations from us will be coming to you next week."

"Now I'll tell you a joke," Janet said.

"Seriously, together we can turn this around."

"That building on the corner where that kid was shot," she said, pointing at the burned-out structure with no intact windows. "Thirty years ago it was a warehouse. A hundred and fifty people worked there. Now it's a crackhouse where people from all over the city come to get high. On any day of the week it has more attendees than Reverend Small's church."

"That abandoned warehouse would be the perfect place to start," Ramsey said quietly.

She snorted. "Face it, Jonathan. There's nothing to build on here."

He shook his head. "Give me six months, Janet, and I'll prove to you this is the place for your foundation's money."

"Six months or six years, no amount of money is going to make a difference here."

"Six months," Jonathan insisted. "Six months and Blue Island will be a spotlight city for every rundown community in America. "

She eyed him skeptically. "I don't know, Jonathan. You're asking the Thornton Foundation to shell out a lot of money on a leap of faith."

"Put two-hundred thousand to start in a nonprofit Blue Island community fund that my company will set up."

Furlong tapped her front teeth with a long turquoise fingernail. "Three months," she countered. "If nothing happens that's it."

"Deal."

They shook hands.

Ramsey settled into the state patrol car for the long ride back to the hotel. As the car rolled along the deserted streets, he pondered Grange's question—"What did we learn today?" He reran in his mind what had transpired over the last twelve hours.

From a geographical perspective the town was devoid of cultural features and resources. The gathering at the church echoed the gang's worldview. Most were angry men and women with little understanding of why they were economically left behind in a country filled with opportunities. But what really had bothered every one of them was why nobody cared. At one point a chant—"We are people too!"—reverberated through the run-down building for over three minutes. Ramsey's body still shivered from the power of their unified voices.

The patrol car pulled up in front of their hotel. Surprisingly the officer, who had said nothing up to that point, turned to Ramsey and asked sharply, "What's your answer to your buddy's question?"

Before Ramsey could answer, the officer's cell phone lit up. He listened for a couple of minutes. Turning back toward Ramsey, he said in a sarcastic voice, "You're gonna like this. The kid who was shot died twice on his way to the hospital but the paramedic was able to bring him back. He's going to be all right. And here's another strange thing. The paramedic wasn't the usual guy for that shift. No one knows who he is and now he's disappeared." He laughed harshly. "Dumb luck."

"Sometimes that's what's needed," Ramsey said. He paused, then said to Grange, "I know what we're going to do. The people of Blue Island are going to build a sacred place where this kid was shot."

48

———————

April 8, 2019
Chicago, Illinois

Ramsey woke up with a start. He was wide awake. He looked at his watch and saw it was 3:10 in the morning. Ideas about what to do with Blue Island rushed into his consciousness. For the next hour he typed feverishly. When he was done he put it in an email and sent it to Grange. Then he sent a phone text telling him to check his email. As quickly as Ramsey awoke he fell back asleep.

Before the first light spread through Chicago's Eastern shore suburbs, Grange had gone to the hotel's business center and printed out Ramsey's recommendations. He read them as he downed three cups of coffee. He highlighted the ones he thought most important:

- Establish a local bank for and run by the people of Blue Island
- Provide educational scholarships controlled by the people of Blue Island

- Create a large fund to incentivize local businesses
- Enforce laws against the upstream polluters of the canal
- Provide internships for Blue Island residents of all ages to join the staffs of representatives of the city and county government, their state-legislature representative, and the Illinois senators.

But an additional one that really caught Grange's attention was to start a series of talent fairs where residents of Blue Island could demonstrate their skills and talents, after which a blue-ribbon panel would find buddies with similar talents in thriving communities and businesses across the country, like the old pen-pal system. If someone demonstrated exceptional computer skills, for example, that person would be paired with somebody from Silicon Valley who would help the resident develop their abilities and contacts.

Grange looked up from his musing and was surprised to see Ramsey sitting across from him at the breakfast table. "These are good," he said.

"They came to me in one of those information dumps in the middle of the night."

"I really like this one." Grange pointed to the buddy system paragraph.

Ramsey was pleased with Grange's grasping the most important point. "It gets at the crux of Blue Island's problem. As Albert Einstein said, 'Problems cannot be solved with the same mind set that created them.'"

Grange replied, "I get it. By always focusing on trying to fix what's wrong, nothing ever moves forward. It's what I call the liberals' blind spot. And then there's the old conservative bullshit that these people are unfixable and it's their own damn fault."

Ramsey nodded in agreement. "I don't know why I didn't see this before." He paused for a thoughtful moment. "Maybe it's the Milagro Shrine's power working through me?"

"What?"

"I'll tell you later. It's so clear to me that people need to shift away from concentrating on fixing their flaws and instead focus on developing new strengths. It's so simple."

"Simple, but hard to do."

"It shouldn't be. That's when it came to me."

"Okay. Go on."

"What's missing are social fields, shared spiritual values that can hold a space for positive development."

Grange's eyes narrowed. "How you gonna make that happen? Have Jesus appear?"

Ramsey leaned back with a wry smile on his lips. "Something like that."

Grange's mouth formed a little "o." Ramsey leaned back in his chair and waited. One thing about his partner, the man never belittled an idea. He always listened, took it in, turned it over, and more often than not added something to it that made it better than the original. This time was no different.

Grange nodded, a smile crossing his broad face. "I see where you're going. The place where the kid was shot. Turn it into a sacred place, right?"

"Bingo."

"You'll need a buy in from the community and I don't mean the elders. Those gang kids would be perfect. Do you have an idea how to get them on board?"

"I'll take a couple of them down to Rio Chama, New Mexico. The young woman Maggie would be perfect."

Ron nodded thoughtfully. "That shrine ... it turned out to be something a lot different than you thought it was going to be, huh?'

"It's not just a place for healing. It's ... it's transformative." A frown came over Ramsey's face.

Grange noticed. "What's the matter?"

"Still missing an important piece of what's going on there. And I just realized, I've been missing it since the day I got interested in sacred places."

49

———

April 10, 2019
Grinnell, Iowa

It had been two days since Ramsey returned from Blue Island. During each of those days his thoughts hovered around his experiences at Rio Chama and the fate of Adam. The shrine was calling him back figuratively and literally. Before he did anything, though, he had one thing to do first. He drew in a sharp breath. He wasn't looking forward to it, but he had to find out something crucial from his mentor Orensen.

It was Saturday morning. Ramsey set his Earl Grey tea aside and turned on his computer. Bringing up the Grinnell college athletic departments webpage, he checked the listings of events. Grinnell was hosting the final men's swim meet of the season against archrival Carleton College. Ramsey knew Roger Orensen would be there. The professor emeritus religiously attended every meet as the psychological and spiritual coach for the athletes.

Ramsey arrived at the natatorium halfway through the meet. The air inside was humid and hot and smelled heavily of chlorine. Spectators occupied bleachers along the far wall beneath a banner proclaiming "Go Grinnell Pioneers." The two swimming teams clustered at the far end of the pool on either side of twin diving boards.

The room was deathly quiet and Ramsey wondered if some athlete had been injured. Then he saw that the diving competition was in full swing with the audience silently watching every performer and politely clapping at the end of each dive.

Ramsey looked for Orensen in his usual spot on the Pioneers' bench beside the head coach. He started in surprise. The space was empty. He scanned the crowd and saw Orensen talking to middle-aged woman. Pointing to the next diver, she bowed her head and Ramsey could see her body shake in silent sobs. Orensen bent beside her and whispered in her ear. The woman suddenly stopped crying and wiping her tears away watched the young man stepping out onto the end of the diving board. She waved. He smiled and then turned around, his body rigid in concentration as he prepared for his next dive.

Orensen leaned back against the bleacher behind him. As he did, a different woman came into view on his other side. Ramsey strained to make her out. There was something about her that was deeply familiar. A chill ran through his body. It was Paige. At that moment Orensen spotted Ramsey and gestured for him to come over.

50

April 10, 2019
Rio Chama, New Mexico

Myriam got up, confrontation burning on her mind. For the past few days she and Hiram, using his connections, had looked deeply into the shrine's ownership and finances. To their surprise they uncovered that the board controlling the Friends of Rio de Milagro Shrine turned out to be a sham. The ownership of the property had been transferred four years earlier to a holding company in South Africa. The agent for the holding company was Raphael Núnez. A bank in Santa Fe had set up a trust to operate the finances of the shrine while maintaining the appearance of a nonprofit organization.

Myriam felt particularly humiliated and angry. She sat on the board and a year ago she had convinced Hiram to ask for a seat as well.

A board meeting was planned for 5 o'clock this afternoon. Raphael Núnez would be there, and so would Father Michael. Both men would have to answer some questions. But before that, Myriam and Hiram needed to do something important. It was Rosa's last day at the Rio Chama Café.

Myriam and Hiram pulled up to the Café. Their usual parking place as well as two others on either side of it had been taken over by an early model Winnebago painted green, yellow, and red. They had to find a spot down the street in front of the hotel.

The restaurant was decked out for a party. Rosa's cousin and his wife and their children and about thirty other family members Myriam didn't recognize swarmed to greet them.

"Thank you for coming," Rosa said, hugging Myriam. "I was afraid you wouldn't be able to make it."

"Almost didn't. Had to park way down the street," said Hiram. He hooked a thumb at the Winnebago. "Whose heap of junk is that anyway?"

Rosa reddened slightly. A booming voice from the back of the room cut through the chatter. "That would be my heap of junk and I think you should apologize for hurting her feelings."

Myriam turned at the familiar voice. "Pete!" she exclaimed. The tall, lanky redhead came over grinning. They hugged briefly and he shook Hiram's hand. "She doesn't look like much on the outside, but if you have a few minutes I'll give you the nickel tour— microwave satellite antenna, solar powered nickel hydride batteries, sonic shower, Tempurpedic bed, MacPherson struts, a fold-out galley with a convection oven, and a hybrid engine that purrs like a Rolls Royce. It'll make touring the U.S. like being in a five star hotel every night."

"You're leaving?" asked Myriam.

"We're leaving," answered Rosa. She held up her hand and showed an engagement ring. "Pete proposed last night."

Hiram asked, "Where did you find the money for that ring?"

"I sold the Café and Pete—"

"I traded in my trusty 1958 Nash Rambler, Nellie Bell, and I had a few extra dollars stashed from working for the South Africans. I figure I won't be seeing them again and I'm no longer needed around these parts. So it's off we go."

"We're going wherever wind and whimsy take us," added Rosa.

51

———

April 10, 2019
Grinnell, Iowa

Ramsey left the swimming meet and strode toward his car. The winds had picked up. A spring storm was on its way. *What a strange twist of fate*, he thought. Some of the old longing for Paige had cropped up, but he also felt a lot of distance from her, a chasm too far to cross. Thinking back on the encounter, suspicion dominated his thoughts and he wondered if her arrival was more than coincidence.

Ramsey had joined Orensen and Paige beside the swimming pool. It had been awkward seeing her and his misgivings must have been plain for her and Orensen to see. The Professor Emeritus had tried to allay Ramsey's suspicions. It was the first time Ramsey had ever seen the man do anything badly. Paige had left saying she'd meet up with them later. While watching the rest of the diving competition, Orensen had explained he was hoping to recruit Paige to join the faculty in the college's religious studies department.

"Her career slid downhill after her PhD and she ended up at UC

Riverside because it was the only place where she and her former husband could both find academic positions. They divorced a couple of years ago and she's on sabbatical looking for something new. Wants to escape Southern California."

"How do you know her?" Ramsey had asked.

"You don't remember? I met her when you brought her for your fifth year reunion here at Grinnell. We've stayed in touch over the years." He chuckled. "After all, we're both stuck in the moribund field of classical religious studies."

"Is she still into that new age Christian thing?" Ramsey asked. "That was a large part of our break up."

"She's matured a lot since then. We're getting together at my place this afternoon. You should join us and see for yourself."

"Old times best forgotten," Ramsey had said.

"New times to be remembered later," Orensen had answered quietly.

Ramsey had agreed to meet them, but now he was no longer sure if he should.

What he really needed was time to think. He took a circuitous route to Orensen's home. The rain pelted down the whole way adding to his sense of unease. He mulled over how, ever since he had received the call from Myriam about the shrine, events had never unfolded the way he had hoped or thought they would. And now Paige.

He turned the corner onto Orensen's street and slowed down to a crawl, stopping his car two doors down from the professor's home. He saw Paige sitting in a large wicker chair beneath the wide front porch's overhang. The Craftsman-style home had belonged to Grinnell College's founder. Rainwater rushed down in sheets from the roof's cedar shingles, spilling over the overhang like a curtain separating Ramsey from Paige. She was no longer the cheery, bouncy flower child he had fallen in love with and who had left him that day in Eugene. She had put on weight and there were more than a few gray hairs. The one time their eyes had met during the swim meet he quickly looked away.

Now seeing at her at a distance, an uncanny warmth swept through him. As thunder shook his car, Ramsey felt a strange urge to tell her everything, seek her out-of-the-box way of looking at things as he once had done when as lovers they shared secrets and dreams. A strange notion swirled unbidden through his thoughts. *Maybe . . . maybe we can rekindle what was once there.* With a start, Ramsey realized he had never stopped longing for her. He had merely placed his work between him and the past. But as quickly as that idea emerged, a darker realization elbowed it aside.

Once more he wondered if her unexpected arrival in Grinnell might be another manipulation by the people or forces that had put in motion his search for Adam Gwillt. He gathered himself together. Now was not the time to give in to paranoia.

Putting the car in gear, he turned into Orensen's driveway. The rain let up and a pale sun peeked through the clouds. With the warm sunlight, Ramsey resolved to be on his best behavior and charm the information he sought out his old mentor.

52

———

April 10, 2019
Grinnell, Iowa

Orensen joined Paige and Ramsey on the front porch with a tray, three cups and a steaming pot of tea. "Thought we should have tea outside today," the old man said with a twinkle as if everything was fine between them.

"Inside still cluttered with artifacts and religious relics gathering dust in shadowy corners?" said Ramsey, forcing a flash of irritation with his old mentor into a narrow compartment of his mind. He couldn't afford to alienate him with pettiness. Not when he needed answers. He had to uncover Orensen's involvement with the shrine, Adam Gwillt, the New Gnostics, and the South Africans. He cautioned himself to go lightly—the way he would with any interviewee.

Orensen laughed. "You haven't been here since your return from New Mexico. I'm in the process of donating my entire collection to Falconer Gallery." Ramsey arched his eyebrows. "There are changes afoot in my future and I don't need them anymore. Though," the old professor smiled wanly, "the house is lonely without them."

The three sat around a glass table facing the street. The maple trees were leafing out and the grass, brown and dormant over the winter, glinted dark green under the rain. The road was as quiet as church. Even the neighbors seemed to be aware this meeting was more than three old friends getting together.

"I'm sorry, Jon. I should have called, but I wasn't sure you'd want to see me after, well, after Oregon." Paige was the only one who called him Jon. "Professor Orensen filled me in on New Mexico, sounds like something you'd want to do."

Orensen chuckled. "Call me Roger. We're all friends here."

"I'm here, Roger, and it's time we talk," Ramsey said, taking great care to keep his tone upbeat.

"You have questions. I may have some answers."

Ramsey glanced at Paige. She leaned back as if taking herself out of the conversation. It made him think she wasn't there as a distraction but for something else. Ramsey reached into his coat pocket and pulled out his phone. He tapped a link with his finger and showed it to Orensen. It was a webpage from the Rio Chama's newspaper telling the story of Adam's disappearance. It showed the shrine's sacred cottonwood tree. At the foot of the tree was Adam surrounded by three people in wheelchairs.

Pointing to the shrine's caretaker, Ramsey asked, "You know who that is?"

The professor gave an apologetic shrug of his shoulders. "I'm sorry, Jonathan; I've never seen him."

Taken aback by Orensen's blatant deception, Ramsey's resolve to tread lightly vanished. "Roger, I don't think I've ever seen you lie so poorly," he retorted, his voice now tight. "You know Adam Gwillt's the source behind the shrine's healing power."

Paige put a hand on Ramsey's arm. Ramsey shook her off. He'd been pushed, prodded, knocked out, tied up, dragged off, and lied to. He didn't have to be nice to anyone. "You need to keep out of this, Paige. It's between me and the professor . . . my old mentor." His eyes bored into Orensen's. "Tell me the truth, Roger. I deserve that much."

Paige started to interrupt again, and Orensen held up a hand. "It's okay." The kindly eyes of his mentor disappeared and Orensen said, "You deserve the truth. There were rumors that Adam Gwillt was responsible for the healing, but the Friends of the Shrine kept it under wraps. They didn't want a repeat of so many of these miracle spots, like the Lady of Lourdes, where worshippers come to idolize the woman and not the place."

That's better. Now we're getting some straight talk for once. Ramsey shunted the rest of his anger aside. It would only get in the way of knowing when Orensen was telling the truth. "That may explain the shrine, but what about Haas and the South Africans?"

Orensen shook his head.

"The DeVere Mining Group . . . businessmen supposedly after diamonds in northern New Mexico but who were really looking for Adam Gwillt. They kidnapped me hoping to find him. It was all part of a plan to capture Adam. Their leader Haas mentioned you. Talked as though he knew you."

"Whoever that was, he was lying," Orensen said.

Ramsey took a breath. His suspicions about the DeVere chairman's duplicity were confirmed. *Unless Orensen's lying to me.* The seventy-five year old professor emeritus smiled and stared guilelessly. Ramsey knew he was telling the truth.

"Do you know where he is?" asked Orensen.

"Hoping you could help with that."

The old man shrugged. "I know nothing about the South Africans or where Adam is. My involvement with the shrine and Adam has been peripheral. It's with a group of New Gnostics here in Grinnell. There's a meeting night. You'll get your questions answered there."

Ramsey grit his teeth. He didn't like being put off, yet he could tell the professor wasn't going to say anything more.

Orensen added, "I urge you to come to our meeting. I'll introduce you and you can ask them what they know."

Ramsey scowled. "You should've told me everything when we first talked."

"Perhaps you're right," Orensen apologized. His eyes narrowed and he said slyly, "On the other hand, ask yourself, even with Peru so far in the past, would you have been ready to accept everything?"

Ramsey jerked in surprise. The professor's words stung him in a way he couldn't deny. He stood abruptly to leave. Paige grasped his hand in hers. "I was hoping to attend the Gnostics assembly. But if you prefer I'll stay away."

He shook off her hand. "Who says I'm going."

53

April 10, 2019
Rio Chama, New Mexico

The Friends of the Rio de Milagro Shrine board meeting took place in the small amphitheater in the Visitor Center, where a movie depicting the story of the shrine was shown four times a day. Myriam and Hiram arrived on time. The day had turned gray and windy and the parking lot was nearly empty. Myriam recognized Carlotta's car and the silver Tundra pickup truck that belonged to the board's president, Raphael Núnez, owner of the largest real estate company in the county. Myriam looked at Hiram. "Looks like a small group tonight."

Hiram nodded. "They must have gotten your message."

Earlier in the week Myriam had called Núnez. As per the bylaws of the organization, she had demanded an emergency meeting about issues relating to the shrine's ownership.

Inside the Center Carlotta greeted them. She led them to two chairs in a small circle near a large window overlooking the hillside. Myriam could see the ancient cottonwood limned by the gray sky. Gusts of wind shook the tree's limbs.

As everyone took their seats, Father Michael rose and said, "We decided to keep this meeting to the core group."

Núnez stood and motioned for him to sit down. He was a short man with bandy legs that showed he spent most of his time on his ranch riding horses. His sun and wind weathered face reflected the somber mood of the chilly afternoon. He cleared his throat and said, "Let's get right to the point. I have some explaining to do. A few years ago the DeVere Mining group came to me with a proposal. They wanted me to buy up land around here. It's what they do when they have a potential mining interest in an area. I told them I would. It was a win-win for everybody." Núnez paused, gripping the back of his chair with both hands. "What happened next was a little unusual. Early last year I urged the company to buy the land the shrine's on. Surprisingly they were more than happy to oblige, even created a trust to keep it running. We made Father Michael the titular head of the trust." Needless to say I was pleased. The growing popularity of the shrine pushed property values up here. The only condition was keeping the ownership a secret. But then about two months ago the company's interest in the land changed. The DeVere group's chairman, Pieter Haas—"

Hiram's head snapped up at the mention of the South African's name. He kneaded the stubs of the little and ring fingers on his left hand. The old parachute injury hardly ever bothered him anymore, but this afternoon it ached. He glanced at Myriam and she was just as mortified. "Cut to the chase. What's Haas got to do with the shrine?" he asked, his gravely voice gruffer than usual.

"Myriam, you might remember I introduced you. He became very interested in the shrine. That's my part in this. Father, please continue."

Father Michael stood. "I want to go back a year. It was becoming clear to a few of us that Adam was somehow the source of the shrine's healing power."

Myriam blinked in surprise. Hiram squeezed her hand. She looked at Carlotta. "Is it true you knew?"

The large woman nodded. "Adam told me he suspected as much.

At the time none of us, including Adam, could explain how it was possible."

"That's right," Father Michael said. "I presume the two of you know about the New Gnostics? The international organization of people impacted by the shrine?"

Myriam glanced at Hiram. "We heard about them recently and looked at their website."

He continued, "It was also becoming obvious to a number of the members of the New Gnostics that the source of the shrine's power was Adam. In the meantime, Adam was slowly fading. This was because of his gradual absorption into a higher plane, as he put it."

Carlotta broke in, "We needed a plan to protect Adam. If anyone else found out, some might see him as a danger and others might try to exploit him as an economic opportunity."

"We tried to find a way to discover how Adam's powers work, but it seemed impossible without letting the secret out," added Father Michael. "Then we learned About the Brothers of the Lord and their foul intentions regarding Adam."

Hiram's face flushed. "I was part of that group."

Carlotta nodded. "We were making plans to move Adam when he suddenly disappeared. You know the rest."

Myriam stood up. "It's hard to believe you're not the ones who took him away."

The board members exchanged glances. Finally Carlotta spoke up. "Do you know something we don't?"

Hiram demanded, "What about Haas? "

Father Michael replied, "He wanted to help us find Adam. He said he had been healed by the shrine several years ago and had joined a small New Gnostics assembly in South Africa. As the chairman of the DeVere Group and now the owner of the shrine he had lots of resources to help us in our search."

Myriam cocked her head to one side. "That doesn't make sense," she said. "I had the impression when Raphael introduced us in February he had never been to the shrine before."

Father Michael's scarred cheeks reddened. He glared at Núnez, who was equally embarrassed. He recovered quickly. "It doesn't matter anymore since we all know it's now hopeless. Adam's gone for good."

Tears formed in Carlotta's eyes. She turned away from the others.

Myriam reached out to her. "I'm sorry for your loss, Carlotta."

"Thanks for your concern," Carlotta replied. "But I'm not giving up hope for my brother."

The meeting ended with no resolution on the shrine's finances or ownership. Beecher and Myriam went out to their car frustrated.

"Do you think we can trust Carlotta? About Adam, I mean?" asked Myriam.

"Can we trust any of them," retorted Beecher. He slammed the key into the ignition and was going to start the car when a sudden thought made him smile. "You know, beloved, there's a way to end all the problems with the Friends of the Shrine."

Myriam caught his lightheartedness. "What are you planning, love?"

"Not here." He glanced back at Núnez and Father Michael standing in the entrance of the Visitor Center. "When we're home alone from any prying eyes."

54

April 10, 2019
Grinnell, Iowa

Ramsey leaned against the wall, surveying the room. Twenty-three people huddled in small groups chatting quietly. Except for two elderly Pakistani men, everyone was white. Most were over forty. He was the youngest person there.

The Sullivan-designed Jewel Box Bank building had its last official financial transaction on May 17, 1999. Since then, it had become Grinnell's visitor center and home of the Chamber of Commerce. Tonight, the building hosted Grinnell's New Gnostic assembly. It was a curious group that had gathered. Gnostics were generally categorized as men and women who quested after a spiritual connection with God. Yet the faces in the room held no such indication of the spiritual journey. At first glance it could have been a meeting of the Elks or the Freemasons.

The room hummed with a whispered energy, so low it was serene. Ramsey felt as if he had wandered into a clandestine meeting of somnambulists. No one acknowledged him when he walked in, offered him a name tag, a cup of coffee, or anything that even hinted at a welcome. He was beginning to wonder if Orensen had given him the wrong time and place, when a woman with blue-streaked, gray hair separated herself from a small group that included the Pakistanis and walked to the front of the room.

She raised her arms and shouted joyously, "I feel it!" Everybody turned their attention towards her and closed their eyes. A look of rapture filled their faces. Her voice carrying the melodic rhythm of a gospel singer, she continued, "May the power of the shrine pour through all of us once again. May the love we all felt at the shrine fill the lives of all who seek to aid a greater purpose. May I fulfill my part in the one work through selflessness, harmlessness, and right speech."

Everyone lifted up their arms and joined in as she finished the prayer: "Let love prevail … let all humanity love and serve."

Ramsey stood silently. He was beginning to feel uncomfortable. After all, he was not a New Gnostic and had never personally experienced a healing at the shrine, just aberrations and illusions.

The woman dropped her arms after the incantation ended and walked to the center of the room. Her eyes met Ramsey's and she came over. Her eyes were green with flecks of coral in them. "You're new here. Welcome." she smiled, extending her hand. She was nearly sixty according to the lines around her eyes, but her skin was soft like a baby's. "My name is Evelyn *Ha-Rishon*."

Ramsey's eyes widened in surprise. "The *first* Eve."

"You speak Hebrew?" she said, surprised.

"Some. I had to learn a little for my graduate thesis on sacred places."

"Fascinating. I'd love to hear more about that," she said, her tone warm and inviting in a way Ramsey could tell was not in the least bit deceitful. "You'll discover that many of us here have incorporated the Hebrew word *Ha-Rishon* into our names from the biblical account of Adam in *The First Testament*."

"I don't understand. I was under the impression that Gnosticism was a Christian tradition."

"Evelyn smiled at his confusion. "Most people don't know that the

Gnostic tradition preceded Christianity. It can be found in Platonism, Zoroastrianism, Judaism, and some scholars believe Buddhism. I'm forgetting my manners. Let me introduce you around, Mr.—."

"Ramsey. I'm a guest of Professor Orensen."

"Of course, you're Jonathan Ramsey. I thought it might be you. Roger told us you would be here."

The way Evelyn said the old professor's name, Ramsey wondered if there was more to their relationship than as acquaintances. "I was hoping to see Professor Orensen here tonight," he said.

"Roger's going to be late, but he said you had information we might need to hear about Adam."

"I don't see how. Never met him."

"Pity, he was quite remarkable. Things here haven't been the same since he disappeared," her eyes narrowed slightly as if coming to a decision whether this was the time and place to speak of such things. She smiled wanly. Her face was luminous and Ramsey had the feeling he could fall into the depth of that smile and never surface again. It reminded him of Paige when they were in love, and he wondered what had really gone wrong between them. Then Evelyn started speaking again and he concentrated on her like he would an interviewee.

"Quite frankly, before Adam disappeared, the Gnostic assemblies like ours were quite vibrant. We thought we were going to change the world. Now we seem to be falling apart. The harmony we once shared is disappearing. It's been very discouraging."

Ramsey shrugged uncomfortably. It was like listening to a writer tell you everything that's wrong with his novel when you were looking forward to reading it.

Evelyn misinterpreted his silence to mean he had heard this complaint already. She asked, "Did Orensen tell you all this? He said you know more about what happened to Adam than anybody else."

Ramsey replied, "Actually, the professor told me nothing except that I would have many of my questions answered by coming here."

"In that case, when we form into breakout groups, come sit with me." The sounds of chair legs scraping the linoleum turned her head around. "We're about to begin. Take any empty seat."

Ramsey chose a seat at the end of the last row. Evelyn moved to the front of the room. She waited for the chairs and people to settle. "To begin, as we always do, let's acknowledge new members and visitors. Tonight we have one of each."

Ramsey listened as an elderly lady stood and explained that she and her newly retired husband had just moved from Chicago to Grinnell. They managed a web app that paired up aikido instructors with students. Then she told the story of visiting the shrine for eighteen days straight and how, on the nineteen day, the ringing in her head that had plagued her for over twenty years stopped and has never come back. When she sat down, the group mildly intoned, "Amen."

Evelyn thanked her and then introduced a visitor from Wales. "He calls himself the Wandering Gnostic. I'll let him tell you all about himself."

From the far corner of the room a middle-aged man rose. Long silver hair flowed down his back. As he walked toward the front, his hair wavered like starlight. His form seemed to shift from stocky to tall and rangy. Ramsey watched the New Gnostics but none of them appeared to notice anything out of the ordinary. He shook his head wondering if the dim light was playing tricks on him.

The man turned abruptly. He peered through the hall, slate-gray eyes piercing the sleepy energy of the attendees. His sharp beak of a nose seemed to point at everyone as powerfully as his glare.

Ramsey started in surprise. He'd seen that look before, had experienced the same fierce mien. He bent his mind to recall, but could not quite lift the veil that was hiding the where and when.

"I bet many of you are having a sense of 'I know this guy from somewhere,'" the visitor said. Stirs and nods followed. "Maybe you think we've met, passed each other on a crowded street or shared a plane to some exotic place. All my life I have been attracted, no addicted, to hallucinogens. I lived as much in the other side, probably more, than the real world. I was at the point where I couldn't tell the difference. I had a vision of the Milagro Shrine and went there, and as they say, the rest is history." He paused.

His audience listened with the same expectancy of the crowd at the Vatican waiting for the Pope to give his blessing. Ramsey found himself like the others leaning forward, wanting to hear more. In fact he felt compelled to meet the man and hoped there would be time afterwards to speak with him.

"And here I am. Wherever my travels take me I always try to visit the local New Gnostic assembly." He paused. Murmurs of thank you and mild applause filled the gap.

"Why are you applauding?" the Wandering Gnostic roared.

The group snapped back in their seats as if a howling gale had slammed into them. From the puzzled expressions on their faces, Ramsey figured this wasn't how visitors usually comported themselves. Curiously, he felt unaffected, as though he were here to witness what was happening but not be a part of it.

"What have any of you done with your God-given experience since you joined? You sit here smiling like inhabitants in the Land of the Lotus-eaters. You chant amen in sappy tones, eyes half closed, unable to see what is happening."

One of the Pakistani men jumped to his feet. "Who are you to tell us we are failing?" Others muttered amen.

"I am *Adam Ha-Rishon*," the Wandering Gnostic stated in a voice like God speaking to Moses in the wilderness. The Pakistani stumbled back into his seat as though he'd been slapped.

Ramsey translated the Hebrew: *the original Adam*. The earlier serenity in the room had long since vanished and now the anxiety was mounting with every passing heartbeat.

"You people don't get it!" the Wandering Gnostic shouted. "You must understand that this is the way it has to be, and always has been. Stop trying to create harmony, peace, and tranquility. You experienced a gift from Adam and now you're closing the door he opened for you, the door that took you across the boundary to the other side, a crossing that you must take again and again. Be like Adam, be like Moses, Jesus, the Buddha, Mohammed. Understand that it's never quite right, never completely safe. You are never complete. It's from conflict that all new and good things come. Accept it, only then can you create a sacred space right here."

The Gnostics sat stunned. Ramsey watched them. They could not take their eyes from the Wandering Gnostic, could not stop listening for his next words. It was as if he held their souls in the palm of his hand. Some of the veil started to shift and Ramsey could almost snatch out of the misty shadows how he knew this strange madman who berated everyone in the room.

Then the Wandering Gnostic rushed over and hauled Ramsey to his feet. He thrust Ramsey at the group and cried, "Follow him into the world of uncertainty!"

It was then that the last of the veil parted and the mists swirled away as if a strong gust of the past had rushed into Ramsey's consciousness. "I know you!" he shouted. "You're Puck . . . the woman who helped me at the shrine!"

The man cackled and leaned in close. He gripped Ramsey by the forearms. His eyes burned into Ramsey's as he whispered, "Yes, and I am the archetype of transformation, Hermes, Loki and Coyote. I am the one who started you on this journey twelve years ago." He cackled again.

Ramsey stiffened. "Glastonbury," he whispered. It all came back to him. He was Loki, the decrepit, one-eyed man who had told him a guide would be provided for him to find his way. Ramsey's body relaxed in the grasp of the Wandering Gnostic and yet an insistent vitality flooded his muscles and his brain was sharper than ever.

The man pushed Ramsey gently back into his seat. He laughed at the group and pirouetted several times, like a dervish gathering strength. When he stopped, heat and light radiated from his skin. "This man is a little crazy, but he knows more about Adam and the healing power of the shrine than he believes."

Dancing and twirling, the Wandering Gnostic started for the door. Orensen entered the room at the same time. The man gently embraced the professor. He whispered in his ear. Ramsey strained and could just make out the feathery voice. "It's time; you've done what you were supposed to do."

"I'm ready," answered Orensen.

The old professor slumped forward. The Wandering Gnostic caught him and laid him gently on the floor.

He bowed to the group. "Honor him," he intoned, then vanished into the night.

55

April 11, 2019
Grinnell, Iowa

Ramsey sat on the edge of the bed. He looked over at Paige who was still sleeping. The late afternoon sun filtered through the latticed window. He was confused and his head swirled with thoughts and regrets of ending up in bed with Paige.

Since the night she broke off their relationship, he had experienced five long-distance romances, all of them lasting less than three months. His moodiness had destroyed every romantic encounter he started. Then, four years ago, he had decided that the effort to make an honest and growing commitment to a partner was no longer possible. He believed his experience in Peru had left him permanently unable to develop the intimacy necessary to be close to another person as a lover, friend, and husband. He had decided his work had to be enough. When his body and mind craved sexual release, he sought out one-night stands.

Then this afternoon had happened. He found himself in Paige's arms as though twelve years had never passed between them.

He stared at her, his thoughts jumbling between happiness, wariness, and confusion. *How's that possible? She abandoned me when I needed her the most.*

Watching the rhythmic rise and fall of her breast, seeing the half-smile on her full lips, the answer burst into his mind in a way that he could only describe as an important shift in consciousness. If anyone could understand him it would be Paige. In that moment, the knot of anger deep within that he had harbored all these years burst out of him like a geyser spewing scalding steam and water. When it was all spent, he saw Paige for the first time for who she was then and now—an imperfect person like himself. For the first time in his life Ramsey was okay with his own imperfection.

"Professor Orensen wanted me to tell you why he did not confide in you," Paige said, opening one eye. She wrapped an arm and a leg over him and snuggled close so her lips were inches from his left ear. "Professor Orensen brought me to Grinnell because he knew the end was near and he wanted to find a replacement for his position before he passed. He specifically asked me not to mention his deteriorating heart condition to you because he knew you would take control of his medical treatment and more importantly press him for answers regarding Adam. Answers that he wanted to take to the grave."

Ramsey lay quietly beside Paige, present to everything she said. Only moments before he would have had tremendous resentment that Orensen would tell Paige and not him about his condition. That was gone too. What he felt for her and his old friend and mentor was only love. It brought tears to his eyes and then he began crying softly.

Paige cradled Ramsey in her arms and rocked slowly. What he received from her was genuine, pure, unconditional acceptance and love.

· · ·

Still immersed totally in his new state, Ramsey set about making dinner. The fragrant aroma of Earl Grey tea mingled with grilled vegetables and chicken. Sounds of the bedroom's shower tickled at his consciousness, reminding him that he wasn't alone. Mindlessly he checked the email on his phone. What he was waiting for was there. A local reporter friend sent him a note that the police were unable to locate the Wandering Gnostic. Descriptions from the people in attendance at the New Gnostic assembly were vague, confused, and contradictory. Ramsey smiled. He had not expected Loki to hang around. In a moment of pure knowing he understood the man was real but not *of* this world. He was the unexpected and disruptive intrusion of the divine into the flow of ordinary life. He had let Ramsey see the divine in its many disguises. For what reason he was unsure. There was something else, but he didn't know what.

Moments later the fragrant aroma of the Earl Grey tea filled his nostrils once again, making his mouth water. Paige called out to him, "Are you still here? You promised me tea almost forty-five minutes ago."

Forty-five minutes! Ramsey blinked and he knew with a slight pang of regret that he was once more in what philosophers and psychologists refer to as the narrative self——telling stories about himself from the past and the present and making plans for the future. He recalled he had a eulogy to prepare.

56

———

April 14, 2019
Grinnell, Iowa

The memorial for Orensen was held on a Saturday at Grinnell College's historic Herrick Chapel. The building could seat seven hundred, and every pew and space in the balcony was filled with colleagues, students he had touched, old friends, relatives, and some of the New Gnostics Ramsey recalled from the meeting. They sat together in a small group beneath a stained glass rendering of Heinrich Hoffman's *The Ascension*.

Ramsey looked over at Paige. "I'm a little nervous."

She smiled reassuringly. "You'll be fine."

He wasn't sure she was telling the truth but it felt good to have her by his side. Although Paige was staying at Ramsey's house, after the first night they decided not to sleep in the same room. Something needed to be worked out. Both said they were fine with the arrangement while she looked for an apartment.

When the College's chaplain finished the benediction, he motioned Ramsey forward. Ramsey walked to the pulpit. On a table next to him was a brass urn with Roger's ashes. Looking down to the first row, Ramsey saw Evelyn. Their eyes met and she smiled encouragingly. His nervousness disappeared.

Turning to the back of the chapel, he pointed at the stained glass representation of William Holman Hunt's *The Light of the World*. "You can see Roger Orensen's face there because he was a light to everyone who ever met him." He smiled as the new Gnostics in the crowd whispered "Amen" among themselves.

"Like many of you, my own life has been far richer because of him."

Again the Gnostics whispered, Amen," this time joined by many in the crowd.

"For Roger, each day was a day to shepherd a friend, a student, anyone he encountered along their path to discovering their purpose in life. That was his gift . . . his genius. . . . He always knew what you needed next. He was the archetype of the wise man. I'm sure everyone here has experienced that wisdom at critical times in their lives. I certainly did on more than one occasion. Roger, you will be missed." Ramsey picked up the urn and raised it above his head with both hands. "Thank you Roger for your understanding, your joy, and most of all for your gift of wisdom that you willingly gave to the whole world."

This time everyone in the chapel raised their voice in unison, "Amen!"

The reception was held under a large canopy on the lawn next to the chapel. Ramsey mingled among the crowd exchanging hellos. He spotted Evelyn in a group of New Gnostics and several college faculty. He steered toward them.

"Perfect eulogy," the Grinnell's Chancellor said to him. "Exactly what Roger would have wanted—short, sweet, and no flamboyance." He was a heavyset man with the hands of a farmer, which he had been until he met Orensen at a roadside diner outside of Ames, Iowa. He told the others, "After talking to Roger for twenty minutes, I decided to sell the family farm and go back to school. Twenty years later, I ended up here." He chuckled. "Like coming home. A toast to Roger."

Ramsey lifted his glass and drank with the others.

Evelyn asked him, "How did Roger change your life?"

Ramsey had not wanted to tell anyone about that, but now the others looked at him expectantly and he realized he had opened the door with his remarks. "I first met Roger as an eighteen-year old freshman with no direction and a lot of questions. Then, when I became his student, it seemed as though whatever direction Roger pointed me in, my questions would be answered, though inevitably more would spring up to take their place."

"He had a way of doing that," the Chancellor said.

"One direction in particular set me on my career path. One weekend in late May he took three of us on a tour of Iowa's sacred places. First, to the Grotto of the Redemption in West Bend. Then we went to Fairfax, Iowa to the Maharishi International University founded in 1973 by Maharishi Mahesh Yogi. At both places we discussed and analyzed the characteristics that made them sacred and how they impacted the people there.

"The final stop was a house in nearby Spillville, where Czech composer Antonin Dvorak wrote some of his most famous music. All of us wondered aloud why Roger took us to this house. After all, it isn't a place ordinarily considered sacred. Historically significant in the music world but not sacred. When we asked him about it, he just smiled that cherubic smile of his and said, 'Wait for it.'

"So, the three of us walked around the house and grounds for about an hour. Dusk was falling by then, and when we got back together it was dark. We stood outside by the front entrance and Roger said, 'Do you feel it?'

"Curiously, none of us had to ask what he meant. We all experienced the same sense of uplifting. I remember it had crept upon me first with a whisper. But as I walked around the grounds, the sensation swelled like Beethoven's *Ode to Joy*."

Evelyn smiled. "I once had an experience like that myself. It was very moving. How do you remember it now?"

"It swept away shadows gathering in corners beneath maple trees and under cars. It seemed as if every bit of darkness were tinged with an aura of light so that hope gleamed through the gathering night in bright colors. By the time we all met up again, we were filled with a giddy kind of energy that could have tamed tigers and bears.

"I remember that I looked at Roger expectantly as though he had the answer to our unspoken question. But true to form he turned the tables on us and asked, 'What is that?'

"We shook our heads. None of us could put our fingers on it. It was at the time, and remains to this day, a mystery." Ramsey smiled at Evelyn. "Although I didn't know it at the time, that mysterious feeling was my call to begin my life's journey."

"Perfect," said the Chancellor, raising a plastic cup filled with red wine. The others echoed his affirmation.

The group drifted way. Evelyn stayed. "What you just said about Roger, I'm sure he would have found it moving."

"Thank you. He was always an unwavering friend. How well did you know him?"

"Very."

Ramsey's eyebrows raised.

Evelyn got the signal and said, "You probably want to know why you didn't know about me. Roger and I had a . . . well, perhaps a not-so-platonic relationship, but it was a based on friendship. We kept it secret. It was a game."

Ramsey thought for a moment. He could see how Roger would delight in the charade. "I'm sorry for your loss," he said.

"Yes, it's a big one. You know we talked about you quite a bit."

"Really?"

"Yes."

Ramsey found himself slipping into his interview persona, inviting Evelyn to share with the way he stood, face neutral.

"There is one thing I believe he wanted me to tell you." She paused as if trying to find the right words. Then, "It's a false choice to believe you can choose between your free will and the destiny designed by the gods for you. The paradox is that they are both true:

You have free will, and your destiny has been laid out. Roger was sure that eventually Adam would tell you this but I'm telling you now. The experience of mystery you talked about just now hasn't gone away, has it?"

It was Evelyn's voice, but the words were the same as if his old mentor and friend were standing in front of him again. Ramsey nodded his head in agreement.

Evelyn pulled him close to her. She whispered, "Keep going!" Ramsey's phone buzzed in his pocket. "Take it," she said enigmatically and walked away.

Ramsey jerked in surprise. He watched her walk toward another group. *She seemed to know the phone was going to buzz.* It was a text from his business partner. Ron wrote, *You're good to go to bring Maggie to the shrine.*

He saw Paige on the other side of the lawn, chatting with the dean of the college. He nodded at her. Moments later she shook the man's hand and threaded through the crowd of mourners to his side.

Paige tilted her head. "Something's different. What's going on?"

"Are you ready for that visit to the Rio Chama de Milagro Shrine?"

57

April 15, 2019
Rio Chama, New Mexico

Beecher sat on the porch of his rustic cabin outside of Rio Chama. The night air was cool and overhead clouds played tag with the moon. Alone at night under the stars used to make him feel uncharacteristically vulnerable as though he were back in Vietnam waiting for an ambush. But the drone of crickets made him sigh with contentment. He knew it was only a moment's peace, because a storm was brewing out there around the shrine and maybe in his personal life. He and Myriam had not really patched things up as a true couple would. They had reunited as lovers and were working together for the betterment of the shrine, but there was still something missing.

His phone buzzed on the coffee table beside him.

He put down his coffee. He swiped the answer icon and said, "This is Beecher."

"Hiram. It's me, Sam. Do you mind speaking with me?"

"No, I don't mind you calling."

Conklin's hesitated. "I wasn't sure. Old patterns die hard."

"What's going on?"

"I felt compelled to call you. Have you heard about the Reverend? Billy Paul?"

"I'm done with all that."

"Of course."

Beecher could hear the disappointment in the man he once trusted implicitly. "Go ahead tell me the news," he said dispassionately.

"He's dying and," Conklin paused dramatically, "he's disbanded the Brothers of the Lord."

"There's a great idea," Beecher said. "Did he say why?"

"The formal notification said the mission of the organization was complete with the closing of the shrine."

Beecher responded angrily. "It's not closed. In fact, I'm going to buy it from the South Africans."

"I didn't know that. Look, I just thought in case you were worried about Billy Paul and the shrine this would set your mind at ease."

"Thanks." Myriam called him from inside the cabin. Beecher got up from his chair and walked through the front door. "Thanks for the update," he said. "I've got to go."

"Anytime. Hey, are you okay?"

He ended the call without answering. As Beecher entered the kitchen, Myriam was all smiles.

"I have good news. Jonathan is coming back here next weekend."

"Taking another look at the shrine?"

"Remember I told you about Jonathan's love interest back in Oregon? A young woman by the name of Paige. They were perfect for each other. I never found out why they split. Anyway, they reconnected in Grinnell and Jonathan asked if we would put her and a young black woman from Chicago up for a few days."

"Sure, but why bring them here?"

"Jonathan's hoping the experience will be transformative for the young lady and will give her clarity about what she has to do back in her own community."

Beecher nodded, not sure what Myriam meant. "It will give me a chance to speak with Ramsey face-to-face. I've wanted to apologize more fully to him for some time now."

"He would like that."

Beecher went to the coffee pot and saw that Myriam had brewed a fresh pot. He poured a cup, idly stirring cream into it for a moment. "I have some news too. Sam called. He told me a bunch of stuff about the Brothers of the Lord, except I can't tell if he's lying or just wanted to reconnect."

"How did that make you feel?"

"A little worried. Surprisingly, it felt good to hear his voice, though I didn't say anything like that." Beecher cleared his throat. "I was probably too short with him."

Myriam went over to him. "You worried about what's going to happen to the shrine?"

"That and other things." He raked his lower lip with his teeth. "I know we've been living here together for the last week, maybe trying to overcome the past for the sake of the shrine's future. But I want us to lay the past to rest for the sake of our future." Taking Myriam's hand, he said, "Myriam, I never asked you to marry me."

"You never had to, Hiram," she said squeezing his hand.

"I loved that about you, still do. But I want you to make an honest man out of me," he joked. He saw the sudden spark in her eyes and added swiftly, "Jokes aside, I can't imagine spending my life without you in it. These last few days alone without the drama of the shrine, I've realized that I want only you in my life as my partner. Myriam, will you do me the incredible honor of being my wife?"

She stood on her toes and kissed him lovingly. "Yes." Then, "And will you do me the honor of being my husband?"

He enfolded her into his arms. "I will."

58

April 15, 2019
Grinnell, Iowa

Ramsey heard the call end and breathed out a sigh of relief. He hadn't been certain that Myriam would be willing to host Paige and Maggie. And he was relieved when he learned that she and Hiram had gotten back together again. There was nothing left for him to do. Ron Grange had arranged the flights for everyone. They would meet at O'Hare Airport midmorning on Saturday.

This work in Blue Island is the beginning of what I'm supposed to be doing, he thought to himself, even though he knew on another level he hadn't finished with what the shrine and Adam had brought up for him.

On the other hand, he was a little worried about Paige. The more he told her about the events surrounding the shrine and his search for Adam, the more he could sense her distancing herself from him. He wanted to ask her about what was going on, but he didn't want to sabotage the trip to the shrine. He needed a female chaperone and she was the logical choice.

At the same time, today was a big day for the two of them.

Ramsey was going to introduce Paige as the new co-instructor of the class he had been teaching with Orensen.

Then he had to drive to Des Moines. Grossinger had left a cryptic message on his phone that he had important things to give him, writings that Adam wanted Ramsey to have. The message ended, "2pm, tomorrow, same place." Ramsey tried calling back but only got Grossinger's voice message. He was being pulled back in again, he thought, but knew he had to go.

Ramsey heard steps coming down the stairs. Paige had gone for a makeover the day before. She looked ten years younger and very much alive with energy. "Good morning," she chirped. "Now I'm the nervous one."

"Wow, you look great. They are all going to love you and that's even before you speak."

"If all goes well. A little celebration after?"

"Actually I have to leave for Des Moines immediately after we finish the class. Remember I told you about Adam's best friend in Des Moines?"

Paige's mood turned somber. "More of that crazy Adam stuff. I thought you said you were done with that."

"I never said that. I said I thought it was done with me." Then Ramsey realized how ridiculous this was. He began to laugh nervously. "I'm sorry, Paige, I didn't mean to put you off. It's just that I have this notion the Adam stuff is going to be important. How about we celebrate after I get back from Des Moines?"

Paige smiled. "Thanks for the apology. I'll make reservations for us at your favorite restaurant." They bumped fists. "Now let's put on a show for these minds hungry for knowledge."

59

———

April 16, 2019
Des Moines, Iowa

Ramsey found Grossinger in one of the two remaining chairs in Adam's old condo. Everything else was gone.

Without getting up, Grossinger said, "I'm glad you could make it."

"What happened here?"

"Adam told me to get rid of everything."

"When? You talked to him?

"Not lately. 'Get rid of it all when I'm dead,' he said."

"Is he dead?" Ramsey asked, settling into the other chair. He kept his focus on the real estate developer, once more using the same techniques he had honed for many years to elicit answers from interviewees.

"That's what I've been thinking. How about you?"

Ramsey shrugged, the gesture inviting Grossinger to elaborate.

Instead, Grossinger handed Ramsey a packet of Adam's writings. "These contain his lifelong interest and research into miraculous healings. They also include materials Adam had written after the accident." Grossinger got up and paced about the empty room. "Last time I saw him, Adam told me he had become quite aware that he was transforming into the purest form of the archetypal healer. He didn't want the world to know about his powers until after his death, or, if possible, ever. He was afraid that he would become like a cult leader or religious figure. Or even worse, people would come to him directly for healings."

Grossinger stopped pacing and returned to his chair, pulling it closer to Ramsey. "I've been instructed to give Adam's writings to you."

Ramsey jerked in surprise. By now he knew that Grossinger was an enigma who never gave straight answers, but this time he thought he should try to get to the bottom of it. "Who told you to? Adam?"

"I can't say."

"You mean you won't say?"

"They're your responsibility now"

"What am I supposed to do with them?"

"Whatever you want. It's your turn now. I am done with it all. Adam was the best friend I ever had." Grossinger began tearing up. He cried deeply until Ramsey touched him on the shoulder. A jolt of deep connection passed between the two men. Grossinger stopped crying and his composure returned instantly. He gazed at Ramsey and nodded knowingly. "Make sure history treats this grand friend and man well."

Ramsey could only promise, "I will."

Back in the car Ramsey looked over the writings. Glimpses of insight flitted through his brain and a certain understanding settled into his being. He began to understand that his searching would always be driven by a state of not knowing, but also that on his journey, each struggle would transform him into a higher state of consciousness and give him a more encompassing perspective. *There is wisdom in the energy and flow of conflict*, he told himself. *To experience that in any moment is what brings about creativity or rebirth. Each rebirth moves us more closely to the purest form of our chosen archetype.*

60

———

April 18, 2019
Rio Chama, New Mexico

Ramsey stepped outside and looked at his watch, 5:35am. First light was glowing in the East. He chose to stay at the hotel in Rio Chama just as he had during his first visit to the shrine.

Although delayed for three hours, the flight from Chicago to Albuquerque had been uneventful. Paige and Maggie had hit it off from the very beginning. It was Maggie's first time flying; in fact, she had never once left Northeastern Illinois, and she was quite nervous. The three of them occupied one row near the front of the plane. Maggie sat in the window seat with Paige in the middle. It was a bumpy landing. It was interesting to see this cocksure, confident woman of the street exhibit raw fear. She gripped Paige's hand. The trust was building and that was good. He wanted Maggie to feel comfortable.

The drive from the airport to Rio Chama was uneventful. Maggie seemed mesmerized by the strange terrain. By the time they arrived at Beecher's cabin, darkness had settled in. Myriam had a meal ready and had many questions for the young black woman, which Maggie answered as best she could.

After dinner, they gathered on the front porch. Here in the New Mexico wilderness where there was almost no light pollution, the sky was awash with stars. The Milky Way glowed. Maggie stared into the night with the awe of a little girl. Ramsey felt her wonder and embraced it, seeing it in his own path, as he grew closer to becoming the archetype that providence had chosen for him. He rose to leave and said to everyone, "I'll swing by tomorrow at eight to pick up Maggie and Paige and drive them to the shrine."

Maggie, having recovered some of her cockiness, said "Why not? That's what I'm here for, right?"

Myriam said. "Why don't Hiram and I take them and meet you there?"

Ramsey agreed, since he wanted to visit the Milagro Shrine himself before he showed it to Maggie and Paige. The last time he had been there, the sequence of events from the chapel to his kidnapping had had such a powerful effect on his psyche that he needed to clear the emotions associated with the place and face it anew.

The Rio Chama Café was open. A few ranchers had gathered for early morning coffee. Ramsey hoped he might spy Rosa and Pete, but the two were nowhere around. He figured wind and whimsy had not yet brought them back to Rio Chama. He experienced a momentary pang of loss, then realized he would see his friend again when the time was right.

Paying the bill, he drove the ten minutes to the shrine and found himself crossing the threshold as he had the first time. Nothing untoward happened. If anything, he felt calm. Looking around, he found himself actually checking to see if Haas might be lurking. But there was only one visitor, an older man standing underneath the cottonwood. Suddenly that sense of mystery he had experienced many years ago at the Dvorak house in Iowa gripped him in a way he had never felt before. Then it came to him: *I am to be the door, the one who can bring truth from the other side and have it manifest in this world. I now know what Adam was saying in his writings and what Jesus was saying in the Gospels.* Ramsey felt a great sense of being uplifted. At the same time he realized that, although it was very clear to him, he could never explain this understanding to anyone else. *Everyone has to get it for themselves.*

Ramsey walked in silence and stillness of mind to the great cottonwood tree. There he bowed. He felt a deep gratitude for the many turnings and struggles and conflicts of his life, now seeing clearly that they were not failures but necessary steps on his journey.

At eight that morning for a second time that day Ramsey found himself at the gateway to the shrine. This time Maggie was by his side. Paige must have sensed the change in him, for she hung back with Myriam and Hiram.

It was a Sunday, and an unusually large number of people had made the pilgrimage to the shrine. Maggie took it all in and finally asked, "Where're the black people?"

"New Mexico doesn't have many Blacks. They have Hispanics," said Ramsey.

Maggie shrugged. "What good does that do me? I'm here because you told me the shrine would help me become a leader for my people. I don't see it."

Ramsey pointed at all the pilgrims. "Why do you think these people are here?"

"It said on the web that the shrine is some kind of super health spa or something like that." She peered at the old and the infirm as they crossed the grounds to the Visitor Center. Some made the laborious climb up the stone steps to the cottonwood tree and the Christ Chapel. She snickered. "Unless you're talking about some kind of scam my gang and I can pull on white dudes back in Chicago, I don't see where my leadership thing fits in."

Ramsey nodded thoughtfully. "I suppose that's one take on it. But let me tell you a story that might help you see it in a different light. Not too long ago no one came here. It was just an empty field with a big old cottonwood tree dying up there on the hilltop. Then a man named Adam Gwillt arrived, hoping to recover from a terrible motorcycle accident. Shortly after, a group of people gathered one evening below that big cottonwood tree up there. Out of nowhere miracles began happening, healings, people changing their lives and relationships. Word spread that it was a remarkable place of healing. People came from all over. They pooled their resources, built the Visitor Center and the Christ Chapel, and put in stone steps to the top of the hill." He paused. "They thought the power somehow came from the cottonwood."

Maggie brandished a brochure Myriam had given her. "That's all in here."

"What's not in there, what they didn't know, and only a few people now know—and now you too will know—the secret of the healing power of this place was a man named Adam."

She snorted derisively. "Come on, how? Some sorta modern-day Jesus thing?"

"The way he put it is that he held the door open to the healing energy coming from the other side. He also said this ability to hold the door open to the other side was once rare but now it's becoming more common, becoming part of humanity."

Maggie eyed him skeptically. Her lips turned down in a frown. "You mean like talking to God? You learn in the streets real quick there is no God, only guns and money and drugs. So, where's this Adam guy now?"

"He's not here anymore and he may be dead. But here's the amazing thing. He left a message for you. You can be like him."

"I can be like some white guy pretending he's Jesus? No thanks. I got enough trouble in Chicago without my crew thinking I'm crazy."

Ramsey grinned. "I see your point. It does sound crazy put that way."

They had been climbing the stone steps as they walked. The

cottonwood had completely leafed out. The benches circling it were filled with young and old sitting silently or praying softly. Little children played and ran about, but those ringing the tree did not call out to them to be quiet.

Ramsey and Maggie walked up the narrow gravel path until they reached the Christ Chapel. A group of pilgrims filed out. They seemed not to care at all that an older man was standing at the entrance talking to a young Black girl dressed in gang colors. Many of them smiled at her and Maggie turned away in confusion at their friendliness.

Ramsey smiled and said. "Yeah, the whole *kumbaya* thing takes some getting used to. Tell you what. This trip isn't costing you anything. So why don't you indulge me and go ahead to sit inside for a while."

"Why?"

"You'll see."

"That's stupid."

"You trusted me once, so please give it a try. Then walk around and explore and see what happens."

Maggie ground her teeth. "This isn't what I expected when you said you'd teach me how to become a leader."

"We'll get to that, but I want you to do this first. You have a watch?"

"I'm not stupid. I have my phone."

"Okay. Someone will meet you down by the gate, say at 2 o'clock."

"Really?"

"Really." He stared at her. "Are you afraid?"

"Fuck no."

With that Ramsey walked off leaving Maggie, arms crossed, glaring at him.

61

April 21, 2019
Seattle, Washington

Ramsey stared at the buildings as the Lincoln Town Car passed through the heart of downtown Seattle. Rain on the side windows distorted the images, elongating some, flattening others. He was suddenly shy. The initial excitement had finally worn off and apprehension crept upon him as a feeling of imminent destiny gathered deep within him. He swallowed, his throat dry. He seriously considered having the driver stop the car so he could get out.

Only yesterday Carlotta had burst into Myriam's cabin and breathlessly announced to him, "If you want to meet Adam, you need to go to Seattle immediately."

The moment was indelibly etched in Ramsey's mind. Myriam's hand had gone to her throat. Hiram stopped talking. Paige and Maggie had shrunk against the kitchen sink as if knowing instinctively they were not a part of the invitation. In that invitation laid the answers to all his questions, questions building over the last twelve years since his misadventure in Peru.

"Of course," he remembered saying, his voice rational and calm, though his heart pounded so hard he could hear the blood rushing in his ears.

"Come with me," she said. Ramsey had gotten up and left without a word to the others. No one said anything. Maggie stared at him for a moment then rushed over and gave him a kiss on the cheek. Her experience at the shrine had changed her. He didn't have to ask; it was written on her face. Maggie had one of those rare experiences that transforms a person instantly. The brash cockiness that had long masked her fear of the future had vanished, and it its place was confidence that comes from accepting fear and using its chaotic energy to find solutions. Paige smiled at him—and then he was gone, through the door.

The driver guided the limo into an underground garage. The lettering above the entrance read "Columbia Center." He stopped before a bank of elevators. A young man with jet-black dreadlocks waited. "We're here, sir," the driver said.

By the time Ramsey got out of the car, his luggage was on a small cart being wheeled toward an elevator.

The young man put out his hand. "I'm Alex. Adam's nephew." He was tall and broad shouldered. His grip was firm. "Please follow me."

They entered the car. The young man hummed to himself as it shot up sixty stories. Ramsey started to ask a question and Alex interrupted. "It's better if I don't say anything, Mr. Ramsey. Uncle Adam would prefer I don't prejudice you in any way."

He ushered Ramsey into an office. Through the rain-streaked glass Ramsey saw Seattle shrouded in mist. Alex opened the door to an inner office and held it for Ramsey, then closed it behind him, leaving him alone in a room with no windows and only the one door.

Along one side was a leather couch and in it sat someone or something. Ramsey immediately experienced a change in visual perception. It was unclear to him if it was a person or an object. Then he heard the unmistakable voice of the apparition he'd encountered his first time at the Milagro Shrine. It asked, "Who do you think I am?" The voice was slow and melodic, almost as if it came from another room or from speakers hidden in the ceiling. Ramsey was unsure if it was somebody actually talking to him.

He focused on the shadow where it occupied the right hand portion of the couch. He said in a low tone, "We met under the cottonwood tree almost four weeks ago." The words acted like a magician saying "abracadabra." The shadow lost its indistinct quality and firmed up into a man wearing blue jeans and a plaid shirt. Graying red hair framed a rugged face with high cheekbones and questing blue eyes. The man was naturally big-boned and muscular. "You're Adam," Ramsey said.

"If you say I am. You've come here for answers. Here's what I say to you. Stop resisting what you have been fighting all your life. Become a master of two worlds like Jesus did, but in your own way."

The door opened and Alex stepped into the room. "The driver will take you to your hotel, now," he said and gestured for Ramsey to leave. Ramsey turned back to the couch. The shadow had regained its amorphous shape. He started to laugh. "Of course."

He walked out of the room. The door closed softly behind him, only it wasn't the sound of closing but of a door opening in his mind and in his life. He knew what he had to do. He would go back to Rio Chama's Milagro Shrine, and sitting under the cottonwood tree, he would go to the other side, and comeback changed. He would merge with his higher-self again and again, emerging each time ever closer to becoming numinous, transparent to the other side in his own unique way. He would become the archetype of transformation, spreading a new kind of sacred place throughout the world.

62

—————

June 21, 2019
Blue Island, Illinois

At the dedication of the Blue Island Sacred Shrine, Ramsey strode up the steps to the stage to acknowledge his part in the founding of the new Leonardo Shrine. On one side of the dais were Ron Grange and Janet Furlong, the only other white people on the platform. Maggie and several of her crew stood beside them.

Reverend Small shook his hand. "Now that you see all this, what are your feelings?"

"Feelings?" Ramsey pursed his lips, looked around at the crowd. He took the microphone from the man and walked back and forth across the narrow stage. "Feelings . . . fear, love, hatred, hope, despair, anger. They come and go like shadow puppets. They grab you and hold you, trap you. . . . I've been trapped many times. Feelings, are not reliable, not reliable at all, not to be trusted."

The crowd looked confused.

At the front of the onlookers Paige projected the sign of a cross with her two forefingers and Ramsey knew he had to be more careful about what he told people in the future.

She's good to have around, he told himself. He was glad he had decided to stay with her. *She's the anchor I need in this world.*

ALSO BY RONALD C. MEYER AND MARK REEDER

Tricksters and Angels

Center: The Power of Aikido

Simulation

Young Adult Books

The Adventures of Andrew Raymond

The Crystal Sword Series

Book 1: A Dark Knight for the King

Book 2: Queen's Knight Gambit

Book 3: Knight to Mate

Other Books by Ronald C. Meyer

Aikido in America

Extinction

18 and a Half Minutes

Other Books by Mark Reeder

Where Memory Has Lease

Shadowloom Series:

Shadowloom

Weft of the Universe

Young Adult books

Marc Holiday Series

Marc Holiday and the Sand Reckoner - 1

AFTERWORD

Go to HangarIPublishing.com to learn more about the Authors and stay up to date with their newest releases.